LOVE DELETED

PAUL INDIGO

rAndom woRd meDia

LOVE DELETED

For information contact :
randomwordmedia@mail.com
PaulIndigo.com

ISBN 978-1-7392973-0-5 eBook.
ISBN 978-1-7392973-1-2 Paperback
ISNB 978-1-7392973-2-9 Audiobook

Published by Random Word Media 2023

PAUL INDIGO

The Letter

The first shock was the letter.
The second, a twenty-two
year old heartache.

Free novelette when you sign up for my newsletter at PaulIndigo.com

When Dr Applegate reads the letter, he is so shocked he needs to sit down. Then his sister calls from Canada inviting herself over and he realises he won't be able to keep the contents of the letter secret. But it's only when he meets an old girlfriend from twenty-two years ago he realises things are conspiring against him, upending his lonely, successful life. Dr Applegate is about to be shaken up by the two people most important to him in the world…

And, of course, the contents of the letter.

Dedication

To Ellen. Who waited patiently for my debut novel.
And Joy. My perfect audience.
And David. Who supported all arts.
And Richard. Who would have loved the science.

Without this cheering family of support, this work of fiction
could not possibly have existed. This novel involves them all.
I'm grateful beyond words. Thank you.

Finally, my beautiful niece, Anita Anne Hogan, who sadly
passed away in December 2022.

Fact

Optogenetics is the ability to control the brain using genetics to turn on or off targeted neurones with fibre-optic light to manipulate thoughts, feelings and actions. It is a genuine science. In 2005, Karl Deisseroth, MD, PhD, a Lasker award-winning professor of psychiatry and behavioural sciences and bioengineering at Stanford University, together with his colleagues, published a paper in Nature on his findings. Since then, more and more funding has piled into optogenetic research for its practical use. One such clinical application could cure a multitude of psychological illnesses through the adaptation of what is effectively a light-sensitive, programmable brain.

The author has taken liberties and projected the science into the near future where it will almost certainly be possible to engineer emotional, thought and memory editing. Already advances in the use of optogenetics for PTSD – a subject mentioned in this novel – is underway. If you'd like to find out more about optogenetics, there are numerous TED talks about this cutting-edge science on YouTube.

Prologue

THE FUTURE

"WILL IT HURT?"

"No Mrs McMillan it won't hurt."

"You're sure?"

"Positive."

"And it really works?"

Mrs Erica McMillan's eyes are red, gritty, sore. She's crumpled and defeated. She cried all morning. She cried for months. For a man she gave her life to. She's hopeful the treatment will solve all her problems.

They're in Dr John Applegate's office. Dr Applegate sits behind a glass desk. He pushes his wire glasses up his nose.

"Yes Mrs McMillan, the treatment really works."

Dr Applegate knows most patients come through the doors looking fragile, wishing on a dream, not quite understanding the treatment, not sure they believe it even. Now the pain in Mrs McMillan darkens into spiteful, narrow eyes.

"I want to forget him. I want my husband gone from my memory." The hate boils inside her for what her husband did to her. How dare he. How dare he. She almost spits the next words out.

"I don't want to know that man exists any more."

Dr Applegate takes this in. He gets this a lot – misunderstanding. The people who sit opposite are exhausted. Weary. Burnt out. In pain. Emotionally, bitterly confused. This treatment is a last lunge at hope. He clears his throat.

"Mrs McMillan, I'm afraid you're thinking of the movie The Eternal Sunshine of a Spotless Mind."

Dr Applegate's seen the film a dozen times himself. The film starts where Kate Winslet's ended a troubled relationship with Jim Carrey and he soon discovers – when she doesn't recognise him at a counter – she has had her memory of him deleted.

Mrs McMillan frowns in confusion.

"Isn't that what you do? Make people forget the person they love? Isn't that what you did with Cooper Hall?"

Cooper Hall. The woman who made the clinic accidentally famous because of her unusual request that resulted in the media frenzy.

"No I'm afraid not, Mrs McMillan."

The confusion deepens.

"But please don't despair. I said we can't erase your memory of your husband. I didn't say what we can do. We do something so much better."

"What is it you do then?"

This is the part Dr Applegate enjoys, giving his patients back the emotional control they so crave. Giving them back command of their lives far from the emotions tearing them apart. He leans forward.

Mrs McMillan leans forward.

He places his elbows on the desk.

She waits, expectant.

He steeples his long fingers.

"It's simply this Mrs McMillan. We erase your love."

1

THE CALL COMES when Harriet's at home in front of the daytime TV programme Loose Women, blowing her nose and feeling utterly rotten about her stupid cold. She's been off from work as Head of Marketing for her husband's fleet of garages recovering and wanted a bit of gossipy television for once.

On TV they're talking about how happy, child-free couples are. How some want to revel in the freedom, how some suffer while others only pretend. Harriet doesn't know if she's pretending or revelling any more.

Her mobile vibrates on the coffee table and pirouettes.

Harriet mutes the TV, checks the phone. Cooper's name flashes up. Strange. Cooper doesn't usually call until the evening. Harriet answers.

"Well that's a first, sis, calling during the working day. Eddsy ask you to give me some tea and sympathy?"

Harriet waits for Cooper to reply but there's just hiss.

"Coops?"

Harriet hears something. Faint noises. It dawns on her Cooper's phone has unlocked itself in her bag or pocket or something and it called the last number dialled. She calls out.

"Cooper?"

Nothing comes back. She shouts.

"COOOOOOOPERRRRRRRRRRRRR."

"I'm here," Cooper says.

Her voice is so close it's like breath against Harriet's ear. Harriet instantly knows something's wrong. On the TV screen

3

the presenters giggle at some joke. One presenter covers her mouth with her hand like she always does when she laughs.

"Coops, what is it?"

"Can I come over?"

"What's going on?"

"Can I come over?"

Harriet's not even sure it IS Cooper. She checks the face of the phone again. It definitely says Cooper.

"Cooper that is you, right?"

"Yeah."

"What's happened?"

"Can I come over?"

"Of course you can come over but what's going on?" Harriet suddenly realises Cooper's crying. She hasn't heard Cooper cry in – what? – years. Not years. This is bad news. Bad bad news.

"Cooper you're scaring me."

"I just—"

"Is Daniel okay?"

Cooper's son.

"Yeah."

"And Jethro?"

Cooper's husband.

Hesitant.

"He's okay."

"Oh my god, are you sure?"

"Yeah."

"Coops, you don't sound sure. What's wrong?"

When no answer comes Harriet tries again.

"Something is clearly wrong Coops. Where are you? Are you in your recording studio?"

"I'm in the car."

"Wait. You're driving?"

"Yeah."

"I hope you're hands-free."

Cooper doesn't respond.

"Oh Coops you should get one of those hands free things."

"Yeah, I know."

Cooper's not only crying, her whole manner is odd.
Cooper's a feisty, pixie-sized, thirty eight year old tomboy,
always in cargos and T-shirts with spiky dark blonde hair. It's
all to tone down the delicate China beauty of her face and fresh
as water green eyes.

"Cooper, I want to know where you are."

"I don't know where I am."

"You're in your car, right? You said so."

"Yeah."

"So you're driving over?"

"Yeah. Guess so."

Harriet really doesn't like this one bit.

"Oh Coops, you're not making sense."

All sorts of thoughts race through Harriet's mind now.
Maybe Cooper had a bad day at work or a friend is ill or dead or
maybe Daniel's done something silly. But that's hard to believe
because Daniel's an intelligent sensible nineteen-year-old.
Maybe… maybe she's been to the doctor and it's— god she
hopes it's not bad news from the doctors. Harriet keeps her
voice as steady as she can.

"Cooper, what's your sat nav say?"

"Hold on."

Beeping sounds come from the phone. Cooper's pressing
icons whilst driving. It means Cooper's eyes aren't on the road.

"Cooper, pull over first, don't do that while you're driving."

The beeping continues.

"Hey I said pull over first."

But there's no response. Cooper can't hear. All Harriet can
do is pray and wait. She thinks to when mum and dad brought
baby Cooper home from hospital. Harriet thought wow forget
all the plastic dolls this is the real thing. It's got warm spindly
arms and legs and opaque eyes that can't quite track you if you
move suddenly. Harriet learned to change Cooper's nappy, feed

5

her, watch her grow, fascinated by her neat tiny fingers. She loved the tiny flat nose you could squish and golly those huge, huge green eyes. Cooper still has a squishy nose. Still has huge, huge green eyes. Harriet can't imagine them crying. Not tomboy Cooper's eyes.

Cooper makes a sudden oh no and Harriet's jolted back. The banshee shriek of brakes, a horrific silence then an explosion of metal-crunching chaos. Then that terrible hissy silence once more.

Harriet stands up.

"Cooper?"

Nothing just silence.

"COOPER?"

More silence.

"COOPER!!!!!!!!!"

2

COOPER OPENS HER eyes. Only one eye opens. She knows what's happened. Her head's crooked at a stiff angle. Someone is screaming her name. There's a warm tang of blood in her mouth with the taste of metal keys. One tooth is loose. She sees a cobweb of light in front of her. Scalpel-sharp sunlight slices through her shattered windscreen, making her blink rapidly.

Cooper notices the airbag has deployed and has already deflated. She tries to move her head, it hurts. She lifts her hands, stares at wet bloody fingers.

A voice continues to scream at her, calling her name over and over. She looks around. The passenger seat is empty the back seats are empty there's no one else in the car. Outside the ground is at an oblique angle. The car has partially driven up a tree. Beside her, a high green hedge. She's in a winding country lane. No one is around. The voice keeps screaming her name. She has no idea where she is, how she got there, none.

Cooper pushes the deflated beach ball of an airbag away. The contents of her rucksack are all over the passenger seat and footwell. The screaming voice comes from the footwell. Cooper's voice is hoarse.

"Who is it?"

The voice pauses then continues but the tone is different. Cooper looks at the footwell, sees the word Samsung in rainbow colours winking at her. She bends forward to retrieve her phone. Her body doesn't move.

Oh god.

Tries again but she doesn't move. She feels a rising tide of panic until she becomes aware of clicking every time she tries to lean forward. The seat belt has locked her into place. She eases forward. The seat belt runs with her this time. Relief.

Cooper reaches, picks up her phone.

"Who is it?"

"Oh god, Cooper." The woman starts rambling but the words come so fast Cooper can't process what she's saying.

"Who is this?"

"Are you serious? Coops it's Harriet."

Cooper looks at the scuffed face of the phone, sees the name Big Sis.

"Are you okay?" Harriet says. "Tell me you're okay. Tell me what's happened?"

Under the crushed tangerine foil of bonnet, something hisses and spits. Cooper's still not with it.

"I'm okay."

Harriet spews out question after question. Cooper can't take it in.

"I said have you broken anything?"

Cooper touches her face. It's tender and wet but the wetness is translucent, not like blood. She's relieved. Then she's not. She's heard when you crack your skull fluid from around the brain can leak out and it's transparent.

She angles the rear-view mirror, studies herself. Looks at her hairline, checks herself all over. Her hair is damp but it's only water.

"Cooper?"

A bruise dark like a storm cloud throbs under her right eye. Her lips are thickening, has blood in the cracks. She opens her mouth, her teeth outlined in blood. She uses her tongue to play with the loose tooth. It rocks and aches in its socket.

Cooper moves her shoulders and her right side complains. She undoes the seat belt, rubs her neck, tests every limb.

Nothing feels broken. She knows the airbag saved her. The airbag, the seat belt, the crumple zone of the car.

"Yeah, I'm a bit battered but everything's cool," Cooper says into the phone.

"You're sure?"

"Yeah."

"Thank god."

Something occurs to her then. She checks her phone. Her phone says it's Tuesday 14:57. She doesn't know what she's doing here. Was she going to do some location recording work somewhere? She checks her phone schedule, the blue glaze of the screen bright as lightning, makes her squint. According to it she should be in her home studio completing the mastering on the Hoffman recording. So why's she in her car? Why'd she call Harriet?

"Harriet, you still there?"

"Of course I'm still here! What, you think I'm going to hang up on you?"

"The car's totalled."

"F the F'ing car! It's YOU I'm worried about."

F the car. Cooper can't help laugh. That's the worst Harriet can do? Her Julie Andrews sis is so sugary.

"Coops, what happened to you? It sounded like you were in a war zone."

"Yeah well this tree jumped out and hit me."

"Oh Cooper, be serious."

"I hit a tree."

"Oh my god. You really scared me. I was pooing my pants."

There she goes again. Pooing my pants.

"Harry, you don't wear pants."

"You realise how long I was calling your name?"

"I heard you."

"About two minutes."

"Shut up."

"I'm telling you Cooper it was two minutes. You screamed then I heard this god-awful noise."

"I screamed?"

"God, I thought you were—"

"Yeah, don't exaggerate."

"IT WAS TWO MINUTES COOPER I'M TELLING YOU."

"All right. Okay. Wow. You don't have to tell the world."

"Where are you?"

Cooper looks around.

"Um…"

"You don't know?"

"Well there's a big tree, a road, a ditch and guess what? I'm in it."

"Oh for heaven's sake, why's no one helping you?"

Cooper scans outside again using her wing mirrors. Easier than turning with her stiffening neck.

"There's a cow in the field."

"What about your sat nav? What's it say?"

"Hang on."

Cooper looks at her phone, goes through icons, gets to her GPS icon, the signal bar saying Connecting…

As she waits Cooper becomes aware her throat is scratchy like it's full of sand. She always keeps a bottle of water in her rucksack but her rucksack is sodden and sloppy and empty. She looks back in the footwell. All sorts of stuff from her rucksack have tumbled out but no water bottle. Cooper feels under the passenger seat, her hand comes across something cylindrical and plastic. She pulls but it's wedged. Pulls again. The car rocks as though on a pivot. Then comes an ominous metallic creaking, a dry door creaking on hinges.

"Uh oh."

"What is it?" Harriet says.

There comes the slow motion sensation of movement as the car teeters and twists away from the tree.

There's an almighty crunch of metal as Cooper's world corkscrews upside-down. The windscreen peels away and hails down with white crystals.

All Cooper thinks is oh crap, not again.

THE SUE BAXTER PODCAST
SUE BAXTER
Hello and welcome to another episode of the Sue Baxter
Podcast Show with your host, Sue Baxter. We look at
controversial issues in the news and ask how did this happen?
Tonight is a special introductory episode we're live streaming
on YouTube and iTunes, Spotify and Facebook. You can send
us your tweets, comments and emails to the links in our show
notes.

Now, Dr John Applegate's book A Mindful Reminder – The
Gateway Programme Trials, has only recently been published
and makes for fascinating reading. Tonight's what if? What if it
were possible to surgically delete your affections permanently
for someone you love? Well in fact we know it is possible from
a surgery pioneered by Dr Applegate and Dr Stewart-Way just a
handful of years ago. This evening our guest is one of the co-
authors of the book detailing this miracle technology. Hello Dr
Applegate.

DR APPLEGATE
Good evening Sue.

SUE BAXTER
Dr John Applegate is a behavioural psychologist specialising in
phobia treatment. He teamed up with Dr Klara Stewart-Way, a
highly regarded neuroscientist, to pioneer a method of PTSD
treatment using a revolutionary new brain surgery called – now
let me get this straight – Fluorogenetic Synaptic Deletion –

which they simply call The Gateway Programme. Did I say that correctly?

DR APPLEGATE

Perfectly.

SUE BAXTER

I gather The Gateway Programme is a kind of brain surgery. Tell us about it.

DR APPLEGATE

Thank you Sue. Yes, The Gateway Programme is an advanced form of optogenetics we call Flurogenetics as you mentioned in your introduction. Before you ask what optogenetics is, I'll admit it sounds like something to do with the eyes doesn't it? It is in fact the science of controlling the brain's internal processes using light in fibre-optic cables. However, Dr Stewart-Way pioneered an advanced method without fibre-optic cables.

SUE BAXTER

By all accounts it seems the results have been nothing short of miraculous.

DR APPLEGATE

We're happy to say Gateway House has treated military personnel and police traumatised in active duty, treated postnatal depression, treated victims of crime and victims of disaster, all with successful outcomes.

SUE BAXTER

And from what I gather, your patients are sufferers who have visited psychiatrists and counsellors for, in some cases, years. Your programme offers to cure them in a single treatment.

DR APPLEGATE

Actually Sue the programme works over a course of a few preparatory treatments but yes the final treatment takes just under five minutes.

SUE BAXTER

Tell us what led to your – and Dr Stewart-Way's – incredible discovery of The Gateway Programme.

DR APPLEGATE

Well, before we set up Gateway House, Dr Stewart-Way had been treating soldiers with Flurogenetics. I was working in an adjacent field treating patients suffering extreme phobia. At the time we were unaware of each others' work. It was a fluke encounter which put us in touch with each other and, as a result, The Gateway Programme was born.

SUE BAXTER

There is one case which made The Gateway Programme famous isn't there? Her name is Cooper Hall and she was the wife of recording artist and performer Jethro T. Hall.

DR APPLEGATE

Cooper Hall came to us seeking help in dealing with something that is sadly the bane of many relationships – infidelity. She approached us with an intriguing question – whether it was possible for us to use The Gateway Programme, which up till then had been used purely to treat PTSD – to undo her affections for her husband. She was going through a traumatic emotional breakdown and suffering from severe panic attacks at the time. We'd never considered using The Gateway Programme for that purpose so Dr Stewart-Way and I had long talks not only with each other, but also with various professionals and independent members of the ethics committee about treating her. As you know, Cooper Hall became the first beneficiary of The Gateway Programme specifically for that purpose several years ago.

SUE BAXTER

Jethro T. Hall first came to fame from a somewhat ironic song Looks Like Love after being a struggling singer for years. It was because of his fame Gateway House hit the headlines.

DR APPLEGATE

We were well-established within the mental health fraternity but yes we attracted mainstream attention after Cooper Hall's involvement.

SUE BAXTER

In fact it's when Jethro T. Hall first made public statements how The Gateway Programme destroyed their marriage your practice became the centre of a media storm.

DR APPLEGATE

Mr Hall has been outspoken about his views against us using a PTSD treatment to treat emotional relationship issues. Cooper Hall however stands in defence of our work at Gateway House and continues to support what we do.

SUE BAXTER

Today Cooper and Jethro remain separated. They're living in different countries I'm told.

DR APPLEGATE

Cooper lives in Ireland now, yes.

SUE BAXTER

I note on your website The Gateway Programme came about in part because of spiders. Is that correct?

DR APPLEGATE

Well yes Sue, you're talking about a patient I treated for arachnophobia when I ran the phobia clinic.

SUE BAXTER

The spider case is itself interesting isn't it? I mean, who'd have thought a spider could lead to a treatment that deletes love.

4

COOPER OPENS HER scrunched up eye to shattered windscreen glinting all around. She's bunched on the upside-down roof of the car, foetal, clasping her leaking water bottle. She puts the phone to her ear. Harriet's screaming her name again.

"I'm here," Cooper says.

"What happened this time?"

Cooper tells her, "Yeah well the car decided to do a somersault didn't it." She says, "The car was hugging a tree and now it's in a nice wet muddy ditch. Oh. And upside-down."

"Upside-down? And you didn't get out?"

"Well, I would've if you hadn't been blabbering on at me for the last six hours."

"You're blaming m— Look are you okay?"

"Yeah, yeah. I've been washed."

"What do you mean?"

"Hang on I need the tumble dryer setting. Where's that fabric conditioner?"

Harriet lets out a restrained laugh.

"Honestly Coops don't joke."

"I'm fine. Mostly."

"You need to get out that thing."

"Yeah I'm trying. I guess it might—"

"It might what?"

"Nothing."

"No tell me."

"God I need a pee."

"Don't change the subject Coops for god's sake what is it?"

"Well, it might blow up or something."

"OH MY GOD don't say that. Get out Coops. Get out quick."

It takes a while but Cooper climbs out. She's in a ditch, her legs in front of her. She feels like Laurel or Hardy after some disastrous, funny incident. Her hands muddy, cargos heavy and muddy, water bottle smeared and muddy, phone muddy, rucksack muddy, T-shirt muddy. She thinks oh wonderful, this can't get any worse. She scans the wreck of her poor Toyota. A question nudges at her head but she can't work out what it is. It'll come to her…

What was she thinking about? Oh yes Hardy. Not Laurel. Hardy always takes the fall while Laurel looks dumbly on.

"He's the fat one isn't he?" Cooper says absently.

"What're you talking about?"

"Hardy. Laurel and Hardy. Hardy's the fat one yeah?"

"What's wrong with you?"

"Yeah, that's what mum and dad used to say, remember?"

"God I love you, you idiot. I hope you're out. How's your sat nav?"

Cooper looks at her phone.

Connecting…

"Nothing yet."

"You need to get to hospital. You could have concussion or internal injuries, god Coops you could have brain damage you could have—"

"Yeah one thing I definitely have."

"What's that?"

Cooper struggles to stand, as uncertain as a lamb's first legs.

"Muddy knickers."

Harriet lets out a snort.

"You really are an idiot."

Cooper's phone pings. She looks at it. The sat nav has located her.

"What the flip am I doing here?"

"Where are you?"

"Three miles from you. I knew I recognised this road."

"I'll come get you."

"I need to call the AA. Or RAC? God I can't remember."

"We'll do it when I arrive. Tell me exactly where you are."

Cooper gives Harriet her location details.

"I'm on my way."

The question returns nudging at Cooper again.

"Harry?"

"Hang on, just grabbing my shoes."

"Why did I call you anyway?"

There's a hesitation in Harriet's voice now.

"You don't remember?"

"That's why I'm asking."

"I'm on my way."

"Yeah but why Harry? There's nothing in my schedule."

"Coops, you weren't just in the vicinity, you were coming to see me."

"How come?"

Harriet's voice is soft and close.

"Oh Coops."

"It's just, I can't work out why—"

Suddenly the gut punch of a memory slams into Cooper.

Cooper remembers.

Puppet strings cut and her knees fail.

Cooper remembers.

She buckles along with the scaffolding of her life, to the tarmac.

Cooper remembers.

Lets out a wail.

Remembers.

The cry that emerges from Cooper's throat is as primal as any wild animal's.

Yeah. She remembers.

5

FOURTEEN MINUTES LATER Harriet races into Farmer's
Field Road in an Arctic white Range Rover. She has no idea
what to expect. The way Cooper howled through the tunnel of
the phone had sent chills through her. Harriet finds Cooper at
the side of the road hugging her knees. She's a pathetic mess in
wet cargos and a mud caked T-shirt. A spray of silver glass and
the black pepper of shattered plastic arcs across the road, a
monochromatic rainbow. Harriet pushes the driver's door open,
rushes out, the car still running. Oil and burning rubber fills her
nostrils. Her first thought is, get Cooper safe and warm. Her
second, to find out why Cooper was heading over to her. She
kneels as respectfully as an alter boy in front of Cooper, puts a
hand on her shoulder.

"Hey." Her voice is soft.

Cooper lifts her head.

"Oh Coops, you're freezing."

Cooper's face is a puffy mess. She has one walnut-swollen
eye sealed shut, the other marbled red from crying. Track marks
of dry tears run through her grimy face, a smudge of blood
around her mouth and nose. Glass speckles her short hair.

Harriet spots the car wheels upside-down in the ditch, the
dirty matt black underside no one but a mechanic has a right to
see. Her sister was in THAT?

She helps Cooper to her feet, helps her hobble to the car.

At the passenger door, and for the briefest of moments,
Harriet realises Cooper's going to mess up her pristine cream
calf leather car seat. It's a new car. The glass flints in Cooper's

cargos might score and puncture the seat. The hesitation is brief but F it no car is more precious than her lil sis. Cooper detects the hesitation, looks at the car seat, looks at Harriet.

"Got a blanket?"

"Course."

Harriet goes to the back, takes out a chequered picnic blanket, returns. Cooper takes the blanket, drapes it over the leather of the car seat with the gentleness of laying it under a baby's chin.

"Oh Cooper, the blanket was for you."

Cooper climbs up collapses into the seat.

Harriet's glad to see Cooper's okay if battered. She'll take her to hospital. She closes her door, goes round to her side, jumps in, clicks the door shut to seal in the warm air. She switches on the fan heater and directs hot air at Cooper. Cooper's arms goose up.

"I'm taking you to St Mary's."

"No."

"Coops I'm taking you to—"

"No."

How can Harriet forget? Cooper's the most stubborn person she's ever known. Harriet takes a brief pause, containing her cauldron of frustration before speaking again.

"Coops, if it were me in the accident you'd want to take me to—"

Cooper twists her head to Harriet, stares at her, eyes as sarcastic as a ventriloquist's dummy's. Harriet knows that look. Cooper really means no.

"You know I have to report this right?"

Cooper stares out the window.

Harriet calls the recovery service, then dials 999 and requests the police. The shiny metal voice of the operator comes over the phone.

"Does the driver need medical aid?"

Harriet looks at Cooper.

"Well…"

Cooper places her hand on the door handle again.

"No."

"Is that a no she doesn't need medical aid?"

Harriet cringes saying it.

"That's right. She doesn't."

"You're absolutely certain of that?"

Harriet thinks NO she's not certain about that. No way in hell she's certain about that. She wants to scream at the operator get an ambulance quick! She keeps her voice as tidy and neat and folded as fresh linen.

"The driver's fine. She's just upset."

Harriet ends the call. She hopes they send one anyway. She makes another call.

"Who're you calling?"

"Jethro, of course."

Cooper clamps on to Harriet's arm with the speed of a cat strike. It actually stings.

"Cooper, you can't not tell Jethro."

Harriet presses a button puts the phone to her ear. Cooper snatches it, cancels the call, hands the phone back to Harriet. Harriet sighs.

"Well, what about Daniel?"

"Not my husband, not my son, not anyone yeah?"

"Oh Coops, look at you!"

Cooper's expression is as hard as granite. It's no use. Harriet raises her hands in the air, her cheeks braised with unsaid words, her tongue held by a safety pin. All she can do is impotently wait for help and hope to god the police make Cooper go to hospital.

6

THE POLICE ARRIVE followed by a recovery truck with two mechanics who chat and debate about how to winch the upturned car out the ditch.

Cooper stays inside the warmth of the Range Rover as one officer in his hi-vis yellow jacket walks along the road, stoops and studies the debris and the skid marks from various angles. The other talks to Harriet as she stamps the cold out her feet and hugs herself. They both glance over at Cooper periodically. The officer says something, Harriet nods and they approach Harriet's car. Harriet opens Cooper's passenger door.

"Coops, the officer wants to talk to you." Harriet steps out the way.

The officer, his jacket glowing radiation yellow, asks if Cooper wouldn't mind taking a breathalyser test and offers it to her. Cooper doesn't look at him, takes it, breathes into it, hands it back. It comes back a big fat zero.

"Mrs Hall, can you scuffle over to the driver's seat and place your hands on the steering wheel please."

"Why?"

"Please."

Cooper obliges.

The officer's face is sharp, all angles. An angry muscle pulses the sandpaper edge of his jaw.

"Thank you."

The officer continues talking but Cooper never once glances his way. She stares out the window, shrugs, answers, nods, answers, shakes her head, answers. Whatever it takes to get him gone. The officer abruptly turns to Harriet, says they need an ambulance. Cooper says no. He reaffirms to Harriet he's going to call one. He walks toward the Toyota as it's winched up. Usually, wrecked cars aren't always taken away that quickly but the road's a hot spot for accidents.

A two-team ambulance crew arrive in green jump suits. The ambulance crew is a man with a rounded jaw of peppery stubble, the woman with a swinging ponytail. They introduce themselves to Harriet as Pete and Casey. Each carry medical packs with them.

Soon Casey goes around to the driver's side, slides into the driver's seat while Pete stays asking Harriet questions. Casey closes the door to keep the warmth in, rubs her hands together, eyes as bright as sunrise.

"Hi. It's Cooper, isn't it?"

"Yeah."

"I'm Casey. Bloody cold isn't it?"

Cooper doesn't respond.

"How you feeling?"

"Yeah, I'm good."

"Would you mind if I took a look at you?"

"Yeah."

"Good. I just want to—"

"Yeah I'd mind."

"Oh. Well what if I looked at your eye? That right one's a real shiner isn't it?"

"Same deal."

"You might have foreign material in there, perhaps even glass."

"There isn't."

"It won't take—"

"No deal."

"How's your neck Cooper?"

"Guess."

"Well, I guess you're suffering from whiplash aren't you? You might find it starts stiffening up pretty soon if it hasn't already. By tomorrow you won't be laughing, I bet I get that right."

"Cool."

Casey asks Cooper question after question but it's clear to Casey, Cooper's not going to co-operate. She's seen this before. Casualties she tries to help who are in such shock they think the accident is a dream. Cooper doesn't seem to be in shock though. None of the usual tell-tale signs. Casey knows her aloofness is more likely due to a personality trait. She steps out the car, joins Harriet and Pete, shakes her head almost imperceptibly at Pete.

Casey asks Harriet what Cooper's like. Harriet says she's stubborn, single-minded, fiercely independent. It reassures Casey. She tells Harriet Cooper's being uncooperative but from observation alone the cuts and bruises appear unpleasant but superficial. She's unhappy with the swollen eye as that's the result of the airbag, as is the split lip and the scorch mark on her cheek. Casey emphasises head trauma is always a concern however benign it might appear, advises Harriet to call medical support immediately there's any change in Cooper's behaviour. She gives Harriet pointers to look out for such as confused or disjointed speech, changes to skin tone, breathing difficulties, erratic behaviour.

When the Toyota's righted after looking as pitiful as an upturned turtle, the police officer halt proceedings. He walks to the car, pushes his head through the near side window. He spends time looking for something but retreats, jaw tight, the tell-tale tic back. He nods at the mechanic to continue winching and goes to his patrol car, talks to his colleague who's leaning on the bonnet and typing in a report. Both officers glance at Cooper, suspicion sparkling in their eyes.

Soon the road's swept, the tow truck gone, the ambulance gone, the police going, the only evidence of a crash being a weeping pale gash in the huge tree trunk and drag marks in the mud bank. Harriet climbs in, buckles up, looks at Cooper.

"Happy now?"

Cooper closes her eye, rests her head into the headrest.

"You know I had to lie to the police officer?" Harriet says. "I had to tell him you called AFTER the crash. He suspected you were on the phone whilst driving but he can't prove it. You know why he checked inside your car?"

Cooper doesn't respond.

"He wanted to see if you had a dashcam. It would've proven you'd been on the phone when you had the accident. He says they catch a lot of drivers like that. He said you have a clean driving record and there's no other reason to hit the tree. The skid marks prove you weren't going at a ridiculous speed and the tree's big and obvious. He said it could only have been either a medical condition or a distraction but you don't have any medical conditions. He said many unexplained accidents are phone related and this has all the hallmarks. He said the last two accidents here were also because of a phone."

Cooper stares out the windscreen, says nothing.

Harriet can't keep the hobnailed boots attitude up.

"Oh Coops, I'm worried about you. I really am. What's going on?"

Cooper says nothing.

Harriet starts the car.

"You know why the officer asked me to put my hands on the steering wheel?" Cooper says.

"Did he?"

"Yeah. Know why?"

"Why?"

"I don't know either."

"Coops look please, let me take you to St Mary's?"

When there's no response, Harriet takes a deep breath and thinks calm deep blue sea thoughts, pushes the car into gear and pulls out. She drives home scared, worried, wishing she knew what the heck was going on.

7

AS HARRIET DRIVES she tries to fathom what's wrong with Cooper.

First Cooper calls distraught. Then she crashes and after a petrifying five minutes of silence Cooper is suddenly all bright and normal. Then out of nowhere Cooper wails over the phone and now she's like… well like this. Silent. Subdued.

Harriet had only ever heard someone cry out like that once before. Years ago when working for the VP of Sales at a local company her boss received a police constable in his office, helmet off. It couldn't have been more ominous. Moments later the boss wailed like that too. Harriet found out later a train guard had discovered her boss's wife slumped against the train window. Turns out she had a heart attack and died in her seat. She was only 43. Passengers thought she'd simply nodded off. Harriet glances at Cooper, head braced against the headrest, wincing in obvious discomfort at the jostle of the car.

"Coops?"

"Yeah?"

"You up to telling me what's going on?"

Silence. Then,

"It's cool."

"You were coming over to tell me something, right?"

"Just said. It's cool."

Before Harriet can say anything else her phone rings from her handbag between Cooper's feet. Cooper pulls out Harriet's phone. It says HUSBAND on the screen.

"Your beloved."

"Answer it for me."

Harriet knows if anyone can make Cooper open up, Eddsy can. He's as blunt as an anvil, doesn't take crap, but he's also quiet and thoughtful. Somehow Cooper's bullheadedness and his bluntness has created a respectful bond between the two.

Cooper puts the phone on loudspeaker, holds it out like a deck of cards.

"The wife's driving."

"Cooper?" Surprise in his voice.

"Yeah."

"How's the rally driver? Heard you took a tumble."

"Yeah."

"Banged up pretty bad?"

"Totally totalled."

"Mean you, not the car."

"I'm cool."

"Heading to St Mary's, right?"

No, your five bedroomed palace, mister."

"Six."

Cooper snorts.

"Hospital let you go already?"

"I'm cool."

"What'd they say?"

"All cool."

"Don't kid a kidder, kid. What you not saying?"

"Ambulance checked me over. I'm a bit roughed up. I'm okay."

"I was about to set off to meet you guys at St Mary's. Know they're sending your car to the pound opposite my garage?"

"Yeah?"

"Martin from the tow truck team says they've seen sheets of screwed up paper less crumpled. What were you thinking?"

"I wanted to play hit the tree."

"Where's Jethro?"

"Not here."

"He knows, right?"

"No."

"Want me to call him?"

"NO."

"What was that? Can't hear you kid. Next time use a megaphone. What about Daniel?"

"Yeah I'll do the rounds later, it's covered."

Eddsy chuckles.

"Missy, sounds like you got a mouthful of cotton wool."

"Lip's busted."

"Airbag. Every time. Burns?"

"No, I escaped the car before it exploded."

"Didn't explode. Referring to the airbag. Gas inside is hot and explosive."

"My cheeks feel kind of fried."

"How do you drive?"

"What do you mean?"

"Hand position on the steering wheel?"

"You're going to give me driving lessons?"

"Humour me."

"No idea."

"Think about it."

Cooper thinks about it.

"Ten-to-two."

"And you survived the airbag?"

"What do you mean?"

"Ten-to-two's old school. They say now to put your hands at quarter-to-three or twenty-to-four."

"Yeah? Why?"

"You have dashcam?"

"No."

"You're lucky. Bet the police checked."

Cooper shares a glance with Harriet.

"Apparently."

"Police ask you to put your hands on the steering wheel, right?"

"Yeah?"

"Ten-to-two the airbag turns your hands into missiles so you punch yourself in the face. Wham! Double shiner. If that was the case you'd have two black eyes."

"You're half right."

"Which eye?"

"My right."

"Right-handed right?"

"Yeah."

"When the police breathalysed you, you probably took the thing with your right hand right?"

"So?"

"He'd have noted it. Left eye not bruised, right?"

"No."

"Means your left hand wasn't on the steering wheel. Likely you were holding a phone. Right-handed people mostly hold their phones with their left."

"Okay, Poirot."

Eddsy chuckles.

"Most say Sherlock. Fact only your right eye's black means more than likely you were on the blower. You know that's an offence right?"

"No comment."

"Gabbing with Harriet right? She said you'd called."

"No comment."

He sighs.

"Kid, she already spilled the beans."

"I deny all knowledge."

"Police take a dim view. Can even check your phone records."

"Yeah, but can't prove the time of the accident."

"You're lucky. Christmas list: Hands-free thingy for Cooper."

"You ever heard of stable doors and bolted horses?"

"Always another horse."

"Yeah well…"

As Harriet drives, she half listens to them, half thinks things through. Cooper's reluctant to call Jethro but she didn't call Daniel either. It's obvious Cooper doesn't want anyone to know what's going on. That secretive streak Cooper's always had. She supposes Jethro and Daniel can't do anything from where they are anyway what with Daniel returning to university and Jethro setting off on some gig or other.

But.

But but but but. Cooper was upset. Why?

Suddenly Harriet's aware she's almost home and slows the car, swings through the gates onto the gravel drive.

When Eddsy and Cooper finish, Cooper holds the phone out to Harriet.

"You guys want to talk?"

Harriet calls out.

"See you later, husband."

"Yeah, wife."

They make smooching noises.

Cooper shakes her head.

"Oh, god's sake."

Harriet pulls in front of the portico, cuts the engine. She turns to Cooper pleased to see Cooper smiling through her swollen lips at their silly banter. Eddsy's call couldn't have come at a better time. Harriet turns to Cooper.

"Right. We're home."

"Yeah? Wondered what that building with a door and windows was."

Her sarcasm's back too.

"We'll get you out those clothes."

"Cool."

"Then I'll draw you a hot bath and we can find out what's going on."

"Okay, mummy."

"Look, I'm only saying."

"Harry, I've like got a nineteen-year-old son. I'm not four."

"Wow, sorry I even spoke."

Harriet steps out the car but Cooper doesn't move. Harriet walks around to Cooper's passenger door, waits. Cooper sits there staring out the front absolutely still, a marionette of loose strings.

Harriet raps the side window.

"Coops?"

Cooper sits there.

Harriet opens the passenger door. Her voice is gentle.

"Cooper?"

Cooper's face drops into her open palms and she starts crying, her shoulders hiccuping.

Harriet leans in, embraces Cooper's shoulders.

"Oh my love, my love. What's going on? What's wrong?"

8

THE SUE BAXTER PODCAST

SUE BAXTER

Dr Applegate, tell us about the strange connection between love and spiders.

DR APPLEGATE

Before Dr Stewart-Way and I created The Gateway Programme, I was running a phobia clinic in which a patient we were treating – Clive, a forty seven-year-old solicitor – had an unusual fear of spiders.

SUE BAXTER

I thought the fear of spiders is quite common. Why was his fear unusual?

DR APPLEGATE

Simply because his phobia was inconsistent. Phobias are by their very nature, consistent.

SUE BAXTER

So the solicitor only intermittently feared spiders?

DR APPLEGATE

It's a little more complicated than that, but essentially yes.

SUE BAXTER

Okay, but how can a phobia possibly relate to love?

DR APPLEGATE

Actually Sue, physiologically, fear and love, or at least intense attraction, looks almost identical. A racing heart, flushed cheeks, dilated pupils and interestingly, the fight or flight response.

SUE BAXTER
(Laughs)
Actually I remember a boy in my class was so handsome he always made my pulse race. He made me want to run from the classroom and hide. Everyone could see my red face and neck. He became aware of my crush which made it all the more excruciating.

DR APPLEGATE
(Laughs)
We've all been there. Now for Clive, his fear of spiders was so intense he blacked out during court. Observers noticed the solicitor stopped to fixate on his legal notes and froze, so even when prompted by the judge, he didn't respond.

SUE BAXTER
So he'd seen a spider?

DR APPLEGATE
At the time nobody knew. However within a minute or so after Clive collapsed, he woke on the floor confused, having no recollection of the incident.

SUE BAXTER
What did people think caused it?

DR APPLEGATE
Well neither Clive's wife, children nor colleagues knew of his fear of spiders. In fact when called on by his young daughters, he'd happily remove a spider from the bedroom, therefore the courtroom incident passed as no more than an intriguing sidebar attributed to a missed breakfast.

SUE BAXTER
And Clive wasn't aware of his phobia either? How intriguing. But why then was he referred to you?

DR APPLEGATE
Because of what happened next.

SUE BAXTER
Which was...?

DR APPLEGATE
A car crash.

9

HARRIET RUNS COOPER a hot foamy bath. She dips her hand in, tests the water. Cooper stands by the bath hands at her side like a child, waiting for her mother to undress her. Harriet used to have to undress and bathe Cooper when they were kids. She takes her cue.

She gets Cooper to raise her arms and removes Cooper's grungy T-shirt first. Then the sodden cargos. Her white bra is grimy and her knickers muddy. Harriet drops everything into a wet pile. Now Cooper's as naked and vulnerable as the soft of a snail. It's the first time in years since bath night Harriet's seen her sister exposed like this, the shell of her clothes gone, her identity a sodden mess.

She studies Cooper's large purple bruise where the seat belt branded her shoulder, sees her bloated lower lip split in the centre crusted with dark blood, sees her eye swollen shut, sees the pathetic slump in Cooper's shoulders. She takes Cooper's hand and eases her into the bath. Cooper slips into the water silently. The water's as blissful as camomile tea, softens Cooper's face, the tension in her law relaxing.

"You soak for a bit, okay."

"Cool."

"How's a cuppa sound?"

"Harry?"

Harriet looks at her.

"Couple of painkillers too, yeah?"

Harriet goes downstairs, makes her a pot of PG Tips, makes it strong, takes it up on a tray with sugar and a small milk jug and two painkillers. Cooper's practically a tea expert and likes sweet brewed loose tea. Harriet places the tray on a wooden drying bench, pours her a cup, pours milk, five spoons of sugar. Harriet only has to look at sugar and she gains two pounds. Cooper though is such a powerhouse she can burn calories blinking. She hands Cooper the cup and saucer and pills. Cooper takes the pills, swallows, takes the teacup and sips and sips and sips and keeps sipping until she drains it. She hands the teacup back, leans against the slope of the bath.

"Another?"

Cooper shakes her head.

"You want me to leave?"

"No."

Harriet draws the bench closer. Cooper only lies there, not moving.

"You want me to soap you?"

Cooper doesn't say a word, only nods.

Harriet kneels on a bath mat, rolls her sleeves up. She hasn't done this since Cooper was her baby sister, feels the thrill of it. She carefully soaps her back first with her almond green tea soap. Cooper doesn't wince, not even once, tough little acorn she is.

"Hey Coops, remember how I always had to bathe you when we were kids?"

Cooper doesn't respond.

"I couldn't believe how dirty you made the bathwater. I always had to wash the bath out twice after a Cooper bath."

Harriet lifts Cooper's arm. There's no resistance. She swabs it, goes under the arm, takes the other arm, does the same. She does her legs, her back, her fingers, even between her toes. Cooper doesn't wince or complain or twist or squirm. Tough little acorn.

Next Harriet takes a soft natural fibre nail brush, cleans grime from under Cooper's stubby fingernails. Cooper's hands are schoolgirl-sized, the nails functionally clipped, not filed like Harriet's.

"Gosh, you were such a tomboy, Coops. You never showed interest in all those Barbie dolls and Wendy houses and things mum and dad bought you. You always preferred to play adventure games. When you were little you'd use a cardboard box and pretend to be a pirate at sea or you'd run around the house pretending to be a motorcar racer and making car screeching noises, remember? When mum asked what you wanted for Christmas she'd stop in front of all the girls' toys but you'd point to the boys' section and indicate a Spiderman outfit or a chemistry set or a cricket bat and she'd say don't be silly Cooper. And at parties mum used to dress us up in pretty dresses and do something nice with our hair and I'd be so excited about it but you never showed an interest. You'd pout and want to be in a cowboy outfit or a spaceman suit."

Harriet uses her silkiest, most expensive shampoo and glugs it thickly over Cooper's head. She carefully massages grit out of Cooper's hair until it's smooth and clean. It comes with the sweet aroma of Japanese cherry blossom. She frees the handheld shower head from its cradle, checks the water temperature with the back of her hand, asks Cooper to tilt her head back. Water froths and sizzles across the terrain of Cooper's head.

"Even on our street you never played with the girls. You called all the girls' games boring and preferred to play with their brothers instead who all had bikes and skateboards and footballs. Remember one birthday mum and dad bought you a pink bicycle with a basket on the front and the name Princess written on the crossbar? Gosh within weeks that bike was as scuffed and muddy as the boys' bikes and you couldn't read the name Princess on it anymore."

Harriet gently showers Cooper's hair, combs the foam out with her fingers. Soapsuds slick down the sides of Cooper's face, past her swollen eye, down her cheeks, runs down her neck in channels. She uncaps conditioner, pours it into a palm, runs her fingers through Cooper's hair. The aroma is heavenly.

"You were always going on grimy adventures with the boys. You'd be laughing, shoving each other around and so happy, calling each other names, telling each other jokes, or settle on the old sofa in the front garden quietly reading from comics while all the girls went around with their Barbie dolls, talked about their hair and clothes and the latest pop stars and actors."

Harriet pauses, remembering something. She tenses before deciding to continue.

"Something changed with you one year, Coops. I think you were eleven or twelve. You suddenly decided you didn't want long hair anymore. You asked mum to cut off all your locks and she wouldn't do it. So you hacked it off yourself."

Harriet snorts out a laugh.

"Mum screamed when she caught you with a pair of kitchen scissors. I came rushing up to the bathroom so fast I thought you'd died! You stood there in front of the bathroom mirror with your hair butchered and all over the floor. Honestly, you looked like you'd stuck your fingers into dad's shaving socket. Mum had no choice but to take you to the hairdressers to complete the job. Even the hairdresser was annoyed you'd wrecked your hair. She had trouble fixing it and you demanded a buzz cut. She looked at mum for guidance and mum went red said no way not on this God's earth. This was the first time I think you faced up to mum. You said if the hairdresser didn't do it you'd do it yourself first chance you got with dad's clippers. Mum had to give in. Even then the hairdresser set the clippers on four though you wanted number one. There was this stand-off between you, mum and the hairdresser. I didn't get it Coops. I didn't get why you were doing it."

Harriet washes out the conditioner, taking Cooper's silence as her answer.

"We came home from the hairdressers like it was a funeral procession. Your hair was so short I could see your glossy scalp.

Mum was seething. Dad looked shocked when he saw you and put down the newspaper to find out what was going on. Then you asked mum if she could buy you some cargos, T-shirts and sneakers and she lost her rag and asked what was going on with you. Dad said if that's what she wants but mum was adamant. Your conduct confused everyone Coops. I remember thinking something's happened."

Silence still.

"Then that same night I woke up because the bed was shaking. You were turned away from me and I realised you were crying. I put my hand on your shoulder and you froze and became dead still. I suppose you thought I wanted you to stop shaking the bed and go to sleep. Actually Coops, I wanted you to know I was there for you. I thought you were crying because of losing all your hair and that confused me all the more because why then would you cut it all off? It's only weeks later I think I realised the truth."

Cooper stiffens but doesn't say anything.

"It was one Saturday. I was in the bedroom fixing myself up in my mirror for a date when I heard you guys playing outside. Funny, isn't it? When you hear kids playing, it's comfort food, like distant church bells or the ice-cream van. But there was something different about it this time. I remember looking out the window. You were playing with the boys but something had changed. Then it hit me. The boys were treating you differently. The way they were looking at you. They'd become awkward and gangly. I'd assumed you'd cut your hair off just to be rebellious and difficult."

Harriet dips her hand in the water and swirls, watching it eddy, a spiral of bubbles.

"You'd cut your hair off because you wanted the boys to see beyond the curls and the dresses they were suddenly aware of. You wanted them to see you as they used to. You'd accepted all the grownups were treating you like this delicate little thing but the boys used to treat you equally. You were one of them. Then suddenly you weren't anymore."

Harriet lets out a sigh.

"You don't know this Coops but I called mum to the window and made her see what I was seeing, how unhappy you looked. Since your haircut you'd been pestering mum for weeks to get you those cargos and sneakers and T-shirts and up 'til then she got her way. This time though mum just pressed her lips together and left the room. That's why the next day you came home and found a bundle of brand new, neatly folded cargos and T-shirts and a pair of trainers on your bed."

Cooper looks up, surprised, looks at Harriet. Harriet holds a soapy palm up.

"Yup. Guilty as charged. That was my fault. But oh Coops, you were so angelic it shone through no matter what you did. The boys still treated you differently that summer, even in your new clothes."

Harriet picks up a wet flannel and gently, very gently, dabs Cooper's face one last time. Soon Cooper is clean everywhere, sweetly fragrant with exotic fruit. Harriet sits back on her heels, appraises her work.

"There now."

She recaps the bottles and clears everything away, grabs a fluffy cotton towel and wraps Cooper's hair. She eases Cooper out the bath, envelops her in a warm bathrobe fresh off the radiator, ties the belt around her waist. The bathrobe is so thick it swallows Cooper up.

Harriet looks at the bathwater. It's dark and grimy, an oil spill. She laughs.

"I'm going to have to wash this bath out twice again aren't I?"

Cooper glances at the water, a half-hearted smile on her swollen lips.

Harriet takes a step back and appraises Cooper at arm's length, seeing that dejected, unhappy eleven-year-old once more. Something inside Cooper is very wrong.

"Coops?"

Cooper lifts her gaze to Harriet with her unbuttoned fresh-as-water green eye, the other eye dark, shuttered down.

"I honestly don't know what you're going through but I'm so happy you came to me. Maybe soon you'll be able to trust me enough to tell me what's wrong, but I won't bother you and Eddsy won't bother you. You can have all the quiet you need."

Cooper stares, not speaking.

"I know you're being brave about something. I promise you Coops whatever it is you're going through I'm with you okay? I'm frightened for you right now. Tell the truth you're scaring the living poop out of me. You could have died today. Oh Coops if I'd lost you..."

Cooper steps into Harriet, folds her arms around her like a little chimp.

"Harry?"

"Yes?"

"Thank you."

At first Harriet thinks Cooper's thanking her for bathing her. For being her sister. For taking care of her. For dealing with the police. For collecting her. For being there.

But when Cooper steps back and Harriet studies her, she sees beneath the thank you. A rock lifted to reveal the truth below, if just for a moment.

The thank you might have been for all the above.

But Harriet knows really it's for those neatly-folded cargos, T-shirts and trainers Cooper found on her bed one summer.

1 0

JETHRO HAS NO idea about the accident.

He's been calling Cooper all afternoon and leaving voicemail messages with his amazing news. He leaves another message to call him back, his voice breathless with excitement. He packs what he needs, talks to every band member over the phone. It's a mad last-minute scramble.

At 6.29pm Jethro calls again, leaves another message. Where is Cooper? Why's she not picking up?

He calls again at 8.20pm this time his voice a little puzzled, a little concerned. Has he missed something? Perhaps she has a late studio mixing job she forgot to tell him about? Sometimes she pulls lates in London recording studios for rush work. She's definitely not answering her mobile and definitely not in her home studio – the phone just rings and rings.

He calls again at 8.29pm.

At 8.43pm.

At 8.52pm, a niggle of concern now.

It follows with a sequence of missed calls with no messages. 9:02pm. 9:08pm. 9:14pm.

He's about to call Harriet to find out if she knows Cooper's whereabouts when his taxi finally arrives with the rest of the band already inside, buzzing and hyper.

Jethro decides that must be it, she's pulling a rush all-nighter and forgot to leave him a note. It's happened before. It eases him a little.

He feeds Kelloggs the remains of the cat food tin then dashes out to the taxi, overnight bag packed, guitar in a case, amazed to be getting such an amazing last minute opportunity.

They all greet him with cheers and back slaps and now he's one of the lads, not thirty-eight anymore, but shiny with the unspent confidence of an eighteen year old heading to his first gig.

THE SUE BAXTER PODCAST
SUE BAXTER
Dr Applegate, you're saying Clive had a car crash due to his fear of spiders?
DR APPLEGATE
We're several months further on from the courtroom incident where he blacked out. After Clive drives his two young girls to school, he pulls away and veers into a parked car. He wakes a little later to ambulance crew surrounding him and he's utterly confused as, once again, he has no recollection of events before passing out.
SUE BAXTER
I'm guessing he blacked out from spotting a spider in the car?
DR APPLEGATE
We believe that now yes. Oddly, one of his daughters reported he'd been waving at them as he pulled away then suddenly froze. She'd described his eyes as becoming strangely glassy. That later proved to be an important clue.
SUE BAXTER
What was happening?
DR APPLEGATE
Doctors believed his blackouts were caused by a medical condition and he was checked out, but scans showed no anomalies. It wasn't until later that evening his wife remembered the car's dashcam with dual cameras which records both the journey and the driver.
SUE BAXTER
What did it show?

DR APPLEGATE

Exactly what one of his daughters had described. When his wife saw the footage she checked the car and found an abandoned cobweb on a wing mirror. She realised the cobweb had been in Clive's field of view when he'd waved his daughters off. This was why Clive was referred to my phobia clinic.

SUE BAXTER

This was before you and Dr Stewart-Way paired up to run The Gateway Programme. Tell us a bit about how phobias are generally treated.

DR APPLEGATE

The treatment breaks into two broad areas – systematic desensitisation and cognitive reframing. In my practice we specialised in desensitisation combined with a unique method I'd developed in memory reconsolidation. Desensitisation is a three-stage affair starting with relaxation techniques, followed by making a personal fear hierarchy table created between the doctor and patient where the patient will declare a stimuli that produces the least anxiety – a picture of a spider, say. The table climbs all the way up to 100% in incremental steps where the final step could be stroking a large living spider. The doctor guides patients through these steps over several sessions until they're able to overcome the fear directly. For Clive, we organised slides of different spiders to flash on the screen one after the other.

SUE BAXTER

Did anything happen to Clive?

DR APPLEGATE

Oh yes. Something definitely happened.

1 2

IT'S LATE EVENING when Harriet holds a food tray outside Cooper's door with a cheese and onion sandwich and bottled water and a down turned glass. She hasn't heard a peep from Cooper since the bath. She expects Cooper's sleeping. She taps on the door. Harriet hates herself for going back on her promise not to disturb Cooper but the girl needs to eat.

"Coops?"

Taps again.

"Cooper?"

Nothing.

"Coops, if you don't answer I'm going to think you've got concussion or something."

Cooper's voice from the other side of the door is croaky.

"Hey yeah. I was asleep."

Cooper hadn't been sleeping. She'd lain in the dark thinking dark thoughts since the bath.

"Sorry hon. I've got a sandwich for you, okay?"

"Yeah, thanks."

"And some bottled water."

"Cool."

"You want them?"

"Leave them there."

"How you doing?"

"Yeah… you know."

Well at least Cooper doesn't have disjointed speech, one of the tell-tale signs of trauma Casey mentioned. She glances down at the tray.

"Coops?"

"Yeah?"

"Can I come in?"

There's a pause.

"Please? There's nowhere outside to leave the tray."

A weary "Yeah, okay."

Harriet steps into the dimness. She places the tray on the dressing table, positions herself on the bed next to Cooper.

"Mind if I turn the bedside light on?"

"Why?"

"I want to make sure you still have good skin tone."

When Cooper doesn't answer, Harriet switches it on. It smarts Cooper's eyes.

Poor Cooper. She looks dreadful. Once more her eyes are rimmed red from crying but at least her injuries don't look any worse. Her breathing too is regular.

"Okay, you'll live." She clicks the light off.

Harriet pauses, wants to ask Cooper what's going on. She wants to help. She waits for Cooper to say something, explain something. But Cooper fills the void with a substantial wedge of silence. It's the silence of a road block. Of pained tolerance. Of waiting for Harriet to go.

Harriet stands up.

"Okay well, don't forget the sandwich."

"Yeah, I won't."

"Night."

"Yeah, night."

Harriet closes the door, rests her head against it, a barrier as solid as that silence. Her voice is too soft for Cooper to hear.

"Oh Coops."

1 3

WHEN HARRIET GOES to bed, Eddsy is snoring, his mouth open against the pillow. Actually he's faking it but he's trying to sleep because being a car mechanic is cold, wet, oily, tiring, bruising, exhausting work and he starts early and ends late and doesn't want to talk with Harriet about Cooper tonight. If Harriet knows he's awake she'll talk and talk and worry and speculate about Cooper and make herself ill and – well, besides – he won't get any kip.

Eddsy likes that he gets to laugh with the boys, his hands slick in the elixir of motor oil, even though he's boss and owns six successful outlets. But he's also middle-aged so he needs more sleep than he used to. People always think because he's a mechanic he's going to rip their wallets from their hands and gleefully savour the leather of it, salting it like steak before banqueting. He doesn't. He's one of the good ones. Running a garage isn't cheap and the labour and the lads' apprentices aren't cheap either. Neither is the loans on the business. Come to think of it the mortgage on the house isn't exactly cheap either. It's not right he's washed in the same greasy water as the shady ones in his trade. Anyway, right now he just needs sleep. He has an important client to impress tomorrow.

Harriet settles under the duvet sniffing the air. Eddsy smells faintly of motor oil, smells faintly of grease, faintly of petrol and is about to complain but realises he also smells strongly of musky gel. He showered. Oh well. He tried. Every night he tries.

Eddsy has already made up his own mind what's happened to Cooper but he keeps it to himself. He never speculates about anything with Harriet. She worries too much about her sister so he doesn't want to add petrol to the fire. Ever since he's known Harriet he's known she carries some sort of duty of care for Cooper. But no he never speculates. Things are what they are and that's that.

Harriet though tries to sleep but can't. Worries tumble about, clothes in a tumble dryer. She becomes aware of Cooper's whimpering through the wall. Harriet lifts her ear to make sure she isn't imagining it. She isn't. She sits up.

"Wife, what you doing?"

Eddsy has a huge Desperate Dan barrel chest so when he talks his voice is so deep and rich it almost shakes your insides, low notes on a church organ.

"Sorry, did I wake you?"

He pressures a dense hand over Harriet's wrist.

"Leave her be."

Faintly of motor oil faintly of grease, faintly of petrol, strongly of shower gel.

"I didn't say night to her."

"You said it five minutes ago, wife."

"Oh... I thought you were asleep."

"Leave her be."

"But listen."

The whimpering continues.

Eddsy lets go of Harriet's wrist and turns over.

"Leave her be."

Harriet decides he's right even though it's torture not to go to Cooper. When Cooper was a baby, Harriet used to jump to her cot-cries when mum was too deep on sleep. But she knows Eddsy is right she knows he is and she knows Cooper will push her away anyway, tough little acorn she is. She settles, pulls the duvet up, faces Eddsy's back in the dark. The heat from his back, a solid sheet of radiator. She traces a line down his spine with a finger, whispers into his back.

"Husband?"

He grunts.

"Eddsy?"

Moans.

"What do you suppose has happened?"

"Sssshhh."

"You know what?"

"Sleep."

"I think she's had a big tiff with Jethro."

"Ssshhh."

"I mean those two are like wallpaper and glue aren't they? They've had a tiff and they never have tiffs. That's what I think anyway. A major tiff. Something huge. What do you think?"

Eddsy grunts again. Talking to her makes her talk back. If he keeps quiet...

Harriet takes a finger and traces a line down his back once more, this time he doesn't respond. She slaps his back. It sounds like she's slapping a solid lump of ham. He stirs, grunts, says ssshhh again.

Blast him, he's being so stubborn.

Harriet can't imagine Jethro ever losing his cool in a tiff. He's so cool himself. Musicians just are, aren't they? Especially ones who play guitar onstage barefoot in ripped jeans and a bolero hat over his long dark hair. Oh, and wears that necklace of wooden dice and leather bangles. Especially ones who are gazelle thin with bony elbows that stick out like chevrons. When he plays guitar those slender fingers slick across the fretboard like a ballerina dancing. And wow the fluid of music that flows out. It's sweet sap from a maple tree.

Harriet also thinks Jethro was almost born a girl but the genes changed its mind at the last moment and reformed before settling. He still inherited the lithe frame, smooth girlish face and silken cheeks like polished mahogany. They make a good-looking couple. They'd look good in paparazzi mags if they were famous. And Jethro is so leisurely he gives the impression he grows weed in a tiny greenhouse with his easy-going manner but in reality he's so straight if you angled a ruler against his edges you honestly wouldn't see light come through.

So.

So…so so so so…What can it be? What can be wrong?

Maybe Cooper wanted a few days with him alone for once rather than all his gigging and they tiffed over it. He's thirty-eight years old like Cooper but by pop standards he's ancient. Maybe Coops has grown tired of all that. Maybe she wants him to call quits on his dream.

Eddsy turns over, faces Harriet in the dark.

"Wife, stop thinking. You're keeping me awake." His voice is gravel.

Harriet smiles a wicked little smile to herself, whispers.

"I should call him – Jethro. I think I should. I don't think Cooper's called him yet."

Eddsy sighs.

"I mean I should, shouldn't I?"

Sighs again.

Harriet gets up.

"Where you going?"

"Well, you didn't see what she looked like."

"Wife—"

"You didn't. She looked all banged up and awful. Jethro should know that. I'm going to ask her if she's called him."

"She's asleep."

"No, she isn't."

They both listen. Harriet realises the whimpering has stopped. They share the silence, complicit in its meaning.

"Oh. Well... She still might not be."

"Cooper needs rest. Leave her be."

Harriet goes to protest but again, she knows Eddsy is right, blast him. Why does he have to be so damned right all the time? She slides under the covers, yanks the duvet up. Blast him. Turns over. Always right. Blasted man. Always. Turns over, flounces on the bed, closes her eyes.

Five minutes later.

Blast it, Harriet can't settle. She turns again, still narked by Eddsy's reluctance to talk even though she knows the man's weary. She shuffles again, half knowing it's deliberate. The rolling of the bed makes Eddsy grunt but within moments his breathing evens out once more. Poor man's exhausted. Gosh he puts up with a lot from her and her infuriating ways. Harriet knows he's beat, she knows it. She rolls over once more pulling away far too much duvet, leaving Eddsy with one thick hairy leg outside.

Eddsy stirs, grits his teeth, cautiously tugs part of the duvet back to at least partially cover his bare leg. He knows the other three feet of duvet are spitefully over the end of Harriet's side but it's all he dares take.

Okay so Harriet knows she's being mean to Eddsy, she can't help it. She's being a real meanie. She doesn't mean to be a meanie, she can't help it. She's frustrated. She reaches over, finds Eddsy's rough as grit hand in the dark. She squeezes. She's sorry. She's apologising. He doesn't squeeze back but he curls his huge ham over hers and pulls her to him. She suspects it's to stop her from flouncing again. She's sure if she pulled her hand away now and sniffed it it'd smell faintly of motor oil, faintly of grease, faintly of petrol, strongly of shower gel.

They lie there in the dark holding hands.

He falls within seconds and his hand relaxes over hers.

Eventually – forty minutes eventually – Harriet drifts away on her own little eddy of sleep.

Until the landline downstairs rings springing them both awake like ill-mannered sunlight.

1 4

THE SUE BAXTER PODCAST
SUE BAXTER
So, what happened when you exposed Clive to slides of spiders?
DR APPLEGATE
The slideshow was going well until one slide caused Clive's brainwave activity to drop into a trance-like state while simultaneously raising his heart rate to panic levels. Clive became glassy-eyed just as one of his daughters described and when my team tried to rouse Clive by snapping fingers and patting and shaking his shoulder, he failed to respond.
SUE BAXTER
What was going on?
DR APPLEGATE
He'd gone into a hypnagogic state – a state between wakefulness and sleep where one can see and hear things not present. It lasted a minute and a half at which point he lost consciousness. When he woke, he had no memory of the slideshow but we learned one important fact.
SUE BAXTER
Which was?
DR APPLEGATE
Clive had held his breath until he lost consciousness. We knew then his blackouts weren't caused by an underlying health condition.

SUE BAXTER

But you obviously found the particular spider that caused it. Isn't it strange it's one particular spider and not spiders in general?

DR APPLEGATE

Yes, it told us something important. Clive wasn't scared of spiders. He was frightened of an implicit traumatic memory.

SUE BAXTER

Implicit? What does that mean?

DR APPLEGATE

Often, trauma memories are not explicit – that is, conscious – memories. They're implicit, meaning that when a trauma occurs, the stress hormone cortisol will shut down the part of the brain that makes memories conscious. It becomes an unconscious memory and Clive didn't know he was frightened by it.

SUE BAXTER

So he doesn't remember the memory.

DR APPLEGATE

(Laughs)

Precisely. Nicely put.

SUE BAXTER

Obviously this memory involved this spider.

DR APPLEGATE

Not so fast. The spider is called the easton parson spider, mainly found in the warmer climes of Central USA. But actually Sue, you're wrong.

SUE BAXTER

Surely Clive must've seen one on holiday somewhere and then perhaps this spider managed to secrete itself into the courtroom?

DR APPLEGATE

Actually Sue, that didn't happen. When we showed him the easton parson slide again, he simply shrugged his shoulders.

SUE BAXTER

Really? What about the slide before or after?

DR APPLEGATE

We tried several slides before and after but nothing happened. So we ran the entire slide show again. This time we even went passed the eastern parson – he was still fine. That is, until he saw the brown recluse spider, also not indigenous to the UK. And no, they don't even look like each other.

SUE BAXTER

How odd. But there must've been a link between the two slides, surely?

DR APPLEGATE

Yes we did discover a link, and it's a rather surprising one.

1 5

WHEN THE PHONE rings Harriet springs out of bed so fast she doesn't even bother with her dressing gown not even her slippers, dashes out the room, thumps downstairs to the hall where the landline phone is. It's Jethro. Must be. Now she'll find out what the heck this is all about.

Eddsy wakes not only because of the phone call but also because Harriet sprang from bed with such abandon it catapulted him from his dreamless slumber. He throws a frustrated arm over his forehead wanting to punch the headboard. He knows it can only be Jethro calling. Eddsy also knows he's being unreasonable. He knows his sister-in-law could have died in the crash, he knows something is up but he's exhausted so he's fighting irritability. He has an important client tomorrow. He sighs. Perhaps after this he'll finally get some kip.

Harriet goes to pick up the phone in the dark, it stops ringing. Blood rings in her ears from all that rushing around. People only usually call the landline if they can't get through on the mobile and Harriet only has the one house phone downstairs. She waits in front of the phone, waits, waits, does an impatient war dance barefoot against the cold parquet in her pyjamas. A minute later it rings again. She snatches up the receiver, says hello.

"Hey Harriet, it's Jethro."

"Hey Jethro."

Harriet hears noises in the background, the sounds of somewhere open and public. She picks up an echoed announcement on a public address. She can't make out the words but she thinks Jethro's at a large train station.

"Where are you?"

"Hey listen, I know it's late and I don't want to worry you and everything but I've been like trying to reach your sister. You heard from her?"

"Cooper's here."

He laughs with what sounds like relief.

"Oh man. Guys she's at her sister's." Then back to Harriet. "What's with her phone? I've been calling and calling. I figured I should call you. Daniel says he got some cryptic message from his mother earlier but I haven't been able to reach her. What're you all doing? It's kinda late."

The public announcement comes back and repeats itself.

"She's sleeping."

"Damn it man, I can't hear you. Hang on."

They wait for the announcement to complete.

"What was that you said?"

"I said she's asleep. Where are you?"

"I'm at Gatwick. I'm like on my way out to Germany. I've been trying to reach Cooper all day, tell her the crazy news."

"What news?"

"We're doing a big Euro tour."

"A Euro tour? What does that mean?"

"You heard of Sabre Light?"

"The rock group? What about them?"

"We're the support for their European tour."

"Really?"

"For real. It's crazy."

"But Sabre Light are huge. They did Wembley and everything."

"Yeah, I know. Call came out the blue. Barkersville pulled out—"

"Who?"

"Sorry, the support band. They pulled out cause of differences in the band over a contract. Wait what did you just say? Cooper's asleep?"

"Cooper's here in bed."

"So, what's she doing at your place?"

That surprises Harriet. Jethro doesn't seem to know anything. Not even about the trashed car.

"You know about the accident, right?"

In the background a woman's voice drifts over the phone. Jethro dips his voice, says hang on to whoever she is. Returns to Harriet.

"Harriet, did you like say something about an accident?"

"Who's that with you?"

"Oh yeah, it's Sophie. You know, she's the new keyboards. The whole crew's here man. The fellas think that's why we got the chance. Keyboards and new harmonies made a difference to the song arrangements. Did you say something about an accident?"

A couple of male voices laugh in the background, a woman's on top. Harriet hears the nervous energy through the line. The band sound amped as though they're come from a party. Harriet sits on the floor. The parquet is cold. She stands up again, back to her alternating feet, back to her war dance.

"Cooper didn't tell you about it?"

"Didn't tell me what?"

Harriet explains about the car and Cooper's injuries. She doesn't tell him how upset Cooper was before the accident. How can she? She doesn't know anything.

"No way. But this is crazy. You sure she's okay?"

"She's fine, promise."

"This is crazy. She didn't call me or anything."

"I'm sorry, Jethro."

"But why didn't she call me? Is her mobile okay?"

"Perhaps the battery's dead."

"What did the hospital say?"

"She didn't go."

More laughter in the background.

Hey guys keep it down yeah? What did you say? Did you say no?"

"I said she didn't go."

"Oh man, that's crazy. Why didn't she go?"

"I tried to talk sense into her Jethro, she wouldn't listen."

"Harriet …Look, I don't mean to lay any weight on your shoulder but you should've made her go."

"I tried Jethro. You don't know Cooper."

"I DO know Cooper... Okay okay, yeah yeah you're right she's a stubborn little minx."

Another public address announcement, more free and easy laughter in the background from the band members. Harriet waits for the address to finish before speaking again, twirls the spiral phone cord of her vintage BT phone, her fingers weave through the coil until she runs out like when she was as a teenager on an epic telephone chat with old boyfriends, perched on the stairs.

"Jethro, do you have any idea why she was coming to me?"

"You mean she didn't arrange the visit?"

"Well… I wondered if you knew anything."

"I don't know anything. What's going on?"

"Okay look, don't worry about it."

"This is crazy."

"Tell the truth I thought you two had some sort of you know some sort of – uh – misunderstanding."

"I haven't seen Cooper since this morning. She was cool then."

"What about Daniel?"

"What about him?"

"Didn't you say Cooper sent him a text?"

"Oh yeah yeah, I left him with his stinky feet fermenting in the bedroom. He's back to university tom— oh man, what's going on?"

"What did she text Daniel?"

"Something about not coming home tonight. But she sent that way early. Look you're levelling with me about everything right?"

"She's a bit banged up Jethro but she's okay."

"This is some crazy stuff going on here. I'm like totally knocked back."

Another voice comes through the line, sounds like Sophie again. Jethro covers the mouthpiece, mumbles something. He comes back.

"Look Harriet, I'm gonna be straight with you, I'm not exactly in a champagne mood she didn't go to the hospital. I mean there's supposed to be a police report and stuff, right?"

"I took care of it."

"You did?"

"They took all the details they needed. They said the road Cooper was on is a hot spot for accidents so they weren't surprised."

"Right. Right. Hey look you said she's asleep?"

"That's right."

"Can you like rouse her? I need to know what's going on."

"Jethro we should let her sleep."

"Oh man."

Laughter bursts in the background.

"Guys cut it out. Cooper's had an accident."

They mumble apologies then concerned enquiries.

"What happens when you try phoning her?" Harriet says.

"I've called and called but her phone keeps going to voicemail. You said she was coming over to you?"

"That's right."

"And like you don't know why?"

"No... The accident you see."

"I need to speak to her."

Harriet doesn't say anything.

"Harriet please, I'm pacing circles here."

Harriet knows it's unfair to leave Jethro dangling like this. Hold on.

Harriet puts the receiver down, goes upstairs, taps on Cooper's door. Taps but there's no answer. She calls out.

"Coops?"

Tries the handle. The door opens. She looks in. A column of light from the hall falls across Cooper's back but she's facing a wall.

"Coops?"

Nothing.

Harriet has a sudden horrible thought. What if she isn't asleep? What if she's in a coma? She steps into the room up to the bed, touches Cooper's shoulder. Cooper stirs, scratches her nose in sleep, settles again. Relief washes over Harriet. She sees the tissues collected on the floor screwed up, all used. Cooper's been crying again. A lot. Harriet sits on the edge of Cooper's bed, touches her shoulder.

"Coops?"

Cooper's voice is croaky.

"What do you want?"

"Sorry to wake you hon. How're you feeling?"

"Steamrollered."

"Jethro's on the landline. Said he's been trying to call you."

Cooper blinks, doesn't say anything.

"Do you want to speak to him? I can plug in the portable phone."

"Not now."

"He says he's been trying to reach you. I told him about the accident. He didn't know."

Cooper says nothing.

"Coops?"

She closes her eyes – eye – and turns over.

"Not now."

Harriet knows for sure now something's going on. Perhaps Jethro forgot an anniversary or something? Harriet continues.

"He says he's at Gatwick. Something about a tour with Sabre Light. Sounds amazing Coops. Says he's flying out tonight with the band. He says—"

"Yeah. I know."

"You know?"

So, nothing's wrong with Cooper's phone, she's been reading her texts or listening to her messages or both. It's obvious to Harriet now Cooper's blanking Jethro but she doesn't know why and it seems neither does Jethro.

"Oh Coops, what's wrong?"

Cooper pulls the duvet over her shoulder.

"Not now."

Harriet pauses but Cooper doesn't add anything. She pats Cooper's shoulder, gets up, leaves the room, closes the door, goes back downstairs, picks up the phone.

"She won't wake up."

"WHAT DO YOU MEAN SHE WON'T W—"

"Sorry, sorry Jethro that came out wrong. I mean she's exhausted, her lips and eye is all swollen. I couldn't bear to wake her."

"She IS asleep right?" The scepticism in his voice is unusual for Jethro. Jethro's the most easy-going person in the world. Harriet cringes at her own lie.

"Really Jethro. She's sleeping."

"Right. Right. Yeah, sorry for wailing at you."

"It's okay, we're all a little rattled."

"Yeah yeah."

The public announcement comes back. Jethro calls out to his crew.

"You guys go on I'll catch up. Yeah yeah I'm cool no worries." He returns to the phone.

"I'm going to be totally on the level with you Harriet, I don't know what to do."

Harriet hears a creak on the stairs, turns, looks up expecting to see Cooper. It's Eddsy. He stands, his huge hulk on the top step, purple circles under puffy eyes, one hand resting on the overhanging wall above the stairs. Poor man looks beat. Harriet mouths it's Jethro.

He sighs so heavily it's almost a breeze, goes to the loo, flushes, returns to bed.

"Harriet, you still there?"

"I'm here."

"Look damn it, I'm coming back. I'm going to tell the guys I'm not go—"

Harriet senses that would be entirely the wrong thing for him to do.

"Don't do that Jethro. Take your flight. This is Sabre Light. Don't blow it. In the morning I'm sure everything'll come right."

"Oh man."

"You know she's okay here."

"I don't know what to do Harriet, I don't know."

Harriet tries to imagine him sweeping his lean fingers though his long dark hair looking flustered, looking frustrated, pacing, biting his lip. She can't. She's only ever seen him chilled with his easy smile.

"Jethro, you've been waiting for a break like this. It's happening. Cooper's comfortable. You're about the only good news there is right now. You need to do your thing. Cooper's safe. Make her proud."

"Yeah yeah I guess. Okay yeah I'll call first thing."

Another announcement comes through.

"Sounds like you'd better go, Jethro."

"Cool."

"What's cool?"

"Nothing."

"No, tell me."

"What you said – you'd better go Jethro. Like a title for a song yeah? Cooper... You know... We play that game sometimes. Song titles. Tell her that one yeah? She'll like it."

"I'll tell her."

He still doesn't hang up. Harriet feels he's waiting for something else to say.

"Why's it feel like I'm missing something?"

Harriet wonders the same thing.

"Go. Go get that plane, go get famous and make Cooper a boatload of money."

Jethro laughs, but it sounds hollow.

"Yeah. Sure."

"Well bye then. Break a leg."

"Yeah, see you around."

Harriet waits for him to hang up, he doesn't. She hears the lonely background of an abandoned airport through the line. After a few more seconds Harriet has no choice but to hang up herself. She feels as though she's just dropped one end of a skipping rope between them, Cooper in the middle. Still, maybe everything will come clear in the morning.

Maybe.

1 6

TEN MINUTES AGO

COOPER WAKES FROM a troubled sleep, aware Harriet's
landline telephone is ringing. It could only be Jethro. Jethro
doesn't know what Cooper knows. Cooper's even been crying
in her sleep, her pillow cold and damp.

When Cooper slaps at the tears on her face a white furnace
of pain explodes over her swollen eye and cheek. She grits her
teeth and waits till the pain subsides.

Cooper hears Harriet's bedroom door burst open.

Harriet's footsteps crashing down the stairs.

The ringing stops.

The phone rings again a minute later.

The thwang of the telephone ring cut short, Harriet
answering.

Next comes Harriet's muted words, the conversation all one
sided.

Cooper is aware Jethro's left lots of texts and messages on
her mobile. She switched it off after the sixth message. Jethro
doesn't know what she knows. He doesn't know what she
discovered about him. What she discovered absolutely. What
she discovered with complete certainty. What she knows.

A couple of minutes later Harriet's footsteps creak the stairs
again, the footsteps pause outside Cooper's door. A light tap on
the door, a whisper.

"Cooper?"

Damn it.

Another whisper.

"Coops?"

Harriet opens the door, tiptoes into the room, sits on her bed and rests a hand on Cooper's shoulder. Cooper fakes being asleep. She knows Harriet's scanning the floor looking at all the used-up tissues. Harriet says her name a few times until Cooper has no choice but to pretend wake up.

They speak.

Eventually Cooper turns over, she can't take any more, she wants to curl up, disappear into eternity. She wants to forget her life. Empty it. Blank it.

Erase it.

Soon Harriet retreats, closes the door, returns to the phone to spend more muted words.

Next Cooper hears Eddsy emerge into the hall, goes to the loo and drags his tired feet back to the bedroom. Cooper feels guilty. So guilty. She's waking her sister's household and disrupting their lives and she doesn't want that. She'll leave tomorrow. Harriet will try to stop her but she'll leave anyway. She'll spend the morning here, wait till Daniel leaves for university then grab a taxi, go home. She doesn't want Daniel to see her beaten up like this. She has to return to feed Kelloggs anyway.

Eventually Harriet hangs up and returns to bed.

Yeah, that's what she'll do. Leave tomorrow. Go home. She'll have the house to herself so that's good. Her and a cat to hug.

Silence now.

Cooper is alone with her thoughts once more and the longest darkest night still before her.

1 7

JETHRO IS AT Gatwick airport, the phone pressed to his ear. He's confused, chest sick with excitement yet stomach heavy, anchored in worry.

He has no idea why Cooper went over to Harriet's when as far as he knew she should have been in her home studio mixing down the Hoffman recordings today. She'd been in what sounds like a nasty accident and refused treatment.

In the meantime he'd been given the Opportunity-Of-A-Lifetime. A Never-To-Be-Repeated Once-Only chance.

He looks about. The airport is empty save for a few people hanging around. There's a guy in overalls sat on a machine polishing the floor. A security guard wandering through, clasping a cup of coffee and nods at the floor polisher. They stop and talk. Jethro slips his mobile into the back pocket of his jeans. The motley crew disappear into the distance, making their way to the gates. Sophie turns at an airport column, looks back. She smiles, signalling for Jethro to hurry. He responds with a raised index finger.

Jethro calls Cooper again, pacing, waits for it to connect, still in two minds about whether to return home or not. It would disappoint the gang though they'd get it. Still, a big tour deal lies in the balance man, it lies in the balance.

The call goes through to voicemail.

Again.

He sighs. He hangs up. Maybe Cooper's phone's damaged. So why does it feel like there's more to all this? If there is something wrong with Cooper's phone couldn't she have used

Harriet's? If he could just speak to her... Still, Harriet was right, what more could he do now? He'll call in the morning, get an update. Maybe then he'd get to speak to his wife.

Jethro spots Sophie hanging back in the distance watching him attentively. She's wearing red lipstick. The bold contrast with her witch-black goth hair is striking. When their eyes meet she taps her watch, mouths come on.

Oh man.

Jethro slips his phone into his jeans, grabs his jacket, straightens his bolero hat and, head bowed, makes his way over.

THE SUE BAXTER PODCAST
SUE BAXTER
Dr Applegate, what was the surprising link you discovered about the two spiders causing Clive to blackout?
DR APPLEGATE
Before I answer that question, I'm going to show you a couple of slides.
SUE BAXTER
Good lord that spider's big. Okay, I'll explain for my listeners. Dr Applegate has just slid across a close up picture of a typical slide of a spider he was showing Clive. The spider's ugly and big and hairy. Dr Applegate, these magnified images didn't bother him?
DR APPLEGATE
Not at all. Now I'll show you the print outs of the two slides that made Clive blackout.
SUE BAXTER
Well, I see what you mean. They're quite different spiders aren't they? But they're also only taking up a small part of the screen. Most of the picture is just plain background. And these pictures caused Clive's attacks you say?
DR APPLEGATE
That's correct.
SUE BAXTER
Yet he was unaffected by the close ups? How strange. So is the answer the further a spider is away, the more likely it is to trigger Clive's attack?

DR APPLEGATE

(Laughs)

You're so close, I'll give it to you. When Clive viewed the
typical slides, nothing happened. Close ups turn most people off
– as it just did you. But we already knew Clive didn't believe he
had a fear of spiders which is why we started with such bold and
startling images. But when two slides inadvertently reset, its
unmagnified state made them both appear smaller than normal.
Remember the backgrounds are neutral so there's no scale of
reference. Now bearing that in mind—

SUE BAXTER

Ah! Dr Applegate are you telling me small spiders are the
trigger?

DR APPLEGATE

Correct.

SUE BAXTER

(Laughs)

My goodness. But… well, why?

COOPER CAN'T SLEEP.

Her front tooth aches, her swollen eye throbs, her bottom lip feels thick and numb, her shoulder complains, she's a mess. But that's not why she can't sleep.

It's her thoughts.

The thoughts in her head.

The thoughts, the thoughts, the thoughts, in her head.

She touches her lip. It's tender and fat, feels like a split sausage. She'd like to text Daniel but if she switches on the phone more Jethro messages will pile through. Texts and missed calls. She can't handle that right now.

Hours pass.

Cooper longs for sleep. She longs to switch off the thoughts in her head. So many dark thoughts. Not just dark thoughts, black thoughts. What she craves now is oblivion. If she had some sleeping pills—

Cooper sits up.

She knows right now, right this minute, right this second, she knows if she had pills, sleeping pills, headache pills, angina pills, any pills, she'd take the lot. She'd tip the rim of the bottle to her mouth and let them scuttle past her teeth, swallow them all, all of them, crunch every last one of them. She wouldn't care how bitter they tasted, she wouldn't care if she choked, she'd shovel them all down.

If she had a razor blade she'd use it, one quick motion, one unthinking slash across her wrist, that'd be it. After all, she'd done that before years ago, once when she—

Cooper shakes the thoughts away, climbs out of bed, slips on a dressing gown over Harriet's pyjamas. She ties the drawstring tight. Harriet's 5ft 6" and Cooper's 4ft 11" so the jacket swamps her, its shoulders hang down beyond her natural shoulders. She leaves the bedroom, makes her way down the stairs in the dark, goes into the kitchen, puts the counter lights on. The tumble dryer rumbles and the noise brings a familiar homey comfort. A green and red light on the machine blinks alternately. It's tumbling with her cargos inside. Cooper goes over to the machine, stoops, pulls it open, pulls out her cargos from the warm insides of the machine, it's damp. Surely it should be dry by now? Yeah well so what? She finds her T-shirt and under clothes. She places them on top of the counter, closes the tumble dryer, the machine restarts.

Cooper stands and runs her fingers along the white granite worktop, sees a thick heavy butcher's block at the far end, sees a set of knives in a rack.

Cooper goes over, selects the one with the thickest handle, extracts it Excalibur-style, rocks the blade under the task lighting. Light skips along its edge. She runs a fingertip across its lip from the hilt all the way to the tip. She shivers at the dangerous thrill.

Cooper touches the pad of her index finger over the point of the blade, testing herself, presses, presses, presses, presses until the pop of resistance of tissue gives way. She winces. A snap of pain. A spot of dark blood swells on her fingertip, becomes a beady red eye. She sucks it off.

Cooper opens a drawer. Cutlery. Opens another, napkins, tea towels. Another, kitchen utensils. Another, phone chargers, wires, scissors, polishing cloths. Another.

Jackpot.

Bottles of pills. They all look old and scuffed. Pain killers, herbal remedies, headache pills. She picks up a brown prescription bottle. White pills rattle inside. On the label it says Temazepam.

Good.

Sleeping pills.

Lots of them. She puts the bottle on the counter. She slides the knife back into the block. Pills. Yeah pills she can do.

She'll dress in the kitchen, silently leave the house, follow the path of the canal in the dark, walk for a while, a mile or two maybe, sit on a canal bench and do it. Later… well later someone will find her. They'll think she's resting. Runners, dog walkers, early morning strollers. Then at some point someone will stop and check on her. The dog walker will return, find her in the chilly morning air, nudge her shoulder. That jogger will pull out an ear bud, ask her if she's okay. The dawn stroller will take his hands out his pocket, sit and try to speak to her.

Then they'll call an ambulance. By then it will be too late. Too late for them that is. Not for Cooper though. Perfect for Cooper.

The important thing is it won't be Harriet finds her. Won't be Eddsy. Just some stranger. No emotional jolt of finding someone they love like that.

Yeah, better that way. Better it's not family.

After that the questions will come. There'll be queries, speculation, guesses. Why did Cooper do this? Why didn't she say anything? Why didn't she seek help? But what's the point? Why go through all that again? There is no point. This is the right way. This is Cooper's way.

Besides.

One person will know why.

Will know why absolutely.

And that person will live with it forever.

So yeah, maybe that's why.

Cooper smiles even though it hurts her lower lip.

A gruff deep voice comes from behind her.

"Hey kid. Can't sleep?"

2 0

THE DAY BEFORE

COOPER KNOWS NO one will be home.

No rush hour traffic so Cooper drives through the flowing streets. She's listening to TM Logan's audiobook thriller The Holiday, gripped already so she wouldn't have minded some traffic. She's looking forward to a quiet afternoon, a pizza, a good film. Daniel's back at university tomorrow but today he's at his mates. Jethro's checking out some venue for a live gig. House all to herself.

Cooper pulls up behind the house earlier than she expected. Lovely. Peace. No music. No work. She has the Hoffman to finish mastering but that's tomorrow in her garden studio.

Cooper parks.

Locks the car.

Goes through the back gate.

Doesn't yet know what she's going to know soon.

Cooper tries the back door before realising she should've come through the front because no one's home and it'll be locked.

The door opens.

That's a surprise. Someone's home after all? Maybe Jethro's back from checking out the gig. Maybe Daniel's back. She calls out.

No answer.

Or maybe someone forgot lock the back door when they left. Cooper hopes it's not that. Who was the last to leave the house anyway?

Daniel probably. Maybe Jethro. She left them both in the house this morning.

She doesn't like the idea the door's been open all day, feels uneasy about it. What if an intruder's in the house? It should make her hesitate but it doesn't. Cooper makes her way through the kitchen into the hall. She hears music.

Relaxes.

The music's so pastel soft it wafts in the air like mist. It's jazzy. It sounds like one of Jethro's.

It is.

It's Dizzy Gillespie with his trumpet. Wooing music. Not Daniel. Daniel's into a fusion of rap and drumstep, an aggressive percussive drum and bass. Jethro played Dizzy on the CD player the first time they kissed twenty years ago in his flat. What's he doing home already? The venue they were checking out was fifty miles away. He was supposed to be checking it out with Sophie, the new keyboardist Cooper's yet to meet.

Cooper shrugs her jacket off, hangs it on the coat stand, calls out.

"Hey."

No answer.

She looks up the stairs, her hand on the banister. The music is louder from there. She calls out.

"Hey, mister!"

He can't hear her over the music.

Cooper climbs the stairs. At the top she glances at the almost closed-in bedroom door. When did he last listen to that? Dizzy Gillespie. Their music. Theirs alone. Maybe he has the plan of a sultry night in and wanted to surprise her. Daniel isn't back from his mates till tomorrow. Then he leaves for the new term.

That'd be nice. A hot bath. Pizza. Time with Jethro.

She steps up to the landing, over to the bedroom door, puts her hand on the door handle. The aroma of Homme aftershave wafts in the air. The music. She smiles. Nice. He IS in the mood. How long's it been since he wore aftershave?

She turns the handle.

Stops.

She stops.

Cooper stops.

Something tells her not to open it.

There.

Jethro is murmuring. His voice soft, indistinct. That's why she stops.

Then there's the other voice.

Two voices.

That's why she stops.

Intimate voices. They ride just above Dizzy's music. One voice deep, the other soft and female.

That's why.

The words are groaned. The scent of Homme aftershave even stronger.

Cooper's insides squirm. She knows she shouldn't open the door.

Soft kisses.

Soft kisses.

That's why.

Soft moans.

Soft moans.

That's why.

Heavy breathing.

Heavy breathing.

That's why.

Then.

God.

Gentle creaking of the bed frame.

Gentle creaking.

That's why.

Cooper has a strange sense of detachment now. A heat-haze shimmer of reality only. Her heart thuds, skin prickles, she feels hot. Quietly, ever so quietly she nudges the door open. It clicks off its latch, barely moves, merely rocks a couple of millimetres. The moans are clearer through the hair's breadth gap. The air is thick around her. Homme stronger. Music louder. She labours hard to breathe, flattens her palm on the door, gives the door a gentle pat.

The door slips open enough for a full eye. She sees a reflection from her dressing table mirror.

It's enough.

She makes out Jethro's lean prostate body, sees the familiar shape of his head, the gazelle of his body. She makes out someone's long sheeny bare olive leg wrapped around him. No. Oh god no. A woman is sharing the bed.

Oh no.

Their bed.

Her chest squeezes to the point she's suffocating.

Oh god no.

Heart hammers.

No.

Pounds, pounds.

Oh god no, oh god no.

Cooper's centre of gravity lurches and she feels the delayed swing of drunkenness. Everything heaves to one side, the house diagonal, the walls converging, the ceiling lowering, the pictures angling, the door frame corkscrewing. Then it all heaves to the other side. Everything is wrong, wrong, wrong, everything is wrong. She feels sick.

No, oh god no.

Cooper steps back from the door.

No, no, no, god no.

Chest tight like a fist.

Oh please please, god no.

Soft kisses.

Soft moans.

Oh god, oh god, oh god, oh god.

Soft kisses, soft moans, the rhythmic creaking, kisses, moans, Dizzy Gillespie, Homme.

Cooper grasps the banister behind her.

Her heart, her mind, her being, her soul, her soul, her soul, her soul, her soul. Everything collapses.

She backs away, turns, stumbles down the stairs, everything plays backwards, backwards.

Finds the coat stand, finds the kitchen, backwards, finds the back door, backwards, finds the car, drives out, backwards, her mind rewinding everything.

Now she has vision like drizzly rain on glass. Tears drip into her lap, she spins the steering wheel, red lights, green lights, amber. It's all mixing up. Kisses, moans, Dizzy, Homme. It's all a jumble of colours, emotions, swirling, spiralling, messy, blurred, spiky. Kisses, moans, Dizzy, Homme. She can't stop crying, can't stop.

Her heart bursts, her heart bursts, it bursts.

Oh Jethro. Oh god Jethro. Oh no Jethro. No Jethro. Please no Jethro.

Jethro.

Jethro

Jethro.

2 1

EDDSY IS IN the kitchen drinking coffee in the dark thinking about children, thinking about his important client, thinking about Cooper's accident when the lady herself appears and clicks the task lights on and tiptoes in. Cooper doesn't see him. He's about to say something but something about her makes him change his mind. He watches her instead. After enough time has elapsed Eddsy clears his throat.

Cooper spins around almost dropping Harriet's sleeping pills. She tucks them behind her back like he can see her guilty thoughts.

Eddsy is in shadow at the breakfast table, a steaming coffee mug in his hand. He's dressed in blue overalls, the logo of a yellow thumbs up and his company's name Tomalin Garages embroidered over the top pocket.

He'd watched everything Cooper did. He saw her taking her clothes out from the tumble dryer and testing them for dampness. He saw her pick up the big thick knife and run her finger along the edges. He saw her prick herself and that strange detached glint in her eye. He saw her rifle through the drawers and find Harriet's old sleeping pills. He didn't like what he saw. Not one bit.

"Jesus Eddsy, I almost crapped my pyjamas."

"Didn't mean to startle you, kid."

"What're you doing skulking there?"

He lifts his mug.

"Breakfast."

"It's only just gone five."

"Breakfast time. What about you, kid?"

Ever since they both expressed their mutual love for Casablanca, Eddsy's called Cooper kid, referencing the line here's looking at you kid Humphrey Bogart says to Ingrid Bergman.

Cooper shows him the brown bottle of sleeping pills. No point hiding them.

"Can't sleep."

"Herbal ones in that drawer too. Don't need Harriet's old prescription. Should've thrown those out."

"Plus everything hurts."

"Paracetamols in the drawer too."

"So, you usually skulk around the kitchen in the dark?" Cooper says.

"Anyone's skulking it's you."

Cooper joins him at the table, rests the bottle of pills in front of her. It's only when he leans into the light he reveals his face the way Orson Welles does in The Third Man. Cooper looks around in a fake conspiratorial manner.

"Is Harry up as well, skulking around somewhere?"

"Wife's sleeping. You should be too. Wife said she was feeling better. Was due to come back to the office this morning, but not with you here. Kid, you look like you been screwed up and thrown away."

"Thanks."

"Coffee? Machine's on."

"Cool."

"It's strong." He grins. "I like it tasting like metal."

"Cool."

He nods at her busted lip.

"Sure you can handle a hot drink?"

"I'll give it a go."

He stares at the pills on the table.

"Coffee'll wake you up."

"Yeah?"

"Still want one?"

"Yeah."

Eddsy gets up, picks the pill bottle up, opens an under counter door, a flip lid bin opens wide like a hungry chick ready for food. He tosses the pills in the bin.

"Know where they are, you really want them. Recommend painkillers though."

Eddsy strides over to a chrome espresso machine, his movements John Wayne slow. Because he's big, 6ft 5" big, every move he makes seems seismic, especially to tiny Cooper.

While he expresses a coffee, Cooper's thinking shit, shit, shit, shit. Should've come down earlier. Shit, shit, shit.

"Cappuccino?"

"Cool."

He presses milk on the coffee machine, it comes out foamy. He deliberates, swirls it into a design by moving the cup as it pours. He takes pride in it. For two years owning the machine he's been doing all sorts of designs with the frothy milk and caramel creme. He's done circles, spirals, lattices, all sorts of things. This one he's been practising a month. He places the cup in front of her. The milk design is a balloon with a string. Cooper looks at it.

"That's pretty."

"Lots of practice at breakfast."

He makes himself a second cup with the same flourish, places it on the table opposite Cooper. His one is the shape of a spanner.

Eddsy sits down, sips his coffee. His fingers are so thick they can't slip through the handle. The mug looks child-sized in his paws.

"Going somewhere?" Eddsy says.

"Why?"

He nods at the clothes on the counter.

"Maybe," Cooper says.

Eddsy rises again. He touches the pile of clothes. They're still damp. He doesn't say anything, strides over to the tumble dryer, opens it, it stops. He shoves the bundle back in, closes it, the dryer starts churning again. He joins her back at the table.

"Know where they are, you really want them."

Cooper doesn't bother to protest. She asks for the sugar. Eddsy slides a bowl across the table. She counts in five spoons. Eddsy looks impressed. She tilts the mug to her mouth away from the most tender part of her lower lip. The coffee's good – hot, wonderfully sweet, so strong she won't have any enamel on her teeth left.

Eddsy nods at the sugar bowl.

"Notice the sugar's as fine as Mediterranean sand?"

"Yeah?"

"Wife only has caster sugar."

"Yeah?"

"Says it looks better than granulated. Costs more. I say to her make your own by whizzing granulated sugar in a food processor for a couple seconds. She don't listen. Just buys caster. More expensive, she buys it anyway. He sighs. Know they call it superfine in the US?"

"No kidding?"

"Superfine sugar. Also call it baker's sugar as it blends better."

"Yeah?"

"Dissolves quicker."

"You know a lot about sugar?"

"Not interested?"

Cooper shrugs.

"So…," Eddsy says, "rough day yesterday?"

"You could say that."

"Just did. Bad news about your Toyota."

"My toy motor."

"Hmm."

Eddsy tips his mug swallows. Cooper watches his golf ball-sized Adam's apple, mesmerised by how much it moves. As he swallows it goes up a long way then down like a sewing machine, needle stitching behind the canopy of grizzled throat.

In social gatherings, barbecues, parties, evenings out, Eddsy sits and watches. He only responds when addressed. Even then it's monosyllables pearled together into short sentences. Cooper wonders whether Eddsy has a mild form of autism. Not enough to nudge any scales, just enough to make her wonder if he does. His presence though is never unsettling. A quiet giant who's just comfortably around. Most quiet people are unnerving. You wonder what they're thinking. Most big men are unnerving too. With Eddsy it's not like that. Cooper gets the impression he's observing, not judging. Eddsy puts his mug down.

"Harriet's crapping herself over you."

"Yeah?"

He glances at Cooper's left wrist. He can't see it in this light but he knows there's a series of faint marks there from when she was younger, vulnerable and a victim of self-harm. According to Harriet, when Jethro came along, Cooper reasserted herself and found a firm footing in life.

So now when he, not five minutes ago, witnessed Cooper choose the biggest knife from the rack, prick her finger, squeeze out a bead of blood with that look of fascination, it troubled him.

"Know what she said last night?" Eddsy says.

"Harriet?"

"No, my other wife."

"What'd she say?"

"Thinks something's up between you and Jethro. But can't work out how you two can quarrel when only one of you knows about it."

"And what do you think?"

"Don't think. Just watch."

Silence passes between them.

"Look kid, you okay?"

She raises her mug of coffee as though making a toast.

"I'm cool. Even if it does taste like metal."

"Are you, he taps the side of his head, okay?"

Cooper slumps in her chair, feels her eyes burn. It takes a while to answer and when she does it comes out a whisper.

"I don't know."

He accepts the honesty, nods. He leans back. The wooden chair crackles against his bulk.

"Seen tons of car wrecks," Eddsy says. "Some fixable. Yours isn't. That tree is easy to hit."

"Yeah?"

"Spoke to the lads who recovered your car."

Cooper sips her coffee through the side of her mouth.

"Yeah?"

"Cooper, mind explaining something? What's going on?"

"You never call me Coops no matter how much I say."

"Cooper's better. Austin Mini Cooper, Gary Cooper, Tommy Cooper. You don't call classics, Coops."

"Yet you're Eddsy."

"It's on my birth certificate. So?"

"I'm a bit banged up that's all."

"Blind man facing the other way can see that. Cheekbone's a beauty, eye's nicely shut shop, lip's fat and juicy too. How's the whiplash?"

"Cool."

"So, what's going on with you?"

"Nothing."

"I'm putting one and one together making—"

"Two?"

"Eleven."

Cooper frowns.

"Eleven?"

Eddsy grins.

"I like binary. So?"

"What're you saying?"

"You call Harriet. You're bawling. You're coming over, you say. You crash. You're knocked out. Then you wake and you're chatty on the phone like you don't have a care. Then you suddenly wail over the phone again and since then you're like... this."

"What's this?"

Eddsy leans forward.

"Kid, something don't smell right."

Cooper looks away.

"Cooper." He says her name quietly. It has the leaden weight of distant thunder.

"It's just stuff."

"Stuff?"

"Yeah, stuff."

"What stuff?"

"Nothing. Just stuff."

"So, what about not going to the hospital?"

"Nah. I'm cool."

"Figures."

"What figures?"

He smirks.

"About as unreasonable as me."

Cooper smiles carefully through her broken lip. It burns when the coffee mug presses against it, but the pain is welcome.

"No laughing matter, not going to hospital. Know how foolish that is, Cooper? Seen enough delayed concussions to know the dimwits should've gone with ambulance crew."

Cooper raises her mug again.

"Cheers."

Eddsy leans further forward in the chair, lattices his thick fingers around his mug, fingernails the size of most people's thumbnails.

"Couple years back," Eddsy says, "truck driver I was chatting to on the M40. Man was in a pile up. Gave himself a shiner when the airbag deployed. Gets a lovely set of bruises, bit like yours."

"Yeah?"

"Haulage company gets another cab out to him, swaps over the trailer. Driver hangs around an hour while they're sorting all this. Me and the lads dealing with a couple cars. Ambulance crew trying to persuade the truck driver to go into the ambulance the last half hour. Truck driver's not having it. I go over, ask him what he's waiting for, get in the blasted ambulance. Deadlines to meet he says, deadlines to meet. Go to hospital I say. Deadlines to meet he says. Guy counts on his fingers. I got a wife. I got kids. I got a sick dog. I got a boss screaming at me for screwing up one of his cabs. I got a late delivery. I tell him the haulage company can get another driver, you need to get seen to. Fella kicks the road, shrugs his shoulder. Deadlines to meet he says."

Eddsy shakes his head.

"Know what happens next?"

"Let me guess. Goes to hospital."

"No. Left eye pops red. Completely marbles it. Fella crumples on the road in a heap where he stands. Starts shaking all over, leg kicking out like he's Elvis doing his fancy leg shake. Know what? Vessel bust in his brain. Man has brain haemorrhage. Now can't use his right side, can't move his right hand, can't move his right leg, lost sight in his left eye and know what else? Can't drive." Eddsy sighs. "No more deadlines to meet."

"You trying to scare me?"

"Trying to make you crap the wife's pyjamas."

"Well, it's working."

"Good. Harriet is gaga over you, kid. Tossed in bed all night. She barely sleeps, I barely sleep. Need my beauty sleep. She barely sleeps, I barely sleep. See these bags under my eyes? That's you."

Cooper pouts. Tries to. Her lower lip feels as though it's covered in leather.

"I'm hearing you."

"So?"

"I'll get out of your hair today."

"Kid, that's not what I'm angling to hear. Won't stop Harriet wearing out the carpet."

Eddsy rotates the handle of the mug all the way around, 360 degrees. The mug says Mechanics do it with nuts. He picks it up, knocks the rest of the coffee back like it's a shot of whisky, stares at Cooper.

"One, take some paracetamols. Two, go to hospital. Three, spill your guts to someone."

"Yeah maybe."

"Cooper, you need to come clean. Maybe Jethro. Maybe Harriet. Maybe a neighbour. Maybe a stranger. Who knows? But come clean. I'm just a mechanic, what do I know?"

Cooper takes in the gleaming kitchen the size of a modest apartment, snorts.

"JUST a mechanic. Right."

He follows her gaze, sees what she's seeing. The sheen, the chrome, the solid granite worktops.

"Don't let stainless steel fool you. All loans and mortgages. The business? The same garage repeated six times in six locations. Not clever, just maths." Eddsy jabs a finger at Cooper. "What you do, that's talent. Seen your recording studio. Heard the results when you mix and arrange all that serious Radio 3 stuff that goes over my head. You could communicate with the ISS on that mixing console you got."

"ISS?"

"International Space Station."

"It's nothing."

"What you do is talent. Me? I just fix stuff. Nothing to it." Cooper sips her coffee.

"Yeah well, that's all I do too."

He levels his heavy-lidded eyes at her. From anyone else it'd look predatory. Once you know Eddsy you know he's about as threatening as a pillowcase of feathers, with family and friends anyway. Cooper also gets the impression he'd defend family with the fierce determination of a rabid dog too.

"Cooper, watch my lips. Go to hospital."

"Yeah, I'll think about it."

"Look, tell you something. Got a fleet of cars from a big sales company to check over this morning. Up to my eyes. Got fifteen days to do the entire fleet. Seventy-two cars. Big job. New client."

"Okay?"

"Even calling everyone from the other branches, right?"

"So?"

"We get this right, we get a five-year contract with them. Biggest deal we've ever signed off. Got to be on site to oversee, right? All pulling our weight. Even then, tight deadline. Still got to look after our regulars. Can't ignore the regulars."

"Congrats."

"Not so fast. Deal not done. Point is, you say to me you'd go to hospital I'd take you, wait with you, everything."

Cooper blinks at him.

"Your sales fleet client won't like that."

He grins. Teeth the size of thumbnails as well.

"Yeah. Staff'll want a pound of my flesh too."

"You'd do that?"

"Kid, not going to hospital, seriously bad judgement. Me in an accident like that? Stubborn as a bully's boot stomping a cat's tail? I'd still go."

"Wow. Nice imagery."

Eddsy stands up, picks up a thick spray of keys. They scrape across the table.

He glances at Cooper's left wrist again. He still can't see the fine lines Harriet told him about he knows are there. What

Cooper did this morning, getting the damp clothes out the dryer, the knife, the pills, it troubles him.

Cooper gets up, goes over to the tumble dryer, opens it. She fishes out her clothes again.

Eddsy watches her.

"They're damp."

She squeezes them.

"They're fine. They've been in the tumble dryer all night."

"It's on eco mode. Takes longer."

Cooper doesn't say anything.

"Fine, put them on kid, I'll shoot you to hospital. I can wait."

"You can't. You've got seventy-two cars to see to."

Eddsy stands in the middle of the kitchen, the task lights making him a menacing silhouette, the stance of a gunfighter.

"Listen," Eddsy says. "Know we can't have kids, right?"

"I know."

"My fault. Balls the size of Russia, they don't do much."

"Cheers for that."

"So, family? Got diddly-squat on my side. Harriet? She's got you, Jethro, Daniel. All we got is what you got."

"So?"

Eddsy counts on his thick fingers.

"Harriet. You. Jethro. Daniel. Me. That's it."

"What're you saying?"

"You got financial troubles, you know where we're at. You got car problems, it's no problem. You got other problems, maybe we can help. Point is, we take care of family. Always. 100%. Right?"

"Now you sound like a Mafia don."

His voice remains deep, the rumble of distant thunder still underhanging it. He sighs.

"Cooper."

"Okay, I appreciate your concern."

Appreciate my concern. Harriet would jump down a well for you."

"Wow, you're up on your imagery today."

"So? Figure it's not money problems."

"No."

"Not Daniel and university?"

"It's not that."

"Trouble at work?"

"No."

"None of you have anything wrong with you, right?"

"Like what?"

"Cancer. Heart condition. Brain tumour."

"God no."

"Something between you and Jethro then." He makes it a statement not a question.

She inhales, lets it out.

"Who knows?"

"Beyond my pay grade. Harriet, your best bet."

Cooper squeezes her cargos again. It isn't less damp.

"Eddsy. What you said…"

"About?"

"Family. All that."

"What about it?"

"Yeah, it's a nice thing to say." Her voice buckles under the words.

"Three Musketeers have a saying."

"Yeah?"

"All for one and one for all."

"Okay?"

"Alexandre Dumas. The man's talking about looking out for each other."

"Who?"

"Fella who wrote it. Point is, struck me as a kid, that saying. See I didn't have family. Was in a home for boys right?"

"Yeah, I know."

"Always wanted a chance to live up to that saying. Got that chance. Harriet, you, Jethro, Daniel. Here for each other, right?"

"Right."

"Always. 100%. Matters not I'm not related by blood. You're all family. Figure I won the lottery anyway."

Cooper can't help it. Her eyes fill. Decision made she shoves the cargos back in the tumble drier, closes the door. It whirrs up again. She rises to her full tiny height, steps toward Eddsy, squeezes his upper arm. It's hard like a pumped up lorry tyre.

"We all fit together, right?" Eddsy says.

Choked up.

"And you say you're just a mechanic?"

"What, The Three Musketeers? Errol Flynn in an old flick."

Cooper considers it.

"You'd take me to hospital even with seventy-two cars to see to?"

He jangles his keys.

"These babies right here? One of them runs the van outside. You say go, we go."

"It's okay, Harriet can take me later."

He grins.

"Good girl."

"Besides she has a hotter car than yours."

"Damn right. Always the best for my girl." He turns to go. "Good. Can't afford the time. Lads and ladies would have my head."

Cooper watches him stride to the front door. She calls out.

"Eddsy?"

"Yeah?"

"You were never going to take me. You were just softening me up to go with Harriet, weren't you?"

He laughs, then Cooper laughs through the rubber of her lips.

He gets to the double oak front doors, opens one. He turns, looks at Cooper.

"Yeah, I would've. Still will, you want."

"Nah. I'm good. I'll ask Harriet."

He steps through.

"Eddsy?"

"What, kid?"

"It's like, appreciated."

He pauses enough to nod, then he's gone.

Cooper decides not to drink the rest of the coffee. She washes the cup under a tap, goes up. On the landing she hears Harriet call out.

Cooper steps into Harriet's bedroom, finds her sitting up in bed, eyes piggy from lack of sleep and the tail end of her cold, blowing her nose.

"He persuaded you to go to St Mary's didn't he?" Harriet says.

Cooper smiles.

"Yeah. Bollocks."

Harriet makes a mini fist pump.

"Yay."

2 2

THE SUE BAXTER PODCAST
DR APPLEGATE
If we knew why small spiders triggered Clive's attacks, we'd understand the source of them. Interestingly, his condition subverted our expectation about the fear of spiders. Large spiders turn most people off, but not Clive. It also answered the puzzle why Clive never blacked out in front of his daughters when removing a spider from their bedroom. He never had to remove small spiders, his children weren't bothered by them. And we now know which spider causes the blackouts. It's called Linyphiidae, and it's common in the UK.
SUE BAXTER
Sounds poisonous, but if it's found in the UK then probably not. You're going to tell me Linyphiidae is an ordinary house spider or something aren't you?
DR APPLEGATE
Actually you're quite correct, Sue. Linyphiidae is known as the money spider.
SUE BAXTER
Goodness. Really? Aren't they about the size of your baby fingernail?
DR APPLEGATE
Indeed.
SUE BAXTER
But surely Clive would've encountered small spiders all the time. Why did he start having blackouts at the age of forty seven then?

DR APPLEGATE

That's a good question.

SUE BAXTER

Now I know you're here really to talk about Cooper Hall's treatment – revolutionary at the time – but please tell us what's so scary about money spiders anyway?

DR APPLEGATE

Another good question. I'll answer the second question first.

2 3

COOPER AND HARRIET are back from the hospital.

Nothing is wrong except minor facial trauma, cuts, a stiff shoulder and a sprained ankle. It took four hours of waiting for x-rays and checks. Everyone told Cooper how lucky she was. The car recovery crew, the police, the ambulance, Harriet, Eddsy, the hospital staff.

But Cooper does not feel lucky.

Take painkillers they said.

She doesn't feel lucky.

Rest for a couple of weeks they said.

She doesn't feel lucky.

Now Cooper's back at Harriet's sinking into Harriet's oval bath. It's her place of solace and thought. The water's high and hot.

No. Definitely does not feel lucky.

Cooper partly floats on the steamy surface. Her flotation tank. She ran it as hot as she could take, an acid of heat etching into her skin.

If she can just silence the thoughts, just silence the pain… She closes her eyes, enjoying the water. The snap of heat brings tears of pleasure to her eyes. Better to cry for this than to cry for…

That.

Dizzy Gillespie. Homme. Soft kisses, soft kisses. Soft moans, soft moans.

That.

It's not the world she needs to shut out. It's what's inside she needs to silence.

As she lounges, Cooper is unaware of a shadowy presence creeping over her. The dark of unconsciousness invisible as it slowly seeps into her.

Her mind starts fabulating. Fracturing thoughts into random pieces and stringing them together in a jumble to mesmerise and distract her like beautiful fireworks. Cooper's unaware her breathing has become shallow. Shallow. Shallower.

The oval bath is so deep Cooper's feet don't touch the end. The basin so smooth her heels loose their tenuous grip. Her head drops forward. Her nose, just above the waterline, ripples the water with every breath.

Cooper is at peace now.

The dark draws night down further on her exhausted body. Her heels slip a little more and her nose sinks below the waterline.

Instantly, autonomically, her diaphragm quits expanding and contracting, ceases to pull oxygen into her lungs as sensitive nerve endings around her nasal lining detect the presence of water. The result is an automatic reflex to prevent her lungs taking it in. Her throat constricts, her lips seal shut. It's the same primitive reaction babies have when dropped into water; they cease breathing and immediately begin to paddle and seek the surface.

Only Cooper doesn't respond as she should. The heat, the silence, the exhaustion, the welcome, eddying waves of comforting black draw her down. The dark, as vast as a night sky on a wide, flat surface of the earth.

Cooper has found peace. Beautiful, welcome peace.

It does not last long.

The next thing Cooper is aware of is an explosion of sharp icicles shattering her awake. She jolts back to consciousness aware she's doubled over on the floor, curled in a foetal position. She splutters, heaving in greedy lungfuls of hot wet air, but she is smiling, high on endorphins from the thrilling elixir of a near death experience, like the dangerous joy of a carnival ride.

Harriet hears a thump on the ceiling, rushes up, knocks on the bathroom door.

"Coops, you okay in there?"

Cooper lies on the floor. The floor is cool and wet and welcome.

"God yeah," Cooper says.

Something in Cooper's voice makes Harriet pause, makes her frown.

"Can I come in?"

"Yeah."

Harriet opens the door, steps in smiling. Then Harriet's eyes widen and her smile turns to one of horror.

2 4

THE SUE BAXTER PODCAST
DR APPLEGATE
True, Clive suddenly started having blackouts from the age of
forty-seven, but we had no idea why. However, we knew the
money spider was triggering a repressed memory.
SUE BAXTER
A spider the size of my hand would scare me to death, but I
don't understand why small spiders would scare anyone.
DR APPLEGATE
Actually Sue you've just answered your own question I'll
explain in a moment. We next brought in a specialist in hypnotic
regression to try to unveil Clive's repressed memory.
SUE BAXTER
I take it the regression worked?
DR APPLEGATE
It did.
SUE BAXTER
You just mentioned I answered my own question. Tell me how.
DR APPLEGATE
You referred to a large spider as being scary then proceeded to
state small spiders aren't.
SUE BAXTER
Sorry, I'm not with you. What's the clue?
DR APPLEGATE
Suppose you wake up in bed one morning to the uncomfortable
feeling something is wriggling under your bed sheets. When you

peel them back you discover you're in a nest of 10,000 money spiders.

SUE BAXTER

Oh my goodness.

DR APPLEGATE

They're crawling all over your body, up your legs, your arms, in your hair, across your face, your eyes, into your mouth, your nose—

SUE BAXTER

(Laughs)

Stop. Please STOP!

DR APPLEGATE

(Laughs)

Well it's itch-making at the very least. When you said you couldn't understand why a large spider didn't affect Clive but small spiders did, you'd mentioned large spider singular but small spiders plural.

SUE BAXTER

Gosh, crawling through my hair and all over my face? Ugh! Makes my skin crawl just thinking about it. So are you saying this actually happened to Clive?

DR APPLEGATE

We believe so.

SUE BAXTER

Oh for heaven's sake. 10,000 spiders? I mean, how's that possible?

2 5

HARRIET DROPS TO the bathroom floor beside Cooper.
Cooper's skin is angry and red and feels as hot as a radiator.
Harriet tries to lift her but Cooper is limp. The steamed up
windows are open, the bathroom door is open. The extractor fan
alone can't deal with all that steam. Steam pours through the
door and window as though the bathroom's on fire.

Harriet cradles Cooper until she feels strength come back
into Cooper's limbs. Soon Cooper is sitting up on the floor by
herself. She laughs.

Harriet stares at her sister. Cooper's lip is glossy with blood,
her teeth stained with blood, her swollen-shut eye weeping, her
whole body the colour of raw prawns. Frowning, Harriet dips a
hand into the bathwater, snatches it out.

"Oh Coops, that's scalding."

Cooper laughs, semi-delirious.

"God yeah."

"What happened?"

"Had a moment."

"What do you mean?"

"I didn't realise how hot I was."

"You look like you've been boiled alive."

The comment makes Cooper laugh until she coughs. Harriet
stares at her. When she's sure Cooper's okay, Harriet grabs a
bath towel, soaks it under a cold water tap and drapes it over
Cooper's shoulders like a cold wrap. Cooper's veins disappear
from the surface of her forehead and the skin loses some of its

raging colour. Harriet sits cross-legged in front of her, staring at her sister.

"Coops, what's going on with you?"

"Like I said. I got too hot."

"Oh Coops, I don't understand what's going on."

"Don't sweat it." Cooper realises the irony of what she's said, laughs again.

"I came up to tell you Jethro called again."

"Yeah? What'd he say?"

"He thinks something's wrong with your phone and he doesn't understand why you haven't tried calling him. I told him you weren't up to speaking to anyone. You ARE speaking to him, right?"

"I'll call later."

"So, your phone is working?"

Cooper eyes her.

"Like you don't know."

"He said something about having to go straight into a sound check. The other band had pulled out completely. They have the whole ten week tour."

"Cool."

"Oh Cooper. That's all you can say?"

"I'm hungry."

Harriet stares at Cooper before continuing.

"Also, Daniel called. He's fed Kelloggs and is heading off to university soon. He wanted to talk to you first but I told him you were taking a bath. Coops, why aren't you talking to anyone?"

Cooper stands, shrugs, totters a bit. The heat's still inside her, still pouring out but she feels so much better. Her face rages and she feels like she's been snapped with elastic bands all over. It's a wonderful sensation and she grins.

Harriet gets up, raises her hands in bewilderment and leaves the bathroom.

"Oh Cooper, you're unbelievable."

2 6

TEN MINUTES LATER Harriet's in the kitchen ripping open a bacon packet about to prepare brunch when her mobile rings. She answers.

"Husband."

"Wife. How's the patient?"

"We went to the hospital, thanks to you. She's fine. Just has to rest."

"Good."

"You're so sweet."

"Shut it."

"I know you're busy with that new client and everything so it's sweet you took time to—"

"Said shut it."

"And you act all mean and sour but underneath you're—"

"Curdled milk."

Harriet laughs.

"She's just had a bath."

"Another one?"

"Had a shaky moment in the bathroom but it's all good. Anyway the hospital suggested salve, painkillers and plenty of rest. You did good husband, persuading her to go to the hospital. I'd never have convinced her."

"Right."

"What's wrong?"

"Nothing."

"Something's on your mind."

"Concerned is all."

"What do you think it is?"

"Wife. Shut it."

Harriet never tires of that word. Wife. His wife. Husband. Her husband. Seven years and she still likes it.

"You heard from Jethro?" Eddsy finally says.

"Yeah. He's bagged a ten week tour with Sabre Light. He called, said Cooper's not answering her phone."

Eddsy sighs.

"Oh, don't be hard on him. This sounds like the real thing. He's been calling her."

"Hell's he doing there then?"

"You know what? You're being a real meanie grump."

Eddsy doesn't reply.

"You are. You're being a grumpity grump. Even more grumpity grump than usual grumpity grump, mister. Honestly I don't know how your employees put up with you grumping all over the place."

"Me, big chief."

"Then you better watch they don't cry mutiny one day."

"They wouldn't dare."

"Anyway, I think whatever upset—"

A phone in Eddsy's office rings. When it rings a few more times he covers the mouthpiece, calls out.

"Ian! Phone!" Then back to Harriet. "Go on."

"I was saying whatever upset Cooper happened yesterday."

"You think?"

Harriet ignores the sarcasm. "And you know what? It's obvious Jethro doesn't know a thing about it. What could it be, you think?"

"Said shut it."

Harriet knows Eddsy never speculates about anything. Not ever, blast him. She wishes she could be more like that. She wishes she could.

"Well anyway, when I spoke to him again earlier he was just as baffled."

"Right."

"Stop saying right."

"Sure thing."

"Listen, you remember once I told you about how Cooper came home from school with a black eye?"

"No. Remind me."

"Well, she said to mum the black eye was because she had a scrap with someone at school, right?"

Eddsy doesn't respond, not even to say right.

"Well, what she didn't tell mum was the person she scrapped with was her boyfriend's other girlfriend."

"He had two on the go?"

"Yes, he did. One Michael Cartwright. He was seeing some other girl from another class."

"How far back we talking?"

"Wait, lemme think. Cooper was fifteen. Turns out Michael had been seeing the other girl for months before Cooper, the little runt."

Eddsy splutters his coffee out.

"Did you just say—"

"I said runt. R U N T."

"Thought you said—"

"So anyway, Cooper had to learn of this love triangle from the girl herself."

"Don't believe that."

"You don't believe what?"

"Something up with those two, yeah get that. But Jethro's not like that."

"I was talking about Michael Cartwright."

"Wife, what you're saying—"

"Well, stop interrupting and let me finish. It's because of what we found out next that made Cooper want to take her own—"

"Harry?"

Harriet spins around almost dropping her phone. Cooper's behind her framed in the kitchen doorway. She's wearing a dressing gown, the belt tight around her, her short hair flat against her scalp.

Harriet's face flushes.

"I didn't hear you come down."

"I'm like after another towel …for my hair, yeah?"

"Airing cupboard behind the bathroom door."

Cooper nods, leaves.

Harriet whispers into the phone.

"Oh crap."

"She heard you?"

"Crappity crap crap."

"Weren't saying anything bad, wife."

"I'd better go."

"Right. And no more four-letter words like—"

"Stop it."

"—runt."

THE SUE BAXTER PODCAST
SUE BAXTER
Dr Applegate, you're telling me the cause of Clive's
arachnophobia came from encountering 10,000 money spiders
as a child? Surely that's ridiculous. What, was he on a spider
farm for heaven's sake?
DR APPLEGATE
When we interviewed his family, his sister recalled an
interesting incident where Clive was about eighteen months. She
was collecting insects and spiders in jam jars in their back
garden. On this particular day she left Clive alone briefly with a
jar of money spiders to collect more. When she returned she
found him apparently snoozing next to an open jam jar which
was now empty. She remembers how struck she was by Clive's
sudden drop off to sleep.
SUE BAXTER
But that's not 10,000 spiders. A handful at most, surely?
DR APPLEGATE
Don't forget, children have vivid imaginations. From an
eighteen month old's point of view it might as well have been
ten thousand spiders. Clive had either knocked the jar over with
a loose cap or he'd opened the jar. The spiders most likely
climbed his arm and escaped over him and this is very likely
why he froze.
SUE BAXTER
He could have shaken them off, surely?

DR APPLEGATE

Remember the flight or fight instinct?

SUE BAXTER

But you're saying he froze – that's not fight or flight.

DR APPLEGATE

Actually there are two other survival reactions not commonly known – to fawn and to freeze. To fawn simply means to comply with a threat, such as being held at gunpoint to get into a car. To freeze is the rabbit in the headlights situation, caused either by indecision or, more relevant here, to hide in plain sight by remaining stock-still. It's the simplest form of camouflage.

SUE BAXTER

So Clive froze. But couldn't he have just brushed the spiders off?

DR APPLEGATE

He probably tried. But some very young children haven't yet developed perfect motor coordination. The most likely explanation after failing to brush them off is he froze and held his breath.

SUE BAXTER

Ah.

DR APPLEGATE

So if our scenario's correct, he'd have tiny spiders running over his face, mouth, nose and so on.

SUE BAXTER

I get it. He held his breath so he didn't breathe them in.

DR APPLEGATE

The spiders had found warmth on Clive's skin and were likely exploring it. Clive had held his breath until he passed out.

SUE BAXTER

Fascinating detective work. But why then after all these years should his condition reappear?

2 8

HARRIET RAPS ON Cooper's door.

Cooper calls out.

"Door's open."

Harriet steps in, hands clasped together, repentant like a convent girl. She doesn't know how to deal with this. She feels bad, so bad Cooper overheard her talking to Eddsy about her boyfriend. Cooper's patting her head with the towel, the bedroom sweet with bathroom scents.

"How's the eye?" Harriet says.

"It's cool."

"Coops, your lip looks worse."

"It's cool. I won't mess your towels up."

"That's not what I mean."

Harriet looks at Cooper, sees something different in her. She looks – oddly – happy. Maybe the bath did her good after all.

"Listen Coops—"

"You were talking about Michael Cartwright?"

Harriet's cheeks flush.

"Oh. You did hear me. We're worried about you Coops. You know Eddsy phoned specially?"

"Michael Cartwright was twenty-three years ago, right?"

Harriet slumps on the bed, repentant hands pressed between her knees.

"I feel awful."

"Harry, it's cool. I don't care who you tell."

Harriet watches as Cooper takes off her bathrobe, slips into her underclothes. She pulls Eddsy's white shirt awkwardly over her sore shoulder and rolls the sleeves up, getting away with the floppy style.

When she's finished, she bundles the towel and dressing gown to the foot of the bed, settles next to Harriet. Harriet wants to reprimand her for leaving damp bathroom fodder around like that. She bets Cooper's also left the bathroom in a state again.

"Coops, I'm so worried about you."

She glances at Cooper's left wrist, tries not to make it obvious. The scars barely visible now. Cooper pulls a sleeve down.

"I know you've been ignoring Jethro's calls."

Cooper doesn't respond.

"Coops, please."

Cooper nods at her phone on the bedside table.

"He called twelve times last night and a bunch more this morning. Sent a bundle of texts too."

"Have you told Jethro why you're so upset?"

Cooper shrugs. Harriet knows Cooper well enough to know she's not going to explain anything. She's so stubborn. Harriet takes the cue to stand up and clap her hands together. A change of subject.

"So, fancy brunch? I was just about to put crispy fried bacon on. If your lip can take it."

Cooper smiles.

"Cool."

"Fried eggs?"

"Ooh."

"Steaming hot baked beans?"

"Oooh."

"Spitting hot sausages?"

"Oooh."

"Fried mushrooms and onions?"

"Oooh."

"Crunchy buttered toast with puddles of melted butter?"

"OOOH!"

"Mustard and ketchup?"

"Lead the way, sis."

COOPER SITS AT Harriet's breakfast bar, bites into the crisp bacon, enjoying the salty burn. It's hot and spicy. She dips a corner of the toast into yolk. It's buttery and tasty. She bites down on fat sausages smothered in mustard and ketchup. It's sweet and savoury. Across from her, Harriet watches her eat with a mother's pride. All that pent-up parenting still surging inside. She clears Cooper's plate away.

Cooper takes her mug of tea, spoons in five sugars and sips. Since the bath she's feeling better but she knows it's not going to last. She needs distraction. She has to work. Lots of work. Work will help.

Harriet clears everything away and Cooper switches her phone on, checks her messages. She deletes Jethro's new phone messages unheard, texts unread. She sees one from Daniel, calls him, chats with him, tells him she's spending a little time at Harriet's. He asks why she sounds so funny, she makes an excuse about a little prang. She's sure he'll get the news from dad before long. It earns a disapproving glance from Harriet.

Daniel reminds her he has to leave for uni today, will he get to see her before he goes? She tells him not this time, she's tied up with stuff.

Next, Cooper runs through three work messages. One from Sennheiser Electronics seeking her opinion on a prototype vacuum tube microphone under the Neumann badge. Another from an acoustical research laboratory who's invented a vibration absorbing panel to line speaker boxes and improve their performance and would love her input. A third from

Graham Chambers of Chambers Music Agency. This is what she needs. Work. Lots of work. Lots of distraction.

She calls the companies, arranges delivery of the Neumann mic and makes an appointment to visit the acoustic labs. Next she calls Graham back.

Graham answers on the first ring, his aristocratic upbringing clear in his Oxford educated accent.

"Ah, finally the lady calls."

"Hey Graham, what up?"

"The lady asks what's up. What's up? Supposed to update me old thing. How's the Hoffman?"

Cooper fills him in about her accident.

"Goodness Cooper, sure you're up to it? Sound dreadful old girl."

Graham is in his wood-panelled office in the east wing of his twenty bedroom manor house surrounded by acres of wooded land. As well as a music agency, Graham owns paddocks, a couple of racing thoroughbreds, several flint cottages and leases an outcrop of land to a small organic dairy farmer.

"What's with your voice old girl?"

"Busted lip. It's like talking through rubber tyres."

He laughs.

"Rubber tyres. Shouldn't laugh but you are a wag."

"I'll finish the Hoffman."

"Excellent."

"But not today."

"Hmm. Anyone else I'd give god almighty. As it's your highly sought-after platinum skills I'm employing… Give me your plan of action. I'll see what I can tell the chappies at the label."

"I need another twenty-four hours."

In the background, Harriet's jaw clenches.

"That's what always impresses me about you dear lady. Not only are you a talented thing, you're also a damned conscientious little worker bee too."

"Hey, watch it buster."

Graham's offhand comment, a hallmark of the good-humoured spar of class warfare they engage in. Cooper makes fun of his upbringing, Graham makes fun of hers.

Graham laughs.

"Much as I hate to disappoint a client, I'll tell the label you're adding finishing touches."

"What else you got?"

Harriet thwacks shut a kitchen cupboard door deliberately. She can't believe what she's hearing.

"Good lord the lady's seeking work," Graham says. "What's happened, your stock fallen overnight? Let me see. You're doing M's Jupiter at the RAH in a couple of months. Also B's 7 with Dominic at the RFH. Dominic always ignores the dynamic markings though. Be careful how you record him, he's bound to over-egg the decibels with his ham-fisted attack on the Steinway. There's also the Scarlatti fest. coming up of course, but not as yet confirmed. Everything else is already booked out to others."

"Is that it?"

"My dear, if you didn't turn your nose up to most of my bookings, I could fly you across the world everyday for something."

Cooper needs work now. Not months from now. She needs something to rescue her from the torrent of dark thoughts bound to return.

Harriet continues to listen to Cooper as she clears up, clattering wares, her anger threatening to boil over. Cooper's being utterly reckless with her own health.

"What about tomorrow?" Cooper says.

Harriet hisses and Cooper glances at her before looking away. She'll have to deal with Harriet after she hangs up.

"Why the urgency?" Graham says.

"Got a new car to buy."

"Dear girl, a little something called car insurance settles issues like that. Look, there's nothing on the books. At least nothing to interest your fascinating shell-likes."

"What won't interest me?"

"Well… there is a pre-master of the heavy metal band the Lance Drewer Group signed up four years ago called – forgive me for this my dear – called The Shitty Squits."

Cooper laughs.

"I like them already."

"Hmm. Actually, you'll know them better as Crimson Pink."

"Didn't the lead singer die from a boating accident, few months back?"

"Well, this is an early demo never released under their original band name. It was so dreadful, the thing was shelved and the whole thing pushed under the floorboards. Now the label want to release the album in honour of the lead singer."

"What's the problem?"

"The spotty engineer who carried out the basic mix made a pig's hide of it. Upshot, it's a bloody mess. Doubt that'll interest your delicate little ears old girl. All those trashy guitars and splashy cymbals will offend thee."

"Who's this engineer?"

"No one you've heard of my dear. Some nine-year-old tyke called Thorn Sharp the label's silly A&R chap signed up at the time. Let's just say his bosses won't be smiling if they get to hear it."

"Send me what you've got I'll see what I can do."

Harriet lets out a low, gritted-teeth growl.

Cooper daren't look at Harriet now, not even for an instant.

Graham is surprised.

"Really? Not exactly up your avenue."

"What's the money like?"

Graham sits up.

"Company are willing to pay extra bullion to anyone who can fix the mess. They've been looking for someone with platinum ears. Fact is, Mr Sharp probably mixed it on his budget Android in some grubby little East End pub while snorting the life out of white sherbet, methinks."

"Graham, your views of us working class peeps is a Möbius strip of clichés."

"Wouldn't dare compare him to common people old girl. Common slug maybe. What's a Möbius strip?"

Cooper puts on a phoney aristocratic voice.

"I'm shocked old man. And you with your public school education."

Graham laughs.

"Last time I was in school, dinosaurs were in short trousers. What's a Möbius strip? Put uncle out of his misery."

"Google it."

"Hmm. Well, you always turn your nose up at this stuff. Can't just be money. Pray tell why."

"I'm experimenting."

"Oh?"

"I've been working on an audio signal processing package with a software company."

"Now uncle is intrigued. Pray tell what this miraculous software can do?"

"Uh uh. Not this side of hell."

"If it's something you developed I daresay it must be good."

"Uh-huh."

He laughs.

"Oh all right, have it your way my dear. Monica will drop the album to the cloud. Oh, and do finish the Hoffman. You have your twenty-four hours. Oh, by the way, how's that little husband of yours? What's his name again?"

Cooper's stomach drops.

Dizzy Gillespie. Homme. Soft kisses. Soft kisses. Soft moans. Soft moans.

"Graham, you know his name."

"Ever decide on a change of scenery old girl there's a rather dapper looking chap with a country pile and a well-stocked cellar of excellent French and Italian plonk to sample."

"I'll think about it."

"Just say the word."

"Swizzle stick."

"Swizzle stick?"

"It's a lot nicer than what I really want to say."

Laughing, Graham hangs up.

Cooper turns to face Harriet. Harriet's glare is so hard it'd crack glass.

Unlike Graham, she's definitely not laughing.

3 0

GLARING AT COOPER, Harriet slams the dishwasher shut, turns it on. She marches over, draws a stool out, sits down and faces Cooper.

"You are kidding me", Harriet says.

"What do you mean?"

"You're going home, aren't you?"

"Reckon I am."

"After yesterday?"

"Still need to keep the bloodhounds at bay."

"Look at you."

Cooper feels good. Great. She points to her lips.

"You see this? It's a smile. I'm cool."

"It's a grimace."

"It's the best I can do with these lips."

"Cooper that's so not funny. You've been lucky so far but don't push it."

"Harry, I did what you wanted. I slept here last night. I went to the hospital. I mean, really? You want me to lie in bed all day?"

"Damn it Cooper, I'd love you to lie in bed all day. You can't open your left eye, your lip's screwed up, you've a swollen cheek and your shoulder's giving you issues. Yesterday you could barely walk and you were a bawling mess. That's not like you Coops. I had to bathe you for god's sake."

"Yeah well, that was yesterday."

"Plus Daniel's back at university today and Jethro's touring Europe FOR TEN WEEKS. I've tried to keep chipper for you but I can't take it. Look if it's money—"

Cooper puts a hand up.

"Already been there with Eddsy."

"Oh Coops, I know what I said yesterday about leaving you alone but you're so different today you're so …I don't know overcompensating or something. Don't tell me you're not."

"I'm cool."

"Look, this is elder sister here. I can see right through you. Don't forget I used to change your nappies."

"There more tea in the pot?"

"Stop it Cooper. Don't change the subject. Tell me what's happening."

For a second, a split second, a rare vulnerability flits across Cooper's face.

"Harry… I have to work. I've just got to."

"Oh Coops, why?"

The moment passes like a shadow and Cooper shakes her head.

"I do need a favour actually."

"Look anything. What do you need?"

"Drive me home, yeah?"

THE SUE BAXTER PODCAST
SUE BAXTER

I mean, what would cause Clive to suddenly fear money spiders after all this time? Something must've triggered it.

DR APPLEGATE

As Clive's condition had originally reappeared in court decades later, we knew something in court must have reawakened his repressed traumatic memory.

SUE BAXTER

Did you find out what?

DR APPLEGATE

According to meteorological records around Clive's eighteenth month, it was a wet balmy autumn – ideal conditions for spiders to thrive. As you know, Clive's older sister collected spiders in jam jars and she placed leaves in the jars with the spiders for something to crawl on. Autumnal leaves turn brown or red or yellow.

SUE BAXTER

So?

DR APPLEGATE

We attended the empty courtroom with Clive for a reconstruction of the day he'd suffered his first blackout. When he took out a legal pad from his briefcase as he had on the day of the session, we realised the legal pad was—

SUE BAXTER

Wait. Let me guess. One of those autumnal colours?

DR APPLEGATE

—A particular shade of autumnal orange. When we visited his childhood family home we discovered a mature maple tree in the back garden. The colour of maple leaves in autumn is also a similar shade of burnt orange.

SUE BAXTER

So your theory is when he spotted the money spider crawling over his legal pad, it triggered his repressed memory of spiders crawling over autumnal leaves in the jam jar?

DR APPLEGATE

Indeed. Now every time Clive saw a small spider it'd trigger a hypnagogic state re-enacting the childhood panic. And because he'd starve his brain of oxygen by holding his breath, he'd lose his short-term memory. Only now the memory lived just below his level of consciousness. It explained why he wasn't aware of the phobia. It also meant anytime he saw a small spider, it'd trigger the original traumatic memory.

SUE BAXTER

He's cured now I'm guessing?

DR APPLEGATE

Well yes but neither systematic desensitisation nor cognitive reframing nor my work in memory reconsolidation could help because, as I've said, Clive had no conscious phobia to fix.

SUE BAXTER

You've mentioned memory reconsolidation before. That's now an important part of The Gateway Programme. Tell us what it is.

DR APPLEGATE

Reconsolidation is the brain's ability to resave a memory. My work in dealing with particularly stubborn phobias is in degrading the brain's ability to resave a stress-inducing memory. If we can do that, we can minimise the emotional impact of a trauma. Few people realise every time you recall a memory, the brain resaves a copy of it rather than the original – like a photocopy. When you next recall that memory, you're no longer accessing the original – it's already been overwritten.

SUE BAXTER

You're saying memories are copies of themselves?

DR APPLEGATE

Precisely. And if you frequently recall a memory, it's like photocopying a photocopy of a photocopy – errors creep in. Unfortunately, with a phobia, the emotional trauma of an event can amplify rather than degrade, exaggerating it.

SUE BAXTER

So I'm guessing this is where The Gateway Programme comes in. How exactly did you treat Clive?

3 2

GRAHAM FINISHES HIS chat with Cooper then calls the arrogant A&R rep Peter March, assigned to Crimson Pink, AKA The Shitty Squits.

Dealings with Peter March always leaves Graham cold. Peter is the type who fawns in the company of powerful people while belittling staff who run after his every whim. A man in love with his executive status and generous expense account. The type Graham hates.

Peter's under-the-thumb secretary fields Graham's call before the great man himself answers.

"Greetings, Peter old chap."

"What do you want Graham?" His voice is almost a sneer.

"About your problem with the Shitty Squits, dear boy."

"What about it?"

"Found anyone who can restore the mixes?"

"I've got an expert making good inroads into it. Why?"

"Ah well. Might have a solution to your petite problem. Graham intends to get serious carats of gold out of the slug."

"What do you mean?"

"Well, can't promise anything old thing but if your other engineer doesn't mind, I have a little someone who might salvage the recordings yet."

"You think the masters can be fixed? Christopher's good but he's not fast. Who's the engineer?"

"You wouldn't know her, dear boy."

"Her?"

"Rather talented young lady. Ears as sharp as fox's. Can hunt out the last known decibel and polish it to a diamond."

"What's her background?"

"Let's just say a secret weapon I use for special occasions. Developing her own forensic audio mastering software with a world-renowned acoustical company don't you know. Can tell you she wields audio gear like a samurai warrior handling a sword though. Turns a drop of water into an orchestra." Okay so Graham is winging it but knowing Cooper's natural talent he's certain he's not skating far from the truth.

"So you – uh – think she can fix the album?"

Graham smiles. The slug's squirming. Graham doesn't want 14 carat. Not 18 carat. Not even 22 carat. He wants the whole bar, 24 carats, so soft you can put a thumbnail into it, you press hard enough.

"Can think of no one better, dear boy. Want my prodigy to have a gander at it?"

"Sure. Why not?"

"And the sovereigns? Sorry to talk nasty little commerce but to earn her interest you'd have to pull her off some serious project. She's truly the best of the best."

Peter's voice is sickly sweet.

"Anything you need, Grey. Anything you need."

Graham names a price and waits. He's sure Peter's shrivelling up and turning brown.

"Whoa. That's a pretty hefty fine Grey."

Another long pause.

"Okay, let her have it."

"Splendid, splendid old boy. Leave it with me. See what I can do."

Graham hangs up, claps his hands, throws his head back, laughs. Peter's mess up must've been so huge and if his Lance Drewer Group bosses discover the costly bad judgement it could mean Graham's out with the morning milk. Rank amateurs running the industry now. Rank amateurs.

Graham picks up the receiver, calls Cooper with the good news. Let's hope his faith in her pays off.

3 3

AS COOPER'S LINE rings Graham thinks about the first time he met Cooper. He was in a London recording studio with a film music commission and had to rush out to find a maintenance person. He spotted a man in overalls disappearing into a broom cupboard and followed him. Turned out the broom cupboard was Studio Z or something, a small project studio a would-be could hire for a few pints.

Graham attracts the technician's attention as the man talks to a slope-shouldered kid in a greyhound hoodie hunched in front of a budget mixing desk. Graham has no idea it's Cooper he's about to meet. The hoodie's recording some band and going about it all wrong.

The technician says don't knock it till you hear the result.

Intrigued, Graham watches. Graham's eyebrows rise, and he passes glances with the technician who's smiling with a told-you-so expression.

Graham's seriously impressed. The guitar sounds huge, modern yet somehow capturing a heritage sound. The whole rig adds energy to the guitarist's performance.

Graham taps the hoodie's scrawny shoulder. The hood's pulled back and Graham's face-to-face not with a pallid male but a girl in her twenties. Graham's surprised once more.

"My dear, where'd you learn that trick?"

"What trick?"

"With the guitar?"

"Dunno. Messed about a bit till I got the sound I wanted."

"Mind if I stay to watch you work?"

The woman shrugs.

"Yeah. Whatever."

Graham studies her from the back forgetting about Lolly in Studio A.

Soon Graham finds out the woman isn't only creative with sound, she's also a problem solver.

An idea occurs to Graham.

In Studio A they're working on an orchestral film score. The recording engineer who stood in for Lolly a few weeks ago had tinnitus so when Graham listened to the result, the recording was fine but bland. It hadn't captured the energy of the performance. Could this woman think up something?

Graham taps the woman on the shoulder, introduces himself, learns her name is Cooper and that the talented guitarist is her husband Jethro. He invites her into Studio A when she's done.

A little later Cooper steps into a room to find Graham and an engineer working in tandem in front of a huge mixing desk in a sumptuous studio. She halts at the threshold, instantly intimidated with its obvious high status. What's she – just someone who messes about – doing here with these top pros? She's used to the stark fluorescence of McDonalds yet she's stepped in the sophisticated glamour of the Hilton and immediately feels out of place. Tasteful spotlighting, padded executive chairs, polished parquet flooring with thick expensive rugs, racks of outboard equipment with flashing lights... even a custom-made mixing desk the size of a running track. This studio is the real thing, these people, the real deal.

Graham spots her, springs up with a smile, guides her in, does everything to make Cooper feel at home. He sits her at the console next to Lolly, introduces her and orders a runner to bring her a cappuccino.

Graham assures her he wants her opinion on something if she'd care to listen. Lolly asks about Cooper's engineering qualifications and doesn't hide his contempt when he learns she's a nobody. Graham asks Lolly to play part of the first movement and he casts Graham doubtful looks but does as he's told, baffled by what Graham's doing. He thinks maybe Graham wants to impress this pretty rebel in her Doc Martens and punk hair.

Immediately the music starts she turns to Graham, says in a quiet voice, classical isn't her thing. Graham pats her hand, asks her to enjoy the coffee and hear it out.

At first Cooper doesn't pay much attention. She's not getting why she's here. But after thirty seconds Cooper's forehead furrows, sensing something not quite right with the sound, closes her eyes and dips her head just as she does when she's working something out in her own studio with the band.

In the meantime, Lolly is throwing confused looks at Graham. What the heck is he up to, asking this amateur to judge Lolly's twenty years of experience? But Graham only smiles.

After the section finishes Cooper turns to Graham, says in the same hushed voice, "Yeah it's amazing. What is it?"

Graham is deliberately obscure. All he says is it's an original orchestral film score for a major production. She nods at that, seriously impressed.

"Recorded with Rupert Heyer and the LSO," Lolly adds.

Cooper's expression doesn't change and Lolly realises she doesn't know who the LSO or Rupert Heyer is. His contempt deepens.

"The London Symphony Orchestra, Rupert Heyer conducting," he says.

She studies Lolly then, picking up on his prejudice and she gives a tight smile.

"That right?"

Graham leans forward.

"Dear lady, I was watching you as the piece unfurled. Know something's dreadfully wrong don't you?"

"Well…"

"Go on my dear, we'd like your opinion. Why you're here after all."

"It's kind of like an ironing board."

"Meaning?" Lolly says.

"It's kind of flat."

Lolly doesn't hide his scowl. Graham claps his hands together, throws his head back, laughs.

"Indeed. Indeed! But how to go about correcting it, dear lady?"

"Rerecord it."

"Ah sorry. No can do, old bean. Tell me what you'd do in that studio of yours."

"Me?" She shrugs. "Dunno."

Graham presses his hands together and puts them under his chin, studying her.

"Give it a go old girl. Talk to me."

She scans the huge mixing desk, all those controls, all those lights, all those switches.

"Talk to me in decibels and Hertz," Lolly says.

Cooper feels his sneer. Lolly's aware she doesn't know the first thing about the science of audio engineering.

"Just walk us through your thoughts my dear. Lolly, be so good as to play the first movement once more, will you?"

Lolly hunches over the desk, presses an illuminated button.

As the piece replays Cooper talks cautiously. She talks in phrases while pointing at the instruments coming through the Dolby surround field of the monitors. That bit's too spongy, this bit's a little lost and needs to sweep over, this bit should be tighter... None of what she says makes sense to either Graham or Lolly.

In the end Lolly stops the playback and says with a clipped voice, "this isn't pop."

"Yeah? That right?"

He continues, tells her how they use multiple microphones to record different sections of the orchestra. How it's all about the microphones doing the work.

"Yeah? That right?" she says again.

Her insipid answers irritate Lolly.

Graham asks Lolly to give her suggestions a go anyway. Lolly sighs, plays the piece and when Cooper says something he makes an adjustment on the desk. Lolly's made it sound artificial and hard. He looks at Cooper.

"So, does THAT make it sound less like an ironing board?"

Something changes in Cooper then. Her eyes narrow to slits and she regards him with the green eyed intelligence of a cat. She asks where all the controls are, what they do, as though planning to take over. He tells her but after a few minutes it's clear she's overwhelmed.

Graham realises he's made a mistake. Cooper has the ear but not the knowledge. He thanks her for her input. Cooper stands, Lolly watching her, looking smug.

Cooper glares back.

"Can you pipe the sound to my studio?"

"You mean PATCH the sound? What studio you in?"

She tells him.

Lolly laughs.

"That junkyard still going?"

"Of course we can, dear lady. Lolly if you'd care to drop the first movement as a WAV file to her desk…"

Lolly bristles at that but organises it then says, "You understand this is a copyrighted project don't you? You can't show it to anyone?"

Cooper dumbs down her answer, winks.

"Yeah, I gotcha."

She thanks Graham for the coffee she hasn't touched, leaves.

When the door hisses shut and seals them in, Lolly turns to Graham.

"What the crying heck was that all about?"

Graham raises an acceding palm, says he only agreed to make a copy of the movement so Cooper could save face. They carry on working on the score, not expecting to hear from Cooper again. They don't know Cooper.

An hour later the studio phone flashes. Lolly picks up, listens, his neck reddening. He covers the mouthpiece.

"It's the punk. Can we come to her studio?"

They go in.

Lolly glances at Graham. The look says what the living crap are we doing in this dump? The room is airless, claustrophobic.

Cooper looks at them.

"Ready?"

They both nod.

Cooper plays back the score. After a minute Lolly leans over her shoulder, stabs the stop button.

"That's not what I gave you. Where the hell did you get that?"

"It's what you sent me."

"Impossible."

"Yeah, it is."

"You're playing back a multitrack. I can see it on your screen. I gave you a single stereo WAV file."

"Yeah, so?"

"So, it can't be what I gave you."

Graham clears his throat. They both turn to him. He points a finger at the monitors.

"Lolly, you hear that old chap?"

"Yeah, I heard." He's scowling.

"What you think?"

Lolly's lips tighten over his teeth.

"It sounds pretty good. But it's not what I gave her."

Graham doesn't care what Cooper's done. He's interested only in the result. It's the same piece all right. It has a soundscape lacking in the original.

Lolly crosses his arms, asks Cooper how she did that, how'd she get it to sound like that? Cooper says "Dunno, I kind of worked in layers." Lolly asks "What do you mean? How'd you manage the instrument separation with only a stereo WAV file?" Cooper says "Pull up a chair, I'll show ya."

Lolly pulls up a battered chair, the PVC arms picked through to the dirty sponge and metal. He squeezes next to her in front of the tiny mixer and computer screen.

Graham's smiling from the back wall. He knows his instincts were right. Lolly is a veteran recording engineer, but this little hooded chit of a girl showed him how she remodelled the original recording on her Fisher Price mixer.

Forty minutes later she's finished explaining her thought processes and Lolly raises an eyebrow at Graham. Lolly's impressed as hell. His expression says holy crap can you believe this punk? If she can produce this in here what the heck can she do in Studio A with the original production?

Lolly's smiling and Graham's smiling and pretty soon Cooper's smiling too. They take her back to Studio A all but throwing rose petals before her tread.

Soon Graham has to leave.

Next morning Graham returns to Studio A to find them tired and wrecked but pleased with themselves, empty coffee mugs and crushed Coke cans everywhere, the peanut and crisps bowls empty. He learns Cooper and Lolly worked through the night. They'd developed a workflow. She told Lolly what she wanted, what equipment or plug-ins she'd have used in her studio, he'd show her the controls, how they work, and together they shaped the piece.

Lolly plays Graham back the score.

Graham has to sit down within six bars. As the piece unfolds he realises it sounds as dramatic as the heave and weight of a tumultuous sea. The piece has theatre.

Cooper puts a cheeky glint in her eye.

"Yeah. We put the ironing board away."

After a moment's silence they all laugh.

Graham usually takes on engineers who have studied years at schools or been in the biz years working with top talents. Cooper is in a different league. She has raw, wild talent he's never encountered before. Graham surprises himself with what he does next. He asks her to go on his books.

Ask Lolly today and he'll go on his knees, misty-eyed over Cooper. He'll say she understands the complexity of sound like no one he's ever met and knows how to sculpt it.

When Cooper answers the phone, Graham is jolted back into his wood-panelled office. He tells her the good news about The Shitty Squits.

If anyone can salvage the album, it's Cooper.

THE SUE BAXTER PODCAST
DR APPLEGATE
Actually Sue, before I answer your question about how we treated Clive, I need to talk about my co-partner at Gateway House, Dr Stewart-Way. Before we met, Dr Stewart-Way was studying optogenetics in Cambridge.
SUE BAXTER
Optogenetics is a form of brain surgery from what I understand.
DR APPLEGATE
Yes but not in the way you think. Dr Stewart-Way is the expert in this area but I can tell you optogenetics in its rawest form is invasive. As you stated earlier it requires passing fibre-optic cables through the skull and uses light to influence the brain's behaviour. However Dr Stewart-Way's unique approach uses x-ray fluorescence which doesn't require fibre-optic cables. We call it fluorogenetics.
SUE BAXTER
You combined your skills to produce The Gateway Programme, which is also the same treatment you use to erase love, isn't that correct?
DR APPLEGATE
Yes, though that wasn't The Gateway Programme's original purpose. As you know Sue, it was invented as a treatment for PTSD. But you're quite correct, it's that reason the treatment has become well-known.
SUE BAXTER
It has the unusual accolade of being both a famous and infamous

treatment. This was because of Cooper Hall's plea for help from you.

DR APPLEGATE

Indeed. Only we didn't bargain on where her plea would lead us.

SUE BAXTER

I'm of course talking about Jethro T. Hall's protests against The Gateway Programme. I believe it was a unique set of circumstances that caused the controversy. However, unfortunately that's all we have time for this week, but in our next podcast, if you'd be so kind as to return, Dr Applegate, we'd love to hear the story behind Cooper Hall's involvement with The Gateway Programme.

3 5

SILENTLY FUMING, Harriet drives Cooper home. She tries to
remain calm and not let her annoyance show. She drops Cooper
back to an empty house and wants to come in

but Cooper persuades Harriet to leave her alone

and Harriet says "Coops I really don't want you alone"

and Cooper stands her ground with her pathetic bruised face
and slumped shoulders

and Harriet says "You're being so silly I could stay with you
if you want, Eddsy would understand"

and Cooper says "No, I really want to be alone please just let
me be alone Harry, I'll call you so you know everything's okay,
just let me be alone just let me okay?"

and Harriet goes to protest again

but sees how stressed she's making Cooper

so Harriet eventually

reluctantly

exasperatedly

drives away.

Cooper watches the car leave. She goes up to the bedroom.
She spots a Post-It note on the door. It's from Daniel. She reads
it.

Hope you're okay, mum.

Why would he ask? What does he know?

Cooper pushes the door open, hesitates.

She stands on the threshold of the bedroom.

Stares at the bed.

The bed.

The one Jethro and that woman slept in yesterday.

THE bed.

The one Jethro and that woman didn't sleep in yesterday.

THAT bed.

Cooper doesn't know what to do about the bed, the bedroom, anything. She doesn't know, she doesn't know.

The smell of Homme is gone. Dizzy Gillespie is gone. The soft kisses are gone. The soft moans are gone. Cooper spots another Post-It note on the duvet. She braves stepping over the threshold, picks up the note, reads it.

Really hope you're okay, mum. Take it easy. Dx.

Harriet must've told him about the car accident.

Or Jethro did.

Another note on the bedside table. I'll call when I get to uni. Dx.

Cooper collects them all, enjoys them all. They're prizes in a paperchase. She reads them all again. Smiles at them. They say laughter is the best medicine.

Maybe it's sons.

Downstairs Cooper's now wearing a dressing gown. She walks past Kelloggs asleep in his basket. He raises his head, watches her pass. There's a Post-It note stuck to his head. It says I had lunch at 12.50pm signed Kelloggs and a penned drawing of a paw print.

Cooper smirks.

Oh Daniel.

Maybe it's sons.

Cooper goes into the kitchen, fills the kettle, boils the water. Kelloggs lazily stretches, follows her into the kitchen, the Post-It note still stuck to his head. In the fridge Cooper finds a Daniel note on the cat food tin. I fed Kelloggs already at 12.50pm. If he says different he's lying. Cooper chuckles.

She gets the milk out, takes the cat food tin out. Kelloggs appears by her ankle. He mews then watches her reaction with the same intensity he gives to watching robins and pigeons from the window and when he sees the tin of cat food, stands on two feet and repeatedly scratches the kitchen cupboard door. The Post-It note on his head flutters off. Cooper picks the bowl up. Inside is a Post-It note.

Really? Do you want me to get fat?

Cooper laughs.

Sons.

She takes the note out, scoops cat food into his bowl, puts the bowl on the floor. Kelloggs purrs loudly, shoulders her out the way, pushes his nose into the bowl and chomps. Soon he's licking the bowl across the kitchen until it gleams. He looks up at Cooper as if to say, so where's the rest?

Cooper brews tea, pours milk into her teacup. She knows the secret formula to the best tasting tea ever. Always use loose leaves. Always leave it for four minutes. Always use water off the boil. Always make it in an unglazed ceramic teapot (unglazed clay absorbs flavours over time). And critically important, crucially important, pour milk first, tea in after.

Milk first, tea after.

Apparently the reason you put milk first is to stop hot tea from cracking the glaze in a delicate China teacup but Cooper thinks it tastes better that way anyway.

She sits at the kitchen table, finds another longer Post-It note from Daniel.

1:15pm. Mum, leaving now. Hope you're not feeling too sore after the prang. From what aunt Harriet's not saying – so it was Harriet – sounds as though it was more than a prang. All she said was it was quite a prang and the car's scrap. Call when you can. Fed Kelloggs. Bet you'll feed him again anyway ;) Mum you know that cat is super evil. The beast could persuade the devil to do a good deed… Feels completely weird you not being here. Amazing news about dad right? Love you loads. Danielx.

Cooper smiles, tucks the note away with the others. Kelloggs curls up under the table, puts his chin on Cooper's foot.

Sons.

And cats.

After four minutes Cooper pours tea into the cup. The milk inside turns caramel. She sets the pot down. She doesn't pick up the teacup. She leaves it there, stares at it, looks at the bubbles spinning on the surface, watches them gather at the rim and pop.

There's nothing but silence. Silence. The fridge humming. Outside, muted cars occasionally drive past. In the hall a seven-day clock ticks. Underneath the table Kelloggs purrs. Cooper feels the throttle in his throat vibrating through her feet.

The tea is steaming.

She stares at it.

Becomes warm.

Stares at it.

Cools.

Stares at it.

Goes cold.

Stares.

Stares.

Cooper places her head in the crook of her arm and rests it on the table.

Sons make you laugh.

Cats guilt you into feeding them.

Husbands, what do they do?

Yeah, she knows.

Some make you cry.

JETHRO IS ONSTAGE of the Antwerp 23,000-seater Sportpaleis. The auditorium empty with nothing but crew milling busy checking rigging and lighting. Lots of hammering and erecting, dealing with stage scaffolding. Jethro's on for a sound check. All the band are onstage sorting their instruments and set-ups. It's buzzy and dusty and chilly. He hasn't seen Sabre Light yet but he met with the manager and sorted out contract details.

Ten whole weeks. Man, that's crazy.

But Jethro's distracted. He keeps worrying about Cooper. He hasn't been able to speak to her in twenty-four hours. This morning she sent him a single text.

Phone was dead. All okay now. Just a bit sore. Car's gone. Congrats on the deal. x.

The message was abrupt and didn't sound like Cooper. He'd called back straight away but the phone went to voice mail. He'd hung up and text her back.

Hey babe glad you're okay. Totally had me worried. Called last night, H said you were sleeping. Get plenty of rest. Maybe catch up later? Stay cool. Love you. JethroXXXXXX.

He'd sent it straight away and waited.

Waited.

Nothing came back.

Several hours later and Jethro's doing the sound check onstage but his head is elsewhere. The audio guy at the back of the auditorium gives the thumbs up and Jethro strums a chord. The engineer's voice crackles through the walkie talkie.

"Jeth, can't hear your guitar."

Jethro runs through all six strings.

The audio guy comes back.

"Still not coming through."

Jethro checks the cables. It all looks fine. He plugs in another cable, strums.

The audio guy crackles through.

"Uh Jeth, still getting zero on the signal."

Jethro screams in frustration, wants to throw his guitar.

Diesel, the bassist, steps over.

"Jethro hey, take it easy okay? Maybe take a break?"

Jethro nods, sets his guitar down back in the rack. He leaves the stage, takes his bolero hat off, sweeps his long hair back with his fingers, puts his hat back on. He goes out for some air.

Gater picks up Jethro's guitar, the volume knob is down. He rolls it up, plucks a note and the audio guy gives a thumbs up. Basic error.

Outside one of the stadium's stage doors a couple of people are smoking joints and stage hands with gaffer tape mill about, sorting out rigging, cabling, lighting. The day's grey and cold and chilly. They nod at Jethro. He nods back as he passes, stepping over cases and cables.

Jethro checks his phone.

No new messages.

Yesterday Jethro sent Cooper a barrage of them. He was all high octane and excitement buzzing with the deal and wanted to share it with Cooper. Today his chest is tight. He left only the one text this morning.

Still waiting for a response.

Something's not right, it's just not right, he knows it.

He calls, gets through to Cooper, talks through a crackly line, but it's no use. The line goes dead.

Before long Sophie appears, gaining hungry glances from the stage hands as she strolls up to him, rubs his back.

"Hey honey."

Jethro shuts the call, acknowledges Sophie with a tense smile. She looks at him funny.

"You okay there?"

"Yeah, yeah."

"Don't worry. It's just nerves honey, that's all. We'll do great."

Jethro slips his phone into his jeans. They return together, Sophie leaning in close, a hand around his waist.

The stage hands watch the pair pass, seeing how they are with each other, all thinking, lucky bugger.

3 7

FIVE MINUTES AGO

Cooper is still in the kitchen, still at the kitchen table, still with a teacup in front of her. Except this time it's not tea, it's her fourth scotch whisky, her fourth. The first time she poured it into cold tea.

Best tasting cold tea ever.

She glugged even more whisky into the second cup of tea using it instead of milk, even nicer. She did away with the tea altogether poured whisky into the teacup for the third, better yet.

Now she's on her fourth and she's wondering if whisky's spelt with an e or not?

Whisky? Or whiskey?

Cooper gives it serious thought as her brain marinates in alcohol. She's beyond tipsy now so they're not just rambling thoughts now she's speaking them out loud running one thought into the next without stopping. Funny how when you're drunk it makes you speak what you think. Funny that. She sniggers.

Her mobile shivers on the table.

Cooper picks it up and answers before she realises it's Jethro.

His voice comes through a heavy crackle.

"Hey babes at last. You're there."

Cooper doesn't say anything.

"Babe? It's Jethro. Can you hear me?"

Breathes.

"Cooper? I'm at the Sportpaleis in Antwerp, doing a sound check. Thought I'd call. Been worrying about you babe."

Breathes.

Cooper ends the call, slams the phone face down on the table. Kelloggs startles awake.

Cooper grabs the bottle of whisky by the neck, pushes back the chair, stumbles upstairs with the bottle. She feels so tired. She spills whisky down the stairs, it soaks into the carpet, she doesn't care. She halts at the bedroom door. No not that bedroom, not that bed, not That bed, not THAT bed.

Cooper goes into Daniel's room. His bed's unmade, she doesn't care. She climbs into bed with the bottle, smelling his familiar teenage sweat, she doesn't care. She rests the bottle against her bosom. Each breath she takes, a little whisky dribbles out the bottle neck, wetting her top, she doesn't care. As Cooper falls asleep the remaining waterline of the whisky settles below the neck of the bottle.

Cooper sinks gratefully into a dark empty place and if she never comes around, not ever, well,

she doesn't care.

3 8

THE SUE BAXTER PODCAST

SUE BAXTER

Dr Stewart-Way thank you for joining us this evening.

DR STEWART-WAY

Thank you for having me Sue.

SUE BAXTER

Unfortunately Dr Applegate is unable to be with us tonight so I'm eternally grateful Dr Stewart-Way has been able to step up at such short notice. I believe Dr Applegate has a pressing engagement?

DR STEWART-WAY

Yes. He sends his apologies.

SUE BAXTER

Now you are Dr Klara Stewart-Way, a neuroscientist who studied optogenetics at the University of Cambridge. However you took the science a step further and coined a new phrase called Fluorogenetic Synaptic Deletion. This is a combining of optogenetics with x-ray fluorescence which does away with fibre optic cables. Before we talk about the important work you do at Gateway House, let's backtrack and explain a little about what optogenetics is.

DR STEWART-WAY

In a nutshell, optogenetics is the science of controlling thoughts, memories and emotions by light. Normally, brain cells won't respond to light. However with optogenetics, we genetically adapt brain cells to become light sensitive.

SUE BAXTER

The first tests with optogenetics were with mice wasn't it?

DR STEWART-WAY

Yes that's right.

SUE BAXTER

You mention optogenetics controls thoughts and memories. What is it about optogenetics that makes that possible?

DR STEWART-WAY

Well, by simply switching a light source on or off, we can prevent specific brain cells from communicating with adjacent cells.

SUE BAXTER

So the brain cells themselves act like a switch?

DR STEWART-WAY

That's correct. And to see it in action, YouTube has a video of a mouse gnawing on a stick of wood. The mouse is unusual because it has fibre optic cables passing into its skull. Switch the light on and the mouse gnaws the wood. Switch it off and the mouse stops.

SUE BAXTER

Is it painful for the mouse?

DR STEWART-WAY

Not at all Sue. Firstly, there are no pain receptors in the brain. Secondly, the stimulus is light, which is painless anyway.

SUE BAXTER

So has the mouse been trained to gnaw wood when the lights switch on?

DR STEWART-WAY

Not at all. There is no training involved. The mouse simply believes it's deciding for itself when to gnaw wood. In reality that decision is coming from the operator of the light source.

SUE BAXTER

So it's basically mind control?

DR STEWART-WAY

In effect, yes.

SUE BAXTER

Isn't that a dangerous science?

DR STEWART-WAY

Any science is dangerous in the wrong hands.

SUE BAXTER

Optogenetics sounds like such an out-there idea – the thought of using light to control the mind. How did it come about?

DR STEWART-WAY

Well it was Francis Crick – one of the four scientists who discovered the DNA Helix – who first suggested using light to control individual brain cells would solve many brain-related issues. It set a number of scientists on an investigative quest on how precisely that could be achieved.

SUE BAXTER

And how did you come across the science? Was it taught at your university?

DR STEWART-WAY

Actually Sue it was a complete fluke, but it changed my life's work.

SUE BAXTER

Oh we'd love to hear how.

3 9

HARRIET ARRIVES HOME after dropping Cooper off. She goes straight to the spare room, clears Cooper's bathroom fodder. The bed's a mess, the carpet is damp where Cooper dropped one of her towels, the bathrobe is draped over the end of the bed. At least Cooper had the courtesy to put all the tissues she'd strewn about the floor last night into the waste bin.

If only Cooper would talk to her. Harriet thinks about how yesterday Cooper was quiet and tearful in a way she hadn't seen in years. Partly caused by the accident, though Harriet knows something else is going on.

Harriet finishes clearing the room and scans it. Lace curtains billow in the open window. All clean and tidy and fresh.

Perfect.

Except no, not perfect.

Not perfect by a long way.

This would have been the nursery. Harriet and Eddsy have five spare rooms. They weren't supposed to be guest rooms, but children's bedrooms. Lots and lots of bedrooms for bundles and bundles of kids. What's the point now? Why did Eddsy insist on building more rooms? One for each new garage he opens, he says. Trophies. To Harriet they feel like empty gestures. She shivers, goes to the window, scans the sky, it looks like rain. She closes the window.

She takes time to gaze into the garden. It's big too. Big enough for a garden swing tied to the big oak, a trampoline, a seesaw, several brothers and sisters who could play tag, run around, causing all sorts of mayhem. She smiles at that.

All that space.

Now it all seems a waste. The smile fades. Two people living in a cavernous home. Most of the time Harriet tries not to think such gloomy thoughts. Sometimes she can't help it. It's a yearning in her, deep, way down deep. A gaping hole so big it swallows everything. It remains unsatiated. Unquenched. Unfulfilled.

Harriet blows her nose, the remnants of her cold. She'll be back to work tomorrow, managing the garages, keeping on top of things, too busy to sit still and think once more. Just how she likes her life to be. But for now, she slumps on to the end of the bed and digs her hands between her knees, feeling alone.

Despite the fact Harriet has professional drive and direction in her life.

Despite the fact she's helped Eddsy build a successful chain of garages by marketing uniquely to women drivers where they feel they can trust the mechanics, trust the quotes and trust the quality of work.

Despite the fact she's brought women mechanics and personnel into the garages and really turned things around for Eddsy.

Even despite the fact male drivers now bite down their macho egos and brave Tomalin Garages for themselves once they realise reputation and honesty is more important than anything else…

For the first time ever, Harriet admits it to herself. She feels utterly.

Utterly.

Purposeless.

4 0

COOPER WAKES TO wet sandpaper raking her ear and the foul smell of meaty breath. Though it's dark she realises Kelloggs is licking her. She tries to move but her neck is stiff. Cooper hasn't moved from her spot since she fell asleep. She opens her eye. She's slept the whole afternoon away.

She sweeps Kelloggs away with an irritated moan. He leaps off the bed, strolls to the open bedroom door and sits perfectly still, coiling his tail neatly around himself and watching.

It takes time for Cooper to work out where she is – Daniel's room. Why's she sleeping in Daniel's room?

Oh yeah. Course.

She becomes aware she's cradling something warm and hard. It's the whisky bottle she took to bed. She puts the bottle on the floor, swings out of bed, feet planting on the carpet. The room swings around a second later and catches up with her. The room smells stale. Her head pounds, her tongue, thick and dry.

Cooper drags herself to the bathroom. She flicks the light on and its brittle whiteness burns her eyes. She leans over the sink, drinks from the cold tap, has a pee. Kelloggs follows her, sits outside the bathroom door, watching once more, patient and silent. Cooper's pee is long and it smells horrible and when she looks at it it's a deep dark yellow. She flushes. She goes to the medicine cabinet, slides the mirrored door, finds the ibuprofen. She breaks open the foil and knocks two into her hand and is about to toss her head back and swallow. She stops.

No.

No she won't take them. Pain is good. Physical pain is so much better than what's inside. Pain is distraction. She drinks more water from the tap until the thirst goes, slips the pills back into the box, puts the box back, closes the cabinet, her head throbbing and welcome.

Cooper brushes her teeth, changes into fresh clothes, returns to Daniel's bedroom. She opens the bedroom windows to air the room, closes the curtains, yanks off the bed sheets to a bare mattress. Next she grabs the whisky bottle by the neck, takes it down, recaps it, replaces it in the drinks cabinet.

In the kitchen Cooper stuffs the bedlinen into the washing machine and finds the rumble of it comforting. She clears up the kitchen table where she abandoned her cold tea stuff from earlier, feeds Kelloggs.

Next Cooper goes through texts. Loads from Harriet. She texts, saying she's been resting and Harriet replies back straight away approving and saying she's here if Cooper needs her. One from Daniel says he's arrived at uni. She texts him back. She sees a text from Jethro. His latest text says he thinks something's wrong with her phone. When he called earlier he thought he could hear her breathing but seems she couldn't hear him and that he's at the venue, they're all preparing but he's excited and nervous. Cooper reads a text from Graham's office with an access code to the Shitty Squits album masters. Good. She'll finish the Hoffman then she'll listen to the Squits. She needs work. Lots of work. Distraction.

Cooper's stomach groans.

Though she had a big brunch at Harriet's she's not eaten since and barely ate anything yesterday. She wants something fast. She grabs a can of tomato soup. Must be Heinz. Only Heinz works for her. She opens it, heats half in the microwave, rips off a hunk of bread, drops a dollop of butter on it, black pepper over it, eats it. It's steaming hot and peppery. She enjoys it, relishes it. Her stomach utters a long appreciative groan.

Cooper finishes it, still wants more so she does it again. The rest of the soup in the microwave, black pepper, hunk of bread, dollop of butter, this time she adds grated cheese on top, a dash of garlic powder. Devours it. Delicious.

She makes herself a cup of tea, sits at the kitchen table. She washes up, dries up.

Her head still throbs. Pain is good.

Cooper heads to her recording studio in the garden, unbolts the door, goes in, flicks the lights on. She sits in front of her console, switches banks of equipment on. The mixer lights up, all the outboard gear lights up, a computer loads up a huge 40" LCD screen displaying recording software with the Hoffman orchestral work. If you squint, the studio looks like a cityscape at night with all the flashing lights.

Good.

Time for work.

Lots of work.

Lots and lots of work.

Lots and lots and lots of work.

Her head throbs. Her head throbs.

Pain is good.

THE SUE BAXTER PODCAST

DR STEWART-WAY

I'd been studying brain surgery in Cambridge and I was at a café one day and picked up a tabloid newspaper someone had left behind. It just so happened there was a small article on page twenty two in the left hand corner.

SUE BAXTER

Gosh you remember the page number?

DR STEWART-WAY

(Laughs)

Yes, yes I do. At first what I read in the paper made me think it was sensationalist rubbish. But it quoted a professor by name from a legitimate American university. I decided to follow it up and discovered he was a real professor.

SUE BAXTER

What was the article?

DR STEWART-WAY

It was about a new science called optogenetics. The professor's name is Karl Deisseroth, and in 2005 he was a professor of Bioengineering and Psychiatry and Behavioural Sciences at Stanford University when he wrote a paper about it. That paper changed my life.

SUE BAXTER

The tabloid newspaper?

DR STEWART-WAY

(Laughs)

Well yes I suppose that one too, but really I meant Professor

Deisseroth's paper. It's because of it I realised optogenetics was what I wanted to do.

SUE BAXTER

Optogenetics does sound more science fiction than science fact though doesn't it?

DR STEWART-WAY

Oh I know. Believe me Sue I sometimes still almost can't believe it. It's remarkable to think science is finally beginning to get a toehold into the physical mechanics of how the brain works and is a real springboard from the earlier works of Freud and Jung.

SUE BAXTER

So optogenetics really works?

DR STEWART-WAY

(Laughs)

It really does, as you know Sue. There's a growing body of research you can find on the net about it. YouTube has a few excellent TED Talks on the subject of optogenetics. There's also, of course, our website.

SUE BAXTER

(Laughs)

But even hearing you, an eminent scientist and doctor in your field qualify it, I find it difficult to believe this isn't a Hollywood movie concept and that oh come on you're having us on aren't you? I mean you're just a Hollywood scriptwriter aren't you, Dr Stewart-Way?

DR STEWART-WAY

(Laughs)

Years ago you'd have been right Sue, it would've been the stuff of movies. In fact it has been.

SUE BAXTER

Now you state you use x-rays rather than fibre-optics in optogenetics. How did that come about?

DR STEWART-WAY

Well Sue, many Parkinson's sufferers do in fact have LED

implants to help treat its symptoms, so it is a well-documented surgery. However I wanted to use less invasive surgery and explored many avenues. I investigated several methods including the modern equivalent of the lobotomy called the Gamma Knife, a legitimate form of brain surgery using gamma rays for destroying cancer cells. However, even at low levels it was too brutal. It's then I became aware of x-ray fluorescence.

SUE BAXTER

How does that work?

DR STEWART-WAY

X-rays can fluoresce genetically adapted brain cells.

SUE BAXTER

So the cells light up? There's no need to drill holes in the skull for fibre optic cables I assume?

DR STEWART-WAY

In essence, yes.

SUE BAXTER

It does sound Eternal Sunshine of the Spotless Mind doesn't it? – the ability to control the mind.

DR STEWART-WAY

Well yes Sue that's the Hollywood movie I was referring to. However, an important difference is The Gateway Programme doesn't interfere with autobiographical memories. The ability to switch off such memories comes with enormous drawbacks as highlighted by the film.

SUE BAXTER

You mean if you delete a memory it can leave huge gaps in your recollections of the past?

STEWART-WAY

Absolutely. In the film, when Jim Carrey comes across his ex-girlfriend Kate Winslet, she doesn't recognise him. It shocks and confuses him. He later discovers it's because she had him erased from her memory. And if your listeners don't mind a spoiler for the film, Jim Carrey decides to wipe his own memory of her leaving them to become attracted to each other once again. The likelihood is they'll make the same mistakes, resulting in the same relationship breakdown. But maybe not. One of the implied messages from the film, despite leaving you on a hopeful note, is that if you erase memory, it leaves you incapable of learning from your mistakes. That's a major flaw with wiping an autobiographical memory.

SUE BAXTER

But you've circumvented that.

DR STEWART-WAY

The Gateway Programme focuses on the emotional content of memories. This is why it's so useful for treating PTSD. Sufferers can recall a traumatic event, learn from it even, without experiencing the emotional trauma accompanying it.

SUE BAXTER

So the horror of a traumatic memory goes but the memory remains?

DR STEWART-WAY

That's it in a nutshell, Sue. If you're the victim of catastrophe, it can leave you nervous, frightened, unable to bond with family and friends. It's a sad fact many PTSD sufferers – post-traumatic stress disorder sufferers – become suicidal. I asked myself what if I could remove the emotional content of a trauma, would it make a patient a normal functioning member of society once more? That was and remains our basic aim at Gateway House.

SUE BAXTER

What qualifies as a traumatic event?

DR STEWART-WAY

Quite simply anything one would find emotionally overwhelming. To witness a murder, or a horrific accident, rape, torture, a nightmare, even a phobia of spiders such as Clive's.

SUE BAXTER

I believe your early work was funded by the British government for the Ministry of Defence to help soldiers returning from tours of duty suffering from PTSD.

DR STEWART-WAY

That's right.

SUE BAXTER

But for some reason it didn't work out. Why was that?

DR STEWART-WAY

Unfortunately Sue, before I met Dr Applegate, my work wasn't yet complete. There was still a long way to go.

SUE BAXTER

Yes. I believe it led to some disastrous results.

4 2

COOPER'S WORKING ON the Hoffman when her mobile rings. Daniel. He'd be at university by now. She stops playback, answers, putting on a voice as bright as tinsel.

"Hey, Daniel."

"Mum. I like arrived a little while back. Just sorting myself out."

She looks at the neon wall clock. It's 8.09pm.

"You get my messages?" Daniel says.

"The Post-Its?" Cooper laughs. "Yeah."

"I bet you fed Kelloggs anyway."

"No."

"Liar."

"I didn't."

"Mum, you are so a liar. I completely get when you're lying you know. You can't hide it from me."

"Okay, well Kelloggs twisted my arm."

"Yeah right. Aunt Harry said the car's totalled. What happened? Someone bashed into you?"

"No. Well yeah, the tree did."

"You hit a tree?"

"It's worse than it sounds."

"You sound a bit funny. You're not pronouncing words properly."

Cooper tells him about the swollen lips from the deployed airbag. She doesn't tell him about the closed black eye, the shoulder, the bruises, the fact the car turned over and showered her in glass and oil.

"I completely knew Auntie Harry was holding back."

"When did you speak to your aunt?"

"Earlier. And again about five minutes ago. I thought you were staying there. She didn't say anything about fat lips though. Send me a picture."

"Yeah, there's more chance of someone shaving off your mush than me sending a picture."

"Like, no one's touching my beard."

"You know it makes you look older, right?"

"So, will you send one?"

"Daniel, you remember when you were fourteen?"

"What about it?"

"I tried to take a picture of you to send to dad's sister in Goa. You wouldn't let me."

"Yeah well, I had Mount Vesuvius on my chin."

"It was a zit the size of an ant's head."

"What are you talking about mum? It was the length and breadth of Africa."

"There's your answer then. No I'm not sending you a picture."

Kelloggs appears through the studio cat flap, pounces on to Cooper's lap, starts nudging at her chin with the top of his head. His purr is loud.

"Uh-oh," Daniel says, "evil cat's on his motorbike again. I can hear the throttle."

"Yeah, I'd better go feed—"

"Wait mum." Daniel's voice takes on a different tone... "Seriously, like what happened?"

Cooper detects the shift in the air. He isn't just updating her. He's trying to find out more.

"What do you mean?"

"Like how come you were going to Aunt Harry's anyway?"

Cooper feels her grip tighten on her phone. Dizzy Gillespie. Homme. Soft moans, soft moans.

"Needed the day off that's all. You know what ear fatigue's like. Sometimes I need a break from work."

Soft kisses. Soft kisses.

"Is she, like, okay? Her and uncle Eddsy?"

"Course, why?"

"It's… well you don't normally take time off do you? It's completely not like you."

"Sometimes I do."

"Yeah mum, right."

An awkward pause.

"You spoken to dad yet, mum? The news is mad, right?"

"What do you mean?"

"Duh. You know, that they're the last-minute support band going on tour with that rock group. You know the band hardly anyone's ever heard of?"

Cooper laughs. Sabre Light's about as big as Queen was.

"That's so crazy, right? I mean wow. Sabre Light."

"It's great news."

"So, have you spoken with dad?"

"Been trying. It goes to voicemail. The last message I got he was part way through a sound check. I expect he'll call later."

"That's funny. I just—"

"Look Daniel, Kelloggs's playing scythes on my thigh. I need to feed him before he shreds me. You settle yourself and this time PLEASE put your clothes in the furniture provided capiche? Don't live out of your suitcase and turn all your clothes into dishrags again."

Daniel lets out a long drawn-out breath.

"Yeah mum, okay."

"Gotta go. I've got a deadline to meet." Cooper realises damn it too late that's not what she should have said. Daniel doesn't miss the beat.

"Wait. Like, I though you said you were taking time off? You know, ear fatigue and your fat lip and whiplash and all that? You're in the studio, aren't you?"

"I'm almost done anyway. But yeah, bed is my next port of call."

Kelloggs mews again, becomes insistent. This time it ends with an irritable growl low in his throat. It couldn't have come at a better time. Cooper scratches him under the chin as reward. Good boy.

"Hear that? Kelloggs is frothing at the mouth."

After the call, Cooper finalises the Hoffman, sends it off, texts Graham it's uploaded, he texts back a thumbs up. Cooper looks at Kelloggs.

"Come on kiddo, time for yum yum."

4 3

COOPER KNOWS SHE'S overfeeding Kelloggs right now. It's not good. Her mind's not in the right place. She'll put him in a cattery tomorrow. She knows he won't like it and neither will she, but she needs to focus on work. She needs work, work, work, work, work.

After a break Cooper listens to the pre-master of The Shitty Squits, shocked the moment she hits play. The contrast between the depth and richness of the Hoffman and the thin scratchiness of The Shitty Squits is vast. She can't fix this. It's a mess.

She calls Graham, tells him the bad news but when he tells her that's all he's got on the books, her chest tightens. If she doesn't work her head's going to explode.

Cooper stalls Graham. She decides on another listen…

Two solid hours later, neck aching, ears buzzing, Cooper takes a break. When she returns she's pleasantly surprised to find she's made headway. She texts Graham, I think I can do this. He texts back a thumbs up and a smiley face.

Cooper works diligently, lost in the first song, enjoying the disaster of it. Teasing and separating the individual instruments like matted hair. She's as careful as a restorer cleaning an old master with Q-tips, meticulous in her methods. It takes patience, it takes time.

Suddenly it's morning, though in the windowless studio it could be any time.

Tired and stiff and achy and shivery, Cooper unrolls Daniel's sleeping bag on the floor, slips in with a bottle of water beside her. Her face throbs, her neck is stiff, her eye aches, her ears ring, but she's happy.

Sort of.

She's relieved from the pain of stomach-churning misery.

Sort of.

She's in a better place.

Sort of.

As she rests, her head fixates on the problems of The Shitty Squits and her eyelids droop. This is what she needs.

Yeah. Definitely. This is what she needs.

4 4

LAST NIGHT
JETHRO IS ONSTAGE to thousands of Sabre Light fans. He's
into his final number of the set with the band and everything's
going great. The audience likes them, the applause between each
song is solid, the buzz is addictive. In five minutes he's off and
Sabre Light come on. Already he can see Sabre Light in the
wings, full of nervous energy, pacing about. It feels like he's
been onstage two minutes not forty. In that time Diesel rode the
bass like a rodeo, Tom thumped out those beats like an African
drum aficionado, Mark's rhythm guitar chopped up the songs
into tight sequences and Sophie's keyboard playing was
spacious and melodic. The band's harmonies twisted around
Jethro's guitar solos and vocals like DNA. The audience likes it.
Sabre Light's lead vocalist RiK Chard nods to the beat of their
final number.

Jethro feels great. Feel fantastic.

Just before he went on, Cooper sent him a break a leg text.
She said she'd been sleeping all day. He didn't think about how
that didn't tally up with the strange call he made earlier when he
thought he heard her breathing. He'd text her back saying great,
he wishes she was here, he's about to kick off.

After a couple of numbers Jethro's noticed more and more
phones lifting above the crowd filming them: A good sign. The
crowd approve and the band passes encouraging glances. As the
last number concludes the applause is solid. Jethro lifts his
bolero hat high above his head, wishes the audience a good

night and they cheer. He introduces Sabre Light and when they come onstage the applause turns to a roar.

Maybe one day Jethro & Crew will get that too.

Maybe.

The band leave the stage amped up. RiK Chard, lead vocalist of Sabre Light, slaps a sweaty Jethro on the back as he passes, says that was immense my man, totally immense. He gets to a mic, praises Jethro & Crew in front of the crowd. They cheer again. Then Sabre Light kicks off with their classic little number, sets the whole venue rocking.

Jethro & Crew grab bottles of Budweiser by the neck from an icebox in the wings, start downing them, watching Sabre Light's performance. The Buds are cold and quench their burning thirsts. Industrious stagehands stop to praise them, shake their hands, pat their backs, tell them how immense they were.

Sophie, glowing, her cheeks hot, perches next to Jethro on rigging as they watch Sabre Light kill it with the fans. Her head settles on his shoulder, the hypnotic thrum of Sabre Light shaking their insides.

"Wow," Sophie says. "Performing onstage to thousands is just like sex, don't you think? Same high after."

4 5

COOPER WAKES, her head splitting, her face tender, her neck stiff, her eye weeping and gritty. She has to unpeel her lip from the pillowcase carefully. A smudge of dried blood remains behind. She uses the studio's loo, washes in the tiny basin, shivers in the brittle air conditioning. She scoffs a cereal bar from one side of her mouth, makes a hot black coffee, drinks carefully. She checks her phone. Couple of messages from Harriet keeping tabs. No messages from Daniel. Message from Jethro from last night's concert and links to YouTube of their performance. Cooper watches a minute of it, replies how it looked great. She doesn't know what she's going to do about Jethro. She needs a clear head. Only way to do that is with time and distraction.

She's grateful Thorn Sharp and The Shitty Squits created for her a custom therapy. This is what she needs.

Work, work, work, work, work.

What she needs.

4 6

THE SUE BAXTER PODCAST
DR STEWART-WAY

Well you see Sue, when the MoD approached me to help treat soldiers suffering with PTSD, at first I refused. I knew I still had a long way to go with my work in optogenetics. However, I was persuaded to meet a couple of soldiers. It made me change my mind.

SUE BAXTER

Even though you knew your work was incomplete and could be dangerous?

DR STEWART-WAY

Even though.

SUE BAXTER

So something must've convinced you to risk that. What was the mental condition of the soldiers you saw?

DR STEWART-WAY

Pitiful. And that was the reason. The soldiers suffered poor sleep, anger, frustration, sudden screaming fits, and often were in extremely poor physical health. They could be described as living wrecks, all but zombies. Many soldiers sadly resort to drug use or alcohol to escape the horrors they've witnessed. There are many theories about the processes of PTSD, but in essence the way I view it is as an exponential backlog of emotional frustrations the brain cannot resolve. These frustrations build quickly to overwhelm the individual and dominate his or her life. It can lead to utter misery.

SUE BAXTER

But it's not just the soldiers themselves who suffer, is it?

DR STEWART-WAY

It also affects family and friends – wives, parents, husbands, children.

SUE BAXTER

You're no longer funded by the Ministry of Defence. Why is that?

DR STEWART-WAY

Unfortunately Sue, as I mentioned, fluorogenetics wasn't by itself a permanent solution. Although I knew the treatments worked, it had no longevity.

SUE BAXTER

So you had fallout, treating the soldiers?

DR STEWART-WAY

Unfortunately, yes.

SUE BAXTER

Tell us about them.

4 7

OVER THE NEXT few days Cooper talks with the software programmers and compilers of Sonic Scalpel to sort out glitches.

More days pass.

Then another.

Another.

Lots of calls from Harriet. A couple from Daniel. A few texts from Jethro, though he's busy on tour. Graham checks in now and then for an update.

Eight days now.

Cooper continues to work on The Shitty Squits with microscopic precision.

Nine.

Ten.

Eleven.

A high-powered microscope.

Twelve days.

Thirteen.

Fourteen. Still working on The Shitty Squits.

Fifteen.

Sixteen.

Still working. Still working. Graham calls, wants to know how she's progressing. She gives him meagre details. She sounds tired, exhausted. He'd love to hear some results but he knows never to ask Cooper for anything until she's done.

Seventeen, eighteen, nineteen days. Busy. She's so busy. The days blur together.

Peter March from the label gets itchy, wants to hear results. His bosses ask how things are going with The Shitty Squits album. Peter March tells them with a fixed, plastic smile, it's all going well, soooo well. Good, good they say. Can't wait to hear it. Peter March sweats behind that plastic smile. He needs to make sure he made the right decision. Is he throwing good money after bad? He insists Graham play him something.

But no, Graham keeps Peter away. Peter March wants to contact her directly, threatens to pull the hefty commission. Can't she send something, just something? No can do old bean. It feels good to have control over Peter.

But Graham starts to wonder if this is going to work out after all. Perhaps this is beyond even Cooper's remarkable skills.

Suddenly Peter March pulls the commission, says he's gone elsewhere, says there's no choice, Christopher is still working on the material and is making huge headway.

Graham doesn't tell Cooper her commission has been pulled. Cooper's never failed. Never. Graham decides to pay her himself out of his own business account. He'll take a gamble.

Still more days pass and Graham becomes more concerned. He'd love to hear a track but no he won't ask. It's all or nothing with Cooper. As binary as that.

More days.

Cooper's working, working, working.

The studio, soundproof, day-proof, air-conditioned, has kept her hermetically sealed from life.

Another track. Another. Another. She has found grains of truth in the recordings. Found a pattern to the flaws. She has deciphered how Thorn Sharp hears. She unwinds his smeary influence from each track, unravels the DNA of how he thinks. She peels him off like untwisting bindweed from the strangled songs.

Another week passes.

Cooper's face heals. Her left eye opens. Her bruised cheek and eye, black and plum, become charcoal and plum, become grey and plum, become purple and orange, become orange and yellow, become cream, fades, fades. The ache in her shoulder aches less, the seat belt brand across her chest lessens and then it's a faint shadow. Her body heals.

Everything heals.

Almost everything.

One thing does not heal.

So now Cooper works even harder. Sleeps even less. She puts tracks on loop so it's loud and brash and brain damaging. Even as she sleeps she remains stimulated.

Never dark.

Never quiet.

A casino of sound and light.

Someone called her a tough little acorn once. She does not feel tough.

Cooper is unaware she's lost weight. She lost three pounds the first week. Two pounds the second. A few more the third. The pounds melt away. She eats, but she doesn't taste anything, doesn't enjoy anything, she doesn't even know when she's hungry anymore. Sometimes Cooper goes a whole day without eating. Her stomach caves in. She stays hydrated on black coffee and tea and water in the dry, staticky air. On those rare occasions she ventures from the studio she finds piles of letters by the front door.

During those weeks Cooper has talked with Daniel, talked with Harriet and tells them yeah she's okay, she's fine, she's mending.

It frustrates Harriet, she can't get anything more out of Cooper. Every time Harriet asks how she is Cooper thinks she's ready to tell her but no she's not. She can't say the words, can't say them.

Cooper has chatted to Jethro as he tours Europe even though it curdles her stomach to do it. She is so tired her defences are down and he's so hyped by the tour the chats are buzzy and sensational and all one way. He drives the conversations.

Cooper just listens. After each call he says he misses her, after each call she says yeah me too. He doesn't notice the distance in her voice, the mechanical autonomy.

Jethro no longer wonders if anything's wrong. The band, Jethro & Crew, are making a name for themselves. The crowd reactions interest the label. Sabre Light praises Jethro & Crew and tells the crowd to buy the album, buy the album, but so far, no, they haven't got an album. Now the record label is keen to sign them on, lock them into a studio after the tour. Everything's happening at once.

One day or night or is it morning or is it evening Cooper completes the final album track, sends a message to Graham and before she can climb into her sleeping bag she is already asleep on top of it.

Later back in his wood-panelled office, Graham sees Cooper sent an email at 4.42am. He's hopeful but he knows not to expect miracles. Cooper's message says, Check out the Spitty Slits or whatever they're called ;) Cx

Graham goes to the cloud, finds her tracks, drops them into a folder. He puts it through his B&O hifi. He sits in his leather Charles Eames chair.

Dear lord he hopes he backed the right horse subbing Cooper, he's down a groaning boat of sovereigns. Here goes.

Graham's mouth drops open.

He listens.

It can't be.

Listens.

Impossible.

Listens.

Utterly impossible.

Listens all the way through, one track after another.

When the entire album is over, Graham remains in his chair, unable to move, silent. He is speechless, utterly speechless.

How? How? HOW? How the heck did she do that?

The clarity, the dynamics, the power of the album is astonishing. As though she wound time back and sat down beside Thorn Sharp as he mixed. As though she re-recorded the entire thing with The Shitty Squits in secret sessions.

Did she make a deal with the devil, what?

He cannot believe it's the same album. He can't. He can't believe it. This is splendid work. Splendid? Did he think splendid? This is BLOODY INCREDIBLE! This is a BLOODY MIRACLE!

He calls her, no answer.

Sends her a text.

WOW!!!!!!!!! The wow is in the biggest font he can send. Streamers, champagne cork, amazed emoticons. Call me when you get this. Gxxxx. PS: Who are you? God?

Later, when Graham talks to Cooper, all she can offer is an unenthusiastic great, yeah cool, glad you like.

Graham hears the utter exhaustion straight away.

"Lady Cooper, you need rest."

"Yeah."

"And big, weighty sovereigns."

"Thanks."

"Go. Don't speak to me. Rest. I have delicate negotiations in your favour to tend to."

"Cheers."

Graham can't wait, claps his hands together, rubs them, calls Peter March, is put straight through, no delay.

Peter March answers, glum, dejected, knowing he has nothing good to show his bosses. His other engineer couldn't hack it. What he sent Peter March wasn't an improvement, just a tonal rearrangement of a car crash. It was as bad as the original, just different bad.

Bye-bye executive office. Bye-bye royal treatment. Bye-bye beautiful Mercedes S Class. Bye-bye glamorous executive secretary. Bye-bye Mayfair flat. Bye-bye generous expense account. He's a has-been. The music rags, the websites, the insider industry critics will speculate why the label dumped him and then it will leak out how he was an amateur wearing outsized shoes.

But Graham tells Peter it's great news. Tells him his engineer continued working on The Shitty Squits after all, even after the money dried up, to demonstrate her professionalism and dedication (implying it's unlike Peter's lack of said professionalism and decorum in rescinding on a commission). Graham attaches one song to Peter's email. Peter listens to it, chokes on his Coke, calls back.

"They're all like this?"

"Every track, old bean."

"I need them."

"I'm afraid it's a hefty weight of gold in coin. The lady's not happy you dumped her, unpaid." In reality, Cooper has no idea.

"Anything Grey. Name your price."

Graham smiles, asks for lots of sovereigns. Lots and lots of lovely sovereigns. A rainfall of sovereigns. A king's ransom of sovereigns. Forget peanuts. Forget walnuts. Forget Brazil nuts. He wants COCONUTS.

"Anything, Grey. Just send me those tracks now."

He calls Cooper and tells her she can buy half a dozen cars if she wants.

Cooper almost drops the phone.

4 8

EDDSY IS WORKING on a car, trying to get his hand
underneath the carburettor to get at that stubborn nut that refuses
to move. He'd loosened it with the telescopic spanner but now
can't get the angle to allow his thick fingers between the narrow
gap to spin it off. The blasted gap is too tight. The other lads
work either side of him on separate cars, one on an old
Mercedes the other on a Honda. In the far corner a Ford bonnet
is up. He needs Jerry, the skinny lad he'd apprenticed eighteen
months ago. Used to be engines had lots of space around them
for access. Nowadays you have to pull everything out to get the
bit you want, or had special tools for. Jerry has an advantage.
He's as flexible as a cat, can contort himself into the crankiest
angles to get access to the most obnoxious parts of an engine.
No one else has Jerry's flexibility.

A voice comes from behind him.

"Hey boss."

Jerry sprouts up from the other side of the bonnet, hair
cropped short, wiry thin, his twenty-three-year-old face twisted
in a dented grin.

"Heck you been, Jerr?"

"Uh sorry boss, had to skip out to pick Chloe up. Jade's
working late."

Eddsy glances over the bonnet, sees Chloe, a girl of about
five clutching a glossy Disney magazine with a picture of a
princess on the cover. She wears a red buttoned-up coat with
blonde ringlets cascading down from a red beret. She sees
Eddsy smiling at her, buries her head into Jerry's leg.

"Chloe, you remember uncle Eddsy don't you?"

She peeks out from behind Jerry with one big blue eye.

Eddsy says "Hey," she ducks behind the leg again.

Jerry scrunches his face up, curiously peering through his John Lennon spectacles at the engine.

"Uh, what're you up to, boss?"

Eddsy explains the problem and within moments Jerry's curved himself into some sort of martial arts preying mantis position with his long spidery fingers. He coaxes the nut out as though he just breathed on it and it dropped in his hand.

Eddsy hands him the spanner and goes to walk away.

"Uh boss?"

Eddsy turns, looks at him.

"You mind looking after Chloe?"

Eddsy looks at Chloe.

"Chipmunk, why don't you go with uncle Eddsy?"

Chloe remains clamped to Jerry's leg like a crab. She talks into his overalls.

"No."

"Sweetie you can't stay here. Lots of big scary machines around."

"No."

"Chipmunk—"

She pipes up. Her voice sweet and light.

"It's cold here daddy. Let's go home."

Eddsy walks around to Jerry's side, looms over her, his shoulders huge.

"Like chocolate, Chloe?"

She keeps her head buried in Jerry's thigh. After a pause she peeps an eye out.

"Uh-huh."

"Hot chocolate?"

Chloe pauses, turns her face to Eddsy.

"Don't be silly, chocolate isn't hot. It'd melt."

Eddsy laughs.

"Had a chocolate milkshake before, right?"

"Uh-huh."

"Drink that, don't you?"

"Uh-huh."

"Hot chocolate'll make you nice and warm."

Chloe puts on an intelligent face, thinks seriously about it.

"Guess who makes it?"

"Who?"

"A big square robot."

Chloe giggles.

"No, it doesn't."

"True. Gurgles and burps as it pours your drink."

She covers her mouth with a gasp.

"That's a bad word."

"It's true."

She screws her face up suspiciously, looks up at Jerry.

"Is that true, daddy?"

Jerry points at the office.

"Chipmunk, see auntie Shirley at the computer in the office?"

"Uh-huh."

"See that big square thing next to her?"

"Uh-huh."

"That's the robot. Keeps the hot chocolate in its belly."

"Oh wowwwwwwwww. It's bigger than a 'numan." She turns back to Eddsy. "Will it make me a hot chocolate drink, uncle Eddsy?"

"Ask nicely, might."

Chloe clamps on to Eddsy's hand, pulls at him.

"Let's GO!"

Jerry laughs.

"Hey boss."

Eddsy turns, looks at Jerry.

"You're a natural, boss."

Eddsy smiles, then feels a pang like an old ache in the pit of his stomach.

Later, when Jerry's finished for the day he finds Chloe behind Eddsy's desk, arms on the armrests looking magisterial. Eddsy is on the other side of the desk where the customers sit. He's checking orders on the swivelled-around computer monitor. Chloe looks up.

"Daddy daddy, look at me! I'm da boss."

Jerry laughs, wiping his hands on a rag, winks at Eddsy.

"You're not kidding, Chipmunk."

"Uncle Eddsy says anyone who sits at this desk 'comes da boss of everything. You get to do lots of 'portant things when you're da boss."

"That's true too."

She screws her face up in serious consideration.

"Think I'll have another hot chocolate."

Everyone laughs.

Soon Jerry and Chloe are gone and Eddsy's office is suddenly so quiet he can hear the clock on the wall ticking. While Chloe was there she fidgeted and asked auntie Shirley and uncle Eddsy a battery of questions. She twisted and spun in his office chair. She jumped and wandered around the office. Even demanded uncle Eddsy read some of her Disney magazine to her. Now Eddsy sits in his office chair feeling a familiar hollow.

Shirley packs up, stands up ready to go.

"Well, that was a gale force."

He grins.

"Handful, that one."

Shirley watches him. Eddsy leans back, vacantly swivelling left and right in his chair, arms settled on the armrests. Usually he's doing ten things at once.

"You okay there, boss?"

He wakes from his reverie.

"Sure. Off you go." Checks the clock. "Long past home time."

Her lips purse into a devious smile.

"Fortunately, I've a boss who pays me double time after five."

"Time and a half."

"Drat. Didn't think you'd notice."

He points at the office door.

"Out."

Soon Shirley's gone. His mechanics are gone. Eddsy is alone in his quiet garage. He logs on to the adoption agency website he checks into occasionally from his desk. Lots of smiling faces of happy parents and lots of laughing children. He scans the pictures, aware his heart is beating just that little bit faster. He's read the blurb so many times, loses himself in it as though reading it for the first time, absorbing every word.

When he next checks the time he's surprised. He hadn't realised Shirley'd left almost an hour ago. He logs out, rubs his face, closes down the computer, switches off the office lights. He steps through the dark garage space, beeps his van open.

One day he'll be man enough to say something to Harriet, ask what she thinks about it.

One day.

4 9

COOPER EMERGES FROM the studio. It's daylight and she's surprised how much the lawn has grown. She hadn't noticed before.

She finds Kelloggs sulking in the cattery. He's miffed, won't acknowledge her, licks himself.

At home, Cooper sinks into a steaming bath. It's the first proper bath in so long ever since that rebirth at Harriet's. She soaks in it, washes her hair, enjoys the hot amniotic fluid. She puts on a bra surprised to find it's too big now. She looks in the mirror.

Takes a step back, surprised.

Her hair's longer but it's not that which shocks her it's that her face is thin, her face narrow, her face is gaunt. She steps on the scales and she's lost tons of weight. Tons. She knows she needs to eat.

The moment she thinks this it's as though her stomach opens an eye. Suddenly it growls at her. She recalls a Royal Institute Christmas lecture where an Arctic explorer talked about having lost so much weight during the expedition when he returned to civilisation he was ravenous for weeks. He kept eating and eating and eating and eating until his body said stop one day. Cooper changes into fresh, crisp clothes. Her cargos have a gap between the waistband and her stomach and she has to create a new hole in a belt to fasten it.

Cooper devours the contents of the fridge, the contents of the kitchen cupboards. It's not enough. She orders lots of food and when it arrives, eats and eats and eats and eats. First she craves cheese. Lots of cheese. Cheddar and Wensleydale and Stilton and Red Leicester and Edam and Stinking Bishop and Roquefort and Danish Blue. Then she feels like fish. Lots of fish. Halibut and cod and sardine and plaice and salmon and sea bass and trout. Then it's meat. Salami and ham and steak and burgers and lamb and chicken and pork and beef. Then she wants bread. Lots of bread. White bread and brown bread and wholemeal bread and cinnamon bread and crusty bread and stoneground bread. Then sugar. Lots of sugar. Cakes and chocolate and biscuits and toffees and wine gums and boiled sweets and marshmallows and liquorice. For two weeks all she can think about is food. More food. Even more food. She puts on weight.

Cooper talks to Daniel more. He's returning in the break. Talks to Harriet more. Harriet keeps wanting to see Cooper and Cooper delaying. Talks to Jethro more. The European tour's over soon. She must be ready to face them. Face them all.

Face him.

5 0

THE SUE BAXTER PODCAST
DR STEWART-WAY
Well Sue, before meeting Dr Applegate, I had three soldiers
who suffered fall-out from my work with fluorogenetics.
SUE BAXTER
How safe were your treatments?
DR STEWART-WAY
Well, I'd insisted many times to the MoD that my work was
incomplete and that it was against my judgement to carry out
such treatments on soldiers. But I had to admit my work offered
a glimmer of hope to these hopeless victims of PTSD. Even the
soldiers' respective families sought help aware of the risk. Both
the Medical Ethics Committee and the General Medical Council
were aware of these trial procedures and set strict guidelines I
adhered to but I kept to even stricter levels of treatment than I
was given. At least the treatment offered the soldiers relief,
however brief. Unfortunately, within months the MoD reversed
their decision when it became obvious one soldier in particular,
Martin Maddock, reacted severely to continual treatment.
SUE BAXTER
I have the names here. Martin Maddock whose role in the army
was as a Rapier Air Defence Gunner committed suicide.
DR STEWART-WAY
Sadly he did. Martin Maddock had a record of self-harm after
returning from three tours of duty in Iraq. Unfortunately, even
though he was receiving treatment, he succeeded in ending his
own life.

SUE BAXTER

Also, Annie Slater, an Artillery Logistic Specialist and David Ranger, an Infantry Soldier, developed such severe psychotic behaviour it resulted in long-term hospitalisation in a mental institution.

DR STEWART-WAY

Yes, they're dreadful outcomes for all three patients. It redoubled my efforts to find a solution.

SUE BAXTER

What precisely was the problem with your treatment as it stood?

5 1

TODAY COOPER REALISES something. For over twenty years she thought Jethro had mended her.

And for weeks since that day.

Soft moans, soft moans.

That day.

Soft kisses, soft kisses.

That day.

She's asked herself so many times why she didn't storm to the bedroom and scream at Jethro. A million million times. She knows the answer now.

Jethro hadn't mended her. He hadn't ever mended her.

Jethro had taken that quiet scared distrustful teenager and turned her into another version of herself. He did it without trying, without knowing. He did it simply by being.

Cooper knew Jethro never looked at her as a girl to be conquered. Instead he saw someone like him. Insecure, despite her confidence, sensitive, despite her bovver boots, frustrated, despite her calm shell, lonely, despite her beauty.

And Cooper herself had been fascinated by Jethro. She saw someone wearing everything on the outside, astonished how he could just do that, be as transparent as varnish, while she'd become a paint-tattered version of herself.

Cooper was fifteen then. Jethro was fifteen.

In the classroom they'd shared their identities as though swapping personal diaries. Their relationship somehow… merged. He didn't coax her. She didn't invite him. Yet they'd shared a world neither his nor hers. A paradoxical third place. An impossible, Schrödiner's Cat place.

So Cooper could never have walked into the bedroom that day her world shuddered like camera shake.

Soft moans. Soft moans.

Couldn't ever have confronted Jethro.

Soft kisses. Soft kisses.

And to confront him now on the phone from whatever stage in whatever country he's in is entirely wrong. To confront him on text, entirely wrong.

They're in two separate worlds after over twenty years of togetherness.

No. Jethro hadn't mended her. He hadn't ever mended her.

Still, her reality dropped her into this whiteout for a reason. It has a purpose. To steel her from that third place so she could be outside it, learn something, not about Jethro, but about herself. What she's learned is this:

For over twenty years, Cooper's been fifteen years old. Fifteen years old holding hands with someone she loved – loves – so it didn't matter.

It hadn't mattered.

Now it matters.

It matters.

The truth is Cooper's vulnerable because Jethro hadn't mended her. He hadn't ever mended her. Not in over twenty years.

He'd preserved her.

5 2

COOPER'S HEART IS beating, her heart is racing for what she's about to do. She goes to the bathroom, slides open the mirrored medicine cabinet door and takes out Jethro's aftershave, Homme. Clasps it so hard her knuckles are white.

Her heart is beating. Her heart is racing.

Takes off the top.

Her heart is beating faster. Racing faster. She wants to test herself.

Inhales.

Suddenly she's sick. Her heart is slamming. She dives to the toilet bowl, dry heaves.

No. She can't face it.

She tries a Dizzy Gillespie track on a streaming website. Listens to the opening bars. The jazzy smoothness fills her ears. She gets a physical, wrenching pain in her chest. She can't listen to it. She can't. That night she dumps the original LPs outside a charity shop.

Cooper hasn't slept in her own bed for weeks, preferring to use the sleeping bag in the studio. Now she uses Daniel's bedroom. But this can't go on.

She forces herself to enter her own bedroom. Stands on the threshold and with a deep breath steps over. She hates it. Hates the room. Wants to trash everything.

She takes a mallet and smashes the bed frame up until it's splintered and crumpled. She drags the mattress outside the door, wants to burn it, but instead offers it on Freecycle.

She goes to a paint shop, buys a refreshing minty green and paints the bedroom, covering the bland magnolia. Mint green is a colour she hates but she does it anyway. She recarpets it. The sales agent recommends a wool mix, something soft and comfortable underfoot for the bedroom. Cooper is hardier than that. She replaces it with jute. Something, robust like her.

She orders a hybrid memory foam mattress online after reading a ton of reviews, orders a new sturdy bed frame, changes the curtains, puts a new lampshade in, gets rid of the furniture, replaces it with Shaker style.

Soon everything's done. The bedroom is made-over.

That night she lies in her new bed, fresh paint still in the air, the chemical smell of new carpet, the duvet crisp and cool. She lies in bed, the pillows are cool and new, the pillowcases still have creases in them. She lies in bed, pushed against the opposite wall so when she wakes in the morning she's disorientated for a moment.

Cooper goes online.

How to deal with a broken heart. Reads voraciously.

How to deal with bereavement. Reads voraciously.

How to deal with loss, reads everything voraciously.

How to deal with depression, reads all she can find. She keeps searching, keeps looking for an answer.

Cooper hears a late-night radio phone-in programme where the guest psychologist has a soft, lilting voice. She calls in at 2.13am, gets on air, doesn't say what the problem is, doesn't use her real name, tells the psychologist she's sad. His voice is so gentle it's like a warm hug from a teddy bear. He gives her comforting words. Says people out there can help her. She hangs up. It's not the answer.

She tries the Samaritans. Talks to them, tells them she's sad. They say soothing things to her. Hangs up. It's not the answer.

She finds a counsellor. She can't say what the problem is even though she's no longer in shock, it's too raw to put into words. No. Not the answer.

She tries a specialist online. It's all text. Perhaps it's speaking that's the problem. What if she writes instead? But no she can't write the words, her fingers won't let her. It's not the answer.

Cooper needs an answer. God please. She needs an answer.

She thinks about going to the doctors to get drugs, dismisses the idea. No it's not the answer.

Cooper reads more articles – doesn't help. Goes into supportive chat rooms – everyone is cynical. Goes to positive thinking websites – they gloss over everything. All the while the Google algorithms intelligently analyses all Cooper's enquiries, funnelling a sequence of ever-tightening search suggestions…

Then.

Cooper comes across a treatment for PTSD.

It's a banner for a revolutionary new process. She reads about the clinic, how it started, reads about Clive a solicitor with his unconscious phobia of spiders. She discovers something called fluorogenetics, something called The Gateway Programme, about how the rewriting of the brain deletes stress from traumatic memories. Cooper has the dawning of an idea. The more she reads the more she becomes breathless with excitement. The idea brightens, turns to day.

Cooper calls the clinic. Their office closed, it's a voicemail. She explains what the problem is. Tells them what she wants – her idea. She leaves her number.

Cooper stops searching, forgets about the PTSD clinic.

It won't be long before Daniel's back for half term.

It won't be long before Jethro's back too.

God.

Anyway Cooper feels a little better. Course she does. Thinks she's beginning to recover anyway. Course she is. Thinks it's only time she needs. That's all. Yeah that's it. Course. Just time.

Besides.

She's way over the worst. Way, way over.

Course she is.

5 3

IT'S LUNCHTIME WHEN Eddsy steps out of the coffee shop
with a giant triple espresso, unsettled about what he's about to
do. He's about to do something that, tell the truth, scares the
crap out of him. He needs the punch of caffeine to brace
himself. He sees the discreet green and white Barnardo's sign he
strolls past every day. He goes up to the door. He sees a metal
intercom, buzzes it. His mouth is dry. Takes a swig of coffee.

A woman's voice comes on the intercom, says hello. He
gives her his name, tells her why he's there. She asks him if
he'd like to make an appointment. His voice shakes a little when
he speaks. He says "No," says "don't worry," backs away from
the intercom.

Relief. He feels relief.

The woman calls out over the speaker, "Hello, are you still
there, Mr Tomalin?" He steps forward, says "Yes" but he
doesn't know really what he's doing there. There's a pause then
a buzz. He hesitates, doesn't want to go in. The buzz keeps
going, doesn't stop, doesn't stop. Eddsy has no option but to
pull the door handle, there's a loud thunk. The door opens the
buzzing stops. He steps in. The door seals shut behind him like a
bank vault. The air inside feels tight around his collar.

Inside the corridor is brightly lit. He sees posters either side,
happy bright children and smiling sunshine, sunshine families
from the website.

A caramel-skinned woman in her forties with big fuzzy afro
hair emerges through a door. She looks Caribbean. She has soft
eyes, a simple navy jacket, skirt long, burgundy lipstick, and

smells exotic, smells floral. She smiles and gold bangles clink when she holds her hand out.

"Hello, Mr Tomalin. I'm Simone Grey, senior social worker."

Eddsy takes her hand, shakes it. He wants to run but the vault-thick door is sealed behind him. She turns, walks.

"Would you care to come through?"

Numb, he follows her through the office.

Three desks, a woman in glasses and long centre-parted hair who looks like a librarian is on the phone, a 30-something man, balding but with youthful shiny skin in faded jeans is writing something in a notepad on his desk. They look up at him, smile. He nods at them. Simone takes him through to a walled-off private room, settles behind a desk. She offers a chair, Eddsy sits. He holds his coffee in front of him, his Boudica shield, feels the heat in his lap. He almost can't breathe. They agree on first names. Eddsy. Simone. Eddsy starts telling her he's been on the website lots of times, looked at YouTube videos, everything, doesn't know what he's doing here really. He rambles.

Simone nods, knows he's nervous, she smiles, hopes she can relax him. She's good at relaxing people, a talent she's always had, the perfect arbiter. Even as a child she could calm her parents when they were arguing just by her presence. Even at school she avoided most fights. People just never stayed angry at her for long.

Simone waits for Eddsy to wind down before speaking.

"Normally," Simone says, "we don't see people off the street, but I've had a cancellation."

She tells him the good news that a single person can adopt. He says no. No? He goes into a ramble again. He has a wife, Harriet. Married eight years, a second marriage for him, Harriet's first. He says he's 46 Harriet is 38. He tells Simone they can't have children. He says the idea of adopting keeps popping up in his head. Simone says, I assume Harriet wishes to adopt? He doesn't know, it's something he wants to discuss with her, but he doesn't want to mention adoption to her until he knows it's possible. Simone says that would of course depend on various factors. He says he'd like to know what the factors are because if it's an automatic no he'll never mention it to Harriet. He just wants to know.

Eddsy likes Simone's gentle coaxing, her gentle guiding. She's warm. Her smile wide and genuine with her burgundy lipstick and her exotic floral scent he finds reassuring. She has motherly brown eyes, warm and comforting like hot Marmite.

Harriet too has motherly eyes.

He notices a sparkly marquisette necklace under Simone's open blouse, it catches the light from the desk lamp, winks at him when she breathes, changes it's Morse Code pattern when she talks, and again when she moves. It's like hypnosis, he feels cradled in the warm sponge of Simone's calm presence.

Eddsy tells her he sometimes catches Harriet gazing at other children in supermarkets, or slows as she walks past the local school playground. It makes Eddsy's throat tighten. Harriet wanted children so much, he says. So much. Simone reassures him. She says usually people who want children but can't are open to adoption. He tells Simone he wants to know if they got a chance.

"Well now, let's see. Any questions I ask I'll assume Harriet will feel the same way at this stage. In an interview with you both it's likely Harriet will have differing opinions. For now, I'll be happy to express my feelings of suitability based on your answers, how does that sound, Eddsy?"

"Okay. Understood."

"Well now, let's see. Let's start at the top. As an adopter you must meet three important conditions. One, I know already is you're both over twenty-one."

Eddsy grins. Big teeth.

"Have you and Harriet been domiciled in the UK for at least a year?"

"Both born here."

"Now, I'm afraid I have to ask this – any criminal convictions or cautions particularly with children for either of you?"

"No way."

"Sex offences?"

"No way."

"What about in the family? Any brothers, sisters, uncles, parents on either side?"

"No."

"Friends, work, colleagues?"

"No way. No."

"Please take your time to think about this."

Eddsy runs through everyone he can think of, shakes his head.

"We will of course have to carry out a DBS check."

"DBS check?"

"A Disclosure and Barring Service check. We will also need to go through your medical histories."

"Okay. Understood."

Eddsy puts the coffee cup on the floor, puts his large hands on his knees, hates that he feels so nervous again. This feels so official suddenly.

Simone sees, notices, observes. She knows the comfort she brings people can flicker out with such brutally frank questions. She quickly flicks the questions away with a hand as though swatting a fly. She smiles. It has a transformative effect. It hypnotises Eddsy. He relaxes, Simone's velvet warmth supporting him again.

"Well, that's the horrible bit over with. I hope you don't mind too much. We do have to ask."

"Don't mind. Understood."

"Is there particular age or nationality of child you're interested in?"

"Anyone."

"Teenager?"

"Anyone."

"Baby?"

"Anyone."

"It doesn't matter if the child is black, white, Asian— ?"

"Anyone."

"What about the sex of the child?"

"Anyone."

"Our children most often come from troubled backgrounds. Is that a problem?"

"Kinda expected that."

She pauses.

"That's good. It keeps the field of opportunity wide open. Well now, I can tell you the adoption process has two choices." She raises an index finger. "One is either a simple Straight Adoption." She raises a second finger. "The other is Foster to Adopt. Do you have preferences?"

"Anything."

Simone appraises Eddsy with pleasant surprise. Most start with a narrow idea what they want but widen their views when they know the facts. Eddsy starts wide to begin with. It's unusual. When she met him, she saw a lumbering giant in blue work overalls many must find intimidating. Then she saw his face. There's a gentleness to him. Consideration in his eyes, like a gardener. A mauve aura surrounds him, hints of a golden haze shimmering at the edges. It's a good sign. Poor man had been sitting bolt upright, his spine, aerial straight, his hands clutching instead of resting on his knees until she'd relaxed him.

"Do you have any questions, Eddsy?"

"Big one."

"Please go right ahead."

"Harriet and me, we never talked about adoption."

"Yes?"

"Well. Kinda scared to ask her."

Simone looks intrigued.

"Oh? Why's that?"

Eddsy takes a deep breath. What he's about to say could close the chance to adopt forever, like that vault-solid, front door.

5 4

COOPER RECEIVES A whopping lump sum into her bank account from Graham Chambers. It's more than she could ever have dreamt of. She organises a hire car now she's able to drive again.

The car arrives and the slender young man from the company stands on the doorstep in a shiny polyester suit, the kind that has snags in it. He likes what he sees in the older attractive woman but as he talks he grows increasingly wary of the look in Cooper's eyes. Even though she smiles there's something broken about her. It unsettles him. He asks if she'd like instruction on the car's controls, she says no she had a car just like it. She signs the form on his clipboard and he drops the keys into her hand, tells her to have a good day, leaves.

Cooper jumps into the Toyota, starts it up, revving it. She goes shopping at a large superstore. All goes well.

But it's coming back something happens.

Drip.

One thought, Dizzy Gillespie.

Drip.

Another thought, Homme.

Drip.

Another thought, soft moans, soft moans.

Drip drip.

Another thought, soft kisses, soft kisses.

Drip drip drip drip.

But it doesn't stop.

Wisps of dark young hair, soft moans, bed creaking, kissing, giggling, slender young body, private, intimate words.

Jethro.

Jethro.

Oh Jethro.

The thoughts come. It gets worse the longer she drives. Worse. Builds, keeps building. Her breaths become shallower, shorter. She becomes otherly, like she's not really in the car anymore. Like she's above the car, hovering above it, looking down on its red roof.

Cooper drives fast. Faster. She drives long. Longer. Drives far. Drives hard.

Cooper needs distraction. The cocoon of the studio is gone. The cocoon of the house is gone. She pulls into the fast lane, the car behind flashes its lights. Then she pulls back to the middle lane, the car behind blares its horn. But she keeps doing it. Slowing down, speeding up, revving the engine in too low a gear, or too high a gear, driving recklessly, tailgating a lorry, a van, a bus, a car, a motorcycle. She switches lanes without thinking, weaves in and out, doesn't care. She's trying to annoy drivers. She wants reactions from the world so she doesn't have to endure this. Distraction. She needs distraction. Control. She needs control. She feels it slipping away like oil on glass.

Her thoughts.

They come back.

Keep coming back.

Drip drip drip drip drip.

Cooper pulls into the slow lane, goes behind a truck belting out black exhaust crawling on an incline. Her car struggles in fifth gear, she has to change down, the car jolts whips her neck. Cars pass her, show her the finger, shout at her, veined red faces, all vicious, all angry.

She looks up at the sky, it's partly cloudy, but there's no rain, no hail, no snow, no storm, just an ordinary sky. Please let something happen. Take me away. Let something happen, please.

Cooper flicks the windscreen wipers on. It screeches, leaves smeared rubbery arcs across the windscreen. She switches the radio onto a current affairs programme. They talk about the economy, about crimes, topical issues, celebrity gossip, the weather, traffic conditions, she turns it up loud. It doesn't help. Turns it to a music channel.

Not loud enough.

Turns the volume up.

Up.

Up.

UP.

UP UP UP UP UP.

The volume can't go any higher. The car booms. Bass-heavy music throbbing through the car.

Tears come. A hurricane. A tornado. A storm. Tears.

Cooper glances at the names on overhead motorway signs, forgets them immediately. Something was thirty miles away. Something else forty-six miles away.

Distraction. Distraction. She needs distraction. Please.

Cooper sees a sign for a motorway rest stop three miles up, takes it. She has no idea where it is. She pulls into the service station. It's a big complex. An acre of parking spaces. An acre of glinting cars in the weak, cloudy sun. She pulls in, parks.

Cooper climbs out rushes to the entrance hits a huge bank of thick glass doors hurts her wrist. Pain. Pain is good. She pushes through. People are coming people are going. She darts past a coffee shop the aroma strong and heavy. She goes past an arcade the electronic noises are loud booming crashing lights flashing. She weaves around everyone they're all walking the other way. She sees a shiny newsagents she goes in walks along the aisles.

People look at her she doesn't notice. A security guard follows her with alert, narrow eyes.

Stark shadowless lights fill the aisles. She feels exposed, a specimen under a microscope. As though someone above is observing her through a lens. She's a microbe on the plane of the earth.

She finds the confectionery aisle. Mars, Twix, Bounty, Snickers, Picnic, Galaxy, Kit-Kat, Toblerone, Crunchie. She wants to shovel all the chocolate down her throat, make herself sick, she wants to shovel crisps, she wants to open the cans of fizzy drinks, guzzle them. Cooper wants to escape her prison. She approaches a long magazine rack.

The magazines are bright and colourful and glossy. DIY magazines and women's magazines and lad's magazines and craft magazines and house beautiful magazines and gossip magazines and television magazines and technical magazines and hobby magazines and financial magazines.

Cooper welcomes the confusing, flashing blur. Distraction. Distraction. Picks up a magazine, flicks through it. She doesn't see the pages, can't read the words. She pushes it back in the wrong place. She picks up another, tries again, the words mean nothing, they don't mean anything to her.

Homme, Dizzy Gillespie, soft moans, soft moans, soft kisses, soft kisses.

Heart pounding in her chest.

Oh god. Oh god, oh god.

A rising tide of hysteria. Panic. Like the sheer cliff drop of dread when you know you're drowning.

Cooper needs to escape. She needs to get out. The air is thick and hot.

No air. No air. Can't breathe. No air. Fear. Terror. All raging inside her, her body taking over. Her frenzied heart, bashing, crashing, wrenching from its moorings to escape her ribcage.

She rushes through the aisles now into people, people, people. They complain, they say hey, they say watch out, they say worse.

An alarm goes off, pierces her thoughts. A security guard's yelling at someone and pointing and shouting and running and it looks as though he's running toward her and pointing at her and shouting at her. Now two are running. Cooper looks down, she's holding a magazine, one she hasn't paid for. She tosses the magazine, runs, runs. She charges into people, twists and spins and turns, bashing into signs, slamming into columns, crashing into doors. Cooper is suffocating, confused, terrified. No air. No air. Can't breathe. Can't breathe. She needs air, she can't breathe, she needs space, she can't breathe, she needs sky, she can't breathe, she needs her cocoon.

Cooper finds the exit, rushes out into a blaze of daylight, daylight, daylight, she's outside. She stumbles on to the curb, rushes into the car park almost hitting into a car crawling along, looking for a parking space. An old woman who rides shotgun swivels her head to stare at Cooper, shock registers on her face as the car passes.

Cooper sees a car, she recognises a red Toyota parked askew, sees the driver's door open, the cabin light on, the radio blasting. It's her car. She runs to it.

Cooper slams the door shut. Heavy breathing. The keys are still in the engine, the engine is still running the radio is blasting, the windscreen wipers are screeching, the vents are belting hot air out. She takes in huge lungfuls of breath. One after the other. One after the other. Slowly, the dread, the panic begins to ebb away.

Cooper winds the window up.

Switches the radio off.

Stops the windscreen wipers.

Cuts the engine.

She can't keep doing this. Something must change. Something has to. Please, something must. She hates that she's like this. HATES it.

It's all Jethro's fault. Jethro. And with that Cooper grits her teeth, suddenly angry, hating herself for being like this. In a burst of frustration her blood rages her blood boils. She smashes the roof of her car with her fists, hammering the side door, stamping her legs on the floor, screaming, shouting, crying, wailing. She's angry, so ANGRY. People stay away from the madwoman bashing her horn, screaming behind the glass.

The two security guards catch up but they stop. They look at her. They stare at her. They exchange sidelong glances. They make a decision. Back away. One has the magazine she tossed anyway. They leave.

Other people watch the spectacle, frightened, fascinated by her. She is performance art. She is TV. She is cinema. She is YouTube. She is Twitter. She is Instagram. She is TikTok. Someone films her on a phone.

Cooper wants to die, wants to, she really, really, really, really wants to. She feels an urge, a powerful destructive urge to start the car, crash it crash it hard, fast, crash just crash, die, burn, die, that's what she's going to do, what she wanted to do from the start, what she always wanted to do, what she's going to do. Lose the misery, lose the pain, lose the crushing desolation, the helplessness.

Cooper shoves the car in gear, revs the engine hard, pushing it harder so it screams, feels the exhilarating drug-rush of control surge through her. She's determined to do it. She's going to die. She's really going to. Do it, just do it do it do it do it DO IT DO IT.

She's about to lift her foot from the clutch, lurch the car into powerful burning motion.

Then.

A moment of confusion, something stops her.

Something.

It stops her.

It's her mobile. It's ringing.

She stares at it in the passenger seat as though she doesn't recognise it. A number flashes up. She doesn't know the number. But she does. It's familiar, she has no idea why. She answers.

"Good afternoon. Is this Mrs Cooper Hall?"

Cooper is panicky, breaths short and quick.

"Yeah."

"This is Dr Applegate from Gateway House. You called and left a message Mrs Hall. We think we can help you."

Cooper speaks. No she doesn't. She can't speak. She screams. She screams the words.

"Please, please, OH GOD PLEASE HELP ME!"

5 5

EDDSY IS SITTING in Barnardo's offices not believing he's there discussing adoption. He finds it difficult to say what he's about to tell Simone. She's gently coaxing him to speak with an encouraging smile, a gentle nod. It makes it easier.

"You know I said we can't have kids," Eddsy says.

Simone knows this is not what's worrying Eddsy. There's more to this. It's his way of leading up to it. Simone nods before speaking.

That's not uncommon with prospective adoptive parents. Her voice is gentle, but she deliberately pushes the conversation on. "Is this a medical issue for one of you?"

Eddsy looks down at his knees. His shame is personal.

"Yeah. My fault. Yeah."

"I'm assuming you explored this with fertility clinics?"

"Yeah." He shakes his head, looks sad, looks disappointed with himself.

She feels an urge to reach across the desk, touch his hand, offer physical comfort. She can't. She's not permitted.

"You're concerned Harriet's not interested in having children? Is that your concern?" Again Simone knows that's not what's on his mind. It's something else. She coaxes, coaxes.

"Nah, she wanted them. But…" His eyes mist over.

"Would you like a glass of water, Eddsy?"

Eddsy shakes his head.

"Nah… When I told her about my condition, she got upset."

"That's understandable."

"We're good together. I propose to her. She says yes anyway. We get married. We're okay. Then she gets depressed."

Simone continues to coax.

"Is she still depressed?"

"Nah. Fine now. But. You know. I ask her about adoption she might get depressed again if we don't qualify."

"I see. Well, it's an understandable concern. I appreciate your telling me, thank you. It is something we'd have to look into."

"Yeah. Guessed that. It's in the family. Her sister had it. Breakdown. She… almost took her own life. Years ago."

"Her sister, I see." Simone smiles. "Then let me assure you Eddsy you've not answered a single question that absolutely strikes you off adopting."

Eddsy looks up, hope in his eyes, meets Simone's.

"Yeah?"

"I can promise you there are no such things as perfect parents. So, I'd be delighted to explain a little more about the adoption process. Do you have the time?"

Eddsy looks at his phone.

"Yeah it's quarter-past one."

Simone laughs.

"I'm sorry. I meant do you have the time for me to explain?"

Eddsy grins, big white teeth, then laughs. It breaks the dark moment. It's relief.

"I'm big chief. I got the time."

Simone's puzzled for a moment, then air-slaps her forehead.

"Of course! You're Tomalin Garages down the road. How silly of me. And oh look, it's even embroidered on your overalls. For heaven's sake I use your garage for my car service. You're the garage for women drivers."

"Yeah. Recognise you as a customer."

"Well, that's nought out of ten for observation on my behalf."

"Face not usually this clean. Uniform's fresh too."

"Well now, getting back to topic, let's say you've crossed the first hurdle on the road to adoption. Let's say the adoption process is in motion. The whole process takes about six months. For the first two months we'll explore your family's background, including medical and criminal records. You've already made me aware of Harriet and her sister's depression so that's something we will have to explore. We will also need to have three referees we'd interview who can vouch for you both. We'll assign a social worker to assess your home which will either be Ian or Pamela, both of whom you passed when you came in. We'd also need to look into the suitability of your home. You'll need to have enough room for a child, even if it's a baby. In fact, when I say child, I am, of course, referring to a child of any age from zero up to his or her teens. A garden would be nice but not essential, and you'd need a second bedroom."

"We got six bedrooms. We got a big garden. Half-acre."

Simone looks impressed.

"Your home sounds lovely."

"Yeah. Empty."

"Well now, if you pass that test, we walk you through something called Training for Approval. You and Harriet will have to take a Home Study course. You'll work alongside prospective adopters and get to know each other. How's that sounding so far?"

"Yeah. Read stuff about it."

"Excellent. We'll continuously assess you along the way but you needn't worry. It's not an examination in the usual sense of the word. It's really an acclimatisation. I have to warn you it will be emotionally draining though. You'll most likely have moments of extreme joy followed by crashing lows. It is going to be a roller coaster ride no matter how prepared you think you are. Do you think Harriet could cope with this?"

"Was like bereavement, you know? Not having kids. Doctor said it was a normal reaction."

"Harriet sounds like a wonderful woman."

"Yeah."

"And I can see you love her very much."

Eddsy tries to say yeah again but nothing comes out. His throat thickens and he chokes up. The woman he loves most in the world and he can't heal her pain. The guilt burning inside him, corrosive.

"Well," Simone says, "I already mentioned we devote the first two months to assessing you both. After that we take all the details and compile it into what's called a Prospective Adopter Report. I'm afraid you won't see that for obvious reasons. This report will go to an adoption panel. Please bear in mind you could stumble at this stage. However, you will have a sense of the likely outcome. Still, we know it is a nerve-wracking time and we'll be just as nervous as you two. You'll no doubt suffer sleepless nights – tears of worry and moments of happy expectation. You'll need to support each other through this period. Ian or Pamela will, of course, help you. If during the process either of you find any part of this overwhelming, you can withdraw. Your decision would be understandable. Many people do withdraw at this stage. The whole experience can be emotionally draining so rest assured you would not be alone in your decision. Importantly the decision doesn't preclude you from future applications."

Eddsy nods, taking that in.

"If you're approved it will be a day of celebration. It's at this stage we'll consider the two ways we have to match you with a child."

Simone raises a finger. "I mentioned earlier an alternative to Straight Adoption was Foster to Adopt. Here you'll have the chance to foster a child who will receive a home placement. If the child happily acclimatises, you'll go to a final stage. It's now you'll have the opportunity to adopt the child."

Simone counts a second finger.

"With Straight Adoption we try to match you with a child who already has an Adoption Plan. You won't meet the child yet but there will be videos and photographs and you will receive a Child Report so you can fully grasp the child's history and background. The child will have your personal details too so they'll know everything about you. You can present the child with a photograph album, letters they can read, perhaps a piece of personal clothing if they're younger. The plan will then go to a matching panel who will make the final assessment on your all-round suitability. Does that all make sense?"

Eddsy nods.

"Any questions?"

He shakes his head.

"Okay well, if the court approves the match it will feel like a lottery win. To the child it's often overwhelming but it's also an exciting time. Your social worker will at this stage work with you and the child on the moving in phase. You'll get to visit your child at the foster placement and there'll be reciprocal visits where your child can stay overnight in your home. If everything goes well, they move in."

"We get to keep the kid?"

"Well not quite yet. It will take a further ten weeks of settling in within your home. After that you can apply through the courts for an Adoption Order. A judge will review the child's placement history and everyone will have the chance to speak. The judge will then decide whether it's a suitable placement. Do note, the judge places the child's own views very highly and will assess the child's reaction to the union. If all goes well – mostly it does – you will now become the child's legal parents. That means you will have complete parental rights under UK law."

"The kid's other parents?" Eddsy says.

Simone nods.

"Ah yes, of course I knew I was forgetting something. Although legally you are now the child's parents, from the child's perspective you'll often be the second family and – as I mentioned earlier – they may have had a traumatic upbringing. However, some children never know their genetic parents. They will have lived in care their whole lives."

Simone leans back in her chair after seeing joy and sadness like passing shadows over Eddsy's face as she explained the various processes. Eddy was there. In the moment. He was living the dream. Living the fear too. This is a man already involved heart and soul in the idea. Simone knows he's lived it a long time.

"It's a lot, isn't it?" Simone says.

"Yeah. Phew. A lot."

"Do you think Harriet can cope with the entire adoption process?"

Eddsy thinks a moment.

"Yeah. Think so."

"And you?"

"Yeah. But we're old."

Simone laughs.

"You are leaning toward the more mature side but it's by no means exceptional. Let's just say your age isn't a barrier."

"Thought it might be."

"Harriet's depression is, as you know, an area of concern we'll have to explore."

"Yeah."

Simone presses her hands together. Her bangles clink.

"Well, that's the whole cake. Any questions?"

"Yeah. What you think?"

"Of your chances?"

Eddsy nods.

Simone gives him her warmest smile.

"Well, from what you tell me, I'd be happy to encourage you to go ahead and discuss this with Harriet. Please bear in mind these are only my thoughts based on what you've said. If you like I can give you an adoption booklet you can take with you. You'll find my name on the inside front cover."

Simone's marquisette necklace sparkles colourfully as she moves to offer Eddy a booklet. He takes it. He opens it to the first page, sees the name Simone Grey, Senior Social Worker/Manager, a picture of her smiling against a white background, a telephone number, an extension.

Simone stands. Eddsy picks up his now cold espresso. They shake hands.

"Well, it's been a pleasure meeting you Eddsy. I'm so glad I had that cancellation. I do hope we see you again with Harriet."

Eddsy leaves, excitement fluttering inside him.

Outside, the solid door slams shut with a hefty ratcheted click. He throws back his head and swallows the rest of his coffee. A shot of brandy.

THE SUE BAXTER PODCAST
DR STEWART-WAY
You see Sue, the problem with my treatments on the soldiers –
despite the temporary relief they experienced – was the
treatments had to be repeated. It is a major flaw that creates its
own problems. As it stood, fluorogenetics was like
chemotherapy – in order to treat the bad cells you have to
destroy good cells. Unfortunately, some soldiers couldn't
mentally handle the relief only to be followed by destructive
lows. But a worse problem was repeat exposure to x-rays,
despite using very low levels, it is still destructive to brain cells
over time. It degrades the protein structures within the brain and
can create dementia-like conditions over time. Thankfully, it's
because of Dr Applegate's work in memory reconsolidation,
combined with mine in fluorogenetics, we finally circumvented
that.
SUE BAXTER
Tell me, how did Dr Applegate's work help?
DR STEWART-WAY
Let me give you an example. I am a keen wildlife photographer
and I still use traditional Kodak and Ilford film. I develop my
own prints in a darkroom and for that I need developer and
fixer. Developer allows an image to appear on an exposed sheet
of photographic paper. However, developer alone isn't enough.
Without anything to fix the image, it will disappear if once more
exposed to light. This was a major flaw in my work. I had no
way to fix its effect. Dr Applegate's work into obstructing
memory recall made my treatment permanent. He'd, in effect,

created a fixative through an ingenious neuro-chemical technique.

SUE BAXTER

So together, this treatment became The Gateway Programme?

DR STEWART-WAY

That's right Sue.

SUE BAXTER

And you used it to treat Clive and his unconscious phobia of spiders?

DR STEWART-WAY

Yes. Clive volunteered himself to be our first Gateway Programme patient.

SUE BAXTER

The upshot is The Gateway Programme cured him, didn't it?

DR STEWART-WAY

I'm glad to say it did.

SUE BAXTER

Even so, you were unaware there was disaster looming around the corner.

5 7

COOPER DRIVES TO Gateway House for a chat with Dr Applegate and Dr Stewart-Way. It's a modern, two-storey, red brick building with Roman columns outside the glass entrance and a mown lawn surrounding a twelve-space car park. Inside is like a doctor's surgery but with more luxurious seating, modern art sculptures and two receptionists. Cooper's invited into one of the offices that looks like a sitting room, and one of the doctors organises tea, which comes in a proper teacup and saucer. They look surprised when she puts five lumps of sugar in and stirs. Can they record her session for their records? Yeah, course. They listen to her story without interrupting, nod in all the right places, look sympathetic in other places, ask probing questions, scribble things down.

An hour later Cooper talks herself out. She feels better. Telling someone has removed all the weight. Now it's her turn to listen.

Both doctors clear their throats and interchangeably explain what they do at Gateway House. They tell her, her phone call intrigued them which is why she's here. They explain The Gateway Programme, about advancing research into the brain, about how it works, about how successful the treatment's been with PTSD. Soon the session is over and Cooper leaves feeling hopeful but cautious. What if it doesn't work? What if it makes her problem worse? How can her feelings for someone, something that now feels so terrible, so soul-destroying, simply vanish? Worse – what if they don't approve her for treatment?

God.

Over the next few days Cooper goes to more appointments. The doctors carefully fast track her. They check her medical history and privately debate it. They're concerned about her mental health. They bring in a psychologist to assess her mental condition. They're aware Cooper tried to commit suicide while still at school over a broken romance that made her fear men's motives. They know meeting Jethro changed her and taught her to trust and love him. Now that security has been shattered and she feels abandoned once more. They have inferred from what she says certain types of men find her so attractive, they seek her out for selfish gratification, skewing Cooper's view of the world about how men use women. They see also for themselves her unconscious defence mechanism of dressing down to protect herself from such unwarranted attention. The way she holds herself, her mannerisms, her demeanour is more masculine than feminine. She is, in effect, a tomboy grown up.

Over several sessions the doctors carefully build a complex profile of Cooper physiologically and psychologically. Initially they'd wanted to speak to her husband but, after some persuasion from Cooper, finally agree her emotional torture is authentic and, because of her medical history, are concerned for her continued well-being. After further points are debated, after all the analysis is over, Cooper receives news.

Approved for treatment.

They warn her how she'll feel nothing for Jethro. Not at all. She won't love him, she won't hate him. She'll have as much empathy for him as she would a stranger.

It makes her hesitate. Of course it does.

Cooper has loved Jethro forever. He made her, she made him. They grew into each other as the years sculpted them. She debates with herself whether she should go ahead with the treatment. It's a big step. It's huge. Dr Applegate tells her we can start treatment as soon as the day after tomorrow if she wishes. God.

Of course she hesitates.

5 8

JETHRO USED TO call Cooper almost every day, but as the weeks pass the calls become more spaced out. He considered how he'd deal with Cooper wanting to see him perform once she'd recovered but somehow it never comes up. She never asks. He never offers. Tell the truth, it's a relief. Jethro's a different person onstage, a different person on tour, a different persona to the studio, a different person. He prefers to keep his two lives separate. Daniel though flies out one weekend, sees him perform once, he gets to meet Sabre Light and then he's gone before he has time to breathe.

Jethro's guitar technique improves quickly, his fingers on fire from the hours of daily workouts on the Gibson. He starts with heavy-duty Martin steel strings until his fingers feel like the tips are melting. Rik Chard from Sabre Light advises him to use extra-light strings. They have a shorter life but yeah, they're so much easier to play, right? When Jethro tries it, it's like playing on silk threads. It brings some relief. Still, his finger pads thicken like the heel of a foot and he moisturises them daily to stop them cracking. After every evening performance, he soaks them in warm milk, another tip from Rik Chard.

Jethro reports all this to Cooper who exchanges his information for hers on her latest projects every few days. But that's all it feels like. An exchange. Like they are on two different wavelengths, living two different lives.

Yeah well, that's because they are right now.

"Babe?"

Jethro looks up, sat at a table on the tour bus parked within the gated grounds of the concert hall they performed at this evening. It's Sophie. He dries the milk off his hands, rubs in moisturiser. Sophie settles opposite, admiring his elegant hands, the way he moves them, how he cares for them. Even the nails are trim and polished, the cuticles pushed back like a girl's.

Sophie's barefoot in her skinny jeans, a white shirt tied at the waist she stole from him, showing off her pierced, blue-jewelled belly button, looking like a cool French goddess from the 1950s.

"The guys are ordering pizza," Sophie says.

"Yeah, give me a tick. I'm like almost done."

She grins, plays barefoot footsie with him under the table where the guys can't see before she gets up and leaves. Sophie grabs Jethro's bolero hat off the table and slips it on.

Jethro watches her go, making her way along the aisle like a model on a catwalk, holding the tip of the hat in that way.

He glances at the clock. Maybe he should give Cooper a quick call. It's been days.

His gaze returns to Sophie as she catches up with the boys. She turns and their eyes meet again. She eyes him playfully, winks, grabs a beer and tosses her head back, taking a lug from the bottle neck while holding the hat in place.

Jethro slips his phone into his back pocket, goes over to join the party instead. He needs to relax, man. Totally.

Hell yeah.

THE NEXT EVENING Cooper lies in bed thinking, thinking.
Turns, twists, turns again, twists again, she can't sleep, thinking,
thinking. Jethro hasn't called in a couple days. She barely
notices. Her head is elsewhere with The Gateway Programme.
Going for a treatment means giving up, means surrendering.
Cooper doesn't surrender. She's not a giver-upper.

She checks the time. It's 8.42pm. No wonder she can't sleep.

Cooper changes into khakis and a T-shirt, denim jacket, Doc
Martens, picks up her keys, goes for a drive. Just to be doing
something like changing the bedroom was doing something, like
shopping was doing something, like working in her studio for all
those hours, those days, those weeks, was doing something,
even eating and gaining weight was doing something.

Now she has nothing to do so she drives.

Cooper drives for an hour thinking, thinking.

She sees a wine bar sign as she's about to pass it. At the last
moment Cooper yanks the steering wheel, pulls into the small
car park. She finds a parking space, pulls in, cuts the engine.
She hears the muffled beat of live music inside. A neon sign
above the door in a swirl of handwriting like a signature says
Cellars.

Cooper steps out. The wind is biting but she welcomes it.
She will go for one drink. Go for the distraction. Too much
thinking, thinking. She needs to be doing something.

As she approaches the door, six smokers are hanging around
outside. Three women, all under twenty, or about twenty, or just
over twenty, short skirts, skimpy tops, freezing, clack their heels

on the pavement to keep warm. Boyfriends, comfortable in leather jackets, in ripped jeans, holding beer bottles by the neck, chat, laugh and ignore their glitzy girlfriends.

Cigarettes with glowing orange butts float in front of all their faces, each brightening then dimming again in unison. Cooper walks past them, pushes the door into the bar. The men watch her go past. The women with angular, tattooed eyebrows and selfie-glossed cheeks watch the men watching her go past, annoyance in their eyes.

Inside the air is hot, thick, mixed with the acetone of alcohol, the malt of beer, a wall of chatter and laughter and music. Now she knows why it's called Cellars. All the walls are brick with arched columns like a wine cellar, painted black. Three guys playing instruments are onstage, one on acoustic guitar, one on bass in front of a mic, a third on a basic drum kit with a snare, a bass drum and a hi-hat.

Cooper looks around for the ladies, spots a neon arrow in pink of a delicate pointing finger and long fingernail and the word Ladies.

She follows the sign, finds the loo. She finds four sinks, a row of four cubicles. An ice-blonde dressed in figure-hugging black with thick charcoal eyeliner stands by an open window, one arm across her bosom, the other elbow resting on it holding a joint. The telltale smell of weed. She blows smoke out the window. The blonde glances at Cooper, pulls on her joint, stares at her.

One cubicle is occupied. The next one isn't. Cooper goes in, shoots the latch.

She flips the loo seat down sits on it. The live music is cushioned through the walls.

Cooper screws her eyes shut, stays there a while. What's she doing here? Really? What's the point of being here?

A couple of minutes later there's a knock on the cubicle door. Three taps.

"You okay in there, sweetie?"

Seems another person wonders why she's here too. Cooper doesn't answer. All she did was go to the loo.

Another tap.

"Sweetie?"

"Go away."

A pause then, "Suits me."

Footsteps clack away. Cooper hears the loo door open, hears music and chatter swell, then the door shuts, it's quieter again.

A cubicle flushes, door lock shoots open, clicking footsteps, tap, gushing water, paper towels, the door opens, the music and chatter swells, recedes.

Cooper's alone now.

She emerges from the cubicle. Why's she doing this? She doesn't know. She doesn't know. Cooper goes over to a basin. Her face looks haggard, tired haunted eyes, faint bruising on her face almost gone. That's why.

Dizzy Gillespie.

That's why.

Homme.

That's why.

Soft moans, soft moans.

That's why.

Soft kisses, soft kisses.

That's why.

The Gateway Programme.

Yeah. Worried.

That's why.

She pulls the taps on, both of them, fills the basin but there's no plug so the basin stays empty. She scoops water and splashes her face. The water is freezing. Her cheeks redden with the shock. When she's done she pulls paper towels out and dabs her face. Her cheeks are so red it looks like rouge.

Outside she goes to the bar, finds a free stool. She perches on it. A young bartender in a pale blue T-shirt appears, curly hair, a nick on his upper lip that looks like an old shaving scar approaches, lifts his eyebrows enquiringly at her.

"Vodka and tonic without the tonic."

He cups his ear. The music's loud. She leans forward. She shouts.

"VODKA."

"Anything particular. We have—"

"Good and strong."

The bartender nods, turns, pushes a glass to an optic, draws out a measure. He puts the glass on the counter. The contents look like a clear, tiny puddle.

"Anything with it?"

"Another one."

"Double?"

Cooper nods.

The bartender doesn't react, goes back to the optic, another shot into the glass.

"Anything else with it?"

Dizzy Gillespie.

Homme.

Soft moans, soft moans.

Soft kisses, soft kisses.

Cooper shakes her head no.

"Ice?"

She shakes her head.

He slides the drink toward her.

He gives her the price. She pulls out a note, he waits and she realises what he said, pulls out another note.

He comes back with the change, moves on to a guy holding a note curled around a finger.

Cooper puts the drink to her lips. Her teeth chatter against the glass. The music is fresh and acoustic with a nasal voice, teetering on it like it's a little too high for the singer.

She hesitates then she downs the vodka. It's a jolt of static. She has a gagging action but she manages to hold on. It burns the back of her throat, burns all the way down. A furnace ignites in her empty stomach, a bomb blast. It hurts. Good. Distraction. She's doing something. That's what she's doing here. She closes her eyes waits for the fire to ease. Needs to be doing something.

Or having something done to her.

When she opens her eyes a guy with a trimmed ginger goatee is next to her leaning back with both elbows on the bar watching the act onstage, rocking his head to the rhythm.

"They're not bad," the man says. "But the guy's singing way too high."

He doesn't turn to her, doesn't even look like he's addressing her. The only clue is the people on his other side are heads close, chatting. Cooper looks at the guys onstage.

"You here for someone?" the goatee man says.

Cooper eyes him. White shirt, black trousers, jacket, a leather manbag across his chest. He looks officey. Every other man in this place wears leather jackets, T-shirt and jeans. The women are dolled up, all younger than her, in couples or groups. She's the only lone woman.

"I'm on my own."

"Yeah, thought so."

"Why?"

He looks at her khakis and a T-shirt and boots.

"You don't look like you're on a social night out."

The alcohol reaches her head, makes her vision shimmery, as though she's under water. A pleasant feeling. Alcohol is doing something to her body. Good. That's what she needs.

Dizzy Gillespie.

Homme.

Soft moans, soft m—

"Want to go somewhere?" Cooper says, feeling suddenly bold. Did she really just say that? It's the drink, the lights, the noise, the chatter.

The guy glances at her, his brow so heavy it shadows his eyes. She looks hard to find his pupils. His forehead wrinkles a little, not much, but enough to reveal pale blue or grey eyes. It's hard to tell in the subdued bar lighting.

Dizzy Gillespie.

Homme.

Soft moans, soft moans.

Soft kisses, soft kisses.

Dizzy Gillespie.

Homme.

Soft moans, soft—

"So?" Cooper says.

The guy still doesn't answer.

Obviously, he's not interested. Cooper rises to leave but the guy touches her arm.

"Hold on." He crooks a finger. "Come with me."

Cooper follows him through the bar, through the entrance out into the cold night, past different girls, different lads. It's unlikely he's a serial killer. Actually, Cooper doesn't care if he is. Let him be a serial killer. Let him.

Goatee man seems to know her car, walks towards it. She hopes he is a serial killer. It'd solve everything. Cooper takes her car keys out but he goes past, turns to her.

"You can't drive."

He walks to a plain white van next to her car. Serial killer cue. Good. Cooper's feeling reckless.

He slides open the passenger door for her. She steps on to the high step, collapses into a seat, surprised she's so tipsy so suddenly. The odour of turpentine hits her. That and paint and salt and vinegar crisps and pork pies.

He walks around the front of the van, slides his side open, slips into his seat, slides it shut, starts up.

"I'm a decorator."

"You're not dressed like a decorator."

He smiles.

"There's a reason for that."

"Yeah? What's that?" Cooper's voice sounds like it's coming from outside her own head.

"I'll tell you about it. Sorry about the smell."

He swings the van out of the parking space into the road. He stops at the traffic light junction. It's red. He turns to her.

"You sure about this?"

"Yeah."

He looks down at her top. She looks down. Her nipples are erect through her T-shirt and open denim jacket. When the lights change and he doesn't move she looks at him.

"What's wrong?"

"Seat belt."

"Really?"

"It's the law."

She finds the seat belt, pulls it across, clicks it into place.

The guy turns on the fan heater, lets air blow into the van. At first, it's cold but then it warms up. He leans forward in his seat, pulls off his suit jacket, gives it to her. She drapes it over the front of her shoulders, covers her front up.

Would a serial killer do that? Cooper nods her gratitude for the jacket.

He doesn't respond, just drives on from the lights.

Cooper realises she's doing this.

She really is.

6 0

EDDSY LIES IN bed. Harriet's asleep tucked in his arms like a squirrel, leg over his thighs, arm across his waist. She nuzzles into him, making mmmmm noises from her place of dreams.

Earlier, as he drove home, he kept glancing at the adoption booklet on the passenger seat, and by the time he'd swung onto his gravel path and parked in front of his home he'd made a decision about it. He's living with that decision now.

He worries about Harriet. He can't help it. She had depression. She almost had a complete breakdown.

Months after Eddsy told Harriet about his condition, Harriet went to a doctor. The doctor prescribed her pills. Harriet said they were to make her feel better. After taking the pills for several weeks and feeling a little better, Harriet said she was sorry she'd been horrid to Eddsy since his news about his fertility.

Eddsy said she wasn't horrid, just in a bad place.

But he'd felt guilty his condition had driven Harriet to that. She said you didn't do it, it's no one's fault. Things will be okay. Now marry me you big oaf.

So Eddsy married her. He loved her. He loves her. She married him. She loved him. She loves him.

Things are okay now. She's content in her sleep, making mmmm noises, happy in her ignorance. Why should Eddsy shake the foundations with this earthquake of a booklet?

So yes, Eddsy'd made a decision as he drove home that evening.

Such a big home. Two people in it. Six bedrooms. Half acre of garden for an entire playground if they wanted. Lots and lots of children.

Parked outside the house he'd picked up the booklet, flicked through it in the shadow of the car. His stomach churning, his hands clammy, he'd flicked through it.

Pictures of happy children.

Pictures of happy families.

Bright sunshine, sunshine families.

Simone Grey from Barnardo's made the whole adoption thing feel so right, and all afternoon Eddsy saw kids. A house full of kids. Lots and lots of kids. Messy with chocolate around their mouths kids. Muddy knees, bright little Wellington boots kids. Childhood drawings stuck with magnets to the fridge kids. Fun cereal packets with silly day-glo green gifts inside kids. Cherios, Snap Crackle and Pop, Sugar Puffs, Coco Pops, Shreddies kids. Cartoons playing on TV kids. Little gloves, little T-shirts, little pairs of jeans, little colourful dresses hanging on clothes lines kids. Princess nightgowns, Spiderman pyjamas kids. Wendy houses, tree houses kids. A swing set in the garden kids. Ball games in the park kids. Girl's hair clips and ribbons on the dressing table kids. Boys football shirts and cricket bats in the porch kids. Colourful, colourful raincoats kids. Tiny duffel coats kids. Stories at bedtime kids. Trampolining on beds kids. Noises thumping through the ceiling when they should be in bed kids.

Eddsy whistled at work as he imagined all this. So much he'd wanted to say to Harriet this evening. So much.

Now in bed, he thinks of the decision he'd made in the van parked outside the house.

Simone Grey's words come back to him once more. Harriet's history of depression is a concern.

It bothers Simone.

A concern.

It'll bother the panel of judges.

224

A concern.

So it bothers Eddsy.

That's why he'd made the decision.

All that time ago when he'd told Harriet of his almost zero sperm count, she'd gone quiet. Eddsy thought of enquiring about sperm donation but waited for Harriet to mention it and she never did. Sometimes when Eddsy came home from work he'd hear Harriet slam the bathroom door and emerge with a fresh face and a smile unaware of her piggy eyes from crying. That was before she started managing Tomalin Garages and changing their fortunes, making the business a success.

Tonight, Harriet thinks Eddsy's asleep. She takes the opportunity to wallow in thought, as she does almost every night.

She yearns for a child. YEARNS for a child.

Just one.

One little mite.

Just one.

When he'd told her the truth about his sperm count, everything shattered. How could Harriet ask him now if he would consider sperm donation? It would be like saying she wanted someone else's child because Eddsy wasn't man enough. She's even thought about asking him about adopting. But wasn't that was saying the same thing, only having the children ready-made? Hasn't Eddsy already suffered enough guilt?

So instead, Harriet turned her marketing skills to her husband's own business. It had changed Tomalin Garages. She'd had the inspiration to market Tomalin Garages to women and it had worked. It was their surrogate children.

Is.

One garage. One bedroom. Two garages. Two bedrooms. Three garages. Three bedrooms... Now they have six. Six bedrooms from six garages.

Yes. It is their children. It is enough.

Eddsy, still awake in bed, thinks how after he'd parked this evening, not leaving the shadow of his van, flicking through the booklet one more time. Pictures of happy happy children, happy happy families. It was the right decision he'd made wasn't it? The booklet only shows the successes after all. It never shows the failures. How many broken hearts aren't in the booklet?

So yes, it was the right decision to open the glove compartment, shove the booklet under the mobile phone charger, documents, an old magazine, a Chapstick, a couple of Bic pens, scraps of paper, chocolate bar wrapper, bag of boiled sweets...

Yes.

Eddsy lies in bed, assured he's doing the right thing. He'll throw the booklet away tomorrow for sure. Best thing.

Now they lie in bed. Neither one asleep.

Unasleep.

Each one dreaming of what might have been.

Unasleep.

Neither one aware the other one's heart breaks every day when they wake. And every night before they fall asleep they lie...

Unasleep.

FIVE MINUTES AFTER leaving the nightclub Cooper and goatee man pull up on a kerb in his decorator's van. He nods at the apartment building, turns to her.

"I live here."

She follows his gaze. An apartment window flickers with blue light and moving shadows behind curtains. Cooper realises it's from a TV screen.

"The TV's to keep burglars away," he says.

"You live on the second floor and you're worried about burglars?"

"You never know."

Cooper laughs.

He climbs out, strides to her side, slides her door open, she steps out. She realises the vodka has made the world as soft as snow. He takes Cooper by the hand, guides her to the door, uses a key to get in. Cooper follows him into a lift. She doesn't know his name, doesn't know anything about him except where he lives, that he's a decorator and owns a white shirt and a manbag and a white van. His clothes don't tally with his van.

On the third floor they get out and she follows him until they stop at a blonde oak door with a chrome number 32 on it. He opens the door, lets her enter his flat first. He tells her to go through.

Cooper goes past a couple of doors in the short, cosily lit corridor. It opens to an attractive sitting room, soft lamps in two corners, the BBC news on a big TV screen. It's a snug with soft furnishings, all buttery creams and mushrooms and chocolates.

The flat's warm but not a moist sticky warmth like at Cellars. One wall has books and Aztec designs and African sculptures. A sofa, a coffee table, a few wildlife magazines on it. Everything is tasteful and tidy. Not what she expected.

"Oh no, you're not, are you?" Cooper says.

"Not what?"

"You're not going to be a gentleman about this are you?"

"That's up to you."

Cooper steps into him to try to kiss him but he's further away than she thinks and she stumbles. She's clumsy. Clumsy with drink, clumsy with inexperience. He catches her and leads her to a sofa. She flops into it. The vodka must've been strong.

"Tea?" goatee man says.

"What else you got?"

He looks at her pointedly.

"I don't think anything stronger's good for you right now."

"Why?"

"Forgive me, you look like someone who had her guts yanked out in front of her."

"Forgive me? Yeah, you are a gentleman."

"I have Earl Grey, Jasmine, English Breakfast…"

"Yeah?"

"What would you like?"

"Something stronger."

He glances at the TV, picks up a remote, changes the news channel to one with soft instrumental music.

"I won't be long."

He's busy in a kitchen opening a drawer, a cupboard, clinking wares. She reclines on the sofa, focuses on the music. It's soft and right. The hum of alcohol makes her relax. She likes it here. It feels safe. This feels like a cocoon. She could get used to this.

He reappears with two steaming mugs. She's surprised. She expected a shot of something. She raises an eyebrow enquiringly.

"They're both Horlicks," he says.

"You're kidding."

"Afraid not."

"Anything with it?"

"Hot milk."

She laughs, liking him. She takes the mug, sips it. It's good, hot, very sweet, feels spongy in the mouth. It's delicious. She looks at the side of the mug. It says …and guest.

You have a lot of guests?

"Mostly mum. She lives on the ground floor."

Cooper looks at him. Grey. His eyes are grey. Misty grey. Misty grey like coastal fog. Who'd have thought she could find that twice? She knows now she's going to do this. She really is.

Cooper looks at the mug he's cupping. It says Thomas. His name is Thomas.

"Your name is Thomas." Cooper realises she's stating the obvious. The vodka is definitely turning her head to mush.

"Steve gave you the good stuff."

"Huh?"

"Steve, the bartender. He gave you almost 100 proof. You asked for something good. He gave it. That's why it cost so much."

"It's gone—"

"—To your head, yes it has."

She sips the Horlicks, relishing the thick, very sweetness.

"This is the best Horlicks I've ever had."

"I made it with whole milk and single cream and added a touch of vanilla. It'll absorb some of the alcohol."

"You don't want me drunk?"

"I was saving you."

"From what?"

Vultures. If I hadn't claimed you someone else would've. You don't want to involve yourself with that crowd at Cellars."

"You're not a vulture?"

"I don't know what I am."

"Why'd you go in there then?"

"It's mine. The bar. Joint ownership actually."

Cooper frowns.

"You're a decorator."

"Five minutes before you came in the bar, I was behind the bar hence the shirt and jacket. The business was dad's. I inherited part ownership with mum. I help her out on alternate evenings."

"How old are you?"

"Thirty-four."

"Is the decorating business yours too?"

"Yes."

"You own two businesses and a flat?"

"The flat is the bank's until it's paid off in a gazillion years. The bar is just breaking even. It's my decorating work that's keeping me afloat." He changes the subject.

"You're twenty-eight right?"

"Yeah, you don't think that."

"In Cellars you looked about nineteen. That's why I saved you."

"I'm thirty-eight."

"Wow."

She smiles lazily. The alcohol in her blood makes everything cosy and slow.

"I think I like you."

"Drink your Horlicks, then decide if you like me."

Cooper leaves her Horlicks unfinished. She puts it on the glass coffee table. He does the same. She leans into him, he leans into her. Lips touch but it's gentle and he cups the side of her head as he does it. The heat of his palm hot from the Horlicks is comforting. His lips feel foreign, his leathery aroma different, his touch exotic, the shape of his body wondrous. The novelty, the thrill stirs her. When he pulls back, he strokes her cheek with his thumb. He's brushing a tear away. The tear is a surprise to her.

"Perhaps you should drink your Horlicks and go home."

Dizzy Gillespie.

Homme—

"Can I stay?"

He considers the question, watches her. Her eyes plead with him. Invites him.

"Are you sure this is what you want?" he says.

Cooper leans in, kisses him again. She hasn't been with anyone since Jethro. Not anyone. Not in twenty years. Never.

Somehow, they migrate to the bedroom, soft music wafting through. She allows the sensations of him to soak into her. It swallows her up and she loses herself, surrendering to his whispered kisses.

Tenderly he pulls her down to the bed as he kisses her. She lets him. He unfolds her. She lets him. He unbuttons her. She lets him. He unwraps her. She lets him. He strokes her bare, she lets him. Her skin is tender, sensitive. She lets him, she lets him. She tingles. She shivers. She moans.

Soft moans, soft kisses.

Hers and his this time, not theirs.

Leather, not Homme.

Instrumental music, not Dizzy.

Soon they're under covers and she's under him. Her hands run over his neck, over the taut sheen of his muscles, over his armoured back, her hands clasp on to his soft, naked waist. Intense sensations flood through her in waves at the newness of everything. The violence of their performance rouse and increase and crescendo until at once their hips meet in a poignant epiphany, suspended in air like trapeze artists poised at the crown of their swing. She's flooded with beautiful pain and catastrophic pleasure. A whiteout. A waterfall of rapture. They tumble, collapsing into the bed as though they'd floated above it, intimately hot and spent, hot breaths, melting, mingling, merging…

Now Cooper lies there glowing with guilty devastation, sensing the alcohol draining from her blood.

Oh Jethro.

She covers her eyes with the shameful crook of an arm, crying silently.

Oh Jethro.

Not the answer.

6 2

COOPER IS ALONE in Thomas's bed.

Cooper has been drifting in a lazy half doze. She lies there lost. She thinks of Jethro.

Jethro.

When they first met at school there was something about him she trusted on sight. Most kids her age ogled her. Big burly types, gym types specially. She hated all that cockiness, all that testosterone, all that macho crap. She'd had enough of that kind of attention.

Cooper remembers in biology class sitting next to a gawky long-haired kid with a ponytail and glasses that had a glazed chromatic tint when it flashed in the light. She was glad she sat with someone quiet, not the bozos who hung around in gangs. She studied the way he was. He was like an artist, the way he moved. His fluidity. The way he sat, held his pen, angled his legs on the stools. It was ballet. His movements mesmerised her. The way his hands moved. Ballet. He'd talk and express with those hands. He could be an artist with hands as poetic as his. Ballet.

Jethro was shy. Pushing his glasses up his nose every time he talked to her, a nervous tic. But he realised she liked him and grew more confident in her company. They became friends over the months. Became closer. Closer. Until they were as close as they could be, still friends.

But there's one day. One particular day.

It was twenty-one years ago.

Yeah, Cooper remembers.

They're in a country field sitting on the grass after he parked his beat-up Vauxhall in a lay by.

Jethro.

Cooper.

They're both eighteen or nineteen now. Still hanging around together. Still friends. Close friends. The day is warm. The summer is in full golden glory. The air is still. He's taken her on a picnic. The smell of grass and hay all around them, on the breeze. She thinks it's nice. He'd never done anything like that before. Even after school, even after college they hung around each other, but their relationship never developed.

So there it was. Fresh sandwiches, French bread, hunks of cheddar and red Leicester, sweet pickle, cucumber, grapes, fruit punch in a thermos, a moist fruitcake, a blanket spread out over patchy grass. Jethro'd prepared everything, brought everything in a wicker basket.

They're both sat facing each other on a blanket. Both cross legged mirroring the other, chatting about anything. Jethro rips at the French bread with his teeth, eats it unbuttered. He turns to her. She's nibbling a sandwich, drinking punch from a see-through plastic cup. Soon they both fall silent as they eat and drink. But Jethro isn't eating any more. He's looking at Cooper. He looks like he wants to say something. Finally, he plucks up the courage.

"Coops?"

"Yeah?"

Pulls at his lower lip.

"Wow, your eyes."

"What about my eyes?"

"They're amazing."

Cooper looks at him. The grass behind her reflects in the chromatic tint of his glasses. It's the first time he's complimented her and he almost says it as a whisper.

Jethro doesn't know how she'll react, whether she'll lay into him like she does when others try to compliment her.

For once Cooper doesn't know how to handle it. This is Jethro talking.

"Yeah, thanks."

"I mean it. They're the colour of the sun." This bit he'd rehearsed in case she did lay into him.

Cooper takes a second bite from the soft cucumber sandwich. He even cut the crusts off. She savours the watery crunch, savours the bite of black pepper seasoning.

"Yeah, thanks."

There's amusement in his eyes.

"You heard me, right?"

"Yeah, you said my eyes are the colour of the sun."

"And you're not mad?"

"No. It's nice."

Jethro looks at her. Waits.

Cooper processes what he said. She looks at him, puts down the sandwich.

"The sun is yellow," Cooper says.

She realises it's not a compliment. Disappointment like a drop of black ink in a glass of water spills through her. She never expected this of him. Not Jethro. She slaps him on the thigh.

"So, you're saying I have jaundiced eyes?"

He laughs, but it's a nervous laugh.

She slaps his thigh again and he laughs, says "Ow!" Turns out he's messing around. She's never hit him before.

"You're saying I have jaundiced eyes aren't you? Thanks a bunch." She slaps him again feeling real annoyance now. She wants to get up. She wants to walk away. Why's she so annoyed? Cooper should've been annoyed he complimented her in the first place but she wasn't. Why is she so annoyed now?

Jethro shies from her slaps, holding up his palms like he's holding up an invisible wall.

"Wait, wait Cooper, I'm saying your eyes are green."

Cooper's not having it.

"Yeah? Last I looked the sun was yellow, moron."

Her annoyance swells to anger. Now she attacks him with a barrage of slaps on his thighs, on his arms, his chest. She IS angry with him. More than angry. He curls up protectively on the grass slender as a coil of spring. The bolero hat he's started wearing tilts off. He starts laughing but her slaps sting. There's force behind them.

"Moron. I thought you were being nice." Black ink spreads through the water, spreads through, staining it, spoiling it.

He tries to explain between laughs.

"Cooper I am—"

Slap.

"— being. Honest I am."

It makes her angrier, his denial. Her cheeks are blazing.

"Moron."

"I'm trying to be—"

Slap slap. Slap slap slap. Slap slap Slap slap.

Jethro surrenders, rolls out of her reach. He stops laughing. He sits up, cheeks flushed. He puts his bolero hat back on. He sees hurt in her eyes.

"You don't understand," he says, suddenly scared.

Cooper crosses her arms, faces away. Her eyes fill. She won't let him see that.

"Honest, I'm not messing Cooper. I can like, explain."

Cooper trusted him. He was a friend. A close friend. She stands up, turns away.

"Wait man. Please. Let me explain."

Jethro stands up, follows her, touches her shoulder, worried. This is all going so wrong.

Cooper stares out at a churned over field, blinks back tears before they spill. Why is she so upset? When she's ready she turns to him. She realises something important. She thought he was going to tell her he loved her. Now she hates him. They stand face-to-face. They can't be friends. Not after this.

Jethro's suddenly gawky, suddenly awkward, pushes his
chromatic glasses up his nose.

"Cooper?"

"Yeah, what?"

"You know the colour of the sun isn't yellow, right?" His
voice is small.

"Moron."

"Did you know when a sun is at a certain temperature it
becomes green?"

"So?"

"Well our sun—"

"Mister moron astrophysicist."

"Our sun—"

"Mr Jethro – Albert Einstein – Hall moron astrophysicist."

"Our sun…"

He waits. Cooper doesn't interrupt this time. Jethro
continues.

"…peaks in the green wavelength. That means—"

"I know what peak means, moron. It means green is the
strongest wavelength, all the others have lower amplitude.
Duh."

"Don't you think that's like, completely cool?"

Cooper pouts. She keeps her arms crossed. What the hell's
he talking about?

"So, all the other wavelengths," Jethro counts on his fingers,
"red, yellow, orange, blue are weaker okay? Green is the
strongest wavelength."

"That's what I said, MORON." Cooper glances at the
blinding sun. Blinks. Looks away.

"So, why doesn't the sun look green then?"

He raises a finger.

"Ah."

"What do you mean Ah?"

"AH!"

"Stop ahhing and tell me what you mean."

"Well, it doesn't look green because when all the wavelengths combine it makes it look white. But most people will never see the sun is like, actually tinted green."

"So?"

"I can see the sun is green."

"You can?"

Now Cooper's confused. Where's this going? So help him if he insults her one more time she's going to punch him really, really hard, walk away, car or no car. No matter that he's sweet and unaware how cool he is, how she's mesmerised by his natural grace, how it reminds her of the artful movements of a gazelle.

"I can definitely see the sun is green."

She narrows her eyes at him.

"So, you have some special Superman powered x-ray atomic eyeballs, is that it?"

He steps forward, tentative, self-conscious, awkward.

"Something like that."

"When have you seen the sun's green? Like at sunset or something?"

"All the time."

"All the time?"

Another inch.

"Uh-huh."

Maybe it's because of the tint of his glasses. She glances at the sun again, blinks away.

"Like now?"

Jethro looks at her, not the sun.

"Definitely now."

"Yeah, that's bull."

Jethro leans in and kisses her. He kisses her. It's so sudden. Cooper's stunned for a moment.

He pulls back, looks at her, expectant and fear both in his eyes. His heart hammers.

Cooper touches her lips with her fingers. He kissed her. She pretends the kiss didn't happen. He kissed her. Her heart is racing, her cheeks are blazing, she has butterflies. She doesn't know what to say. He kissed her. She says the only thing she can think of.

"When have you seen the sun is green?"

"Every time I look at you, I see flames of green."

Jethro is parodying poetry or something.

"What are you talking about?"

"Beautiful flames of green."

"My eyes are green."

"That's right."

Cooper stares at him. Doesn't know what to make of it.

"And your pupils. Oh wow."

"What do you mean, my pupils?"

"They're black."

"Everybody's pupils are black."

"Only your pupils are like moons, Cooper."

He's talking in riddles.

"The moon isn't black."

"It is with the sun behind it."

"Like a solar eclipse?"

"Yeah, that's it, a solar eclipse. The moon can hide the sun but it can't hide the flames of the sun right? There's a ring of flame around the moon in an eclipse."

"The corona."

"That's it the corona, except your coronas are amber."

"You can see that? They're barely there."

"I saw them in biology class."

Her eyes are green and they have amber surrounding the pupils except she'd call it pale orange not something as beautiful as amber.

Jethro removes his glasses, studies her eyes. Studies the stain of colours in her eyes. Their faces drawn so close she can feel the heat in his breath, can see his eyes too. She sees the true colour now the chromatic glasses are gone. His eyes are grey. Misty grey. Misty grey like coastal fog. Oh wow. Beautiful misty grey.

Fascination begets fascination. She becomes fascinated by his fascination, he becomes fascinated by her fascination.

"I've, like, wanted to say that so many times."

Her heart. Racing. Is he saying he loves her?

"You have?"

"I tried to say it, but…"

"Yeah, it's okay. It's you."

"Honest?" Jethro looks hopeful now.

Cooper nods. He continues.

"I… I love your eyes Cooper. No matter how old we get, your eyes, the flames, the colours, they'll always be the same. They'll always be in total eclipse."

She smiles.

"Where'd you get that?"

"What do you mean?"

"Those words."

He looks confused.

"I don't know. They just come to me."

"They're yours?"

"Guess so."

"They're nice."

He smiles.

"You like them?"

"Yeah."

Jethro makes a decision.

"I have a surprise for you."

"What is it?"

"Hold on."

He rushes over to the Vauxhall, opens the boot. Cooper has no idea what's happening. He lifts a tartan blanket. Underneath he takes out a guitar.

"Where'd you get that?"

He sits down cross legged. He tunes the guitar.

"I've been learning to play."

She joins him on the blanket, sitting opposite again.

"Since when?"

"Like, last year I guess."

"Really?"

"Uh-huh."

"You never said."

"I've been trying something."

"Trying something?"

"Like, to write a song."

"What's it about?"

"Well uh…"

"Tell me."

His cheeks flush.

"It's about your eyes."

"My eyes?"

"Uh-huh."

Her head is swimming.

"You mind?" he says.

"No."

"Sure?"

"You gonna play it?"

"I thought you'd like, mind. You know cause you don't like compliments and stuff."

"What's it called?"

"Eclipses."

He starts singing a simple melody and oh wow. His voice, it's sweet and pure and clean and soft and delicate. If a gazelle could sing that's how it'd sound. He sings about suns. And moons. And total eclipses. A song about how her eyes are two suns, two moons in eclipse. How her beauty is so bright sometimes he can't even look at her because he's staring at suns and moons. He sings about colours, about if all he ever did is wake to twin eclipses for the rest of his life it would be all the world and everything.

As he sings Cooper's clenched heart unfolds, smoothes out, releases. Up till now she's been squeezing her heart like a fist so her feelings for Jethro never surfaced, never saw light. She read about how Chinese mothers used to bind their daughter's feet tight. It was fashionable for women to have tiny feet. Now the binding on Cooper's swelling heart splits, rips off, unable to contain it anymore. Everything spills out. She feels an overwhelming rush of emotions. An expansion of feelings floods her.

Then the song is over.

It's over but it hangs in the air and trails away like a flock of swallows over the horizon. Her love. It's so big, so huge, she doesn't know what to do with it. Cooper cries, silently.

Jethro leans in.

"Hey man, don't."

Cooper can't help it.

She cries.

Jethro leans over the guitar, cradles her face. He's never seen her cry. She's tough like a kernel of unpopped popcorn. She looks up. Her lashes long and wet. He lengthens his slender neck, angles his lean jaw, his mouth meets hers. Softly. The second kiss thoughtful, profound, full of meaning. Full of unspoken history. He pulls back and she pulls back and they're gazing, gazing.

She sees his gaze flit between each of her eyes. His eyes are misty. Misty grey. Misty grey like coastal fog.

He sees beautiful green eclipses with a ring of amber coronas.

"I just don't know which of your eyes to settle on. It's like they draw me in, you know? Every time I switch between them I'm kind of trapped in the vortex and it pulls me closer."

To Cooper it's the most beautiful words she's ever heard. The most beautiful song. The most beautiful day.

"And I'm like completely in love with you, Cooper. I always have been."

Oh god. Those words those words those words wow those words. Somehow they're even more beautiful. Beauty upon beauty.

Cooper falters. Falters and tumbles. Tumbles and falls. Falls and falls and falls and falls. She doesn't just love him. She is tremblingly, tumblingly, spinningly, somersaultingly in love with him. She laughs as she cries. Cries with the joy of it. She flings her arms around him, the guitar in the way, it doesn't matter. The guitar, the declaration of their feelings, unites them.

Cooper snaps open her eyes.

Oh.

Back on goatee man's bed.

Oh.

Her face is wet. Still crying, silently. Love. So big. So huge, she doesn't know what to do with it. She cried for the birth of something. Now she's crying for the death of something. Dying suns. Dying moons. Dying eclipses.

Oh Jethro.

She too collapsed into his vortex that day. Tumbled in and swallowed into a swirling maelstrom, knowing she would tumble forever.

Now she's trapped in a black hole that's impossible to escape. Nothing ever comes out a black hole. Not ever. She will tumble forever. Tumble until she dies. Until the end of time.

She knows.

Yeah she knows.

No matter what, she will love Jethro forever.

No matter where she is, she will think of Jethro forever.

No matter who she's with, she will suffer forever.

She gazes at her wrist, at the scars on her wrist.

No matter what, she'll never cope with suffering.

Stares at her wrist.

Not forever.

Cooper angrily slashes at her tears with the back of her hands. Naked and exposed she rolls over, finds her phone in her bag on the floor by the bed. She makes a call. Resignedly, she makes a call. Is that what she's doing? Resigning?

A voice answers. But it's voicemail. Cooper waits for it to finish.

"It's Cooper Hall. I'm ready for treatment."

Yeah Cooper knows that's exactly what she's doing. Resigning.

6 3

AFTER COOPER LEAVES the message on Gateway House's voicemail, she gets up, searches for her clothes. She feels naked and vulnerable. She finds them, not strewn about as she'd remembered but folded on to a wicker chair beside the bed.

Cooper listens for the man who's flat she's in. She's forgotten his name. There's movement from another room. She scrambles into her underclothes, her khakis, her T-shirt, her denim jacket, feels instantly better. Cooper leaves the bedroom, finds the bathroom opposite. Afterwards she follows the sounds back to the kitchen.

The kitchen is clean and bright with a small counter space. It's enough for a hob, a small oven, microwave, fridge, toastie maker, kettle and a couple of overhead cupboards. The man has his back to her.

"Hey," Cooper says.

He places the last of the wares on to the draining board, turns around and wipes his hands into a tea towel. He smiles.

"Hi Cooper. I'm Thomas."

"Yeah. Hi Thomas."

She glances at the green microwave clock. It says 1:15am.

"Yep, you been asleep about three hours," he says. "No hangover?"

"My head's completely cleared up."

"It should be. The good stuff Steve gave you is not only strong but also leaves your body fast. You're married, right?"

Cooper instinctively glances at her ring finger. No ring. She took the ring off weeks ago.

"Yeah."

"What're you looking for?"

"My shoes."

"I meant—" He smiles. "Well, they're under the bed."

Cooper goes back to the bedroom. It smells of sex in there. She looks under the bed and finds her Doc Martens, a sock in each. This is a tidy man. She puts them on.

Thomas appears by the bedroom door.

"Here are your keys. You dropped them in the car park by the way. You're not used to drinking, are you?"

"Not that stuff."

"I'll drive you back to your car if you're in a hurry but otherwise can I fix you something?"

She doesn't look at him.

"Cheers, I just want to go."

*

When they arrive at the car park she sees the bar is dark, the sign off. She turns to Thomas.

"How come your bar is only breaking even? It was heaving tonight."

Thomas shrugs.

"You came on a popular night. Open mic. I wish it were like this every night."

"Then do open mics every night."

He shakes his head.

"Not enough local talent."

"What about hiring in bands?"

"I do that already."

"Someone more popular?"

"Can't afford it."

"Quiz night?"

"Every Tuesday."

"Karaoke?"

"Once a month."

"Taster evenings?"

"Taster evenings?"

"You know, trying out all the different brands of wines ...or expensive vodkas."

He laughs.

"You want a job? You're full of ideas. I could pay you in salted peanuts."

"You could offer food."

"We could but we're a wine bar."

"Try it. People like simple things to eat."

"We do crisps and the aforementioned peanuts."

"You've got a toastie machine in your flat, I've seen it."

"I have."

"Try cheese and onion toasties first. They smell great."

"I'll need licences."

"What licences?"

"Catering, insurance, fire."

"You can extend insurance to cover cooking. Fire I guess you already have under your building insurance. Catering is a basic food and hygiene course. But you'd need to contact Environmental Health and get a Food Safety Officer to check over everything. If it all checks out, you're set. There may be a couple of new hoops to jump, I guess."

Thomas looks impressed.

"You know about this stuff?"

"Worked in a café as a teenager."

"I'll give it some thought."

Cooper turns to leave the van.

"Cooper?"

"Yeah?"

"Don't do what you did again. There are better ways of dealing with whatever you're going through."

Cooper's jaw tightens and her hands turn into fists like she's ready to fight.

"I'm going through something am I?"

"You know you are."

"You didn't mind a few hours ago."

"I don't mind at all. But you do."

Her car keys bite into her palms. She stares at him. The colour of his eyes are grey. Grey but not misty grey like coastal fog. It's not Thomas she's angry with. Not Thomas who hurt and betrayed her.

"What makes you think I mind?"

"I'm a bartender. Unofficial psychiatrist. Or psychologist. I never know the difference. You deserve to treat yourself better is all I'm saying."

"Yeah well, cheers for showing me your flat."

"Oh, and your catering advice…"

"What about it?"

"I'll consider it."

"Yeah?"

He grins.

"I just might."

Cooper slips out the van, slides it shut, makes her way to her own car. Inside it's cold after the warmth of the van. She rubs her hands together, starts the engine. She sees the tank's almost empty. Thomas's van swings around, flashes its headlights twice, nips back the way he came with practised agility. Then he's gone as though he never was.

Cooper drives home.

Just as empty as her car.

6 4

THE SUE BAXTER PODCAST
SUE BAXTER
Tell me Dr Stewart-Way, why is it two people sharing the same terrible event can result in one getting PTSD and not the other?
DR STEWART-WAY
What a good question. To answer that, I need to explain how the brain learns to cope with everyday stress.
SUE BAXTER
Please do.
DR STEWART-WAY
Have you ever noticed when you've had an unpleasant experience, you'll linger on it – if you're the victim of road rage for instance?
SUE BAXTER
Well yes. Sometimes I live with it for days when a driver explodes at me for making a blunder.
DR STEWART-WAY
Exactly, and another word for lingering is dwelling. You might ask what's the purpose of dwelling? Why would the brain want to torture itself like that?
SUE BAXTER
I suppose it's to do with learning from an unpleasant experience to avoid it in future.
DR STEWART WAY
Yes, the brain is ultimately a puzzle-solver. We now know every time you recall a memory you're actually recalling a copy of the last time you recalled that memory – well-documented

research tells us that, and it's something Dr Applegate's work takes advantage of. Though there's no absolute proof, we personally stand by a theory that by dwelling on something upsetting, you're recalling the event so the brain can re-enact the situation to gain insight into it and learn how to avoid it in future. In each re-enactment, the brain rewrites a copy of the memory in order to progressively strip away the negative emotional content connected to it. We call this memory loop, desensitisation.

SUE BAXTER

So you're saying the act of dwelling, as well as being a kind of rehearsal process, is also an emotional repair mechanism?

DR STEWART-WAY

We believe so, and is utterly out of our control. We don't want to dwell. We can't help it, but it has an evolutionary benefit encoded into our limbic system and in normal circumstances the brain operates this mechanism flawlessly. Once emotion is stripped away – and usually the puzzle solved – the dwelling ceases. Dwelling, though unpleasant, is a learning mechanism. Unfortunately it can lead to a form of PTSD where the sufferer marinates in an endless loop, haunted by the dreadful event. For some reason the brain doesn't – or is unable to – strip away the emotional content of the trauma. The longer the loop continues, the more it fatigues your natural sense of wellbeing.

SUE BAXTER

So you consider PTSD a natural dwelling process gone wrong?

DR STEWART-WAY

That's a very good way of putting it. And the result is persecution. And as we know, any kind of persecution will affect anyone, no matter how positive we are to begin with.

SUE BAXTER

Why then does it happen?

DR STEWART-WAY

No one knows for sure. However one of the theories is, because the sufferer can't work out a solution to the puzzle, the brain

behaves like a stuck record. Even if there is no logical solution –
a senseless accident for instance – the brain will continuously
re-enact the memory anyway, to the detriment of the sufferer's
mental health. This is where doctors normally intervene with
drugs or psychological tricks to help sufferers, but it's not a
cure. The Gateway Programme however circumvents that by
severing the emotional connection to the memory thus
terminating the dwelling process.

SUE BAXTER

So hold on, does that mean a memory and the feelings for that
memory aren't in the same place?

DR STEWART-WAY

Actually that's true. They're located in entirely separate parts of
the brain linked by neural pathways. And that's very fortunate
for Gateway House.

SUE BAXTER

So you cut the link that travels from a memory to, where?

DR STEWART-WAY

Two almond-shaped clusters of nuclei seated in the brain called
the amygdala. Think of the amygdala as the seat of emotion, a
sort of superhighway of the limbic system. When you recall a
memory, specific neural pathways from a memory to the
amygdala ignite. If it's a positive event, it's in the brain's
interest to preserve that connection so you'll feel good whenever
you think of it. If it's a negative event, it will erode the link
through persistent dwelling. Unless of course it misfires to
become PTSD.

SUE BAXTER

I see. The Gateway Programme is like lifting a needle from that
stuck record.

DR STEWART-WAY

Correct. And the relief is instant. It's incredible to see the stress
on faces melt away after treatment. Patients come in looking
pitiful, exhausted, depressed and defeated. When they leave,
they'll walk straighter, laugh, express joy with a disbelieving

enthusiasm that's infectious. They'll often look rapturous. It's wonderful to witness that.

SUE BAXTER

In that case Dr Stewart-Way, what went so wrong with Cooper Hall?

6 5

OVER THE NEXT few days and weeks Eddsy forgets and keeps forgetting to find the booklet he left piled under all the debris in the glove compartment in his van. Every time he thinks of it, he's having a shower, or he's under the bonnet of a car, or he's out somewhere with Harriet, or he's at lunch walking past Barnardo's. He never remembers when he's actually in the van.

This goes on for a while. And each time he thinks, must take it from the van, must take it from the van and throw it away. Must remember.

But he never does.

In time, Eddsy forgets it's there altogether.

He has no idea what this negligence will cost.

6 6

THE TOUR WITH Sabre Light ends next week and course, Jethro's sad it's coming to an end. It's been a complete white-out frenzy of organised mayhem. The buzz, the noise, the dust, the crackle. Jethro & Crew become better known, and they receive almost as much reception from the crowds as Sabre Light, their fame spreading on Vimeo and YouTube and TikTok and the management company's own website. Hits on their personal website vlog have increased a thousand-fold. To fans, they're getting two for the price of one on their tickets – Sabre Light and that new band, Jethro & Crew. The management agency are even hammering for a deal to be struck with Jethro after the tour.

Crazy.

Jethro calls Cooper, she doesn't answer. It doesn't bother him. He hasn't called for several days. It's just the way things are. He waits for her outgoing message to complete.

Coops? Just a few more nights and we're done. Man, I'm beat. He waits. Doesn't know what else to say. Then, almost as an afterthought. Yeah. Love you.

Jethro ends the call, makes another.

This one is secret.

Important.

One Cooper can't know about.

COOPER VISITS GATEWAY House for several scheduled appointments over the next few days. They carry out an MRI scan to map her brain. The machine draws Cooper inside a tunnel so close she can barely lift her head. It feels claustrophobic – like being buried in a coffin. The operator notices the familiar spike in heart rate and assures Cooper through speakers everything's going to be fine, Mrs Hall. He plays calm ambient music to help her relax. Cooper is told to lie absolutely still and focus on the music. She does it easier than most, listening to the harmonics. All sustained open chords. Forths and fifths. The machine starts and builds to a washing machine-like rumble, spinning in its own vortex of magnetism around her. Tumbles. Spins. Somersaults. Line by line a scan of her brain appears on a computer screen. The doctors are pleased. It's a good image. Before Cooper can stand it any longer it's over and she's drawn out.

In the next appointment Cooper is injected with something. She's told it's to reprogram specific brain cells to fluoresce under x-ray.

Then comes the final day.

Dr Stewart-Way escorts her into a room with a small x-ray machine. She settles Cooper into the seat below the machine and draws it over her head like a hairdryer. Dr Applegate sets up a needle in a device that rests on the side of her neck over a vein. He quietly explains he will run the auto injector remotely to deliver a precise micro dose of a chemical to put her in a state of mild suggestibility and that it'll be over before she notices. Dr Stewart-Way says she has time to change her mind if she wants.

Cooper hesitates.

She thinks of that day she and Jethro declared their love. The one where he strummed the first song he ever wrote and played for her. A song about moons and suns and eclipses. Her heart swells with love. Tremblingly, tumblingly, spinningly, somersaultingly.

Oh Jethro.

She thinks of the day, the one with Dizzy Gillespie, Homme, soft moans, soft moans, soft kisses, soft kisses. The Red Robin of her heart has been shot and tremblingly, tumblingly, spinningly, somersaultingly, drops to the ground, struggling, wanting to die, unable to. There's no escape. Not ever. Not from this kind of love.

"Mrs Hall?"

Big breath.

"Yeah. I'm ready."

The doctors nod, leave the room, settle in the control room with an observation window. Dr Stewart-Way powers up the machine. Dr Applegate is ready. The doctors acknowledge each other.

A psychologist gently guides Cooper through speakers. "Mrs Hall I want you to think of your husband. Think of Jethro."

How can she not? How can she ever not?

In silence they work. In all, the process takes four minutes and thirty-three seconds – by coincidence precisely the same duration as the experimental piece by composer John Cage. Cage's composition is called 4'33 because it also consists of four minutes and thirty-three seconds of absolute silence where the orchestra plays not a single note, makes not a single noise.

During that time Cooper's love for Jethro fades. His song to her fades. The swallows disappear over the horizon one by one.

Then they are gone.

Where there was love.

Tremblingly, tumblingly, spinningly, somersaulting love.
Now it is silent.

AFTER THE TREATMENT, the doctors asks if Cooper would like to be alone for a few minutes?

Yeah she would.

They say they'll return in twenty minutes to go through a post-treatment check.

They close the door.

Cooper is alone.

She's nervous. A part of her thinking this hasn't worked. She doesn't feel any different.

Cooper takes a breath, closes her eyes. Okay here goes.

She thinks of when she first meet Jethro in his chromatic glasses in class.

She's surprised when nothing happens. Not a blip.

His familiar, sweet, musky smell?

No.

Dating him?

Nothing.

Okay how about something more exciting? How about the shape of his mouth on hers?

Nada.

Restaurants?

Cinemas?

Walks in parks?

Picnics?

THEIR WEDDING?

She thinks of amazing holidays they've had together. That time when he was stung by a jellyfish on his thigh in Spain and

he said between gasps she has to pee on it to take the sting away
and she said she didn't think that was right but he insisted and
so she did and it didn't do anything, it still stung. Then when he
explained it to a Spanish doctor the doctor laughed and said it
was a myth and Jethro's cheeks blazed with embarrassment
which made Cooper's heart swell all the more.

Nothing now. Now it's just an amusing anecdote.

What about that surprise romantic getaway where he'd
sprinkled rose petals and lit candles around a hotel bath and they
both got in? The petals were a complete disaster because it stuck
to their skins and gave them red patches the size of coins. Hotel
guests thought they had some infectious disease. Plus all those
candles kept going out and Jethro burnt his backside and she set
fire to a towel and set the hotel's smoke detectors off. Complete
disaster. So funny. She always showered him with kisses after a
disastrously funny reminisce like that, laughing in bed together,
and she'd say you're an idiot and he'd say yeah, I'm a total tool.

A funny story now, that's all.

What about the biggie? Declaration Day. That wonderful
day, that amazing day, that incredible day he took her to the
field and sang her a song about love and eclipses and moons and
suns and all her pent-up love for him tumbled out and wrapped
him in her heart forever.

No.

Nothing.

Holidays. Cuddles. Christmases. Life's events. She
remembers them all. None make her heart move.

It's like all those memories are encased in see-through
plastic. Pieces of Jethro, something to observe only. Specimens,
preserved on glass slides. Something to pick up, study under a
microscope, put back and move on.

Cooper hardly dare believe it. But no wait. Cooper braces
herself. Okay, there's just one last thing…

Dizzy Gillespie.

Homme.

Soft moans, soft moans.

Soft kisses, soft kisses.

Wow. Wow. Wow.

Cooper's heart doesn't hurt, her mind doesn't fret, her eyes don't cry. She really, truly, honestly, feels nothing.

But actually Cooper does feel something after all.

Tremblingly, tumblingly, spinningly, somersaultingly feels it.

The vortex is gone. It's absence, a relief.

And she smiles.

THE SUE BAXTER PODCAST

DR STEWART-WAY

In answer to your question Sue, nothing went wrong with Cooper Hall. Not as far as the treatment went. The Gateway Programme was faultless. It was personal reasons in her own life which caused complications.

SUE BAXTER

Can you explain then what it feels like after you've had treatment?

DR STEWART-WAY

Well for that I'd like to ask you to do something.

SUE BAXTER

Okay?

DR STEWART-WAY

Think of someone you care about very much.

SUE BAXTER

Charlotte, my best friend. What about her?

DR STEWART-WAY

She was present throughout your childhood?

SUE BAXTER

She was. We were and still are very close.

DR STEWART-WAY

So you'll have thousands of memories of her.

SUE BAXTER

Of course.

DR STEWART-WAY

You'll be aware you've lost most of those memories. You may remember specific events, a birthday party or trip out somewhere together, but you won't remember everyday moments with her.

SUE BAXTER

Yes I expect that's true.

DR STEWART-WAY

I'm sure you're aware of the term avatars as used in computer games?

SUE BAXTER

Of course.

DR STEWART-WAY

In Hindu mythology an avatar is the presence of a deity in human form. In the context of a computer game it's a participant of the self in the game. A second self if you will.

SUE BAXTER

But how does this connect with The Gateway Programme, Dr Stewart-Way.

DR STEWART-WAY

I discovered our brains hardwires fractal structures of the people we know into avatars. And importantly they reside in specific geographic locations in our brains.

SUE BAXTER

(Laughs)

So I've built a mini version of Charlotte inside my own head, is that what you're saying?

DR STEWART-WAY

Absolutely. I mentioned the brain isn't very good at remembering mundane events. But it is exemplary at developing avatars. However, this isn't simply a mental image of Charlotte. The avatar encapsulates everything you know about her.

SUE BAXTER

And the purpose of building avatars is… ?

DR STEWART-WAY
Well to answer that Sue, I'm going to have to ask you a rather strange question.

7 0

COOPER ARRIVES AT Paddington station, checks when her train's due (not for another twenty minutes), finds a coffee shop, goes in. She feels so different. So light. This morning before the final treatment was another world. Thank you Dr Applegate and thank you Dr Stewart-Way. Thank you Gateway House. Thank you beautiful amazing world.

Cooper's been testing herself with thoughts of Jethro ever since she left Gateway House. Every time she tries to find something heart-warming about him, her mind wanders. Wanders wonderfully. She has not a care.

She steps up to the coffee shop counter, orders a croissant and a coffee, puts in five spoons of sugar. Cooper takes them to a large leather sofa, picks up a magazine, flicks through it. The cover has an article title, Ten Things He Doesn't Have To Know.

She smirks at the prescience of the headline. A few minutes later someone sits at the other end of the sofa. The man puts down his coffee and pulls out an orange Penguin Classic from a canvas rucksack. She looks at the title. Dracula by Bram Stoker. She returns to her magazine.

Ten minutes later she's already exhausted the magazine. She goes to pick up another from the table, only too late she realises it's underneath Dracula man's coffee cup. The coffee goes everywhere, all over the table. The man glances over his book, realises what's happening, springs up. He uses his napkin to stop the coffee running down the side of the table and together they pick up drenched magazines, holding them by the corners.

He takes his wet napkin, wipes the covers when an assistant appears with a damp cloth and clears the mess away. The assistant is annoyed because this happens at least once a day and the owner never does anything to solve the problem because it's not him who has to do the clearing up. Embarrassed, Cooper says sorry to the assistant. The assistant gives a half-smile. Cooper says sorry to the man.

"Ah, don't worry about it," the man says. "You've probably saved my life anyway." His voice has a soft Irish lilt to it. Cooper appraises him. He's in skinny jeans, black top, and black leather shoes, almost looks beatnik. She guesses he's in his late twenties.

"Now, you know caffeine's a poison don't you?" the man says.

"Yeah?"

"Oh, it is. If you ate a whole jar of coffee powder all that caffeine would kill you."

"Yeah, I must stop doing that."

He chuckles, rises from his seat and heads to the counter. Cooper grabs her purse, follows him. The man orders a decaf cappuccino. Cooper calls to the assistant.

"I'll pay for that."

The man turns.

"Will you look at my wallet? All bent out of shape by these coins. I'll be glad to be rid of them."

"Yeah, but it was my fault."

"Now, don't you worry about that. I prefer money you can fold anyway. There's nothing sweeter in your wallet than a picture of the queen on the back of a ten pound note. Or twenty if you happen to be so lucky." He pulls out a ten pound note, kisses it, replaces it. He tips out his coins and passes them to the assistant.

Cooper looks at him.

"Sweeter on a fifty pound note then."

"Now, you'd think that wouldn't you? The amount of hassle I get trying to buy something with one of those little rascals if one happens my way. Not that they have the good grace to find a home in my wallet you understand."

The cappuccino made and paid for, they return to the sofa. He holds out his hand and Cooper takes it.

"I'm Adrian, but you can call me Adrian."

He kisses Cooper's hand. Heat rushes to her face. She's slapped a man for less. Cooper introduces herself.

"Cooper."

"Now that's nice. A nice sturdy name. Very nice to meet you, Miss Cooper."

"Cooper's my first name."

"Is it now? Adrian happens to be my first name too. You'd care to join me?" He points to the same sofa they'd already sat at.

"You're sure you can trust me?" Cooper says.

"Trust you?"

"Not to spill more poisonous coffee over you?"

He laughs.

"My old mam used to say once bitten twice shy but you know sometimes it's just a playful little nip."

They settle next to each other on the sofa. Cooper dives into her purse.

"Look, let me pay yeah? I'll feel bad if you don't."

Adrian dismisses the offer with a raised palm. He's about to put his coffee cup down on the table then gives Cooper a sidelong glance. An impish grin appears and he puts it down anyway. He's teasing her and she likes it. Close up, Cooper notices the crows feet around his blue eyes. Maybe mid thirties.

For a moment neither has anything to say. Adrian studies her.

"You know, you're what my mam would call a handsome woman."

Handsome? To Cooper it sounds like something from a Regency romantic novel.

"Yeah?"

"You're a very attractive person."

Cooper nods, doesn't speak. For once she doesn't mind the compliment. But neither does she respond.

He laughs.

"Honest, it's not a pick up line. It's from When Harry Met Sally, that classic from the 80s. You've seen the film, of course you have."

"Yeah, um, Billy Crystal and Melanie Griffith."

"Ah well…"

"I'm right, aren't I?"

"One point for Billy Crystal but sorry nil for Melanie Griffith."

"What're you talking about? Of course it's her."

"Ah, but you're wrong."

"No, I'm not. She sits opposite Billy Crystal in that famous café scene."

"Oh, I'm with you there but you're wrong."

"Who is it then?"

"Well now, that's for me to know and you to find out."

"I have. It's Melanie Griffith."

"Tell you what, I'll give you a bit of a second guess?"

"Melanie—"

He playfully narrows his eyes at her.

"Now, you're sure you're sure about that?"

"I've seen the film like four times. It's you who's wrong. I'm sure of it."

"Are you now?"

"Absolutely. Melanie Griffith. Yeah. Definitely."

"Want to phone a friend?"

Cooper shakes her head, enjoying the banter.

"I'm sticking with Melanie."

The shop assistant reappears with a fresh pile of magazines and places them on the coffee table. She ensures the magazines are out of Cooper's spill range.

Adrian addresses the assistant.

"Miss?"

The assistant looks at him.

"You've seen When Harry Met Sally? Of course you have."

She nods.

"Can you tell me who stars in it?"

"Billy Crystal and Melanie Griffith," the assistant says.

"Hah! See?" Cooper says.

"Sorry, you're both wrong."

"Who is it then?" the assistant says.

"Well, I'd love to tell you who it is but I don't think either of you would believe me, so hold on."

Adrian pulls out a tablet from his rucksack. He taps on the screen, types something then turns the tablet towards them both. They see on IMDB a poster of When Harry Met Sally. It says Billy Crystal and…

The assistant smirks before leaving.

Cooper turns to him.

"What's it like being a film nerd?"

"Tell the honest truth Meg Ryan and Melanie Griffith are often mixed up. You know the paparazzi resort to checking which one has the tattoo of Antonio on the top of her arm to make sure? So, you remember the scene?"

"Which scene?"

"The one where Billy says to Meg she's so pretty?"

"I remember the I'll have what she's having café sex scene."

"Ah, the old I'll have what she's having café sex scene. Everyone remembers that. People always remember the popular scenes. Nobody remembers the others."

"And you do?"

"Sure, I'm weird like that. For instance, Billy doesn't just say Meg's pretty. What he does is he leans on his arm just like you're doing and he says you're a very attractive person."

"And what does Meg say?"

"Thank you."

"Is that all?"

"Well no, she complains he's coming on to her. You should know this if you've seen it four times."

"Yeah, I should."

Cooper checks her watch and realises her train's going to leave soon. She gets up.

"You're off already?"

"Yeah my son is—"

"You have a son? Get away."

"Daniel. He's at uni. He's back tomorrow."

"At university? And a husband?"

"Yeah. One of those too."

"Now, that's unusual."

"What do you mean?"

"Somehow you don't look married. It's not just the missing ring. I can usually tell."

Cooper collects her things. She holds out her hand.

"Well, it was funny meeting you Adrian. Sorry about the poisonous coffee."

"Now, before you go…"

Adrian goes into his rucksack yet again and pulls something out, pushes it into Cooper's hand. She looks at it. It's his business card. She reads it. It says Adrian Andrei sculptor.

"You're a sculptor?"

Adrian holds his hands up.

"So they tell me."

"Adrian Andrei. That doesn't sound very Irish."

"Italian father, settled in Galway. That's why I'm in London. Had a meeting with a gallery."

"You must be good."

"Now, don't you believe it. I've had masses of meetings with tons of galleries all over the shop. Doesn't mean a thing." He leans in, lowers his voice as though about to pass on some conspiratorial fact. "Fact is, I'm a chippie mostly. You'll find me putting up stud walls and hanging doors on some freezing building site come Monday."

"What kind of sculptures you do?"

"Now, let me see. I like working with found wood. Like to preserve their natural form. Nature as art, you know?"

"Bits of old tree trunk, branches, that kind of thing?"

"You've got the idea."

"Yeah, I've seen that before."

"Not like mine you haven't."

"How come?"

"Website's on my business card. Give it a gander."

Cooper promises she will, then leaves, catching her train.

She sits down in an empty window seat as the train leaves the station. Adrian had called her handsome. The compliment that sounded like a phrase out of a historical novel. Cooper, the woman who hates compliments finds herself smiling at one. Maybe because he was good-looking. She didn't think it was that though. She thinks on what he said, how she didn't look married. Cooper realises she doesn't feel married either. The treatment really has changed something deep down inside.

She takes her phone out, logs into Adrian Andrei's website but can't get a signal. She gives up, leans back closes her eyes and thinks of her meeting with Adrian Andrei, sculptor and chippie. That's when she gets the text.

THE SUE BAXTER PODCAST
SUE BAXTER
Go on then, surprise me with your question Dr Stewart-Way.
DR STEWART-WAY
When you meet up with your friend Charlotte, do you ever have to ask yourself, is she a threat to you?
SUE BAXTER
What a strange question. It wouldn't even cross my mind. Why would she be a threat to me? She's my best friend.
DR STEWART-WAY
Sounds like an odd question doesn't it, Sue?
SUE BAXTER
I doubt I've ever asked it.
DR STEWART-WAY
Actually you're constantly asking that very same question of her and anyone else you come across in your daily life, stemming from your brain's flight or fight mechanism.
SUE BAXTER
(Laughs)
But I've known her forever.
DR STEWART-WAY
Perhaps this will help: When you lift a rock and find insects under it what's the first thing they do?
SUE BAXTER
They scuttle away.

DR STEWART-WAY

They run from perceived danger.

SUE BAXTER

But Charlotte isn't perceived danger.

DR STEWART-WAY

And that answer comes to you instantly because of the existence of her avatar in your brain. You went through the process faster than a blink so you didn't even notice. You will however notice when meeting a stranger. The first question you'll ask is, is that person a threat?

SUE BAXTER

Well I suppose that depends on context. A strange man down a dark alley at night I'll assume he's dangerous even though most of the time he'll be a passer-by. But meeting him at a party I'll assume he's safe because it's a safe environment.

DR STEWART-WAY

That's a very fine example you've given Sue. Context is vital.

SUE BAXTER

So that's why we build avatars – to ask if people are a threat?

DR STEWART-WAY

To ask if they're a threat, quickly. The brain has an incredible agility to process multiple pieces of information at once, you see. When you read a novel, the story unfolds in sequence. Action follows reaction follows action follows reaction as the plot develops. But try to think of a whole plot at once and you can't. It takes time to run through the story sequentially. However you can grasp how the story made you feel all at once. You can then summarise the entire story as an emotional experience, describing it generically: It's a romantic comedy about neighbours in a dispute over a tree. Or I could say it's a psychological thriller about neighbours in a dispute over a tree. Instantly you know which story has feel-good overtones and which has tension and suspense. Well an avatar is a kind of genre-building structure too. Emotion is a billion year old intelligence and it all stems from the parallel processing capabilities of the brain so you're not even aware you asked if Charlotte is safe.

SUE BAXTER

Can you give me another example?

DR STEWART-WAY

Of parallel processing? Why not? Perhaps a non-emotive one. Boogawapwapfallypop.

SUE BAXTER

(Laughs)

I'm sorry? What did you just say?

DR STEWART-WAY

(Laughs)

Tell me Sue, what does it mean?

SUE BAXTER

Well it's a nonsense word of course.

DR STEWART-WAY

How long did it take you to work that out?

SUE BAXTER

The moment I heard it.

DR STEWART-WAY

You didn't have to go through your brain's filing cabinet of words one by one. That's the beauty of parallel processing. From your point of view you just knew it was a nonsense word. In reality you searched the relevant centres of the brain in nanoseconds to find another example of that word and came back with zero in an instant. The avatar of your friend Charlotte is also an example of parallel processing, instantly summed up in how you feel about her.

SUE BAXTER

Okay you've convinced me. But in that case Dr Stewart-Way, if an avatar reveals the emotional insight of a person, The Gateway Programme surely sabotages that by severing the emotional link you just talked about?

DR STEWART-WAY

The beauty of the human brain is it abhors a vacuum, so when we apply The Gateway Programme, the brain short circuits to make a recursive analysis of the avatar instead. The result is the same. You know instantly if that person is safe but this time, without feeling anything for them.

SUE BAXTER

And this is what you did with Cooper Hall for her husband Jethro T. Hall?

DR STEWART-WAY

Correct.

SUE BAXTER

Well, Dr Stewart-Way, that leads us to one question I'm sure all our listeners want to know the answer to.

IT'S EVENING WHEN Cooper arrives home. She opens the front door to a wall of music. Daniel's back, the music, coming from Daniel's bedroom, is bass heavy with muffled, monotonous, spoken words. Wasn't he supposed to return tomorrow? She calls out but he doesn't respond.

Cooper removes her jacket, stares at the mirror. Takes off her boots, stares at the mirror. Takes her socks off, stuffs them into her boots, stares at the mirror. She sees an indefinable difference about her. Or perhaps it's a perceptual shift.

Kelloggs appears, mews, rubs against her leg to tell her he's there. Then he saunters away, flops in front of the kitchen doorway, lifts a leg and starts licking his fur.

Cooper steps over him, finds a can of cat food, opens it, drops it into his bowl. Kelloggs stands, stretches, strolls to the bowl with all the time in the world. He stops by it, sniffs it for approval. He tests a chunk then bites, chews, swallows and repeats.

Before she knows it, Cooper is preparing a meal. Lancashire hotpot. She has everything out on the kitchen table.

The music stops. Daniel's bedroom door crashes open.

Footfalls descends the stairs, the thumps bearing the weight of a man in the bound of a child. He appears and leans against the doorframe, teenage-thin, hands slipping under his armpits.

"Hey mum, thought I heard noises. S'up?"

Cooper turns to him, feeling the instant pride of a mother. She made that. Made those eyes, made that face, that smile, those arms, those legs. Every part of him came from her right through to his bones. She made him and nineteen years later he's standing in front of her, his own portable existence, her satellite, her trophy. A recording of a love that once was.

"I called out earlier," Cooper says.

"Yeah?"

"Well? You gonna give your old mum a hug?"

He makes a face then reluctantly swaggers over, hugs her. She peels away.

How tall he is. How handsome he looks.

"How come you're back early?" Cooper says.

"Yeah, Stacy's parents picked her up this morning. I like noped myself out of uni and cadged a ride."

"Noped?"

"Just an expression, mum. Mum, your hair."

"Won't your professors be unhappy you left early?"

"Nah, they get it. Saves me a few quid on the trains. It's only one day. Mum, your hair."

Cooper sweeps her hand through it. She can hold a whole fistful now. It's longer even than Kellogg's fur.

"Yeah, decided to grow it."

"It's sick. For real. That gelled-back look is way funky."

"Thanks."

Daniel scans the bowls on the table, the wooden spoon, the meat on the chopping board, the sliced vegetables.

"What're you doing?"

"Building a spaceship."

"Yeah mum, you know that is—"

"—so not funny, yeah I know."

An endearing one-sided smirk kinks the corner of Daniel's mouth.

"That's dad's favourite. How come?"

"He's back tonight."

"Yeah?"

"He texted."

"Thought there were a couple extra gigs?"

276

"Apparently not. They were cancelled early on."

Daniel eyes the table, sees enough only for two.

"So, none for me?"

"I wasn't expecting you till tomorrow."

"Yeah well, what am I going to eat tonight?"

"I don't think you'll starve."

Daniel doesn't wait. He swans over to the fridge, yanks it open, clinking bottles in the door so it sounds like the early doorstep milk delivery. He stares at the contents, becomes still, hands slipping under his armpits again. One of Daniel's habits is standing before an open fridge, entranced. Cooper usually chides him for letting all the cold air out. Thirty seconds later she can't bear it.

"One day you're going to freeze in front of that thing, buster."

It breaks Daniel's spell. He loads his arms with bread, cheese, pickle, butter, peanut butter, jam.

"You know I'm cooking right?"

He grins.

"Like, I thought you were building a spaceship?"

Cooper grabs a tea towel, lashes at his hollowed bum with it. He snorts, expertly arching his back away.

"That is so not funny," she says.

Barefoot, Daniel kicks the fridge door shut, goes over to the table, drops his treasure. He grabs the breadboard, a knife from the cutlery drawer, settles at the table, one long leg shot out to the side.

Next, he artfully arranges everything around him like an artist arranging paint pots, slaps down a slice of bread, butters it, chops cheese haphazardly with the short stubby knife, presses it to the bread, opens the pickle jar, scoops a huge dollop on to the cheese, spreads it. Cooper continues on with the recipe at the opposite end. They face each other, neither saying anything for a moment, the comfortable silence of a mother and son in the homey jigsaw of their relationship.

"So, you going to tell me about uni?"

"Nothing to tell. Just the usual stuff."

Cooper thinks about her treatment. Thinks about Dizzy Gillespie. Homme. Soft moans, soft moans. Soft kisses, soft kisses. They mean nothing.

Daniel eyes her.

"Why're you smiling?"

Cooper doesn't hear.

Daniel clicks his fingers.

"Mum, like yo?"

Cooper looks up.

"What's the joke?"

"What joke?"

"You were smiling about something."

"Yeah nothing. Something at work."

Daniel chews on a sandwich, head tilted, watching Cooper.

"Why do you keep staring at me?" Cooper says.

"It's not just your hair."

"What're you talking about?"

He cocks his head the other way. It reminds Cooper of a caged budgie finding itself in a small birdcage mirror, trying to work out how a full-sized mate can live inside a small round porthole with empty air behind it. He shrugs, loses interest, hunches over his food once more. He finishes his sandwich and starts again on more bread, spreading it with peanut butter this time.

"Daniel, you do know there's enough here for you."

"Yeah like, that's ages away. I'll die of starvation first."

She watches him gouge into the jam, smear it on top of the peanut butter.

"And what have I said about using the same knife you've used for pickle in the peanut butter and jam?"

He grins, licks the knife.

"It's clean now."

Cooper rolls her eyes.

He continues to chew, watching Cooper as she works. Chews, stares, chews, stares, chews, stares.

"Will you stop it," Cooper says.

"There's something different about you."

Cooper's intrigued.

"Yeah?"

Daniel's about to speak when the front door opens and a gust of air punches through the house. The kitchen door rocks slightly as it always does when the front door opens. Jethro's voice calls out.

"Hey, the dude has entered the building."

7 3

TONIGHT AS EDDSY and Harriet eat their meals at the kitchen table, they discuss the direction Tomalin Garages should take. Harriet talks about how hybrid cars changed the industry a few years ago. Eddsy too recognised the change – with hindsight – but now he realises Harriet made the right call to equip their existing garages with expensive new tools and training to accommodate those changes. He remembers how he resisted her, but finally agreed when he saw her winds of change was right.

This time Harriet is talking about how fully electric cars are going to make an impact on their business if they don't react. Already several manufacturers sell electric cars off the forecourt. It's time to acknowledge fossil fuel engines are one day going to be a thing of the past. We need to react to the changes. Eddsy says maybe they should wait a few years, see what happens. Harriet shakes her head, says at the moment dealerships who sell electric cars also service them, but it's time for independent garages to acknowledge that change. We should get in early. Retrain in the new technology. Besides, she's been researching government subsidies into it. Tomalin Garages should grab them while they're offered.

Eddsy doesn't even hesitate to consider it. He almost didn't listen to Harriet last time.

"Maybe it's time to open a seventh garage then," Eddsy says.
"Yes. Make it for electric cars."
Eddsy grins.

"Then if things take off like you think, won't be long before we can build a seventh bedroom either then, wife."

Harriet presses her lips together at that.

"Don't."

Eddsy looks up from his meal.

"No more bedrooms. Please."

Eddy smiles at her request then, but it's with sadness. He reaches out, touches Harriet's hand across the table, squeezes it.

"No more bedrooms," he says.

THE FRONT DOOR slams and the house shudders. Jethro's in the hallway. He dumps his Gibson guitar case and a suit case down, calls out.

"Do I smell me some mean cooking or what?"

Daniel and Cooper call out.

"We're in the kitchen."

Cooper pauses, not knowing how she'll deal with this situation. She has to be normal right now, if only for Daniel's sake. She stands with the sink behind her, pastes on a smile, waits. This is Jethro in person. The real thing. The real test.

For a second Daniel looks at her funny. Then he pushes half a sandwich into his mouth and seems to dismiss whatever it was he saw in his mum. He turns to see his father.

Jethro appears in the doorway, tired and unshaven. He stops, takes everything in. Flecks of grey glisten on his chin. His hair, long and lank under his bolero hat. He has on a grey Sabre Light Euro Tour T-shirt, a lightweight blazer over it, thin blue scarf, ripped jeans, suede moccasins, no socks. He looks exhausted, his eyes craggy. But even tired and sweaty and crumpled, he's still attractive, a rock star now.

Jethro musses Daniel's hair first.

"How's ma boy?"

Daniel pushes his hand away. "Oh dad. God's sake, I'm like nineteen. God's sake!" Jethro goes to snatch half a sandwich Daniel has on his plate and Daniel possessively curves his shoulder around it, blocking him.

They laugh through the ensuing mini tussle, an excuse for a father-son embrace.

Jethro straightens up, runs his eyes over Cooper approvingly, taps two fingers against his hat in greeting.

"Well howdy pard'ner."

Cooper looks at him. She feels…

Yeah two things.

Nothing.

Absolutely nothing.

And surprise.

First nothing.

He is here. Jethro. In the kitchen. This adulterer. Pretending happy families. This destroyer. Pretending everything. This cheat. Pretending. He does it so well. Cooper's alternate future would have screamed and shouted and sworn and cried right about now. But here, even its shadow is absent. Thank you Dr Applegate. Thank you Dr Stewart-Way.

"Howdy back," Cooper says. "What brings you to town mister?"

"Well now, I got me a wifey and a young buck I needs to reacquaint myself with."

The second thing, Cooper's surprise.

The treatment means Cooper sees Jethro without the tonality of emotion. She didn't realise its absence also removed a blind spot of familiarity. Suddenly she sees Jethro the way others who meet him for the first time see him. A slender, amiable, attractive man, confident in his casual style. Someone who knows his identity. Confidence oozes from every ounce of him; the way he expresses with his hands, his fluidity of movement. She'd forgotten that. Even his persona is silk smooth and easy. Easy as melted caramel.

As Jethro gazes at Cooper, his eyes soften, his voice takes on a husky quality.

"Well, hey," he says. His words travel the span of kitchen, yet it's somehow intimate, as though tenderly whispering into her ear.

"Well, hey back."

There's a third thing Cooper notices.

Appreciation in his eyes.

Cooper didn't expect that. Despite Dizzy Gillespie, despite Homme, despite soft moans, soft moans, despite soft kisses, soft kisses, Jethro still loves her. She sees it with the fierce clarity of a crisp, alpine day.

No. Didn't expect that.

Jethro holds Cooper's gaze as he strides up to her, looking as purposeful as a man determined to land a sensuous kiss. Instead, he takes her around her waist and, at the last moment, rotates her. He kneels and theatrically kisses her bum, his hands flaring out behind him as though bowing before a magisterial presence.

Cooper laughs, turns back around.

Daniel rolls his eyes, pushes back his chair.

"God's sake you two."

A fourth surprise. This one of herself.

Cooper realises she can admire Jethro, yet not want him. She didn't expect that. She can laugh with him, yet not need him. No. Didn't expect that.

And that means Cooper realises she can be perfectly normal too. Act perfectly normal.

Yet never love this man ever again

THE SUE BAXTER PODCAST
SUE BAXTER
My question is this Dr Stewart-Way: Does The Gateway
Programme alter my feelings for anyone else?
DR STEWART-WAY
No, only for the avatar targeted. This is why we place such
importance on locating specific brain cells. You see, once we
locate the avatar in question, we simply obstruct it's connection
to the amygdala.
SUE BAXTER
Brain cells interconnect, yes?
DR STEWART-WAY
That's correct.
SUE BAXTER
So if you block the road from A to B might you not also cut off
the route that takes you to C?
DR STEWART-WAY
That's a good argument. Remember, I said the brain works as a
parallel processor. It means each route is unique – not reliant on
another route – yet can share neural pathways.
SUE BAXTER
But the shared paths… By cutting off one route aren't you also
cutting off routes you didn't want to?
DR STEWART-WAY
Okay let me give you an example. Let's once more use your
poor best friend, Charlotte.

SUE BAXTER

(Laughs)

Goodness she'll never forgive me if she hears this podcast, but please do carry on.

DR STEWART-WAY

You know Charlotte's landline number?

SUE BAXTER

Of course.

DR STEWART-WAY

You have it stored in your phone I expect?

SUE BAXTER

Absolutely.

DR STEWART-WAY

If you tried to call her, how would it be possible to ensure your call never gets through?

SUE BAXTER

Well, I suppose by cutting her telephone line.

DR STEWART-WAY

That means nobody could call her. There's a far less radical procedure. I'm assuming you've programmed her number into your phone so you can speed dial her, is that correct?

SUE BAXTER

Yes.

DR STEWART-WAY

So to call her you select her name and press call.

SUE BAXTER

Okay I think you're going to say the Gateway Programme is like deleting her name and number from my phone.

DR STEWART-WAY

Actually no Sue. Let's say your phone is your brain and Charlotte's name in your phone represents your brain's avatar of her. Let's further say her telephone number represents the neural map from the avatar to your feelings for her.

SUE BAXTER

I'm with you so far.

DR STEWART-WAY

What if I deleted one digit of her number from your phone's memory but keep her name in the phone?

SUE BAXTER

Obviously if I tried to call, it would never connect.

DR STEWART-WAY

Would it affect any other call?

SUE BAXTER

Well no.

DR STEWART-WAY

With The Gateway Programme we can silence individual neurones. This blocks the unique links between the avatar and amygdala whilst preserving the integrity of the neural pathway. Any shared links remain undisturbed.

SUE BAXTER

You'd need to know the precise location of Charlotte's avatar in my brain to do that, down to the last cell, surely.

DR STEWART-WAY

Indeed. And finding it with the degree of precision we've achieved in The Gateway Programme had, up till then, been impossible.

SUE BAXTER

So how did you manage to achieve what other scientists couldn't?

DR STEWART-WAY

Well that's to do with a statue.

SUE BAXTER

A statue?

DR STEWART-WAY

Indeed.

SUE BAXTER

What statue?

DR STEWART-WAY

Well there's something particularly striking about this statue, and it's its striking feature that holds the secret to how The

Gateway Programme was invented.
SUE BAXTER
Oh? And what's this striking feature?
DR STEWART-WAY
The statue is extremely ugly.

AFTER JETHRO KISSES Cooper's bum he stands up, winks at Daniel. Daniel slow claps and once more rolls his eyes. Jethro takes a flourishing Shakespearean bow.

"I thank you."

He pulls out a chair, collapses into it.

"Am I completely bushed or what?"

Cooper joins them at the table.

"So, you going to tell us?"

"Tell you what?"

Daniel chomps down his peanut butter and jam sandwich, pushes it into a cheek, talks through the other side of his mouth.

"Mum means are you like gonna tell us about the tour?"

"Yeah yeah, totally. Looks like we're getting a record deal. If all goes through, Jethro & Crew is gonna be locked in a studio for the next six months. The folks loved us. Sabre Light are my new best buddies."

"So, what're they like?" Daniel says through his food.

"Sabre Light? Cool bunch of guys, what can I say? You should know, you met them."

"Yeah like, for two minutes."

Jethro shrugs.

Daniel and Cooper exchange glances over the spartan answer.

"Yeah, sorry guys I need me a good hot bath and some kip. I smell like a hog's armpit."

"What's the lead singer like?" Cooper says.

"RiK Chard? Yeah, he's a good guy."

"He seems a bit full of himself," Daniel says, "the way he prances about."

"That's called owning the stage. It's all front. You know he calls his mum every night?"

"No way."

"Totally."

Cooper looks pointedly at Daniel.

"Unlike a certain someone I know."

Daniel side steps the comment.

"What about the rest of the gang?"

"They're cool."

Another exchanged glance between Cooper and Daniel.

Jethro holds his hands up.

"Guys, look tomorrow I'm all yours, okay?"

Silence.

"Guys, really my ears are still ringing from listening to big decibel music for three months. I need me some rest and recuperation. Some good ol' R&R. Oh hey I've got tons of stuff in my case. Programmes, mugs, signed CDs, hoodies, all that stuff. You guys saw all my tweets and Facebook updates right?"

"Yeah, totally dad. I'm like not doing anything else at university."

Jethro turns to Cooper.

"You saw them, right?"

"Course."

"You guys missed me though, right?"

"Like you gave us a chance," Daniel says. "You were completely calling or texting every five minutes."

He grins.

"Only keeping tabs on my number one fans."

Cooper smirks.

"Cause that's all you have."

Daniel sniggers, curls the rest of the bread into his mouth.

"Nice one, mum."

Jethro turns to Cooper.

"Anyway, where's this old lady invalid I've been hearing about? All I see is hotty totty."

"Yeah mum, didn't you like have a fight with a tree?"

"Well thanks for all your sympathy cards and flowers... Three months ago."

"You know I'd have been over here faster than a bullet if you needed me," Jethro says. "Harry said you were okay, just a bit bruised. She had to totally twist my arm NOT to come back that first night, but know what? Every day I felt more guilt than the guy who dropped the baby. Plus, I had no idea they'd extend the tour did I? The regular money's been good though, right? You seen our latest bank statement?"

"Cool, you can buy me a car," Daniel says.

Jethro ignores him, once more gazing at Cooper, drinking her in.

Tonight, after my bath, I think I'm going to put on some good old Dizzy and get us in the mood. "How's that grab you babe?"

Daniel shoots up scraping his chair on the floor tiles.

"God's sake, I'm like totally out of here."

"Hey, where you think you're going mister?" Cooper says.

Daniel turns to her, puts on a wary face, full of guilt.

"What is it?"

"You know what. That."

Cooper pointed stares at the battleground of food on the table.

Daniel exchanges looks with Jethro but Jethro raises his eyebrows with his best Better Do What The Lady Says Or She'll Make Your Life Living Hell expression.

Daniel grabs everything from the table and jams it into the fridge. He shoves them anywhere there's shelf space, no organisation. He goes to leave again.

Cooper glares at the mess he left on the kitchen table. Breadcrumbs, daubs of jam and pickle, bits of grated cheese.

"Do it properly."

Jethro grins.

"You're totally busted, mister."

Daniel gives a theatrical sigh, gets a dishcloth, wipes the table free of breadcrumbs and flecks of cheese into a cupped hand, tosses it into the bin. He wipes the table down, tosses the cloth into the sink like landing a basketball into a net.

"Happy now, Mutherrrr?"

"Thank you."

He backs out the kitchen before he's told to do any more boring stuff.

"Call out when the meal's ready, yeah?"

Daniel leaves, thumping back upstairs. The bedroom door slams in, the music starts. Suddenly Cooper and Jethro are alone.

Jethro gets up, goes to the wine rack, opens a bottle of red, hands Cooper a glass.

"At last," Jethro says, "some us alone time."

Cooper takes the glass. This, she thinks, will be interesting.

7 7

THE SUE BAXTER PODCAST
SUE BAXTER
(Laughs)
You're saying Dr Stewart-Way, a statue you discovered holds the key to The Gateway Programme because it's ugly?
DR STEWART-WAY
(Laughs)
Indeed, but I'm being fanciful. Let me explain. You may not be aware of this, but your brain has a distorted neurological map of your entire body. In the Natural History Museum in London, there are two grotesque figures – two statues if you like – called the Penfield Cortical homunculi. Do you know of them?
SUE BAXTER
I don't think so.
DR STEWART-WAY
(Laughs)
Believe me you'd remember if you saw them. Dr Wilder Penfield, an eminent Canadian neurosurgeon, created them. The sculptures are, as I mentioned, profoundly striking in their ugliness. Yet Dr Penfield didn't create them on a whim.
SUE BAXTER
What's it to do with The Gateway Programme?
DR STEWART-WAY
Well, the homunculi represents the brain's neurological map of the body. However there's something unique about it – each homunculi distorts the size of each body part to represent the

proportion of cerebral cortex devoted to it. Would you care to guess which part of the body is largest?

SUE BAXTER

(Embarrassing laugh)

Um…

DR STEWART-WAY

Go on. Take a guess.

7 8

COOPER TAKES A sip of the wine, winces.

"What's wrong?" Jethro says.

"The wine. It's like battery acid."

"You're kidding?" Jethro sniffs his own glass. Tastes it. "Seems fine to me."

Cooper takes another sip. Bitter. Bitter, sharp, acidic. Something metallic about it she doesn't like, like drinking wine after brushing your teeth. She remembers what Dr Stewart-Way said. There will be side effects. For some it's a new judgement of colours. For others, certain sounds or smells. The most common thing reported is an alteration of tastes and flavours. Cooper never asked whether the side effects are permanent or temporary.

She hands the glass to Jethro. He takes it, sniffs it, shrugs, pours it into his own, takes a sip, puts his glass down.

He moves in front of Cooper, slips his hands around her waist. She slides her hands around his. This adulterer. This cheat. This man she does not love. This destroyer. This wrecker. This man she cannot hate.

Jethro gazes into her eyes.

"Wow."

"What is it?"

"Wow. I've forgotten how much I've missed them. Total eclipses."

Cooper gazes into his. Grey. Grey but not misty grey like coastal fog. Just a blank, grey slate.

Even though she knows what she's done, Cooper still feels surprise for feeling nothing for him. Not distrust, not anger, not anything. How many frivolous girls have propositioned him on one of his mini jaunts across the clubs and pubs of Britain? Suddenly it seems so clear. He's used to audiences admiring him. So smooth, so relaxed. So—

"I totally missed you," Jethro says.

Cooper accepts that with a nod. She believes him. She sees that in him at least.

An uncertain look comes into Jethro's eyes.

"You missed me too, right?"

"Course."

How strange. An insecurity in Jethro Cooper's never noticed before. Is that also guilt speaking?

"Is that what you want me to say?"

He laughs.

"Oh man, that'd be like a Stepford wife Cooper. I like that you're a brick wall to most people. I love that brick wall. And I love I'm safe behind that brick wall. You're my fortress against the world."

The music upstairs ends, another track starts kicking, another muffled pillow over the rap voice of the singer.

Despite what Dr Applegate and Dr Stewart-Way said, Cooper still expected to feel outrage for this cheat, this adulterer, knowing what he's done. This destroyer, this wrecker, knowing what he'd done. That seeing him in person would stir… well something. Resentment. Bitterness. Fury. Anything. But there's not a ripple. Her neutrality is mirror smooth.

Jethro nuzzles into Cooper's neck, a sybaritic sensation she always enjoys. She lifts her chin to allow access, a cat accepting a scratch. He stitches a line of kisses to her throat, speaking between words.

"You did miss me though, right?"

Cooper inhales the familiar tang of his sweat, the thick heat coming off him. She thinks back to that night.

THAT night.

Cooper stepping up to the bedroom door, pushing it enough to expose her eye through the gap. The cool breeze through it. Observing. A doll's house view.

"Course."

"How much? Come on, hit me baby."

Cooper thought The Gateway Programme would be like a tooth cut from its nerves. No feeling left in the tooth. It's not like that at all. It's more like a gap where a tooth used to be. She wants to explore that gap, relish the novelty of that vacated space. She wants to play with it. Taunt it.

"I miss you," Cooper says, "like nothing on earth."

THE SUE BAXTER PODCAST
SUE BAXTER
(Awkward laugh)
Um… This is rather embarrassing… I'm guessing the genitals are the largest on this homunculi?
DR STEWART-WAY
(Laughs)
Many people guess that. In fact the face and particularly the lips take up a huge proportionate part of the brain. On the female version of the homunculus created by artist Haven Wright, the tongue is especially large. However the answer is…
SUE BAXTER
The eyes?
DR STEWART-WAY
It's the hands.
SUE BAXTER
The hands? Really?
DR STEWART-WAY
Think about it. Our hands touch the world to a far greater extent than most other parts of our body combined. We're always picking things up, pushing things around, opening and closing things, feeling the texture and temperature of things, searching our bags, drawers, pockets, purses, wallets. We're in constant physical contact with our world through our hands. We hold mobile phones, swipe icons and messages, jingle keys, touch door handles, chairs, light switches, mugs of tea and food. Coming into this studio you probably touched objects and

surfaces over a thousand times in the time we've been here. You also touched your face, scratched your head, adjusted your clothing, your seat and so on. In fact right now you're doodling on a notepad. That means you're simultaneously touching a pen, notepad, and the desk, three completely different surfaces and textures.

SUE BAXTER

(Laughs)

Ah you've caught me.

DR STEWART-WAY

By contrast, while your hands touched perhaps 5,000 different articles today, your feet has only been in contact with the insole leather in your shoes.

SUE BAXTER

When you put it like that, I can see why the brain is so receptive to hands.

DR STEWART-WAY

Indeed. The brain dedicates a huge surface of cortex to the hands. Some who lose their hands in accidents talk about the sudden isolation they may feel. They often report how their world feels dreamlike. It can take time to adjust. They have in essence lost more than 95% of their physical contact with the world. To give you an inkling of what that's like, when you repeatedly see a famous celebrity on TV, in the cinema or in magazines, the celebrity will become increasingly familiar to you. But because you can't physically touch her you'll lift her existence to mythical proportions.

SUE BAXTER

That never occurred to me. Famous people appear mythical because we can't touch them.

DR STEWART-WAY

In fact the greater the media coverage of that celebrity the more her mythic qualities elevate. Our brain reinforces that status. We consider objects and people we're unable to touch – a priceless work of art, a rare gemstone, the Queen – as precious. So powerful is the effect it ultimately creates a godlike aura. It's the same reason religious figureheads and the dead take on this mythic quality. If you meet this celebrity, the desire to touch her can be almost irresistible. Only social etiquette prevents you. Think of over enthusiastic football fans hanging over stalls to touch their heroes as they trot onto a pitch.

SUE BAXTER

Or even screaming teens reaching out for their pop idols on stage.

DR STEWART-WAY

Indeed.

SUE BAXTER

Okay understood, but what's the point you're making about the hands? What's that to do with avatars?

DR STEWART WAY

Well, it's because of a remarkable scientific project that started in 2009 The Gateway Programme is possible at all. In fact it will make your jaw drop to see what the scientists did.

SUE BAXTER

Why, what did they do?

OVER THE NEXT week Cooper and Daniel hear all about Jethro's experiences with the tour. Sabre Light had a huge reception in Europe, emerging onstage from a sleek green limo to a roar of cheering fans.

They'd toured Sweden, Belgium, Greece, Germany, Italy, Spain. Sabre Light's lead vocalist RiK Chard only has to pump a fist in the air and the audience would roar, like he was conducting an orchestra of audience.

In the meantime, Jethro & Crew's website hits have been steadily rising and his twitter account has almost 14,000 followers and climbing. There's talk of an official music video. Jethro knows the money isn't in CD sales alone anymore. Now it's about online streaming such as Spotify and Apple Music, advertising royalties, merchandising such as mugs, T-shirts, book deals, exclusives, film cameos and so many other things. They've a rising presence on TikTok, YouTube, Pinterest, Instagram and a gazillion other sites.

During that week Cooper talks to Dr Stewart-Way and Dr Applegate. They tell her it's too early to say whether her sense of altered flavours and smells will become permanent. Already, she's adjusting to the difference. Cooper's progress pleases the doctors.

Today, Jethro's at a Maida Vale recording studio. Daniel's out with mates. Cooper's in the garden studio when her phone rings. It's Harriet.

"What's up?" Cooper says.

"Well, you sound brighter."

"Yeah?"

"Why you no call?"

"I'm working."

"And catching up with your boys."

"Yeah, that too. It's a mad house again."

"Daniel pumping out his music from his bedroom you mean?"

"Yeah."

"And Jethro's doing pretty good. I've seen the official footage on the website."

"Yeah."

"So, things working out?"

"They're trying to sort a deal with a record label. Jethro's in a studio today."

"I mean you, Coops."

"Oh... Course. Yeah."

"Really?"

"Course."

"So, what was it all about?"

"What do you mean?"

"Oh, you know, like twelve weeks ago you, sobbing into the phone, like the car crash, like the not going to hospital protest, like the whole I Vant To Be Alone thing."

"Yeah, I wasn't that bad."

Harriet splutters a laugh.

"Yeah right… Oh Coops you're always so guarded. It's me! Harriet. That lovely, attentive older sister who not only bathed you she also changed your nappies too. Remember her?"

"Things fell out of control in my head that's all."

"You know that first phone call from your car, I thought someone had died."

Cooper recalls that alternate version of herself. That woman is the same woman who's speaking to Harriet right now. Only that walking piece of China, easy to shatter, is now titanium.

Then the next day, Harriet says, the VERY next day, you want to go home and almost break my arm forcing me to take you back to that empty house."

"Kelloggs needed feeding."

"Yes, I know Kelloggs needed feeding but I thought you and Jethro had broken up or something. Even saying it now it sounds utterly impossible."

Cooper thinks about that. Maybe not so impossible anymore.

"Yeah well, it's sorted now."

"What's sorted?"

"I am."

"Oh come on Coops, give me something."

Cooper thinks for a moment.

"I worked stuff out in my head that's all."

"You and Jethro?"

Cooper remains silent.

"God, you are SO infuriating!"

Cooper laughs.

"Know what I thought? I thought it was because Jethro went on this tour thing."

"Okay."

"Then I thought no that wouldn't upset you. You'd be supportive. Especially since it's with Sabre Light."

"Okay."

"Then I thought… well actually I pretty much dismissed everything else."

"Right."

There's a pause. Harriet's waiting for something.

"OH COOPER!"

Cooper laughs again.

"You're really not going to say, are you?"

"I'm not trying to be mysterious."

"Yes you are. You're better though, right? I can tell."

"Everything's cool."

"You know what? I believe you sis. You sound like your old self."

"Yeah, and what's that?"

"Furtive and sarcastic."

Cooper laughs. Harriet laughs.

"What am I gonna do with you, eh?"

"Nuffin'. I is perfeck as I is."

A piercing Tannoy-like voice comes through the phone.

"Car at pump number four, please turn off your mobile phone."

"Where are you?" Cooper says.

"Opps. Sorry sis, gotta go. Eddsy's filling up at a petrol station. Shouldn't be using my phone… Hey Coops?"

"Yeah?"

"Welcome back."

HARRIET HANGS UP. She's waiting in the van at the superstore petrol station for Eddsy to pay. She's pleased to hear the old Cooper back. If only she could find out what the problem had been. God that sister of hers.

Harriet glances over the forecourt to the checkout queue. Eddsy is fourth from the till.

Eddsy sees Harriet looking, signals if she wants a chocolate bar or something. She shakes her head no. He grabs one for himself. Harriet instantly regrets her decision and signals to him. Only now he's turned away. Drat. Oh well, she can steal some of his chocolate. Then she remembers the lemon drops in the glove compartment he always keeps there.

Harriet opens it. Stuff tumbles out. Phone charging cable, cereal bar wrapper, a pen, an old mobile, receipts, scraps of paper. She tuts, picks them up. Messy pup. Throws the wrapper into the pull-out ashtray, puts the pen and cable and old phone back. She rummages around for the boiled sweets. He must have some, he always does. She finds a crumpled paper bag. Yes there they are. She takes a sweet out. Pops it into her mouth. Lovely and hard and sharp and bittersweet.

Harriet flips the glove compartment shut. The door bounces open again. The phone cable's caught in the hinge. She pulls it away. A booklet comes out with the cable.

Harriet picks them both up, coils the cable up, in it goes. Goes to shove the booklet back in.

Freezes.

Harriet freezes.

She reads the front cover of the booklet: Thinking of Adopting?

THE SUE BAXTER PODCAST
DR STEWART-WAY
When I was attempting to map the human brain Sue, the first thing my team located on the surface of the brain was the neural links to our hands. This was due to the results of a famous 2009 project called the Human Connectome Project.
SUE BAXTER
The Human...?
DR STEWART-WAY
The Human Connectome Project. It's a brain-mapping project that involved scientists from several continents and is a major advance in neuroscience. The results are truly spectacular. Prior to that, the only useful map of the brain we had was a rather rudimentary model created in 1909 called the Broadmann Map. Though the map has proven essential to science during that time, it's the Human Connectome Project that has made it possible to create a detailed three-dimensional computer-generated model that intricately traces the billions of fibrous interconnections within the brain. It's an incredible feat.
SUE BAXTER
You were part of the project?
DR STEWART-WAY
No but we benefited from it. During that time I was head of a small research team studying the living brain of a deep sea fish called Macropinna microstoma. We were selected to explore specific areas of the fish due to our pioneering work.

SUE BAXTER

Why a fish?

DR STEWART-WAY

For one very useful reason: Macropinna microstoma has a completely transparent head. You can literally see its brain through its flesh. It's surprising because it looks like a see through jelly representation of a fish with all the organs inside. In reality you're looking at a living animal. If you want a surprise, Google it.

SUE BAXTER

(Laughs)

I'm intrigued. You'll have to tell me how to spell it.

DR STEWART-WAY

Our first breakthrough was in mapping brain cells dedicated to the fish's lips. Before you ask why the lips I'll tell you it's the fish's equivalent of us touching the world through our hands. It takes up a huge portion of the fish's cortex. We then developed painstaking techniques to map smaller areas within the brain such as the various fins, the lateral line, the eyes and so on. After that we applied the same procedure to small mammals. Eventually we were able to use the methods we'd developed along with data from the then completed Human Connectome Project to study the human brain.

SUE BAXTER

How? We don't have transparent heads like the fish you mentioned. Well most of us don't.

DR STEWART-WAY

(Laughs)

Well indeed. In effect, we made the human brain transparent by overlaying highly detailed neural maps from The Humane Connectome Project. We then applied a method called Diffusion Spectral Imaging, the same technology hospitals use today to map a patient's brain. Incidentally I have a printout of an image of the brain created by The Human Connectome Project. Here, take a look.

SUE BAXTER

Oh my. Gosh I never expected that. Goodness that's beautiful. Forgive me Dr Stewart-Way I'll have to explain to my listeners what I'm looking at. Dr Stewart-Way has just slid over a photograph of the human brain, but it's not like any picture I've ever seen. In this picture the brain looks more like those stunning fibre optic light fountains you can buy. Gosh it looks like a work of art.

DR STEWART-WAY

Yes, it's utterly exquisite. And before we frustrate your listeners anymore, I can assure them there is a beautifully illustrated website dedicated to the project that's easy to find. I guarantee the images of the brain you'll see will astound you. Most importantly though, this work has been enormously beneficial to our work in optogenetics.

SUE BAXTER

So tell us Dr Stewart-Way, what's so special about the spectral imaging you were talking about?

DR STEWART-WAY

Diffusion Spectral Imaging. DSI allows us to create the equivalent of a Google map of an individual brain. With it we're able to precisely locate specific neural links and trace their pathways. To put that into perspective, the new James Webb deep space telescope can see further than any telescope on earth. However, it's so precise it can study a piece of sky the size of a penny piece placed 62 miles away and capture an image of billions of stars and galaxies through that penny piece. Our work on earth is multiple times that resolution. It is spectacularly precise.

SUE BAXTER

Well that leads us to a question I'm sure all our listeners would love to know. Suppose I had the treatment to erase my feelings for my best friend Charlotte. How would I feel about her now?

8 3

COOPER HAS BEEN planning how to tell Jethro about everything.

She'll do it on Friday.

By Friday Daniel will have left for university. They'll be alone. She'll tell Jethro she knows all about what she saw that day in the bedroom. She'll say it straight out.

Make it plain.

Clear.

Matter of fact.

She'll tell him she's not sure she didn't crash the car on purpose that day.

She'll tell him though he broke her heart, she doesn't hate him, isn't angry with him, isn't upset.

He'll be confused. He'll want to know why.

She'll say she can never love him ever again. That it's impossible.

He'll ask why it's impossible.

That's when she'll tell him about The Gateway Programme.

At first he won't believe her. Then when he does, his face will drain of colour. He'll say he's sorry.

Too late.

He'll say he'll make it up to her.

Too late.

Or maybe he'll want to end their relationship too. But no, Cooper doesn't think that. She saw the insecurity in his eyes, the adoration wrapped in his words, the tenderness in his touch. It will matter to him. Their relationship will matter.

When the first night after he returned from tour, they made love...

Jethro made love.

Cooper didn't mind. She didn't hate him. She didn't love him. He was just a man on top of her. A man who is her husband who she knows everything about. And yeah, course she enjoyed the familiar pleasure of it. But that was all.

So, when Cooper tells Jethro everything, it won't be with spite.

It won't be with venom.

She won't be indignant and self-righteous.

She won't scream or rip things.

She won't rage.

Cooper will tell him calmly she doesn't intend to leave him just yet. Not while Daniel is at university. It wouldn't be fair on Daniel. Jethro will have to agree, no it wouldn't be fair on Daniel. She won't tell him about meeting Adrian, the sculptor-carpenter after the treatment, and liking the attention. She won't mention Thomas, her experimental fling before the treatment either. Why hurt Jethro just because he hurt her? It's so unimportant now.

But Cooper will tell him her emotional clock has reset. How it's at zero. How since the treatment all the crazy, poisonous noise scalding her insides has gone.

Cooper is calm.

Cooper is clearheaded.

Cooper is Cooper once more.

In fact, Cooper wonders, is love important at all? Alligators don't love. Spiders don't love. Frogs don't love. They get on in life just fine. Maybe not loving anyone is a simple kind of paradise. Maybe true contentment is to just exist. Just to function. Just to be. No emotion to cloud the day. Sunshine forever.

Yeah.

So Zen.

Cooper initially thought the treatment would be a sweet kind of revenge. It hadn't occurred to her it wouldn't matter.

Still.

Cooper won't be cruel.

She won't be bitter.

She won't be anything.

She'll just be Cooper.

But once Daniel has his qualifications and is ready to face the world on his own, that's when Cooper will go. Cooper's willing to wait. By then they'll have done everything, prepared everything. They'll have planned their financial separation. He'll have his money, she'll have hers. They'll have divorce papers drawn up. Decree nisi and Decree absolute. Sort bank accounts, sort the sale of the house, sort possessions, sort everything.

Methodical.

Clean.

Practical.

Cooper is willing to do that because no matter what Jethro says, no matter how he reacts, no matter how repentant he is, no matter what he does, he cannot alter Cooper's decision one bit.

How can he alter her feelings for him?

She has none.

8 4

HARRIET IS SO absorbed in the adoption booklet she's unaware Eddsy has finished paying for the petrol and is making his way back. Excitement bubbles inside her, makes her dizzy. She flicks from page to page, absorbing everything. She finds out anyone can adopt a child, you don't have to be a heterosexual couple. You don't even have to be a couple. That surprises her. Who knew? She reads you can be any age between 18 and 65 – something which makes her and Eddsy eligible. She reads adopted children can be of any nationality.

Eddsy pushes through the petrol station door, makes his way on to the forecourt. He rips into his chocolate bar, takes a bite. Where did he park? He scans the petrol station, spots his silver Toyota Proace van at Pump No. 4. Oh yes. He sees Harriet, head bent over, reading something.

Harriet can't focus on what she's reading anymore She's overwhelmed. A question pops into her head: When did Eddsy get it? And another: How long has it been in the glove compartment? Since they'd married, their garage business had grown and grown. He'd bought a second garage. Then a third. A fourth. Now they had six. He'd worked harder and harder longer and longer hours.

Six years, six garages.

Six years, zero children.

For years the idea of adoption had played on Harriet's mind. Several times she'd tried to find a way to ask Eddsy. Only one thing stopped her: Eddsy never once hinted at the idea. Her default feelings are that adopting a child would make him feel inadequate. That he'd believe he wasn't man enough to produce his own offspring. Okay, so Harriet had no way to know if that were true but his medical issue had obviously damaged his ego, how could it not? He is such a proud man. She sees the success of the garages in a new way; surrogate children.

Eddsy strolls around a car and approaches his van. He's about to open the van door when he drops his keys. He stoops to pick them up.

Harriet's on the ninth page of the booklet when a noise like dropped keys makes her look up. Suddenly Eddsy is standing by the door. She shoves the booklet back in the glove compartment, clicks it shut.

Harriet quickly rummages around her handbag, tries to pull out a novel she's partway through, but she doesn't get to it in time. Eddsy opens the door.

Six years, zero children.

"Good?" Eddsy says.

Harriet looks at him.

"Huh?"

"What you were reading – good?"

Six years, zero children.

Harriet nods blankly. Eddsy climbs into his seat, starts the engine, pulls away.

Doubt creeps into Harriet's mind. So why has Eddsy said nothing? Perhaps someone shoved the booklet into his hand as he passed by one day. Do they hand out things like that? Harriet doesn't think so. Perhaps she should ask him. Wouldn't it be amazing? Wouldn't it though? Harriet opens her mouth. She almost does.

Almost.

Another thought occurs to her.

What if he says no? What then?

Besides, she's sure Eddsy has his reasons for not mentioning it. Perhaps he's thinking about it but wants to be sure first. And if he's sure he's bound to ask her then, isn't he?

So no, Harriet won't say anything. She doesn't want to pressure him.

What if he never mentions it though? No, stop that. Harriet won't jinx it. She's so excited her lip quivers, has to try hard to hide her excitement.

Eddsy opens the glove compartment, throws the petrol receipt in, frowns for a second as he stares into it, then shuts it, glancing at Harriet. He clears his throat.

"I know what you were reading."

Harriet looks at him.

"What do you mean?"

"I bet I can guess."

Harriet's heart thumps.

"Want to take the bet?"

"What's the prize?" Harriet says.

"If I get it right, I win."

"Win what?"

"A smooch from you."

"And what do I win if you're wrong?"

"A smooch from me."

Heart thumps.

"Okay. What was I reading?"

Heart thumps, heart thumps.

"A Japanese invention."

Harriet frowns.

"What do you mean?"

Eddsy grins.

"Know the Japanese invented the novel?"

IT'S LATE, DARK, cold. Cooper is on one of the twin side by side swings in the blackness of the back garden. Daniel's already back at university, so tomorrow Cooper will tell Jethro everything. All she's been through, all she's done. She's ready now.

She's in a puffer jacket, her hood up. Jethro appears in the doorway, a silhouette against a rectangle of lit kitchen behind him. He's in T-shirt, shorts, hands under his armpits leaning against the doorframe. His breath, visible.

"Hey, what you doing?" Jethro says. He rubs his hands together. "Wow, it's colder than a hater's stare out here."

"I'm thinking about Daniel," Cooper says.

"Daniel?"

"Yeah, you know, our son."

"I mean like why? Why out here in the cold?"

"I'm missing him, now he's gone back."

Jethro's silent in agreement for a moment, then he responds.

"Hold on, let me grab something warm, I'll join you."

A minute later Jethro reappears in a coat, takes a seat on the swing beside Cooper. It's Daniel's swing. The red swing. Cooper's on the blue swing. At night red looks black, blue looks black. Jethro rubs his hands together, takes his tobacco tin out of his coat pocket, pulls out a pre-rolled rollup, lights it.

Cooper gently rocks, staring at the black earth. She's thinking about how Jethro will be after she tells him what she knows. She's almost tempted to tell him tonight, now, this moment. He's so relaxed, so easy in his ways. Tomorrow it's going to be a different story. Let him have one last night of calm. She has no anger. No bitterness. No urgency.

"So," Jethro says, "like did you use the swing a lot while I was away?"

Jethro hears the swish of her puffer as she shrugs.

"Couple times maybe. Wasn't this cold though."

They gently sway together, human pendulums, the earth teetering one way then the other, the fulcrum of the planet at their feet. Jethro slows down and Cooper detects a change, opens her eyes.

Jethro is looking up and she follows the lean tilt of his jaw, face upwards, the shadowy profile angled at the night sky. The stars nip tiny spots so colourlessly white and so brittle it looks like it could crack the sky.

"You know what they used to think?" Jethro says. "They used to think stars were the pinpricks in the floor of heaven letting the light through."

"Yeah? Cool."

Cooper keeps the gentle swinging up. Preparing herself. Tomorrow will be tough on Jethro. But he needs to know she knows what he did to her. What he made her do.

Jethro tries again.

"You know our sun is a star?"

She sighs.

"Yeah Jethro, I know."

"Hey." Jethro touches her swing to slow it. "Cool it a moment."

Cooper catches her feet on the grass. Jethro twists on his seat to face her.

"Like, what's eating you?"

"What do you mean?"

"Coops, I can totally tell your head's not on straight."

Cooper glances up again. The Milky Way, a faint lacy gauze across the sky. Most nights you never see it – too much light pollution. He gazes up, shares her view as though inferring she's as unreachable as the stars tonight.

"You've been like elsewhere since I've been back."

"Yeah?"

He lets out a long slow sigh.

In that familiar sigh Cooper hears the troubled crease of his forehead, the confusion in his eyes, vague worries forming in his head. He has no idea. She realises how much she's absorbed of Jethro's tics from having lived with him. Like classic TV commercials from childhood. Not learned, imbued.

For mash, get... Have a break. Have a... You can be sure of—

"Cooper?"

"Jethro?"

"Something IS cooking inside. What is it?"

Without The Gateway Programme Cooper would have screamed at him again. Just like she never did in the kitchen when he first returned from tour.

She would have.

She would have torn at his face.

She would have.

She would have kicked him in scalding rage.

Yeah she would have.

She would have hammered his chest. She would have taken disgustedly infested words she's never in her life uttered and hurled them at him. She would have crushed him like an insect until he was a smear, a black stain of blood on the grass. She would have wailed, screamed, wailed, raged, wailed. Neighbourhood windows would have illuminated, lanterns bearing witness.

Instead, Cooper is calm, a fascinated observer of herself.

"Nothing's eating me," Cooper says.

"Since I've been back, things've felt different. I don't know whether it's me or what."

Intrigued, Cooper turns to him.

"Yeah?"

"It's like you're keeping back something."

This surprises Cooper. Even though she feels nothing for Jethro she knows everything about him. She knows his story. She knows their history. Yet she can't fathom what she's giving away that makes him think what he thinks.

"How come?"

Jethro kicks the earth, his voice sulky, like Daniel's can be.

"I wish I knew. Just something about you."

Jethro looks at her. He's glad it's just a silhouette of her he sees facing him. It's easier to ask her without seeing her. A tone of voice has greater clarity than the words themselves.

"Tell me you're okay, I'll believe you."

"Yeah, I'm fine."

"Like really?"

"Yeah, really."

In the darkness Jethro can't hear a lie. The words she says are without sharp edges. An untroubled voice. Cooper's telling the truth. He lets out a held breath.

"So, like why'd you think something's bothering me?" Cooper says.

"I guess I've been away too long. I've never been away from you, like, three months before. Crazy times, just crazy times. Stuff's going around in my head."

"The recording deal?"

"The tour. The deal. Being away from you so long. Means a lot of changes for us. I mean, what if we hit it big?"

"Then you hit it big."

"It's kind of scary."

"Why?"

Jethro pulls on his rollup, shoves his hands between his knees.

"I've been waiting my life for something like this. But know what? I never thought I'd be like out of my comfort zone. First night onstage before Sabre Light came on, thousands of pairs of eyes staring at us. I was totally unprepared. The whole crew were like jelly."

"Well, I've seen YouTube. You performed great. Your songs sound great. You all did great."

"Yeah, I guess. We practised years not till we got it right, but till we couldn't go wrong."

Cooper knows he hasn't revealed a hint of what he's done to her. For some reason infidelity doesn't stain his skin, doesn't darken his tongue, doesn't bleed from him.

Jethro finishes the roll up.

Hey, let's grab some Zees.

*

An hour later Cooper is drifting off to sleep, barely aware she's leaving Jethro behind on the surface of the bed. Sleep. That great hulking cruise liner half immersed into the mattress has launched. As Cooper leaves the last remnants of consciousness behind, she feels Jethro lean over her, whisper into her ear, tastes the mint of his breath. She won't remember this.

"Cooper Hall I... never meant to leave you behind. You're like totally my whole world."

His way of apologising? Is that what this is? What does it matter now? It's all too late.

Cooper responds to him, answers him. What comes from her mouth is barely a moan deep in her throat. She won't remember this. No. Not this moment. Not any of it. She answers anyway.

Yeah? You're not my whole world either.

JETHRO WAITS FOR Cooper to fall asleep. Her hair's no longer buzz-cut short, her clothes more feminine. She wears a touch of colour now. Reds. Yellows. Pinks. All subtle changes since his absence. He slides off the bed, careful not to wake her, goes downstairs with his phone. He calls, his voice a low, intimate whisper.

"Yeah. She's asleep. You good? Yeah great. It's all cool. Nah, she doesn't know. I thought tonight she guessed, but nah. I can't wait to see you again tomorrow. Yeah? You too. Love you. Can't wait. Night."

Jethro hangs up. Returns to bed.

THE SUE BAXTER PODCAST
DR STEWART-WAY
Post treatment, your best friend would have no more emotional significance to you than, say, a character from a TV soap, Sue.
SUE BAXTER
Goodness.
DR STEWART-WAY
You'd still know everything about her because of course your brain has built a version of Charlotte and therefore your knowledge of her would remain intact. However your feelings toward her would be entirely neutral, certainly nothing beyond basic empathy.
SUE BAXTER
Forgive me Dr Stewart-Way but that sounds horrific. Charlotte's my best friend.
DR STEWART-WAY
Agreed, but what if your treatment's for someone who's harmful to you?
SUE BAXTER
Such as?
DR STEWART-WAY
If you have an abusive partner, perhaps. We receive countless cases of mistreated partners – sadly usually wives and girlfriends – where the victim continues to return to their ceaselessly repentant partner in the desperate hope they'll change. Unfortunately it usually ends with another barrage of physical or mental abuse and, tragically, the cycle repeats. With

The Gateway Programme it's possible for the victim to permanently leave the relationship the same day after the final treatment. They're no longer trapped in an endless forgive-and-return behavioural cycle.

SUE BAXTER

Surely their partners turn their aggression towards you and Gateway House?

DR STEWART-WAY

So far not, since the abusive partners also receive the benefit of treatment once they realise the finality of the situation.

SUE BAXTER

Tell us the process a patient goes through. What's it like to have treatment?

DR STEWART-WAY

When a patient first comes in we meticulously explain everything about The Gateway Programme. They'll usually go away afterwards to digest the information. Some however want to book the second appointment straight away. Some we never see again.

SUE BAXTER

What happens during the second appointment?

DR STEWART-WAY

We go through a detailed questionnaire with the patient. By then we'll have their medical records. We also try to explore anything relevant in the patient's background. We need to ensure The Gateway Programme is appropriate for them. If approved, we'll schedule an fMRI scan.

SUE BAXTER

I believe hypnosis is part of the brain scanning process?

DR STEWART-WAY

Indeed, though hypnotism is an often misunderstood term Sue. Many believe if you're hypnotised, you lose control of your body. Actually that's not true. Hypnosis is a highly focused act of concentration, rather like reading a book so absorbing you become unaware of your environment. If you're on a train, perhaps you'll miss your stop. In fact there's an incredible true story of a businessman who was reading a novel by L. Ron Hubbard at an airport waiting for his flight to be called. Not many people know Hubbard was a bestselling science fiction author. The novel saved the businessman's life. Would you like to hear the story?

SUE BAXTER

I'm intrigued. Do tell.

DR STEWART-WAY

Well, the businessman found the novel he was reading so absorbing he didn't hear the repeated announcements calling him by name and missed his flight. Fortunately he was able to catch the next flight out but when he arrived home he found his family gathered inside, many crying and white faced, utterly shocked to see him. It's then he discovered his original flight had crashed. Well, the businessman's absorption in the novel at the time his flight was called was so intense he didn't hear the call. That is a perfect example of hypnosis.

SUE BAXTER

(Laughs)

I'd like to know the name of that novel.

DR STEWART-WAY

(Laughs)

I'm afraid I don't know, but I'm sure it's easy to find out. With our patients, we place them in a relaxed, dimmed environment with perhaps the sound of the sea or forest or something else, whatever their preference. We use a certified psychologist and hypnotherapist on-site. Once the patient is sufficiently relaxed, we introduce a precise microdose of psychotropic substances into their bloodstream.

SUE BAXTER

Psychotropic substances? Aren't they Class A drugs?

DR STEWART-WAY

That's correct.

SUE BAXTER
Surely that's illegal. How on earth do you get away with it?

IT'S SATURDAY. The day Cooper intends to tell Jethro the truth. But Jethro has a surprise for Cooper himself. He tells her at breakfast.

"We're doing something different tonight."

"What do you mean?" Cooper says.

"I want you beautified."

Cooper looks at him.

"Why?"

"Because tonight I want to go crazy and dine out with my beautiful wife."

Cooper thinks maybe that's a good thing. Maybe telling him in a public place he won't be so unpredictable.

"Table's booked for six thirty."

"For real?"

"Yeah totally, for real."

Later, she starts to get ready, puts her smart black cargos on.

"What," Jethro says, "about one of your evening gowns?"

"I haven't got any evening gowns."

"You've got that black number. You know the one. Wore it to your friend's 80th." Jethro grins. "You looked so hot you totally boiled water."

"You want me to wear that?"

"Like seriously, all the men went googa."

"Yeah, and all the wives drew claws."

He laughs.

"I just want to show off my beautiful wife. Tonight's special."

"You know I don't wear dresses."

A shadow of disappointment casts over his eyes. "Well, find something nice. Car's here in forty-five minutes."

"What car?"

"The one I ordered."

"But you said we're booked for six thirty."

"Totally."

"That's ages. Where're we going?"

Jethro's gives her a deliberately enigmatic smirk, "Somewhere nice man, somewhere nice," and leaves the room.

Cooper keeps the cargos on, tries on various tops, not really liking the overall effect. Then she spots the black dress hanging alone at the back of the wardrobe, laundry plastic covering it. She considers it for a second, takes the plastic off, slips into it. The dress rests light and insubstantial against her skin, held only by thin straps over the shoulder. It fits, but it makes her feel insecure and bare. She catches herself in the mirror and blinks in surprise at her reflection.

Later, Cooper comes down the stairs in the dress. She's wearing Oxford Allure red lipstick, short hair gelled back, funky yet feminine, a mushroom-coloured chiffon wrap, a string of her grandmother's small, gently aged golden pearls around her neck and a pair of thin strappy heels. She feels overdressed and overexposed, vulnerable, yet it's the first time in years she also somehow feels liberated from her own – what? – confinement? Is that what it is? She likes the feeling, enjoying the heady effect like the first blush of alcohol. Gone are the aggressive cargos, the informal T-shirt, the bovver boots. This is her first outing feeling like this in forever and it scares yet thrills her.

Jethro gazes up at her as she descends the stairs. His eyes widen.

Cooper feels self-conscious.

"Is it too much?"

"Oh man, oh wow. Forget dinner. Let's go upstairs. I'll cancel the car."

Cooper laughs. She feels nothing for Jethro, yet once more, she enjoys the compliment.

The second surprise comes when the doorbell rings. Jethro calls down from upstairs.

"That'll be the car."

Cooper answers.

A man in an immaculate uniform stands on the doorstep, a pristine grey cap in his hand, buttons up the side of his jacket.

"Good evening, Mrs Hall. My name is Ross. Your car is waiting."

"You're the taxi? You look like a chauffeur."

Ross angles his shoulders to reveal a gleaming black Rolls Royce sitting on the curb.

Coopers mouth drops open.

"No way."

Jethro appears beside Cooper beaming, fixing his cufflinks. The aroma of Homme around him, stirring nothing in her. Jethro's in a black dinner jacket, crisp open-necked white shirt, long hair combed and draped behind him. Even his bolero hat is smarter than his usual everyday one.

"What's going on?" Cooper says.

"Shush. Let's follow the man."

Jethro takes her arm and they leave. A neighbour from across the road stands in a window, silently calls to someone behind them through the mime of glass. Another pedestrian walking a dog stops to look. Ross opens the car door for Cooper, she climbs in. Jethro goes around the other side, opens the door for himself, whistling.

Inside, the seats are creamy soft, the aroma of expensive leather filling the space. Cooper sinks into the seat as though sinking into a moist doughnut. The chauffeur climbs into his seat and the Rolls purrs to life.

The journey is like riding on marshmallows it's so smooth and quiet. The windows are gently tinted so buildings outside take on a soft glossy sheen. She turns to Jethro.

"What's with all this?"

Ross clears his throat.

"If you'll allow me, Mr Hall?"

"Yeah, carry on, spill the beans man."

Ross tells her it's a Rolls Royce Phantom. He asks if she'd like the provenance of the car.

Course.

Ross tells them about the politicians, heads of state, famous celebrities, actors, singers, Nobel prize winners, writers, artists who sat in the very seat they're sitting in. As he talks Cooper becomes aware they're heading into central London. Cooper watches as they pass the Edgware Road flyover, Madame Tussauds, Marble Arch, Oxford Street, Selfridges and Tottenham Court Road's Centre Point building. They're heading towards Covent Garden. She interrupts Ross, asks where they're going. Ross remains politely silent. Jethro answers with an enigmatic grin.

So Cooper asks again. And again. And after too many times Jethro finally caves in.

"All right, I'll give you something. You noticed the number plate of the Rolls?"

"No. Why?"

"Ah."

"What do you mean ah?"

"AH!"

"Stop ahhing and tell me what you mean."

Jethro smiles.

"If you saw the number plate you'd know where we're going."

"Stop the car. I want to see the number plate."

"We're almost there."

"Where?"

"You'll see."

Cooper runs through possible answers in her head. Did she miss something? An anniversary or something? A special birthday? Anything? Nothing, absolutely nothing comes to mind. It must be something to do with The Gateway Programme wiping some memory after all. She'll have to tell them at Gateway House.

That is the second surprise.

The third surprise is the destination. Not just any destination. They pull down a lane and stop outside—

THE SAVOY HOTEL.

Cooper can't believe it.

A doorkeeper in a top hat and long blue coat stands at the entrance. He steps up to the door, opens it and assists Cooper out.

"Am I dreaming this?"

Jethro laughs. The doorkeeper laughs. Ross laughs. They've seen this reaction so many times.

Cooper turns and looks at the number plate. It says S8 VOY, the hotel's own courtesy Rolls.

"Did you notice?" Jethro says.

"No. Notice what?"

"Like, we totally drove down the entrance in the right-hand lane."

"Oh yeah. How come?"

The doorkeeper steps forward.

"If you'll allow me, Mr Hall?"

"Yeah, go ahead."

"Wait," Cooper says looking at Jethro. He knows your name?"

"We knew you were coming, Mrs Hall," the doorkeeper says.

I'm in an alternate universe. I must be.

Everyone laughs.

The doorkeeper coughs into a grey gloved hand. A cloud of breath leaves his mouth.

"Regarding driving on the right hand side of the road, Mrs Hall, it's because of this building here on your left."

Both Cooper and Jethro turn and look. Above the doors in gold and red it says Savoy Theatre.

The doorkeeper continues.

"You see, the theatre was here before the hotel was built."

"I don't get it. What's the connection with driving on the right hand side?"

"Well, it was so hansom cabs could alight theatregoers in front of the entrance. The tradition is now part of British law."

Cooper turns to Jethro. His eyes glinting with pride, watching her bewilderment with amusement. Infidelity. Really. It doesn't stain his skin.

"Would you like to know more?" the doorkeeper says.

"Yeah, okay."

He continues his well-rehearsed speech.

"Notable guests to the hotel include Thomas Dylan, Judy Garland, The Beatles, Marlene Dietrich, Charlie Chaplin and his wife Oona, Alfred Hitchcock, Ingrid Bergman. Fred Astaire danced on the roof of the Savoy back when we had a roof garden. Monet painted more than 100 views of Waterloo Bridge from his room here. Marilyn Monroe and Laurence Olivier had cocktails here. More recent celebrities include Gordon Ramsay and, in fact, his new restaurant opened here recently. Also, Lily Allen, who had her hen party here, Stephen Fry, Taylor Swift, Rhianna, and even Sabre Light."

Cooper glances at Jethro at the mention of the band, wondering if that was a deliberate name drop.

"Also, as I'm sure you'll discover, Mrs Hall, some of the hotel's most iconic guests have cocktails named after them. For instance one can order a Frank Sinatra and a Coco Chanel. Coco's cocktail arrives with the scent of Chanel No. 5. And if you happen to be hosting a dinner party for thirteen, the fourteenth place setting will always be our famous cat."

Cooper stares at the doorman.

"You're kidding. The Savoy has a cat?"

"Indeed we do, Mrs Hall. Kaspar the Cat. It's a sculpture by artist Basil Ionides, complete with full place setting and a napkin around his neck. But unless he's dining, you'll find him perched on his own pedestal in reception ready to greet you."

Cooper regards him playfully.

"So, what does Kasper like to eat? Whiskas?"

The doorkeeper laughs.

"I believe he's partial to Norwegian smoked salmon, Mrs Hall."

"Yeah, figures. And drink?"

"He, of course, enjoys our finest Somerset full-cream milk."

The doorkeeper opens the door and they step through into an envelope of cushioned warmth.

Cooper stands inside in awe. Everything is grand yet surprisingly homey. She admires the high ornate ceilings, the chessboard floor, the polished wall panelling, the huge black-and-white columns, the deco hanging lights, the soft lighting. She glances around, sees guests relaxed in comfortable seating in conversation pools with rugs, sofas, coffee tables, lamps. Some are reading, others quietly conversing, all smiling, sipping something. Some look of obvious wealth. Others wear jeans and casual wear. All look happy and relaxed.

Jethro takes her hand and leads her to one of the hotel's restaurants, Simpson's In The Strand. A Maître d'hotel greets them, leads them to their table and they're seated. Immediately a waiter returns with a bottle of champagne in its own ice bucket with glasses. The whole thing is a heady, disorientating experience. Cooper realises there are four glasses.

"What's going on?"

"Ah."

"What do you mean ah?"

"AH!"

"Stop ahhing and tell me what's going on."

That is her third surprise.

Her fourth surprise is when Jethro looks over Cooper's shoulder with a smile of recognition and stands up. Cooper twists in her seat to see who he's looking at.

Then Cooper sees her.

Her.

HER.

A svelte woman in a flowing maroon evening gown approaches, glossy brunette hair cascading down her shoulders.

It's that woman.

Her.

Dizzy Gillespie.

Homme.

Soft moans, soft moans.

Soft kisses, soft kisses.

Her.

God, how young she is. Not much more than a girl. No more than nineteen. But no emotions rise in Cooper, not anger, not pain. There are no tears. The only thing that rises is confusion. Why would Jethro do this to her? Why would he introduce his mistress like this?

That is her fourth surprise.

The fifth surprise comes when Cooper sees a slender young man emerge from behind the girl.

Cooper's mouth drops open a second time and this time she stands up.

Daniel.

He's in a dinner jacket and trousers identical to Jethro's. They are both grinning, looking at Cooper.

"Hey, mum."

Cooper turns, looks at Jethro, looks back at Daniel.

"What is this?" Cooper says. "Why aren't you at university?"

"Wow mum, you look like, totally amazing."

Cooper looks at Daniel. Stares at the girl. Looks at Jethro.

"Will someone PLEASE tell me what's going on?"

The girl steps forward, smiling, holding her hand out.

"It's a pleasure to meet you, Mrs Hall. Her voice is articulate, educated."

"Mum, this is Araminta."

Cooper takes her hand, distractedly shakes it, lets it drop. Araminta is holding a small gift-wrapped parcel in matt red paper with a silk ribbon bow. She offers it to Cooper. Cooper looks at her.

"This is for me?"

"I made it myself."

"What is it?"

"You'll have to open it to find out."

That is the fifth surprise.

The sixth surprise, the biggest surprise, comes when Cooper turns back to Jethro and the surprise occurs within Cooper's own head. Jethro's smile couldn't be wider. He looks tall, trim, handsome, beaming.

Turns back to Daniel.

Tall.

Trim.

Handsome.

Beaming.

Looks at Jethro, the set of his jaw, the grey of his eyes, the breadth of his wide smile.

Looks at Daniel, the set of his jaw, the grey of his eyes, the breadth of his wide smile.

She looks down at Daniel's hand. He's clasping Araminta's hand.

Daniel and Araminta.

Cooper sees it now. Sees it. It's so obvious. So clear, oh god so clear.

No.

Oh no.

No.

She sees it. Daniel is a copy of Jethro. Of course. A boy. No. Not a boy. Not a boy any more, Daniel is a man now, yeah a young man.

Cooper knows.

No.

Like a car crash it hits her she knows.

No no.

Like almost drowning in a hot bath she knows.

No no no.

Like having a meltdown in a motorway service stop she knows.

No no no god no.

The truth slams into her. She is beyond shock. Beyond surprise. With terrible horrific comprehension, she knows.

No. Oh god. No. No. No. Please no.

It wasn't Jethro she'd glimpsed in their bed with that woman that girl this Araminta that day.

Not Jethro.

It was Daniel.

HARRIET IS IN bed. Eddsy is asleep beside her. Harriet can't though. She tries to, but the excitement of finding the adoption booklet yesterday in Eddsy's glove compartment keeps her awake.

Thoughts continue to race through her head. When exactly did Eddsy get the booklet? How long has he been thinking about adopting? IS he thinking about adopting? Why hasn't he told her? Has he told anyone else? It's the same questions she's been asking herself all last night and all day today.

"Wife?"

Eddsy's voice is heavy through the mattress and, through her ear pressed to the pillow, she hears the springs sing in sympathy. She lifts her head.

"Husband?"

"You're wide awake."

How does he know that? How can he tell?

"So?"

"Don't need to worry about Cooper anymore."

"I'm not."

Harriet's response comes too quickly, before she has time to think. So quick it can only be the truth.

Eddsy turns over.

"So, why you not sleeping?"

Damn it. She should have agreed with him.

"How could you tell?"

"Just could. So?"

"I am a bit worried actually." It's the only lie Harriet can think to tell.

"Okay?"

"I know Cooper's in a good place now but I'm her sister. I can't help it."

Eddsy furrows his brow in the dark. Something doesn't fit. Harriet's not telling him the truth this time. He reaches over, places a hand on Harriet's face.

She feels the cushion of it. Faintly of motor oil, faintly of grease, faintly of petrol, strongly of shower gel. Her face, pressed between two cushions, one the warmth of his hand. It makes her want to cry suddenly. Dad used to do that. Press his palms to her face at bedtime, the warmth, gentle evidence of his love, his support, just being there, being a father. Eddsy is doing that right now.

Being a father to her.

But Harriet doesn't cry at the familiar gesture. No. She holds back.

At that moment, for some reason he can't fathom, Eddsy wants to tell Harriet about his visit to Barnardo's. Wants to tell her about meeting with Simone Grey. Wants to tell her about the amazing things she had to say. Wants to tell her about the adoption booklet in his glove compartment he keeps forgetting to get rid of. He almost feels the words lightly surface to his lips.

"Actually," Harriet says, "I was just thinking about Cooper and Jethro at The Savoy. They must be loving it, all that glitz. Must be amazing."

Ah. Eddsy thinks about it. Of course. That must be it. It's not worry. It's vicarious excitement and curiosity for her sister.

"Yeah. Guess so."

So Eddsy doesn't say anything more. Doesn't say what almost steamed from his lips.

And Harriet doesn't tell him she found the adoption booklet.

And they fall together into frustrated, dreamless sleeps.

THE SUE BAXTER PODCAST
DR STEWART-WAY
Yes, you're right Sue, the pharmaceuticals we use on our patients are considered Class A illegal drugs. However, back in 2020, UK regulators allowed the use of DMT – dimethyltriptamine – in official trials to treat depression. It opened the way for other such trials.

SUE BAXTER
Surely that can't be safe?

DR STEWART-WAY
For drug users, that's right. However, we are doctors. And because we microdose – which has long been acknowledged as a legitimate medical treatment for mood enhancement – the patient is hardly aware of the effect. Plus it's only ever performed once. The procedure is completely safe.

SUE BAXTER
What's in the doses?

DR STEWART-WAY
Mescaline and phencyclidine. Hallucinogenic compounds. It's to carry out a practice called narcosynthesis – it aids hypnotic trances. Many patients aren't susceptible to deep hypnosis. Microdosing guarantees it, especially as it is auto injected in the neck, close to the brain. It's fast acting and has to be. It lasts only minutes.

SUE BAXTER
You're hypnotising your patients. Why?

DR STEWART-WAY

So a hypnotherapist can guide a patient to cognitively evoke the person they wish to have emotionally deleted. It's how we monitor increases in blood flow and glucose levels in specific areas of the brain from an fMRI scan.

SUE BAXTER

So you're locating the avatar?

DR STEWART-WAY

That's right Sue. In the general vicinity.

SUE BAXTER

Wait. The general vicinity? That sounds a bit… well, unspecific. You said earlier your work was precise, down to singular neural route levels. Which is it?

COOPER'S BEEN IN the Savoy's restaurant twenty minutes with Jethro and Daniel and Araminta, talking, chatting, clinking champagne glasses and marvelling at the plush experience while enjoying the ambience of their intimate circle.

As they talk, as Cooper tries to smile, tries to enjoy herself, tries not to keep staring at Araminta, she tries tries TRIES to feel love for Jethro, tries to force it out of herself. She covers his slender hand with hers, squeezes it, rubs his arm with a semblance of affection. But when she's presented with the Savoy Bill of Fare menu, the words scramble before her eyes like black grit. Her mind her mind her mind keeps flitting away. No one notices. Or if they do they think it's the shock of where Cooper is. After all, they all knew about the Savoy. For Cooper it was a complete surprise.

Plates arrives.

For Cooper it's clear crab broth. On the table is also smoked haddock omelette, potted rabbit and pea and leek tart. For the main course she has roast lamp rump while the others tuck into pan-fried duck breast, roast Scottish lobster and salt baked whole sea bass, all with various steaming vegetable side orders.

Cooper eats the lamb, tries to enjoy the aromas, the textures, the complex arrangement of flavours tinting her mouth, but she can't. They sample each other's plates, hunt with forks. All are delicious but once more Cooper's taste buds barely register.

As they eat, Jethro glances at Cooper repeatedly, such love in his eyes, such huge, overwhelming love.

"Coops, you've like barely said a word," Jethro says finally.

"Yeah. Can't believe any of this."

Glances at Daniel.

"Seeing you all dressed up."

Looks at Araminta.

"Meeting Araminta."

Cooper takes in the whole restaurant, expressing with her hands, slightly tipsy.

"The Savoy. The Rolls. Champagne. It's all a bit mad."

"Yeah, crazy right?"

They laugh.

They believe her. But inside Cooper's head she's thinking how she can't have got it so wrong, so monumentally wrong. She can't have. But she has. Monumentally wrong. So so so so monumentally wrong.

She knows Daniel and Araminta are holding hands under the table. They hunt out each other's between courses, sending lovesick glances, secret smiles.

Araminta, who has long brunette hair cascading down her shoulders, who looks so young, sounds so educated, is so obviously intelligent, so attractive.

Daniel, who keeps attentively sweeping silken strands of hair away from Araminta's mouth when she talks, smiling, smiling, happy.

And Jethro. Happy, tipsy, beautiful Jethro.

Cooper is in the centre of it all, feeling as incongruous as an oily nut and bolt on this delicate watercolour of the evening.

Cooper tries to imagine Daniel in their bed with Araminta but can't. She sees Jethro no matter what. Even though she knows the truth she can't delete the image. Her brain has hard-wired the information, soldered it in permanently.

Cooper turns to Daniel and Araminta, suddenly wanting to verify something for sure.

"How long you guys been dating?"

Daniel and Araminta glance at each other.

"It's been like a while," Daniel says.

"How long?"

He shrugs, looks at Araminta.

"Dunno. Six months maybe."

"Actually, Mrs Hall, it's five months, four days, seven hours and…" Araminta checks her sparkling dress-watch, "twenty-four minutes and sixteen seconds." Daniel looks at Araminta, surprised.

"Yeah? Is that like true?"

Araminta laughs, pokes him in the ribs.

"Hah! Got you."

Daniel makes a sour pout.

"Awh, I love it when he pouts like that, Mr and Mrs Hall. It's so sweet. I bet he did it when he was little."

They insist Araminta calls them by their first names.

"Man, he did it all the time," Jethro says. "He was a furious little cub."

"Will you guys, like, cut it out?" Daniel says.

No one says anything, pursed lips to dam the laughter.

"I wasn't like that. Mum, back me up here."

"All I know is you used to take it out on Theo," Cooper says.

Araminta raises an eyebrow.

"Theo?"

"Yeah mum, don't."

"Theo was his teddy bear. When he was frustrated, he'd throw Theo out the cot. But every night he'd fall asleep with Theo tucked tight in his arms."

"Oh my goodness he had a teddy bear! Awww, that's so sweet."

Everybody looks at Daniel whose cheeks braise with heat. They burst out laughing.

Araminta pokes him again.

"Oh sweetie, you're soooo easy to tease."

Cooper tries to get tactfully back on track.

"So, you met at university?"

They both speak.

"In Professor Jameson's class."

Daniel and Araminta look at each other at their unison reply, giggle like children, tipsy on love and champagne.

Cooper turns to Jethro.

"You knew about Araminta?"

Jethro picks up his champagne glass, smacks his lips after sipping.

"A couple days. The little tyke's been totally keeping this treasure from us. Big surprise, right?"

"I had no idea you were seeing someone, Daniel."

Daniel turns to Araminta, admiration in his eyes.

"Mum, like I completely can't believe it myself. It's totally sick."

Araminta scrunches her face into a cute smile.

Cooper studies Daniel's expression. So like Jethro. That love. Shining out. Misty grey like coastal fog. Cooper turns to Jethro. Love. Shining out. Eyes, misty grey like…

No.

No.

Just grey.

Dessert arrives and Cooper spoons a mouthful of triple chocolate mousse. It's light and sweet with a bitter undercurrent of dark chocolate. Once more her taste buds don't register. She looks at Jethro and Daniel. Daniel and Jethro. Jethro and Daniel. Look closely, look carefully, there are differences. Daniel has the wiriness of a teenager, not the dense solidity of a man who though slender, is approaching forty. Why didn't she see that? Also their hair's different. They both have dark hair but Jethro's has fine grey strands. Also his hair is far longer than Daniel's. Why hadn't she registered that too?

The way they move has subtle differences too. Jethro's movements are fluid, musical. Daniel's movements have some of the same fluidity, but it also has elements of inexperienced boyhood, as though still not quite used to his height. The gazelle has grown too quickly, too fresh born into adulthood.

If Cooper'd only opened the bedroom door that bit wider, despite embarrassingly finding her son in bed with a girl, she'd have known the truth. She'd have known the truth and with it, relief. There'd have been red faces and Cooper would've reprimanded Daniel's use of their bed, but none of what followed would have happened.

All that torment.

The car crash.

All that destruction.

Thoughts of suicide.

The whole breakdown.

Sleeping with another man... God. Cooper really did that. The guilt inside Cooper drills down deeper.

Then, of course, The Gateway Programme and the cleansing of everything.

Cooper turns to Araminta.

"I expect you've seen our home?"

Araminta and Daniel speak simultaneously. She says yes he says no.

Cooper and Jethro look at each other, smile. Araminta turns to Daniel with a scrunch of her eyebrows. Daniel squirms, talks when he sees all attention on him.

"Well... yeah okay but like only once... We didn't stay long... You guys weren't home... Araminta, like wanted to see where I lived..." His cheeks are furnace red.

"A Wednesday, right?" Cooper says.

Daniel and Araminta look surprised, look at Cooper.

"I didn't see you, mum."

There it is. Proof. Absolute proof.

"I popped back to the house to get something. I thought I heard... well music from your bedroom, that's all."

"I like thought I totally checked out your studio."

Cooper ignores Daniel's comment.

"I called out but you didn't hear me so I went on to my next job." Cooper wonders if she's explaining too much.

"So, like, did you come upstairs?"

"I didn't have time."

Cooper sees a flicker of relief on Daniel's face, knowing what he's thinking. Cooper sees every flicker, every expression, every hand gesture Daniel makes. Every movement is a dictionary index to a page of his personality. She sees it so blindingly, so brightly it surprises her no one else ever does.

She thinks back to Daniel as a child, spending his afternoons on the swing in the garden, the shy little, sweet little, awkward little, quiet little boy. But Daniel isn't nine anymore. Daniel is nineteen now. Daniel is at university now. Daniel is a man now, he's a man.

"Mum?"

"Yeah?"

"You're like totally staring me out."

"I'm admiring you all dressed up. You're so handsome."

Araminta pokes him playfully.

"My handsome gentleman."

IF Cooper hadn't finished early that day.

IF Daniel hadn't taken Araminta into their bedroom.

IF he hadn't played Jethro's Dizzy Gillespie records.

IF he hadn't worn Jethro's aftershave.

IF there hadn't been soft moans, soft moans.

Or even having done all that…

IF Cooper had stepped into the bedroom.

IF she'd never heard of The Gateway Programme.

IF Daniel had never met Araminta.

IF they'd never had a son…

Soon they're downing dark coffees and sampling chocolate mints. Cooper watches everyone, all so happy, yet she's utterly numb. She tastes the coffee, separated from it, numb. Puts a mint into her mouth, doesn't taste the mint, the chocolate, numb. She tastes nothing, experiences nothing.

So when Jethro looks at her with such love in his eyes, such love such love cascading out, a brook, a stream, a tumbling frothy waterfall of love.

And whispers all this is crazy right?

And looks at her for approval and validation with his wide, loving eyes.

And squeezes her knee under the table.

Cooper only nods. That's all she can do. Because all she feels is.

Numb.

THE SUE BAXTER PODCAST
DR STEWART-WAY
Yes Sue, our work is precise. However, we use the fMRI to locate an avatar in the brain rather like the way one would use a finderscope.
SUE BAXTER
A finderscope? Isn't that something you'd get on a telescope?
DR STEWART-WAY
Indeed. On most high-powered telescopes you'll often find two scopes, the telescope itself and a second smaller eyepiece connected to the telescope called a finderscope. The finderscope has a wide field of view and helps aim the telescope at the general area a star sits in. Using the fMRI is rather like using a finderscope. It shows us the area of brain we need to focus our attention on.
SUE BAXTER
Then what happens?
DR STEWART-WAY
Well, the fMRI allows us to build up a blueprint of the patient's brain. These include cubed grid references rather like on an ordinance survey map. These three dimensional grid references are called voxels. From there we pattern classify—
SUE BAXTER
(Laughing)
Stop STOP! I'm afraid you're blinding us with science.
DR STEWART-WAY
(Laughs)

Forgive me I do rather become involved in the technical aspects of the work.

SUE BAXTER

I think we get the gist. Basically you find out where the avatar is and I assume you home in on one of these mapped grid references with something more precise?

DR STEWART-WAY

That's correct.

SUE BAXTER

So, tell us how you zap the brain cells of the avatar?

DR STEWART-WAY

Actually Sue, we don't zap brain cells. If we did you'd become aware of huge gaps in your memory. You would be conscious of this vacuum and that alone could have consequential effects on related memories. I'll try to explain what I mean by way of an example. In the '70s Christopher Reeve Superman film, there's a scene where Superman saves Lois Lane from plunging to her death by swooping in and catching her. He says to her something like don't worry miss, I've got you. She looks down and says you've got me, but who's got you? The line makes me laugh every time. Well, memories can't exist in isolation the way Superman's flying abilities can. Memories are scaffolding. Each memory supports another and is itself supported by another. Removing even a minute amount of scaffolding would compromise the infrastructure and could create a house of cards effect where huge swathes of memories cave in. We have to respect the integrity of the structure.

SUE BAXTER

So what do you do?

DR STEWART-WAY

Let's refer to your friend Charlotte. You want your feelings for her deleted in this hypothetical scenario. We know the avatar you built of her and your feelings towards her are in separate locations of your brain. Earlier I mentioned the amygdala is an area of brain which gives meaning to your feelings, a sort of junction box between memories and emotions. We know therefore whenever you think of Charlotte, precise neural pathways between Charlotte's avatar and the amygdala increase in activity.

SUE BAXTER

So you locate these routes?

DR STEWART-WAY

We do, and select a portion of it for priming by applying a fluorescing chemical marker. This attaches to single neural pathways. It's a little like applying dye to a specimen to see it better. After that, we do something most people find even more shocking than using psychotropic substances.

SUE BAXTER

Oh? What's that?

DR STEWART-WAY

We inject a virus into the brain.

THERE IS, OF course, one last surprise for Cooper.

It's after the evening is over. Jethro stops at the Savoy Hotel reception desk. He asks the concierge for his room key.

"Of course, Mr Hall."

Cooper looks at him.

"For real?"

Jethro winks.

They all go up and stop at a door. The plaque on the door states The Savoy Suite. They go in. Cooper is utterly dazed. It has an amazing view of the River Thames and Waterloo Bridge. They stand by the window all in a line and look out. They point out Big Ben, the London Eye, Hungerford Bridge, Waterloo Bridge, the Houses of Parliament, cranes with spotlights dotted around the city, all sparkling with city lights. The other way is St Pauls, the Shard, that funny Spongebob shaped tower, the Gherkin. From their window London looks a bit toytown, a bit glittery, a bit unreal.

Next they wander around the suite saying it's amazing mum, wow isn't it special. Yeah, totally crazy.

The suite is huge. A sofa room with widescreen TV above a fireplace, a separate dining space. Mirrors are everywhere. There's a luxury shower, and the bedroom is stunning. Cooper wanders around in silent awe. She touches everything lightly, as though confirming reality. Jethro organised this whole evening for her?

They find a coffee machine, crisps and chocolates, Toblerone and Snickers in the bar stacked with full-sized alcoholic bottles. Araminta finds a Beauty & Fitness folder, perches on the sofa, learns there's a swimming pool in the building, treatment rooms, a fitness suite, a steam room and sauna. Gosh she says, you can have all sorts of pamperings; facials, aromatherapy, massage. I'm so jealous.

Jethro emerges from the bedroom looking pleased with himself.

"Hey, look what I've just found me."

He pulls out slippers from a Savoy drawstring pouch and grins.

"Crazy, right?"

Soon Daniel and Araminta are gone and Cooper and Jethro are alone.

They are alone.

They have a suite and Cooper can't believe it all. They have a suite at The Savoy Hotel. Jethro has changed out of his dinner jacket and trousers, sits against the headboard in T-shirt and Flintstone boxers, gazes out at the Christmas tree colours of London through open curtains. Cooper stares at herself in the bathroom. Stares at the woman in the mirror. Wipes her Oxford Allure lipstick off. Cleanses her face.

Soon Cooper's finished and in pyjamas – Jethro had thoughtfully packed an overnight case for her. She emerges.

"Now this is what I'm talking about," Jethro says staring out at London. "Crazy, right?" He turns, looks at Cooper.

He scans her all over, grins.

"But know what? Nothing beats the sight of my wife in pyjamas. For real."

She laughs.

"Shut up."

Oh Jethro she doesn't say. If only she could turn everything back she doesn't say.

Cooper slips between the sheets beside Jethro. The bed is firm and soft. Nothing like fresh sheets. Jethro switches the bedside light off, the ceiling lit only from the dapple of city lights and undulating watery daubs. Cooper rests against the headboard, both sharing the view.

On the Thames, lit barges glide elegantly over the black water. Listen carefully and the vague buzz of a city comes through the double-glazed windows. They watch a silent star of light from a distant helicopter slide over the horizon in a straight line.

"It doesn't look real, does it?" Jethro says. "This is what I'm talking about." He turns at Cooper looking contented, buzzy with champagne.

"You happy?"

No.

"Yeah, course."

"A surprise, right? I totally had to keep this one under my bolero hat. We kept it good and secret, Daniel and me. It was worth it to see your face. Oh man."

"Must've set you back a bit," Cooper says.

"What the heck? I haven't seen my woman in months. We needed some serious make up time."

Cooper wants to cry. Wants to. Look what he's done for her. She faces Jethro, cheeks dry. There's nothing to cry for. No heartache. Jethro looks so pleased with himself, so happy.

"How long you been planning this?" Cooper says.

"Not long. I knew it had to be a like completely cool surprise for you. Then when Daniel asked if he could bring someone and I heard about Araminta, figured it'd be a cool way for us to meet her and to completely overwhelm you all in one."

"Won't they get in trouble with the university?"

"Nah. They don't start back till Tuesday."

Cooper looks at him.

"Yeah?"

"I'm telling you, it was all a ruse. Daniel even stayed at Araminta's last night."

Jethro slides down to the dense pillow. Cooper shuffles across and rests her head against his shoulder, presses her ear to his heart, listens to the thump thump. It's a familiar, comfortable position. A favourite cushion.

Used to be.

"And whooee, did you get a load of Daniel's gal?"

"Yeah, he's definitely punching above his weight."

"Wow, the way they strode into that restaurant looking like a Hollywood power couple."

Suddenly Cooper wants Jethro to want Araminta. To want everyone. Anyone but her. Yeah, that's what she wants. That'd make it okay.

Earlier today Cooper thought everything would change between them. She'd be in control. And yeah everything has changed. But now she is rudderless.

"So, like, what did you think of her?" Cooper says.

"Araminta? Did you hear that silky voice? Like someone drizzled melted dark chocolate over golden honey. She's totally into Daniel. You see the way they were drooling over each other? What did you think of her gift?"

Araminta had painted a small watercolour of Kelloggs from a photograph and put it in a gilt frame. Cooper opened it at the dinner table. Now it lies flat on the dressing table, cradled in the gloss of open wrapping paper.

"Yeah, really thoughtful."

"Is Daniel getting some posh totty or what?" Jethro says. "She's like debutante material right? Finishing school and all that stuff. Probably had a coming out ball. I always fancied a bit of top class totty myself."

When Jethro makes a deliberately provocative remark Cooper usually throws a pillow at him or playfully slaps him. She says nothing this time.

"One day Daniel's gonna be leaving the nest even if it's not with Araminta. It kind of brings it home. Our boy's a man."

"Yeah, he is."

Jethro senses something he can't define in Cooper, pecks her on the forehead.

"You know, I'm luckiest of all."

Don't say that.

"Yeah?"

The guilt tears at her, as sturdy as prison bars.

Pecks her again.

"Yeah. Definitely."

Cooper closes her eyes willing herself to feel something for this man. Feel anything.

"Know what?" Jethro says. "Call me crazy, but you're kind of sombre."

Cooper eyes snap open, unaware she'd closed them.

"Yeah?"

"I guess it's all this. Totally overwhelms, just totally overwhelms. But whooee seeing you all girlified and stuff when you came down the stairs. You looked a total knockout Coops. You didn't just blow my socks off, you popped all my toes like soap bubbles."

"Yeah, thanks."

"Far as I'm concerned, you're like the most beautiful woman ever walked this earth. I'm totally not used to seeing you in a dress. And your hair. I mean. I can't believe you grew it in the time I've been away. I never remember it ever being that long."

"It's still short."

"Yeah, but it's longer than I ever remember it."

"Never got round to cutting it, that's all."

"I'd love to see it grow."

Cooper looks at Jethro.

"Yeah?"

"Totally. I like seeing you girlified. I don't know, you have this enigmatic aura going on suddenly. Like where did that spring from? It's a version of you I've never seen before. Even our boy noticed."

"What do you mean?"

"Ah, you know it. You caught him looking at you this last week, said it made you feel all self-conscious."

"Oh yeah."

"It's like you've turned beautiful to eleven. Makes me want to bite you." Jethro nips her nose, growls like a lion. "Oh yum. Delicious."

Cooper laughs.

He tickles her around the waist.

"Oh yum yum yum."

She laughs, squirms away, pushing at him with the heel of her hands.

He goes in for the kill, tickles her ferociously. When he's finished he hangs over her. He cranes his head, kisses her.

"Damn it man, I'm so crazy happy right now. Everything is coming right Coops. I feel it. You feel it too, yeah?"

"Yeah, course."

"I mean the gigs. The record deal. Daniel and Araminta. Even your work. It's all working out. It's like the world's put a red carpet out for the Hall family."

Jethro rests his hand on Cooper's hips, slides them past her flat stomach, her nipped waist, circles her breasts through her pyjamas. He cups one like cupping a baby's head. With reverence. Cooper didn't think she'd be doing this with Jethro ever again. She thought today was going to be the end of everything physical between them. She thought there'd be tears his tears, and guilt his guilt, and shame his shame. But that was before everything.

The Rolls Royce.

The Savoy.

Champagne.

Daniel and Araminta.

Jethro and Daniel side by side.

Dawning and realisation and

God.

Cooper stops thinking. She kisses him back, just as ferociously. She will defy her emptiness, try to evoke something, stir something. She knows Jethro. Knows every nuance of him. Every fraction of him. Every day of him. She wants to want him. She runs her fingers through his long hair. Tries to arouse herself, runs her fingertips along the back of his neck. Uses her nails along the curl of his shoulders, under his T-shirt. She feels a stirring sexual interest awaken but nothing else.

Please. Something happen inside, please.

Jethro responds, switching up a gear and presses his lips to hers, tongue exploring her dark mouth. She lets him, wanting him to burst her open, let light flood in, release something from her.

His weight shifts and Cooper is beneath him. She feels the familiar shape of him. The weight of him. The knowledge of him. But.

No wonder.

Not anymore.

No awe.

Not anymore.

Pyjama jackets unbutton, hands explore. The elastic of pyjama bottoms pulled away. Hands explore.

Cooper strokes him in the right places. Responds the right way to his strokes. Rises and falls at the right moments with him. Their timing familiar yet new. Moist spicy lips, damp salty skin, hot sweaty bodies.

Even when the intensity increases, even then nothing changes inside her. Arousal but that's all. No thrill. No stirring whirlwind. No overwhelming emotions to drown in.

No love.

God.

Cooper's measurelessly, infinitely empty of love for him. This must be what a lobotomy feels like.

Before long he burns and rages with passion so strong it would blister skin. Yet she can only witness it. Watch it through a screen. Not an experience, merely sexual observation, bodily gratification.

Then.

Then they are spent.

Cooper nuzzles into him. Jethro cradles and loves her, strokes and holds her, whispers and caresses her.

Cooper's glad of one thing. Jethro didn't notice how empty she is inside, slides into sleep with that knowledge at least.

Only he did.

SOMETHING'S WRONG WITH Cooper.

Jethro knows it.

He feels it.

Since they made love that first night after he returned from the tour he knew then like he knows now as they lie in bed in the Savoy Suite. It's like she knows a secret he doesn't and is keeping it to herself. Cooper had said all the right things making love, did all the right things making love, made all the right noises making love. But it's like she wasn't making love.

In the Invasion of the Body Snatchers film, aliens replace people by copying them then devouring the original so no one notices the replacement. They look the same, know the same things but they're different and people notice it in the replacement's personality.

Yeah well, Cooper is different.

Then there's the bedroom makeover. It surprised him and Daniel. It's minty green for a start. Cooper hates minty green. What was wrong with the way it was anyway? She'd bought a new bed, new furniture new carpet. Everything new.

Why?

After they went to bed that first night after Jethro had returned from tour, Cooper had stayed on her side of the bed until Jethro asked how come she wasn't resting her head on his chest like normal? Cooper made an excuse she was out of the habit. True, they'd never been apart almost twelve weeks before. Then she'd rested her head on his bare chest and settled.

But in bed at The Savoy the thought troubles Jethro. Ten minutes of staring at the ceiling later he can't keep it in.

"Coops? Remember when you like had the car accident…?"

Cooper doesn't answer.

"Coops?"

Nothing.

Jethro nudges her, she doesn't respond. He lifts his head, looks down at the top of her hair. She's a vague shadow. She must be well and truly gone.

Then it happens. Jethro knows for certain. Cooper's not asleep. He knows.

Her eyelashes, see.

Her eyelashes man, her eyelashes.

Her eyelashes tell him because it sweeps against his bare chest and he knows Cooper's awake and blinking. He tries again.

"Coops?"

Another sweep of her eyelashes.

Jethro gazes at the city colours reflected on the ceiling.

Her butterfly kisses keep coming. Keep coming and keep keeping him awake. Jethro lies still. The last twelve weeks have been a flash, a whirr, blinding lights and deafening cheers and coach travelling and historic cities alive with music. An intoxicating, boozy, exhausting, bizarre, amazing event.

Only Jethro knows the bizarre isn't over yet. Cooper's awake and pretending not.

No. It's not over.

COOPER'S EYES SNAP open during a troubled sleep. They open wide in the dark. It's 3.22am. Of course. Of course of course of course. Why didn't she think it before? She gazes at Jethro.

He's contorted in sleep, head shoved into a pillow, arm thrown over the edge.

All Cooper has to do is call Gateway House and say she wants the treatment reversed. Didn't Dr Applegate say something about isolating emotional memory rather than deleting it? That means her feelings for Jethro must still be contained inside her. If The Gateway Programme blocked the pathway, surely they can unblock it? What is done can be undone, right?

She looks at Jethro, his mouth crushed into the pillow as though his skull is the weight of an anvil. She closes her eyes into what she hopes is a better sleep. Cooper will call Dr Applegate tomorrow. Secretly of course. Jethro never has to know.

Yeah.

Tomorrow things are going to change.

They have to.

COOPER'S HAD SEVERAL hours more sleep when Jethro nudges her awake with a toe.

"Hey Coops, shift it."

Cooper wakes. Opens an eye, feels sluggish.

"Hey."

Jethro is bright, already up in a white courtesy dressing gown, bouncing on his heels at the side of the bed.

"You know they have a pool and gym here? Sauna and everything."

"Yeah. I know. Araminta read it all out."

"Come on. I gave you an extra ten minutes already."

Cooper rubs her face.

"What time is it?"

"Seven-ten."

"That's early."

He grins.

"Totally. Got to make the most of the SA-voy experience."

She drags herself up into a sitting position as Jethro goes to the window, gazes out.

"Get a load of the view. It's wild."

Cooper crawls out of bed, goes over to the window. The Thames looks romantic in the hazy morning sunlight. Boats and ships grey in the sun, slide along the Thames in silhouette relief against the water. Cars and buses silently cross Waterloo Bridge.

"That's so crazy right?" Jethro says.

"Yeah, amazing."

Cooper drags herself to the loo. Jethro calls out.

"You need to move your backside, Coops."

She calls out.

"You go."

"You got to come sample the delights."

"Yeah I will. Just need coffee."

"Would madam like me to set it up for her?"

"Yeah, thanks."

Jethro goes to the coffee machine, puts in a pod.

"Espresso, right?"

"Make it strong."

He laughs, makes the coffee, brings it to her when she emerges.

"How you doing?"

"Champagne completely knocked me out." Cooper eyes him. "So, how come you're okay?"

"'Cause I'm not a wuss like you. You coming down?"

"Later. I feel blurgh."

"Long as you're ready by eight."

"Why?"

"Breakfast man, breakfast."

Cooper doesn't know if she can face breakfast.

"Yeah? Okay I'll be ready to go down by then."

"Forget it. Happening in our suite."

"Here?"

"That's what I'm talking about. Full butler service. The works. Crazy, right?"

"Sounds cool."

Cooper is glad for that. She definitely can't face other people.

Jethro heads for the door, slings a towel over his shoulder, turns, winks at her.

"See you laters, lazy girl."

THE SUE BAXTER PODCAST
SUE BAXTER
Um… what did you say? Dr Stewart-Way am I understanding
you correctly? You're saying part of the Gateway Programme
involves injecting a virus into the human brain?
DR STEWART-WAY
Yes, but it's not harmful. Viruses have unique properties
medical science can take advantage of; a virus can invade a
living cell with new instructions without damaging the cell. It's
a powerful tool in medical research, the biological equivalent of
a Swiss Army knife. Part of The Gateway Programme involves
introducing a virus that will only respond to brain cells with a
chemical marker. The virus then reprograms those specific
brains cell to photosynthesise and fluoresce.
SUE BAXTER
Viruses are contagious, yes?
DR STEWART-WAY
We've disabled the code to replicate.
SUE BAXTER
So the way I understand it, you make certain brain cells glow
when you use x-rays, and also make them light sensitive?
DR STEWART-WAY
Yes to both parts of the question.
SUE BAXTER
Why?
DR STEWART-WAY
This is where my work with optogenetics has advanced. We call

it flurogenetics. We don't need to use fibre optics as a light source. We can fluoresce the brain cells remotely, wirelessly through x-rays. Therefore there is no invasive treatment. No drilling through skulls.

SUE BAXTER

But this is what I don't get about optogenetics or, in your work, fluorogenetics. What is it about light that makes it possible to alter how the brain works?

DR STEWART-WAY

Well, light has an amazing property. It weighs nothing. Therefore the ability to control brain cells without physical intervention preserves the integrity of the brain. It's also where the magic happens. By making a brain cell light sensitive, it transforms it into an on/off switch whenever we fluoresce it by x-ray. It's now possible to code brain cells to detect a single photon of light, so low luminance fluorescence is perfect for our purposes. Instructions that pass through the neural circuits terminate at the fluorescing cluster of brain cells, disconnecting the avatar from the amygdala which – as in the case with your friend Charlotte – switches off your feelings for her. The process is called silencing a cell.

SUE BAXTER

And how long does it take for brain cells to adopt these new features?

DR STEWART-WAY

About a week. But unfortunately it isn't a solution on its own.

SUE BAXTER

Because?

DR STEWART-WAY

Because the moment we turn the x-ray off, the terminating brain cell switches back on.

SUE BAXTER

So my affection for Charlotte returns?

DR STEWART-WAY

Precisely.

SUE BAXTER

So this was your problem with your soldiers – why you couldn't cure them permanently of PTSD?

DR STEWART-WAY

We could give the soldiers repeat treatments for temporary relief from PTSD during the session, but repetitious exposure to x-rays, as we all know, is damaging at a cellular level, which is why when you have your bones or teeth x-rayed, medical staff stand behind a lead shield. My problem was I didn't have a method to permanently silence brain cells.

SUE BAXTER

But then you discovered a solution.

DR STEWART-WAY

Yes. Dr Applegate was, to quote a cliché, the knight in shining armour.

SUE BAXTER

Well okay so I've had The Gateway Programme treatment and I no longer have feelings for my wonderful friend Charlotte. Let's say post treatment I change my mind. I've realised I've made a huge mistake and want my affections for my best friend restored. Is that possible?

DR STEWART-WAY

You mean is The Gateway Programme reversible?

SUE BAXTER

Yes Dr Stewart-Way, is the treatment reversible?

DR STEWART-WAY

You're referring to Cooper Hall.

SUE BAXTER

I am.

DR STEWART-WAY

Well of course we all know the answer to that question.

COOPER WAITS UNTIL seven to call Gateway House's 24-hour emergency helpline. She makes another Tassimo coffee from the machine, sips it while gazing out the window at London. The coffee's good and strong. When she's ready Cooper goes in the bathroom, locks the door, puts the shower on. She knows Jethro's going to be back for breakfast by eight so she has plenty of time but she takes precautions in case he's early. Locking herself in the bathroom is the safest bet.

Five minute later she's through to Dr Applegate, apologises for the early call, asks her question and waits for Dr Applegate to speak. His pause is long.

Too long.

"Dr Applegate?"

"Yes, Mrs Hall, I'm still here."

"So, it's possible, yeah?"

Dr Applegate lets out a long sigh.

"Mrs Hall, what you're asking, I'm afraid it's not that simple."

"Yeah, I just need to know if you can do it."

"In theory."

"Cool."

"The problem is we've never done it. Never reversed treatment for anyone."

"You can try though, right?"

JETHRO WALKS ALONG the corridor, pleased with his forty-minute swim. Cooper was missing out and tell the truth he's a little disappointed. But okay she looked wrecked this morning. All that champagne. Anyway he didn't have the heart to make her do something she wouldn't appreciate so early. Still, he didn't want her to miss everything. She's bound to be up now. She could try the facial or maybe even a full spa day. They're booked in till six this evening. Breakfast. Lunch. Pampering in between. Afternoon tea, then they go home. Pure luxury.

He makes his way back along the corridor in his bathrobe, the desire to whistle strong. He doesn't. There are sleeping guests. Everyone's just so nice. Staff. Everyone.

A smartly dressed white haired couple, the man wearing a blue blazer with an emblem on the pocket and the woman in a camel-coloured poncho and a hat walk pass him. The rings on her tanned and wrinkled fingers glint so much it's unreal. Jethro guesses just one of those sparkly little kissers could probably buy his whole house and then some. He says good morning as they pass. They smile, say it back.

A butler in full livery glides by with a bronze breakfast trolley, acknowledges him with a smile, stops and gently raps on a door. Jethro's stomach groans. Yep, he was working up a wicked little hunger space. After a bath he'll settle down to a huge breakfast in the best hotel in the world with the woman of his life. He could get used to this. Yeah he could. Totally.

He thinks back to last night. That look on Cooper's face though! The surprise. Bam! One surprise after another, bam

Bam BAM! It'd all been worth it. But next time he goes away that long he's taking Cooper with him. No way he wants to be away from her that long again. Since he's been back things have subtly changed in ways he can't really define. It's decided. If she won't go, neither will he. Somehow those twelve weeks have distanced her.

He almost passes his own door, stops outside, uses his key card, goes in.

Cooper's not in bed. She's nowhere to be seen. Then he hears the shower. He can just about hear her talking over the shush. He smiles. Probably talking to herself. He tries the bathroom door.

Jethro is surprised.

It's locked.

DR APPLEGATE CLEARS his throat.

"I'm afraid we can't just experiment on you like that, Mrs Hall."

"You can't just undo everything?"

"First, every new procedure we carry out has to go through the medical council for approval. Second, it's not an avenue we've considered. We wouldn't know where to start."

"What if I volunteer myself to be your first guinea pig?"

"I'm sorry Mrs Hall. It would be irresponsible of us to even consider what you're suggesting."

"There must be something."

Dr Applegate takes a moment to gather his thoughts.

"Mrs Hall, what you must appreciate is we're still in the early days of neural editing."

"Yeah, but my feelings for my husband are still inside me, right?"

"That's correct."

"The treatment switched them off, yeah?"

"In a manner of speaking."

"So, if you switched them off, why can't you switch them back on?"

"Because it's not really a switch. That's just a term we use. It's really a rewriting."

"So, you can't undo it?"

"The truth is we haven't explored how to."

It was Cooper's last hope. Her last hope.

"I'm afraid what you're asking is science of the future. It's going to be years of research before we can approach anything like this."

"What about oxytocin?"

"Mrs Hall..."

"Please."

"What about it?"

"It's a love drug, right? Isn't it called the cuddle drug?"

"Colloquially it's called that. Why?"

"It's a bonding hormone, right? When couples get together I've read it increases in the brain."

"That's correct. But in your case Mrs Hall your brain can't induce it with your husband."

"But I can take it right? A tablet or an injection or something? When I'm with Jethro? Something to make me want to bond with him."

"No, Mrs Hall, I'm afraid not."

"Why not?"

"The reason is simple. It's impossible to feel anything for your husband. The oxytocin won't have anywhere to go."

Cooper doesn't let up.

"I signed your legal forms."

"Absolutely you did. To clarify you understood the ramifications of our treatment. All our patients have to."

"So, couldn't I just sign a waiver stating I'd take full responsibility for anything you try to do to reverse the treatment if it goes wrong?"

Dr Applegate sees where Mrs Hall's going with this.

"Mrs Hall, again please understand you're not grasping the gravity of what you're asking. Even if we could somehow gain the approval of the various boards and committees – something I guarantee they will not agree to – we would have to carry out years of extensive research first."

"BUT I JUST WANT TO LOVE HIM AGAIN!"

A long pause.

"I'm truly sorry, Mrs Hall."

1 0 1

JETHRO TRIES THE bathroom door again. Cooper can't really have locked it. But the door doesn't budge.

Jethro frowns, presses his ear to the door. He thought he heard her shout something. Now he can hear her talking again. Can't hear what she's saying though.

Jethro knocks.

"Coops?"

Cooper doesn't hear.

He raps harder, calls louder.

"Coops? Cooper?"

The knock startles Cooper. She almost drops the phone.

She cuts the call, pushes her head under the forceful shower, drenches her hair. She grabs a towel.

When she opens the bathroom door, she's already shoved the phone into the pocket of her bathrobe, hair dripping.

The first thing Jethro notices is her surprised smile. If he didn't know better he'd say it looked pasted on. She's flushed, her cheeks rosy. Shower must've been hot. But something else on her face. Some other expression he can't quite grasp the meaning of. He doesn't mention the locked door.

"Thought you'd have been done by now," Jethro says.

"Yeah, really enjoyed that."

He laughs, doubt vanishing like vapour.

"I bet. You totally missed out on the morning swim though. It was amazing. I was the only one there. Except a couple of people in the gym."

"Yeah?"

"One of them was coming to use the pool after going on the treadmill. They don't call it a gym though, they call it a Fitness Centre. One of the staff came up and asked if I'd like an electrolytic energy drink or mineral water or something after my swim. I had me a freshly squeezed orange juice when I got out with real bits of orange floating on top. It was delish. Then I said something totally cool."

"Yeah? What did you say?"

"I said to the guy, put it on my room. I always wanted to say that. Put it on my room."

Cooper laughs.

"How come you're back already?"

"He rubs his hands together. Well, we need to get this day started man. Don't forget the massage and a spa and everything."

"Yeah, I know."

Cooper scrunches her wet hair, her phone deep in the pocket of her bathrobe.

"Then I thought we could go maybe visit some land sites around this joint. You know, like Buckingham Palace, the National Gallery and stuff. What do you think?"

"Cool."

"Then come back for more pampering and grub."

"Sounds great."

"So, like how was the shower?"

"Yeah, it was great. You got to try it."

Jethro eyes the freestanding bath.

"Nah, I'm gonna have me a soak." He picks up something from the bath rack. "Look, they even have their own Savoy rubber ducks. Sweet. You think it's okay if we like, you know, steal it?"

"The duck?"

"Yeah."

She takes it. Looks at it. Turns it upside down. Smirks.

"What is it?"

Jethro grabs the rubber duck.

"Look what it says on the bottom."

He looks, laughs. Pinched from The Savoy Hotel, London.

1 0 2

THIRTY MINUTES LATER Cooper has changed into her
cargos from the overnight case when Jethro emerges from the
bathroom, his skin scorched red and glossy, his long hair wet
and dark against his scalp. In the bath he had to keep reminding
himself Cooper's readjusting to everything, his being back, the
Savoy, Daniel having a girlfriend, all that. It just takes time with
her. It's just time, that's all. That's why she's been so quiet.
That's why she's hardly said a word. She's dazzled and dazed
by everything. That must be it.

Now Jethro holds bottles of courtesy gels like little trophies
and dumps them on the bed. Cooper sees his are half used. She
sees all her bottles are still full. Good thing Jethro hasn't
noticed.

"What did you think of the gels and stuff?" Jethro says,
staring at the hoard.

"Yeah, great."

"Crazy, right?" He sniffs his armpits. "I totally smell like
I've come out from a Turkish massage parlour." Cooper wants
to gather them up before he notices. She sorts out her bra,
panties, puts them on, grabs a T-shirt from the suitcase.

"Was it work?" Jethro says. He slips into his jeans.

"What do you mean?"

"Like, you were on the phone, right? In the bathroom?"

Cooper pulls her T-shirt down, her brain scrambles to think
of something.

"Yeah, Graham lining up some stuff."

Jethro grins.

"You tell him where we're at?"

"Yeah, I told him."

Jethro glances at the basket of gels. Sees his are all squashed and hers are so neat and tidy.

"What'd he say?"

"He said lucky old me."

"That's all?"

"Yeah, basically."

"The Savoy. I mean The S-A-V-O-Y, man. Hah!" He laughs. "I mean, wow."

"Yeah."

He looks again at Cooper's collection of gels and lotions. Penhaligon's it says on the posh label. So neat. So tidy. Glances from bottle to bottle, admiring the simple white labels on the clear bottles. He reads the labels. Atmosphere filtered shampoo. Atmosphere filtered? What the heck is that? Then there's body lotion and shower gel.

Then he looks at the top of a bottles. The liquid goes all the way up the neck. Picks one up, sniffs it through the top. He can just about smell the aroma. He looks at the next bottle, about to sniff it.

Notice the liquid goes all the way up the neck.

At the next.

All the way up.

At the next.

All the way up, all the way up, all the way up.

"How come—"

Jethro stops when he sees Cooper staring at him through the dressing table mirror. She looks away. She's slapping moisturiser on her face but her eyes were hard on what he was doing. It's the same look she had when she opened the bathroom door. The one which almost brought a word to his head. What is that word?

"What were you going to say?" Cooper says.

"Nah, not important." He takes the gels, shoves them into the overnight case. All her bottles are full, her hair is wet. Full bottles, hair wet. He didn't pack any shampoos for her. What's she been showering with?

Suddenly the word comes to him. Yeah that's it. It's—

There's a knock on the door. Jethro gets up, rubs his hands together. He opens the door. A smiling butler greets him with a bronze trolley and breakfast covered in glass domes.

"Good morning, Mr Hall. I hope you both slept well. Your breakfast for two."

"Yeah, thanks. Wheel her in my man, wheel her in."

The butler wheels in the breakfast trolley, bids Cooper good morning, sets the trolley by the dining table. He's meticulous about everything. Lays the tablecloth flat, smooth, fits the table perfectly. White plates laid. The butler takes out a tape measure, measures the distance between the silverware and the table edge.

"You're messing with me, right?"

The butler looks up.

"Mr Hall?"

"The tape measure."

"Oh no, we take great pride in the table setting sir. I'm still learning." The butler looks contrite. "I shouldn't really have the tape measure on me."

"That's like, crazy."

"We try to take care of your every comfort, sir. You ordered the Savoy Breakfast for two?"

"Yeah, yeah, the works. Coops, you gotta see this."

The butler lays each item out and points at each in turn as he talks.

"We have fresh juices, fresh coffee, a selection of white, wholemeal, sourdough, and granary toasts, English muffins. We have croissants, Danish pastries, free-range eggs, scrambled with smoked bacon, Cumberland sausage, semi braised vine tomatoes, baked beans, Stornoway black—"

"Heinz, right?"

"The baked beans sir?"

"Yeah."

"Actually, it's the chef's own recipe. Would you like me to request the ingredients?"

"Nah, that's cool."

"You also ordered blueberry pancakes with maple syrup."

"Yeah. Cool. I want to stuff myself silly today."

The butler laughs.

"Yes sir, I can see that. Will there be anything else?"

"What other things you sort out? Other than food I mean."

"We'll be happy to arrange anything sir… Providing it's legal of course."

"So, if I like wanted a MacDonald's you could like fetch that for me?"

"Yes sir, anything you wish. We have many guests who request fast food."

"What about entertainment?"

"Well, I could recommend sites to visit sir. There's a fashion show on at the South Bank Centre this morning at ten featuring the latest work of designer Frederico Benelli. Or perhaps you'd like a spot of theatre. Dream Girls at the Savoy theatre or perhaps The Lion King at the Lyceum or Kinky Boots at the Adelphi. You could go on a Jack the Ripper tour travelling around Victorian London, or Sherlock Holmes or Dickens. If you're interested in historic buildings monuments and landmarks dotted throughout London we have—"

"What's the craziest thing a butler's done for a guest here?"

"Well, I would say unusual rather than crazy. I'm told we have many unique requests."

"Unique requests. I like it. Like what?"

"I believe we had a celebrity who wished to bathe in goat's milk."

"You're kidding."

"She wanted our chauffeur to drive to Wales to—"

"To WALES? For real?"

"Yes sir. It was to fetch enough goat's milk to fill a bath."

"You couldn't like go to Tesco or something?"

"She insisted on unpasteurised sir. None of the supermarkets had unpasteurised."

"Jeez, that's a long wait for a bath."

He laughs.

"I'm sure it was ordered in advance."

"Yeah, guess so. Who was it?"

The butler's voice drops to a whisper and Jethro has to lean in.

"Well, I CAN reveal she was a supermodel."

"Yeah, figures."

"If there's anything else, Mr Hall?"

Jethro stares at the banquet.

"You think there's something I missed?"

The butler laughs again.

"No sir. I think you've ordered just about everything."

"A feast for my gal and me."

"Bon appétit Mr Hall, Mrs Hall."

When he's gone Jethro scans the table, grins.

"Whooee sister, get a load of this."

Cooper comes over, glances at the table, smiles.

"That's ridiculous."

They sit opposite each other and throw white linen napkins on their laps and dive in. Jethro makes appreciative noises. Cooper eats in silence. Finally, Jethro can't hold it in.

"Coops?"

"Yeah?"

"You're enjoying yourself, right?"

"Yeah, course."

"Like, you're sure, right? It's not too much?"

Cooper looks up then. Sees the concern in his eyes. He looks… frightened. A little boy.

"Course. It's amazing." She leans over the table, clasps his hand, smiles.

"Sorry hon, I can't take it all in that's all. It's really special. Almost makes up for you being away so long."

There. That look on Cooper's face again. That look. That same expression. He knows what it is for sure now.

"What's wrong?" Cooper says.

"Just enjoy breakfast. We got a big day ahead."

"Yeah. I am. Really."

There was no doubting it now, Jethro knew the word fit. That expression on Cooper's face. He knew what it was.

Guilt.

THE SUE BAXTER PODCAST
SUE BAXTER
So even after all these years of running your practice Dr
Stewart-Way, The Gateway Programme is still not reversible?
DR STEWART-WAY
I'm afraid not.
SUE BAXTER
Will it ever be?
DR STEWART-WAY
I'm sure it will one day.
SUE BAXTER
You were telling us earlier you didn't have a means to make
your treatment permanent until Dr Applegate came along. I've
read the story in yours and Dr Applegate's book, but I'd love to
hear you tell it in your own words. It's an amusing story.
DR STEWART-WAY
Yes. We came across each other completely by accident. If it
wasn't for him, The Gateway Programme would never have
existed.
SUE BAXTER
And good heavens, from the way Dr Applegate tells it, what an
accident.
DR STEWART-WAY
(Laughs)
It was terribly embarrassing.
SUE BAXTER
Do tell our listeners.

DR STEWART-WAY

I was at Gatwick airport heading to a convention in the States when I tripped over a suitcase. It just so happens the suitcase was next to a public waste paper bin and I grabbed onto it and sent the whole thing tumbling, scattering rubbish all over the place. It was dreadfully embarrassing both for myself and the owner of the suitcase. Anyway he was apologetic as we tried to clear up the mess. We got talking and became increasingly aware we were both scientists and doctors.

SUE BAXTER

The owner of the suitcase was Dr Applegate no less, your co-partner at Gateway House.

DR STEWART-WAY

Indeed. We started chatting and I learned of his work in memory reconsolidation. He mentioned one particular case which was causing him frustration. It was about a solicitor with an unconscious phobia. Well, after he learned about my work, we had a quiet moment of dawning where our combined efforts might prove mutually beneficial.

SUE BAXTER

So Clive's case, at that precise moment, was part of the coincidence.

DR STEWART-WAY

I can't possibly fathom the astronomical probability of two scientists whose separate projects could be matched more perfectly. Out of the seven billion people who inhabit this planet, the chance encounter of meeting at Gatwick airport on that particular day at that particular time with this particular case… well, there were no two other people more opportune to meet.

SUE BAXTER

(Laughs)

And all because you fell over his suitcase.

DR STEWART-WAY

(Laughs)

Well yes. They say all success is half luck. I'd say in this instance it was 99.99 percent luck. Dr Applegate's work in memory consolidation is utterly brilliant. Applying his methods we can now anchor brain cells into a permanently silenced state. It's completed the treatment we now call The Gateway Programme.

SUE BAXTER

And that's the whole treatment?

DR STEWART-WAY

That's it.

SUE BAXTER

Which is the treatment Cooper Hall had.

DR STEWART-WAY

Indeed.

SUE BAXTER

But, tell me Dr Stewart-Way, doesn't it come with its own issues?

DR STEWART-WAY

You mean because the treatment cannot be reversed?

SUE BAXTER

Yes, it leaves no room for a reparation of the couple.

DR STEWART-WAY

By the time the patient has contacted us for such treatment it's usually well beyond any chance of reparation. The other party can of course also have the treatment.

SUE BAXTER

Still, that leaves no chance for reconciliation.

DR STEWART-WAY

Which is why psychological evaluation is such an important precondition of the treatment.

SUE BAXTER

So you don't accept everyone?

DR STEWART-WAY

Absolutely not. Every applicant has to go through rigorous

assessment. We accept almost every PTSD case but only one in five relationship issue cases.

SUE BAXTER

How come?

DR STEWART-WAY

It's in the best interests of the patient or relationship.

SUE BAXTER

Can you elaborate?

DR STEWART-WAY

We have to ensure the treatment is without the aftertaste of regret – jealousy or anger for instance. Therefore we reject or defer cases if we believe the patient is making an impetuous decision. We have a psychoanalyst, relationship therapist and psychologist on our team.

SUE BAXTER

What about divorcing couples where one of them is still very much in love with the other?

DR STEWART-WAY

That's often where we apply our treatment. One party has already left the marital household, perhaps having already begun a new relationship. The remaining member, if still suffering, can opt for treatment.

SUE BAXTER

What about children? Might it not prove distressing for children to discover one or both their parents have had treatment? Won't they be in a broken home with no hope of reconciliation?

DR STEWART-WAY

The fact their parents have already split up will already be distressing. If it's acrimonious it can be even more harmful to the child. The treatment negates such issues. Parents can be civil to each other without harbouring jealousies or hostilities. This can only be a healthy environment for any child involved.

SUE BAXTER

And grieving widows or widowers?

DR STEWART-WAY

We do try to discourage it. Grieving is natural. But prolonged grief leading to clinical depression will obviously have a bearing on our decision to approve a patient for treatment.

SUE BAXTER

Dr Stewart-Way, how was it then Cooper Hall managed to have treatment when the marital home hadn't been broken? As far as I'm aware Jethro T. Hall didn't even know he'd been wrongfully suspected of infidelity.

DR STEWART-WAY

That's easy. Cooper lied.

1 0 4

AS COOPER EATS breakfast she considers herself a prisoner in a dull grey room wishing she can escape.

But there's no door. There's no window. It's an empty airless room she's trapped in and will be for the rest of her life. An amazing man is sitting opposite Cooper at the breakfast table, loving her, enjoying his feast. But more important than that, he's doing everything he can to make her happy. Once Cooper loved him without even trying. Effortlessly. Powerfully. She can't believe that was just days ago. It feels like never. But it was a love so right no one else could ever fit the way Jethro does in her life.

Did. Did fit. Past tense.

Cooper misjudged him.

Just once.

She sips her coffee, sips her orange juice. Jethro is making a pig of himself, scoffing everything, sampling everything, and it makes her laugh. Yeah, he can still do that to her.

The Cumberland sausage is gorgeous. The bacon is spicy. The eggs, perfect. The bread is sweet and heavenly. And London. Gosh, it looks amazing, sunny, bright, busy. She never realised just how many buses there were all over the place, on practically every road she can see. It's a perfect morning. A perfect breakfast.

It should be perfect.

Cooper looks at him. Jethro. Beautiful, beautiful Jethro.

Oh god.

They were almost childhood sweethearts. That's what it felt like when she met him in the sixth form. Now she has only memories of him. Photographs in an album. Piles and piles of them. But she feels nothing for them. They are not fond memories. They are merely accounts of their past. Jethro and Cooper on a beach. Jethro and her at the Parthenon in Athens. His last birthday with all three of them devouring pizza. One with him onstage at a local gig.

The memories stir nothing.

They're not fond memories.

Merely accounts of their past.

HARRIET'S WORKING FROM her home office, updating the Tomalin Garages website with a special offer for exhaust replacement at a discounted introductory price. She's been toying with the idea of setting up a Tomalin Garages membership club where for just a few pounds a month, members get simple maintenance like replaced windscreen wipers, oil and brake fluid checks, tyres, windscreen washer and a few other things, plus discounts on larger jobs. Once customers are part of a membership, you basically get the customer for life. She needs to think it through though before raising it to Eddsy, work through the finances of it. It has to be profitable while at the same time offering a genuine benefit to customers. But she also needs to do research into setting up a garage for servicing electric cars, find out what government-assisted funding there is. Perhaps it's about time she had an assistant. Harriet knew she was stretching herself too thin.

Still.

Harriet's mind's not on it today. She pulls open her desk drawer, takes out the adoption booklet she stole from the glove compartment.

She opens it to the front page. It says Simone Grey, Senior Social Worker/Manager, and a telephone number, and a lovely picture of a generously smiling woman with a warm glint in her eyes.

Where did Eddsy get the booklet? Why did he have it in his glove compartment? When is Eddsy going to mention it to her?

Will he, ever?

Harriet looks at the phone number. In a sudden impulse she picks up the telephone, dials the number. It rings. Someone picks up.

"Barnardo's, Simone Grey speaking, how may I help you?"

Harriet wants to ask about Eddsy. Wants to. Has he been there? Really wants to. Did Simone Grey meet with him? Truly, she wants to. She feels her chest heaving. The words are like Velcro, catch in Harriet's throat.

"Hello?" Simone Grey says again.

Finally, Harriet can't hold back.

"Oh, I'm sorry. Wrong number."

She hangs up.

1 0 6

IT'S BEEN A few days since The Savoy.

Jethro lies in bed next to Cooper. She's sleeping. He lies there with his arm over his head in the dark, frustrated. He hates himself for what he's thinking. What he's about to do. He thinks it again, unable to help himself.

Is Cooper seeing someone?

It hurts his heart to think that, a dull pain in his chest.

Not Cooper. Can't be. They are life-long soul mates. They were teenage sweethearts. They are bound forever. Those were the rules.

Were?

The thoughts persist, keeps him awake like a dog nudging him with its nose, pushing for attention.

Jethro tries to fight it.

No, of course she's not seeing someone. Definitely not. No. No. No way. Not Cooper, no way.

Minutes slip by.

2.26am.

2.39am.

3.08am.

3.24am.

4.17am.

At 4.18am Jethro snaps.

Oh man. These are crazy thoughts.

Jethro studies Cooper's back, curved into her own quiet third of the bed. He needs to stop thinking and do what he doesn't want to do.

Jethro eases himself out of bed. Careful. Don't wake her.

In the grey darkness of night he spots the familiar shape of her rucksack on her dressing table. He makes his way over, slowly unzips it, slips his hand inside. He can't see the contents but he finds familiar and unfamiliar objects: Tissues, a purse, a couple of pens, something flat and oblong and small, and something tubular, it feels like lipstick. She doesn't wear lipstick casually. He takes it out, drops it, hears the soft thud on the carpet. Damn it how's he going to find it in the dark? He goes on his knees, pats his hands around. He finds it, picks it up. In the shadowy darkness he can see it's not lipstick, it's lip balm. He replaces it. He's searching for her mobile.

Thoughts fire through his head. Cooper isn't like that, why am I doing this? Go back to bed.

But what if she is seeing someone?

But she's not, that's not Cooper.

But what if she is?

Come on, man.

Her phone's not in her bag. Yeah, course not. The phone must be recharging. He spots her mobile phone on the bedside table. Should have checked there first.

Jethro creeps around her side of the bed, picks up the phone, pulls out the charging cable. Something on top of the phone falls toward the table, he catches it in time, lets out a breath. He's tense. It's Cooper's reading glasses. He places her glasses back on the table.

Jethro opens the bedroom door holding her phone, slips out.

Downstairs in the sitting room, feeling like a criminal, pacing, he swipes Cooper's mobile phone. Pacing. Criminal. Pacing, pacing.

The sitting room door opens a little and Jethro freezes.

It's only Kelloggs. He pushes his nose and nudges the door a bit wider, saunters in, makes a low acknowledging noise, aware it's odd for Jethro to be up at this time, watches Jethro pacing. Kellogg's tilts his expressionless face up at Jethro.

The phone is locked. Jethro's faced with a four-digit number request. That isn't a problem. He knows the four digits because it's the same as his. If they accidentally took each other's phones they'd be able to call each other, let them know. But that was a few years ago when they had identical phones. Now they have different phones but still they use the same four digits.

Don't they?

He tenses. He taps in her four digit number, the phone unlocks. The relief is instant. The knot in his stomach relaxes. That alone should be enough. Just knowing Cooper's not hiding access to her phone should be enough.

But it's not.

Jethro swipes into her texts. There are hundreds of them but they're mainly from him, from Daniel, from Harriet, from work colleagues like Graham. There isn't a name he doesn't know.

Okay, enough now.

Jethro switches the phone off, returns to the bedroom, plugs her phone back into the charging cable, watching her shadowy form, hoping he hasn't disturbed her. She remains motionless.

He returns to bed, eases in.

Cooper also has a laptop.

Damn it.

Sometimes she sits at the kitchen table surfing the net, sometimes in the sitting room, sometimes in bed. He doesn't remember seeing it in the bedroom tonight and doesn't want to take the chance of looking for it in the dark and stumbling and waking Cooper.

Damn it, stop this, stop this craziness.

But Jethro can't.

He's not going to sleep. He's been fretting four days, four days.

He rises, leaves the bed again, makes his way downstairs feeling guilty, so guilty. They've been together for like twenty years but he can't help it. Something is up. Something is up with Cooper. It's sending him crazy. Jethro makes his way into the kitchen, finds the laptop closed on the kitchen table. It's in plain sight. Another good sign but it doesn't help.

He flicks on the kitchen lights and the brittle starkness of the halogens hurt his eyes. He blinks, adjusts to them.

Jethro settles into a seat, opens the laptop, starts it up. The laptop whirrs into life. He doesn't know whether it has a password, he's never used it. Everything loads up and he's straight through to the desktop. No password. Good. Yet another good sign.

But. Yeah, not good enough.

He looks in the documents folder first. Music contracts, Performance Rights Society royalty statements, basic correspondence.

He looks on the C drive for other folders.

Regular work stuff.

Goes into the trash can.

A few old documents, nothing important.

He goes into Word and looks at recent documents in the drop down menu. All are correspondence. Nothing out of the ordinary. He finds the photograph directory with lots of family shots. Restaurants where they ate, birthday celebrations, Christmas, pictures of Kelloggs with his blank face.

Jethro clicks on the Firefox browser and several tabs load up. Facebook. Twitter. Google. Nothing incriminating in any of them, all accessible.

Now he feels so bad. It's almost worse than being wrong because the fault is with him not her. Then he remembers Facebook has private messages. His heart races when he finds some but realises they're nothing special, mainly it's Harriet or Daniel or him, hating himself for spying on her like this, unable to stop himself.

He checks the bookmarks meu, finds a few more websites: Yahoo News, BBC, Wikipedia, YouTube, some recipe websites, a few film sites, lots of music sites and recording studio sites.

He checks the website history, finds nothing out of place there either.

Enough now, stop this craziness. Imagine if Cooper came down and saw what he was up to, what would he say?

Jethro closes the laptop. He returns upstairs, climbs into bed, his night vision gone after the brightness of the kitchen, lies there in the dark, arm across his head like before, feeling bad for even thinking what he thought.

Everything is okay between him and Cooper, it's only odd because he's been away, that must be it. Yeah sure that's all it is. He feels so bad now.

An hour later he starts to drift off when he's jolted awake once more.

Check her phone.

Yeah, he already did that. You didn't check her phone records you only checked her networking sites. But he checked her phone, he checked her laptop.

Check her phone record.

No, enough.

Check it, check her phone record.

No.

4.41am 55 seconds.

Check her phone record.

4.42am seven seconds

Check her phone record.

4.42am 12 seconds.

Check her phone record.

DAMN IT!

Jethro gets up. Glances at Cooper making sure she's still asleep. She is. He goes to her phone. He doesn't bother to unplug it this time, feeling braver. He unlocks it.

He finds an unlisted number part-way down, almost a month ago. He checks the history. It seems Cooper called them first. Then they called her. Then she called them back. There are a few back and forth calls. One as recently as four days ago early in the morning.

What were they doing four days ago?

They were at The Savoy.

But he doesn't remember her calling anyone.

Wait.

Wait.

The Savoy hotel suite bathroom.

Cooper said she was speaking to Graham about work. Didn't she say Graham called her? Jethro couldn't remember. But in that case why didn't Graham's name come up with this number? And why would Cooper be speaking to him so early anyway?

It didn't fit.

Jethro, memorising the number, closes the phone. He returns to his side of the room. He lies carefully back down, feels the dip in the bed careful not to wake her once more. He picks up a pencil from his bedside drawer, starts scrawling the number in the dark on a sheet of paper.

"What're you doing?" It's Cooper. She sounds alert, startling him, making him freeze.

"Oh, hey."

"What're you doing?"

How long has she been awake how long how long? He was right by her bed looking at her phone, she was facing him, all she had to do was open her eyes how long?

"Oh, nothing."

"Why were you prowling?"

"I wasn't."

"You were on my side of the room."

Cooper saw she must've seen. Jethro doesn't know what to say. He sees the window.

"I was looking out the window."

"How come?"

"Like I thought I heard something. A fox maybe."

She doesn't respond. After a few moments she still hasn't said anything.

"Cooper?"

No response.

He leans over, whispers.

"Coops?"

Cooper responds with a groan. She's fallen back to sleep.

Relieved, Jethro scrawls the rest of the number, hoping he remembered it, puts everything back in the drawer, closes it.

He rests his head on a pillow. Finding an unlisted number, probably just a new work contact despite the 7am call she made seems to have settled his mind. But why so early? Why? Jethro is too tired to answer, feels sleep dragging at him.

This time sleep comes fast.

JETHRO WAKES LATE, not due in the studio till tomorrow.

He turns over, Cooper's not there. He spots a sheet of notepaper next to the clock. He puts his glasses on, reads Cooper's handwriting.

To: Sleepyhead. Gone to Tear Studios. DO NOT CALL UNLESS YOU'RE DYING :). She adds a skull and crossbones and xx.

Jethro turns over. Her phone is gone, the umbilical phone cable sticking up.

Jethro goes into his side drawer, pulls out the slip of paper with the phone number on it. His first thought is to call the number. His second is to obey his bladder and freshen up.

As he freshens up, he thinks instead of calling the number he should do a search online and see if it brings anything up. Better than calling. After all he has no idea who's going to answer, and what would he say?

He dresses, uses his phone to search the number online. No results. He calls the number, heart thumping in his ears, wondering what he'll say if someone answers. Nothing happens, it never connects, silence. He wrote the number down wrong. Must've.

He looks at the number scrawled on the paper. Looks at it. Studies it. Cooper'd interrupted him last night writing the number down so maybe he mixed up the digits or something. He sees where he wrote the first part of the number before Cooper startled him. Then the second part of the number at an angle to the first almost runs off the edge of the paper. It'd been dark, he couldn't see the paper he was writing on. He counts the numbers, there's a digit missing. A thought occurs to him. He checks the surface of his bedside table. There's a single 8 in pencil written on the table, missing the paper entirely. He almost laughs. He tries the full number in Google again. Result.

Jethro clicks on the link.

Jerks his head back as though surprised by a snake.

1 0 8

THE SUE BAXTER PODCAST
SUE BAXTER
Dr Stewart-Way, you say Cooper Hall lied in order to receive treatment, but she did believe her husband was having an affair.
DR STEWART-WAY
She did. Unfortunately, as the world knows, Cooper Hall was very much mistaken.
SUE BAXTER
What was her lie then?
DR STEWART-WAY
Cooper Hall told us Jethro T Hall had fled the marital home when in fact he was on a concert tour in Europe. We acted at once treating her. Perhaps too hastily.
SUE BAXTER
So you accept it was a mistake?
DR STEWART-WAY
Her state of mind concerned us. We maintain it was the right decision nonetheless, even in light of later discoveries.
SUE BAXTER
But do you think you might have been blindsided by her unique idea to use the treatment to mend what was effectively a broken heart? It was, after all, a novel use of The Gateway Programme at the time.
DR STWART-WAY
Perhaps so, but we guided Cooper through a complete psychological evaluation just as we do with all our PTSD patients. After considering her medical history and our

psychological profile of her at the time, we decided to act. However, in light of what transpired, we now have far more robust systems in place.

SUE BAXTER

So, lessons have been learned?

DR STEWART-WAY

Indeed.

SUE BAXTER

Returning to Cooper Hall… What in her medical history, influenced your decision?

DR STEWART-WAY

I'm afraid I'm unable to answer that.

SUE BAXTER

But there was a sudden change in circumstances wasn't there? Cooper suddenly called you out of the blue one Sunday morning.

JETHRO SPENDS FORTY minutes reading the details of the Gateway House treatments. What the heck is this? Nothing makes sense to him. Gateway House claims to help people with PTSD. In that case why would Cooper call them?

Jethro reads how two doctors pioneered a treatment: Dr John Applegate and Dr Klara Stewart-Way.

He reads about a revolutionary brain surgery for treating PTSD. It sounds utterly Frankenstein to him. He reads glowing testimonials of victims of depression, horrific accidents, child abuse, disturbed soldiers, victims of crime, the bereaved. The results all seem too good to be true. What the heck had this got to do with Cooper anyway? He reads of the issues the centre treats.

Grief.

Yeah but no one's died recently.

Traumatic accident?

No. Well she had the bad car accident but she's been driving since then.

Child abuse?

She never hinted at it.

Depression?

Come off it man, what for?

All Jethro can think of is last year Cooper was a little beat-up about Daniel leaving for Durham university, but that was last year. The event meant sadness and pride for both of them right? Sadness and pride. He continues with the list.

Loneliness.

Cooper doesn't strike him as lonely.

He must have written down the phone number wrong. He must've.

Sexual assault.

No. No way.

Wait.

Hold on.

Sexual assault?

They'd been to bed together since he'd been back. If it was sexual assault, that wouldn't have been the behaviour of a victim. Didn't people go off sex or something? Panic when they try to get intimate after something like that? Or change? And like there'd have been a crime report. Harriet would've known about it. So would he.

…If Cooper had reported it.

Jethro's scalp crawls.

Sometimes victims blame themselves, don't they? They carry it around like a secret and it eats them up. Like it makes them feel guilty.

Wait.

Yeah, wait wait wait wait wait.

Cooper looked guilty at The Savoy. What if Cooper feels guilty about an attack and is carrying it around like a sack of rubble, like it's her fault? What if she was speaking to a doctor while in the shower at the time when Jethro interrupted her? Cooper never really relaxed at the Savoy, never got into the spirit, not even with all the pampering, the sauna, the spa, all that fine food, fine drink. Yeah he'd expected her to be dazed by it all at first, course. But not like that. Not in the way she had. Cooper wasn't just dazed. She was distant.

Sexual assault? Jethro runs a hand through his hair. Don't let it be that. Jethro doesn't want it to be that.

He hadn't been around at that time though had he? He'd been so wrapped up in the European tour he didn't know what was happening. He wasn't around, Daniel wasn't around and Cooper was going over to Harriet's when she had the crash.

But if that's the case why wouldn't Cooper have told him? He'd have been back on the next flight, forget the tour. Years ago he remembers hearing Woman's Hour on Radio 4 of a rape victim whose boyfriend dumped her when he found out. That had doubly traumatised her. With the attack. And with guilt. Apparently there are men who behave like that with their wives and girlfriends when they most need love and support.

Maybe instead of support, maybe some husbands accuse. Maybe instead of comfort, maybe some husbands push away. Maybe instead of acceptance, maybe some husbands become jealous.

But Jethro's not like that. Cooper would know that right? It had to be something else.

Jethro's hands are shaking. The thought of someone else touching his wife, hurting her... And Cooper, being alone, feeling abandoned, unable to cope...

Jethro squeezes his hands into fists. Try as he might he can't think of any other reason Cooper might have phoned them. Think this through.

He'd been away doing the tour right? How was Cooper then?

Harriet said something about Cooper driving over, upset. Yeah wait. Upset BEFORE the crash. Whatever happened must've happened that day. He wasn't there. Daniel wasn't around. Cooper was alone. Cooper had been seeking refuge and Harriet had been her only choice. Cooper'd rushed over to Harriet's for some unknown reason, had the car crash on the way. And wait, fact number two – for a couple of days he couldn't even get hold of her. And didn't Harriet describe Cooper as out of it? That could've been the shock of the accident. But even when Jethro'd managed to speak to her, she seemed far away. He'd been so jazzed about the tour he hadn't realised how different Cooper'd been at the time.

Worst of all, since then Cooper's changed in some way... like she's had some sort of trauma.

Like she's been assaulted. Like she's been r...

Oh man.

It's not possible. Is it possible?

Hands through the hair.

He won't believe it. Not that.

Is it possible? Is it Jethro, come on man, is it?

Jethro's stomach turns over.

"Yeah," he says, his voice quiet, trembling. "Yeah, it's possible."

1 1 0

JETHRO DECIDES TO call Harriet. She answers, her voice
cheery.

"Hey Jethro, what's up?"

"Harriet, I don't mean to worry you, but—"

"What's happened?"

"It's cool it's just—"

"What's happened? Tell me."

"Nothing's happened."

"It has though, hasn't it? Something's happened."

"I just need to ask you something."

"Go on."

Jethro hesitates, runs a hand through his hair again.

"You like, ever heard of The Gateway Programme?"

"The what?"

"The Gateway Programme."

"Should I have?"

So that was a no. That's good. Or is it?

"Jethro, what's going on? Is it about the time she came over?
The car accident?"

"I don't know what to do."

"Oh god I've gone cold. My skin's gone all clammy. I have
to sit down."

"That night Cooper stayed with you, like how was she?"

"She'd had the car accident, remember?"

"You ever find out why she was driving over?"

"You mean you don't know?"

"No. Know what?"

"Didn't you ask her?"

"No."

"Well, I did and she didn't say diddly-squat."

"What was she like?"

Harriet thinks back to that terrible day.

"Well, other than that she was pretty banged up, Coops was quiet. Really uncommunicative. Eddsy even said when they chatted the next morning, she seemed preoccupied. In the end we thought it was mainly shock from the accident. Whatever she was coming over to tell me paled into insignificance. Oh Jethro, I'm all worked up again. What's going on? What's this about?"

"I'm kind of so worried for her."

"Why?"

"She's different."

"How do you mean?"

"I can't figure it out. You wouldn't know it just seeing her. I've spent time with her."

"Where is Cooper now?"

"She's working."

"In her garden studio?"

"No, a commercial one."

"Okay, I'll call her mobile."

"NO!"

Harriet's surprised by his outburst.

"Ooookay."

"Harriet, sorry man, but I don't want you to do that."

"You're worried about her. I'm worried about her again now too. I somehow knew this wouldn't go away."

"You've spoken to her on the phone since though, right?" Jethro says.

"Sure. Tons."

"She seems okay to you?"

"Sure, that's why I haven't chased her up on anything. Look, I won't say you called me first. It'll be one of our chatty chats sisters do."

"I don't even want her to, like, suspect anything. If you called this early without reason, Cooper'd suspect something."

Harriet hesitates.

"I suppose so. Okay, I'll call later."

"Don't say anything about me calling you though, yeah?"

"What's this programme thing you were asking me about, anyway?"

Jethro looks down, spots something on the carpet. Harriet says something but he doesn't hear. It looks like a business card. Blank. The back of a card. He remembers last night dropping the lip balm in the dark. Maybe this dropped out too.

Jethro picks up the card. He turns the card over. He reads.

Jethro goes cold.

"Harriet, I'll catch you later."

"Okay. Call me if—"

Jethro hangs up and stares at the card. Stares at the logo of the card. Stares long. Hard.

The business card says Dr John Applegate, Gateway House.

Jethro knows what it means. It wasn't just that Cooper'd called Gateway House. The card says so much more.

So much more.

It says she's already been.

1 1 1

THE SUE BAXTER PODCAST
DR STEWART-WAY
You're referring to Cooper's phone call out of the blue one
Sunday morning?
SUE BAXTER
Yes, Dr Stewart-Way. She called you several days after
treatment seeking a way to reverse the programme.
DR STEWART-WAY
Yes, and as you know Sue, it's something we're unable to do.
SUE BAXTER
So what could you do to help Cooper and Jethro's relationship?

1 1 2

FIVE MINUTES LATER Jethro calls Harriet again, pacing the bedroom.

Harriet answers before the second ring.

"Jethro?"

"Harriet, I don't know who else to turn to, man. I'm scared, I'm totally out of my mind."

"Oh hon, I can hear it in your voice."

Jethro tells her about the business card. He backtracks and tells her how Cooper acted strangely at The Savoy and about the Gateway House website.

"Jethro, we need to talk to her. YOU really need to talk to her."

"I tried. Spoke to her a while back. She tried to convince me nothing was wrong."

"Is Cooper definitely a patient at this clinic?"

"I don't know. She has their card. There are phone records even."

"Phone records?"

"I checked her phone when she was asleep. Oh man. I've never done that anything like that before."

"Oh hon."

"That's how I found the number. I feel so bad."

"I understand. We're both worried. I'd have done the same. Honestly that girl can be a clam. She doesn't release so much as an air bubble."

"You think I should call them? Gateway House?"

"They probably wouldn't tell you anything anyway. Jethro, sorry to ask but what do you think's happened to make her go there?"

"I think…" Jethro struggles to say the words.

"Jethro?"

"I think she might've been… when I was away… she…" He feels sick, stomach squirming.

Harriet's voice is soft, patient.

"Go on."

"She's so attractive, right?"

"Oh, she's gorgeous all right and wears it like a weight around her ankles."

"And she's tiny. She'd be easy to overcome. It wouldn't take much for her to be… for her to be… assaulted."

Jethro lets the sentence hang. The word, less harsh than the word rape but they both think that horrible word anyway. The word hangs between them, swings back and forth as obvious as a squeaky shop sign in the wind.

"Oh Jethro. Oh no, no. Oh gosh no."

"It's something in my gut, just something in my gut." Jethro's voice is strained. "And that's something they treat."

Harriet tries to reassure him.

"If THAT happened there's no way Cooper would bounce back like that."

"The website says different. Says they cure 99% of cases."

"Not that, Jethro. People take years to recover from trauma like that and many never do. I mean, the way Cooper sounds on the phone now she's more spirited than I've heard her in years. It's like someone's turned the brightness up on the TV."

Jethro turns the business card over in his hand.

"You think?"

"All I can say is Cooper and I have been having some really nice conversations lately. She's more chatty. She's laughing more than I've ever known. When we finish I end thinking I enjoyed our little goss."

"I don't know, Harriet."

"In fact, the more I think about it the more I honestly think you don't have anything to worry about."

Jethro goes quiet.

"Okay, this clinic, what's the web address?" Harriet says, hearing the doubt in his silence.

Jethro gives her the web address. Harriet spends the next few minutes scrolling through their blurb as he paces.

"I see what you mean. They claim a lot."

"Yeah."

"But you know what, Jethro? Snake oil comes to mind."

"That's kinda what I thought."

"Look, sit down with Coops, tell her all what's worrying you. Something bad obviously happened that day but probably not anything as bad as you think. You two are like… I don't know like salt and pepper. Ham and eggs. Fish and chips."

Jethro laughs but it's half-hearted.

"What I mean is you guys are sooooo compatible. You ask her directly, maybe she'll talk."

"I guess."

"Don't worry. I'll call her this evening too, find out what I can. I'm sure whatever happened to Cooper that day sorted itself out. It'll be okay. I'm sure of it."

"Thanks Harriet. Thanks man. Thanks a lot."

After Jethro hangs up, he paces. He can't settle. Should he call Cooper? He sees the note. The skull and crossbones. He looks at the business card, makes a decision.

Jethro finds his boots, puts them on. He puts his leather jacket on. He puts his bolero hat on. He leaves a Gone Out note on the kitchen table. He grabs his keys. He leaves the house.

1 1 3

DR APPLEGATE IS in his consultation room when his desk phone rings. He picks it up. It's his PA, David.

"Yes, David?"

"Dr Applegate, it's Mr Hall. Mrs Cooper Hall's husband."

"I see. Put him through."

"No sorry, I – uh – I mean he's here."

Dr Applegate takes off his spectacles, rubs the bridge of his nose.

"I – uh – I tried to tell him he needs to book an appointment but—"

Dr Applegate thinks about the early morning phone call Cooper made just days ago.

"Okay David. Please ask him to wait. I'll see him in a moment."

Dr Applegate calls Dr Stewart-Way's adjacent office but her phone immediately goes to voicemail. Oh yes. Klara's away. He hangs up, collects his thoughts. When he's ready, he buzzes David.

"David, could you prepare the Hall file please. Also, a disclosure form?"

"Right away."

"And please send Mr Hall in."

The door opens. Jethro Hall steps in.

1 1 4

WHEN JETHRO WALKS into Dr Applegate's office, he expects the consulting room to be a white, stark room, a desk, a chair for patients, a couple of medical cabinets, a telephone. He doesn't expect to walk into someone's sitting room. The room is softly lit, the carpet, thick. In the centre is a sofa, generous cushions strewn on it in a kind of designer way that's supposed to look casual. In front of the sofa, a polished wooden coffee table, two brass reading lamps with green shades either side of the sofa. On the wall, tasteful, classical art in a gilt frame, an oil painting of a Mastiff standing erect, head held high beside his master. It looks baronial. It also doesn't look like a print. Dr Applegate smiles as he rises from his desk, wedged into a corner as though it's an unimportant part of the room. The sofa's the important bit. Behind the sofa, a wall of books. They look like encyclopaedias, medical books.

Dr Applegate approaches Jethro, shakes his hand, introduces himself. He looks like a trendy architect. He's tall, lean, grey at his temples, a cracked, friendly face, maybe forty-five, maybe older. He looks polished in his wire-frame glasses, a crisp, pencil grey shirt, one button open at the neck, black trousers.

Dr Applegate offers Jethro a seat, offers a drink. Jethro asks for a glass of water.

Dr Applegate makes his way over to a small tea and coffee making area. He opens an inset fridge full of waters, juices, a carton of milk, a quartet of soft drink cans. He takes out a small bottle of mineral water, twists the top off the bottle, it fizzes. He takes an upturned glass, rights it. He pours the water into the glass. He cuts a lemon in half, floats a slice of it into the water. The water fizzes. He walks back, hands the glass to Jethro.

Jethro takes the glass, takes a sip. The water is cold and so mineral sharp it's almost bitter. He didn't expect restaurant grade water. He takes another sip, another, puts the glass down on the table. Dr Applegate settles on the other side, clears his throat.

"Mr Hall—"

"It's Jethro."

"Jethro, first I'd like to say thank you for coming along. I'd also like to disclose I'm recording this chat with you as part of my client files. Do you have any objections?"

"How come?"

"Nothing sinister. We do it with everyone."

Jethro flicks a hand.

"Yeah, whatever. It's cool."

"Also, before we start, would you mind signing a form?"

"A form?"

"Just a formality. In summary it states you have voluntarily become a client with us and that you're aware of the recording."

"I don't need to be a client with you."

"Forgive me, but you already are, at least as an original absentee half of the client agreement."

Jethro tilts his head, brow furrowing.

"Let me explain. Before I can discuss your wife's case I need you to assign yourself as a client as part of the contract we drew up for Mrs Hall."

"So, she's a client?"

"That's correct."

Jethro's knee starts bouncing.

"Like, forgive me doc, don't you guys have patient confidentiality agreements?"

"You are of course correct. But as stipulated on your wife's form, and because of the unusual nature of Mrs Hall's request, you are inclusive as part of the client consultation. In it we state we can fully disclose to the other party the full terms of treatment if they're originally absent from the consultation. This form authorises that approval."

Jethro shrugs.

"Yeah, whatever."

Dr Applegate opens the folder, hands it to Jethro, twists open a fat black ballpoint pen, hands it to him. Jethro scrawls his name, hands the pen and form back.

Dr Applegate thanks him, pockets the pen, slips the sheet of paper back in the folder, places the folder on the sofa beside him, puts a possessive hand on it.

"Now we can begin."

Dr Applegate tells Jethro about Cooper's account of seeing Jethro in bed with another woman in their bedroom. He tells Jethro about Cooper's distressed state. Her suicidal thoughts. How without intervention she almost certainly would have self-harmed, perhaps fatally. He tells Jethro about the treatment. How she became involved in The Gateway Programme. He tells Jethro, Cooper no longer has affections for him. Dr Applegate is blunt in his explanation. Clear. To the point. Each point is a bullet in Jethro's gut.

At the end Jethro is quiet, his mouth dry. At first he hadn't really believed the website. He thought, like Harriet, it was all a sham. Now he knows, far-fetched as it sounds, it isn't a sham at all. This is for real. He picks up the glass of mineral water, drinks. Tastes the bite of iron. Mineral sharp. Puts it down. The knee still bouncing up and down, only faster.

"No way Cooper would do that. No way."

Dr Applegate pats the file in front of him.

"I'm afraid it's all here, Mr Hall. Jethro."

Jethro stands up.

"This ain't right. Cooper wouldn't do that. You got it wrong."

"Jethro."

"I'm going now. This is someone else. I'm like sorry I disturbed you."

"Jethro."

Jethro makes for the door, goes across the wide expanse of soft, expensive carpet.

"Jethro, she's attempted suicide before hasn't she?"

Jethro pauses by the door.

"It happened before she met you, isn't that right?"

"She had a bad rap as a schoolkid," Jethro says. "She was fourteen. Yeah, before I met her. How'd you know that, doc?"

"Her full name is Cooper Marie Hall. She used to be Cooper Fisher before she married you."

Jethro feels his head go woozy.

"Jethro, please take a seat."

Jethro closes the door again. He walks across the carpet. This time the carpet feels spongy. The air, spongy. Everything spongy. He slumps into the sofa, hands clasped together, knee bouncing. Starts playing guitar finger exercises on his bouncing knee. Barred F root chord. Barred A chord. Barred D. He tries three different inversions of diminished sevenths.

Dr Applegate waits with the patience of a doctor.

Jethro stops with the chords, picks up his glass, drinks half the mineral water, puts the glass back down. A silver crown of bubbles rush up the glass. It sizzles, settles around the half cut lemon.

"This ain't right, it just ain't right."

"I can see this is a shock for you."

Jethro stares at the glass, looks at a stubborn bubble crawling up the side, slower than the rest.

"You got anything stronger, doc?"

"You mean spirits?"

"Yeah, spirits."

"I have but I'm afraid I don't normally—"

"What you got?"

Dr Applegate pauses.

"I have whisky, gin—"

"You got any vodka?"

Dr Applegate rises, walks back to the drinks area. He slides open a wooden panel, pulls out a bottle of vodka, unscrews the top, pours it into a shot glass, tightens the top, returns the bottle, slides the panel shut, returns, hands Jethro the glass.

Jethro raises the glass to his lips, snaps his head back and swallows in one go. The liquid slips down. It's both cold and hot. Cold in his mouth, hot as it fires its way down. He places the empty glass on the table. He turns to Dr Applegate.

"Cooper doesn't love me anymore, that's what you're saying, right?"

"It's a bit more complicated than that."

"This ain't right. This ain't right." Jethro's face screws up. "She thinks I'm having an affair?"

"Well, that was her motivation behind the treatment."

"So, she like saw me in bed with another woman?"

"Yes."

"Like, in our bed?"

"In your marital bed, yes." He listens as Jethro scrambles to make sense.

"Look, I got a son. WE got a son."

"Daniel."

"Yeah, Daniel. You know he's at university right? He's studying something on Ancient History right? You know what he got?"

"What's that?"

"He got a girlfriend. His first proper one. She's lovely. She's elegant. She talks like she comes from Mayfair or something. She got a waist, thin as a straw. She got long, thick brunette hair. She got Audrey Hepburn eyes, dark like molasses. She's lovely. Cooper only found out like on Friday night about Araminta. I only found out a couple days before."

"So?"

"So, Daniel didn't tell us till recently they've been going out like months. Turns out Araminta's been to our house. Same day I left to do a music tour in Europe, turns out. Cooper must've... well she must've spied them. She must've run away. Daniel had no idea she was there. Cooper called you right? Last week, early in the morning, right?"

"You know about that?"

Jethro takes that in, accepts it. The information is spongy. Soft. It's lost its impact. Like punching him with hands inside oven gloves.

"You got another one of those vodkas doc?"

Dr Applegate takes the glass, refills, returns, hands it to Jethro.

Jethro downs it. The second one hits him solidly. Spongy and fuzzy now. He tries an augmented A chord on his bouncing knee. A C# F. You resolve the F it becomes a plain old A major chord. You flatten the C# instead it becomes first inversion F major. Or root A minor 6.

"Now I get it, I get it."

"I'm sorry Jethro, I don't follow you."

"You know we went to The Savoy in The Strand? Me and Cooper?"

"No, I didn't."

"A treat for my wife man, a treat. Did the whole Roller thing from the house. She didn't know what hit her when she saw the car outside our house and a chauffeur on the doorstep and everything. She didn't know."

"It sounds like a lovely surprise."

"Should've been man, should've been. Listen, I got a story to tell you doc. So me and Cooper, we're led to the dining table in The Savoy, she notices like four champagne glasses then in walks Daniel and Araminta holding hands. Cooper looks shocked. I thought at the time it was way shocked. More than I'd have expected, seeing Daniel there with a girlfriend. But yeah, I get it now. Cooper recognised her. Araminta. Oh man.

Cooper recognised her from seeing her in bed. Then she realised she made a crater-sized mistake. You getting me doc? Just figured it out. It was Daniel in our bed with his girlfriend. Cooper saw Daniel making out but I'm guessing she didn't hang around long enough to realise it wasn't me. He's the spit of me, right? Hey, you never been to Simpsons in the Strand? Restaurant inside The Savoy?"

"It is a very pleasant eating experience, I agree."

"Yeah, yeah you got that right. Only we spent a night at the Savoy too. Booked a room with a river view. The Savoy. Should've been amazing. Should've been."

"Mrs Hall called me on Sunday morning."

"Somewhere around seven or eight, right doc?"

"That's correct. And now I think I understand why."

Jethro looks at Dr Applegate.

"Yeah? Why's that? What'd she want?"

"Cooper asked whether it's possible to reverse the treatment."

1 1 5

COOPER ARRIVES HOME from a location recording at Tear Studios. It was a good session. She intends to go to her garden studio and do a quick mix down. She opens the front door, walks in.

The door to the kitchen is wide open. Cooper spots Jethro, his back to her, seated at the kitchen table, head bowed.

Cooper calls out.

"Hey."

Jethro doesn't move, doesn't respond.

"Jethro?"

He doesn't move, doesn't respond, head bowed.

Cooper stares at him as she shrugs her denim jacket off, hangs it up. Surely, he heard her?

He doesn't move.

She takes her boots off, being deliberately noisy, puts them on the rack, stares at him.

Doesn't respond.

"Jethro?"

Cooper walks to the kitchen. Jethro's head, still bowed. Something is wrong, Cooper knows something is wrong. Jethro's head is bowed, his hands crossed in front of him, he is still, very still, very very still. She touches him on the shoulder.

"Jethro?"

Jethro looks up. His eyes, swollen red.

She pulls the other chair from under the table next to him, sits down.

"What's happened?"

"I know," Jethro says.

"What do you mean?"

"Like I said, I know."

Cooper looks at him, her face a mask.

Jethro unfurls his fist on the table. In his palm is a crumpled sweaty business card.

Cooper only utters one word.

"Oh."

1 1 6

"I SPOKE WITH your Dr Applegate," Jethro says.

"Oh."

"He told me everything. He told me, according to you, you saw me in bed with another woman."

"Oh."

"He told me, according to you, I'd gone off to Europe with this other woman from the band, and wasn't coming back. With Sophie Cordroy. Then you know what?"

Jethro looks up, stares at Cooper, eyes wet, red.

"Then he told me you had the treatment so I asked what, The Gateway Programme treatment, and you know what?"

"Go on."

"He said yes."

"Oh."

Jethro's face screws up.

"I thought something had happened to you. I knew something was up when I found this." He spreads the business card between his fingers, flat on the table.

"And then with what Harriet told me, I put it together."

"You spoke with Harriet?"

"We thought someone had assaulted you or something."

"Oh."

"Tell you what though. I didn't expect to hear what the doc said."

Jethro's face crumples. Cooper notices for the first time his boots are on. Beside him on the table, his statement bolero hat.

He looks like he's just come in and slumped into the chair and hasn't moved since.

"I wish you'd talked to me, Coops. I wish you had. But I guess it's my fault too. I should've come back that first night. I should've."

"Did Dr Applegate tell you I'd called him afterwards?"

Jethro continues to study the card, flicks at a corner, turns it around and around.

"Yeah, he did."

Confusion, anguish, pain, disbelief passes over his face like flickering shadows. He looks at her, so crumpled. So broken. Pain. Distress. So tortured. Love.

Love.

Cooper feels something for Jethro too. Not love, but it's something. What is it?

"I'm sorry, Jethro."

"Yeah, I kinda get that."

"I'm sorry."

"Only one thing I don't get. Why'd you think I'd do something like that?"

"I didn't. Not in forever years. Not until I saw…"

He looks at her, his eyes sodden, his mouth twisted in misery.

"I wish you'd stepped into the bedroom. I wish you had."

"Yeah, I wish it too."

"I'm guessing you thought it was me with Sophie, right?"

"Yeah."

"Well, for the record, nothing's ever happened between us. Sophie flirts like mad yeah, but I'd never do that to you, Coops."

Cooper presses her lips together, leans over, covers his hands with hers. It's her way of saying she's sorry for doubting him.

Jethro freezes then. Stares at what she's done. He doesn't look at her. He carefully extracts his hands from under hers until they're free. Jethro stands up slowly like an elderly man, shoulders stooped.

"Oh yeah, forgot to say, I like spoke with the label."

"The record label?"

"It's not happening."

"What isn't?"

"I told them I can't do it."

"Oh Jethro."

"I've pissed the band off."

"Jethro, you can't back down."

"The label said they're gonna sue me. Said I signed the contract. They already thrown money at us."

"Oh Jethro."

Jethro picks up his hat, walks into the hall like he's dragging something heavy behind him. He grabs his scarf. Cooper sees Daniel's overstuffed rucksack by the front door. Jethro hooks it over a shoulder. He takes out his keys.

"Where are you going?" Cooper says.

Jethro tests the weight of the keys. He opens the front door. Jethro pauses at the front door. He doesn't turn around to face her. He faces the world.

"Jethro?"

"I wish you'd stepped into the room. I wish you had."

He puts his hat on, steps through the doorway, clicks the front door shut.

Cooper is up instantly. She rushes to the door.

"Jethro?"

Opens the front door.

"Jethro!"

She races out on to the porch. His car, his crappy Fiat 500 rust bucket is backing out.

Cooper rushes up to it, slaps the driver's window, calls out. "Wait."

He stops the car but doesn't look.

Cooper doesn't know what to say. She doesn't know what words to use. Doesn't know. She works out what she feels for him though.

Jethro nods to himself, doesn't wait any more. He pulls out. Drives away.

Cooper stares after him, feeling what she feels for him, remembering what the doctors said about feeling basic empathy. And yeah, what she feels for Jethro.

It's pity.

1 1 7

COOPER HASN'T HEARD from Jethro in weeks.

When he'd first left she'd called almost every thirty minutes. Then she found his mobile phone switched off in a drawer five days later. He'd meant to leave it behind.

After charging it up, Cooper listens to messages from the band. "Jethro like for Christ's sake where the heck are you? We need to talk to the label, get this stuff sorted yeah? Come on man, you can't throw this chance away. Call, yeah?"

Calls from the record label threaten Jethro with lawsuits. No one knows where Jethro is. No one knows how to get hold of him.

Cooper calls the band members one by one. They have no idea where he is. Time moves on. They get an occasional email from him, they say. "Sorry sweetheart that's all I know. Yeah I know sweetheart we'll let you know if he contacts, yeah yeah, sure sure, course."

Cooper keeps Jethro's phone charged, it rings all the time every day. People she doesn't know wants to get in touch with him, venues, bookings, friends. She listens to messages left when she didn't get to pick up. Calls people back. Explains Jethro's not on this number at the moment. No, she doesn't know how to contact him.

Harriet calls all the time. Cooper doesn't answer, just sends texts. She feels lost. An empty house with no one but Kelloggs. A sister who phones all the time, worried about her. Daniel calls, confused by everything. Eddsy's been around a couple of times but stands on the doorstep saying Cooper should come stay with them till stuff is sorted.

Thing is, Cooper doesn't need all that. She doesn't need the attention. Cooper doesn't miss Jethro. She can't miss him. She doesn't love Jethro. She can't love him.

Still.

Her life feels strangely vacant, like a missing tooth. The tongue keeps flicking over the empty gap. Even though it's gone she notices it's absence all the time. All the time.

She speaks to the doctors. They tell her it's probably due to the habit of routine that's thrown her out. In PTSD cases people are happy to be rid of what tormented them. In this case, well, it's different. It's a person you loved, one you set up your life around. Now you're having to unravel your life from around theirs. It's bound to be strange.

More weeks pass.

Mail for Jethro piles up. Unless it's a bill, Cooper leaves them unopened on the hall table. He has to come back one day. Has to. The house remains empty of his music. No more waking in the middle of the night to Jethro's impromptu playing from an unplugged electric guitar. He kept the guitar at the side of the bed for ideas. He'd wake up, try something out, jot something down in a notebook, go back to sleep in seconds. He says sometimes he finds gold dust in that notebook.

The guitar gathers a faint film of dust, faded grey like cobwebs.

The notepad on his bedside table stays untouched. The pen hasn't moved. Jethro didn't take a single guitar with him. Cooper keeps to her side of the bed. She never stretches out to find it empty.

No, she doesn't love him.

Daniel knows the truth.

Araminta.

They know the truth.

And though Daniel's in Durham, he calls almost every night. His coursework hasn't been going so well since the separation. When he'd heard about dad he'd rushed home and learned everything. But he couldn't stay long. They'd embraced and he said he was sorry for using their bed and making the whole mess happen.

Daniel blames himself. He blames himself.

Araminta is with Daniel in Durham though she's on a different degree. She's helping him through this time. Araminta phones Cooper, explains how guilt-ridden Daniel is. She apologises again and again, again, again, again. Cooper says no one could know the disastrous outcome. It's no one's fault. No one's fault.

Months pass.

On the nightly calls Cooper learns from Daniel about Jethro. Jethro started calling Daniel a few months back. Daniel tells Cooper dad's working on new material.

"You know where he lives?"

"No, dad never says."

"You have a contact number for him?"

"No mum, his number totally comes up unknown."

After their chat Daniel always says "I'm so sorry mum, I messed up, I'm like completely sorry."

Sometimes Daniel cries over the phone. Cooper says it's not your fault, it's not your fault. One day he says he's sorry too many times and Cooper says don't you ever tell me you're sorry again, yeah? He pauses, registers the anger in her voice, collects himself, says yeah mum okay.

Cooper hears Jethro one day. On Capital FM. A DJ is interviewing him. Jethro sounds relaxed. He sounds calm. He's with his band. They're called Jethro & Crew.

Cooper calls the record label.

Yes, he's cut a new deal with them. He's doing a promotional tour.

428

They release a debut album. They have a good social media presence. On the radio they joke that it's not called song writing anymore, it's called being a topliner. Supposed to mean someone who writes lyrics and melody over an existing composed beat but it's used interchangeably with the term songwriter nowadays.

Cooper calls the band members.

"Yeah sweetheart, we're working with him. Nah love he's not here at the moment. Yeah sweetheart we'll give him the message. Sure sure, no probs."

Cooper goes online, sees a tour lined up from the official Jethro & Crew website. They're doing 34 large venues. They have a Twitter following, an Instagram following, Tumblr, Snapchat, Facebook, YouTube, TikTok, Vimeo. There's already several fan clubs. Should Cooper try to see him backstage at one of his concerts? She goes down the list of some of the locations. Birmingham, Brighton, Glasgow, Liverpool, London, Manchester, Norwich, Nottingham...

Then decides no, it's not the right thing to do.

Next thing the label release the album. It's on special edition vinyl. No CDs. Not online anywhere. You can only buy vinyl. Jethro calls it an LP in interviews. People don't know what an LP is. He laughs, says it means long playing record. Says that's what oldies used to call it. People put the tracks on YouTube or on torrent websites and other streaming sites.

All the illegally uploaded tracks are taken down within hours.

The exclusivity makes them even more popular. People go out of their way to buy the album. They get out their dads' old turntables from the loft or from second-hand shops or buy new ones. Jethro & Crew gets into the newspapers. He's interviewed on radio, on podcasts. Isn't he and the crew a bit old to be a new thing? Jethro laughs. Yeah, yeah, we're ancient. He's thirty-eight. But it's the music, the music everyone goes for.

Cooper buys his LP, goes into her studio, pulls it out of the sleeve, then out of the white inner paper sleeve. She enjoys the tactile moment. The record is a picture disc. It's a bolero hat, the grooves cut into the wide rim, the centre label is the centre of the hat. Under the spotlights the grooves of the record glisten like the surface of the sea in moonlight. Cooper places it on the turntable.

Plays it.

A few familiar tracks. Ain't It So. The Lives of Others. Time and Time Again. It's Only a Song. Smoky Dusty Foggy Mist. Some new tracks she's never heard. So & So. Captured. Motley Disaster. Zoom Me. The Gun on Me. Promise. Undone.

Jethro & Crew surf the fame. They go on an international tour. Climb the charts in the US.

Then.

Then.

One day reporters, photographers, TV crews and journalists are outside Cooper's house.

Seems Gateway House is in the news.

Seems Cooper is in the news too.

Jethro mentioned he has a wife. Yeah they're separated. The media find out how, why, when, who, what.

Cooper hears an interview where he tells how things went wrong. How things got all messed up. Gateway House starts to become famous (or infamous) for dealing with broken love. They hadn't offered that service, only the PTSD treatment. But people bomb Gateway House with phone calls. All they want is their hearts' mended. Thousands of hearts. Thousands. Millions. Billions. Trillions.

Phone calls from the press journalists ask to speak to Cooper. In the street journalists press contact cards into her hand. Even when she's shopping in Tesco. Even when she jogs. Phone calls to her mobile all the time. She hears Dr Applegate and Dr Stewart-Way on radio interviews. They mention Cooper. They consider Cooper a brave pioneer. She was the first to undergo the treatment for love. Love deleted. People want to know what it's like. When journalists can't get through to Cooper, they go after Daniel. Approach him in the streets of Durham outside the university. He's the son of Jethro and Cooper Hall. Things go crazy for a while.

Another six months.

Seven.

Ten.

A year.

Jethro & Crew are doing well.

Gateway House has had a massive influx of business, they've just opened another clinic.

The news frenzy is quieter. Starts to die. Starts to go. One day there's nothing in the news about them. Silence again.

It's 2.02am.

A mobile rings. It's Cooper's.

Cooper fumbles for her phone in the dark, picks it up, answers it.

"Hey there," the caller says.

Cooper recognises the voice at once. It's Jethro.

1 1 8

AT FIRST HARRIET waits for Eddsy to say something about the adoption booklet.

She waits and waits.

But he never says a thing. Days of excitement and anticipation had turned into weeks of expectation, had turned into months of resigned acceptance, has turned into a year or more. It isn't going to be. Harriet used to think about asking Eddsy about the booklet but somehow she couldn't bring herself to do it. It was obvious Eddsy had already decided. Well, she knows that now. She was never supposed to see the booklet anyway. It was in his glove compartment. It wasn't exactly hidden. Still. She could have asked him anyway couldn't she? No. Harriet could never have done that.

Eddsy too forgets about the adoption booklet in that time. Then when he remembers, he searches in the glove compartment. He can't find it. Funny. He was sure he put it there. Perhaps on one of his clear outs he'd thrown it away without thinking. Must be what he did.

One day, a year later he goes to visit one of his six garages to welcome a new employee. As he drives along the high street he glimpses a billboard. The headline is All You Need Is Love, the title of one of the Beatles' songs, and a bunch of children of all ages, nationalities, all in T-shirts, ripped jeans, a couple are babies, some are young children, others are teens, they're all laughing, hugging each other or holding hands. They're all in a queue disappearing off into infinity. It's a happy queue. It has the Barnado's logo and a website. Then Eddsy remembers the booklet again. Suddenly he knows the right thing to do. Of course. Why didn't he think that before? He pulls off at the next junction, postpones his appointment at the garage. Calls an office number. He talks to someone and they chat.

Eddsy ends the call, smiles.

He has a place to be.

"JETHRO?"

"Yeah, it's me. Did I wake you?"

Cooper sits up straight, sleep evaporated. She turns her pillows portrait, leans back.

"It's okay," Cooper says.

"Sorry, I wasn't thinking."

"Yeah, don't worry about it."

"I kept meaning to call but I kept scaring myself off. I finally grabbed the horns, just finally grabbed the horns."

"How are you?"

"Yeah I'm cool. Busy."

"That's great."

"Yeah. You?"

"I'm doing okay. Where're you calling from?"

"I can't tell you, you'll hate me, Coops."

"Why? Where are you?"

"I'm sitting on a beach in Malibu."

"For real?"

"It's a gorgeous evening. I'm at a producer's beach house. Ocean's blue, sand's like gold dust and I'm holding a Malibu Martini. It's total heaven."

"What time is it there?"

"Just after six."

Cooper laughs.

"Yeah, I hate you."

He chuckles.

"Look Coops, I like owe you an apology."

Cooper's surprised. She didn't expect this.

"Yeah?"

"The publicity to do with Gateway House. That wasn't my doing. That was Spanish Monroe. He blabs to the A&R guy one day and they use it for publicity. Tell the truth it completely pissed me off. Then the whole thing took over. All the newspapers, TV, radio, podcasts, blog sites. Apparently, it blew down Twitter. I had to do interviews man. It went crazy. I know reporters pestered you like they pestered Daniel. Fact is all we could do was ride this out."

"I saw the interviews."

"Yeah. Label's laughing but I'm not. I'm glad it's over. I wanted to stick Spanish's drumsticks so far up his backside they'd come out the top of his head. You know how he is. One drink and he blabs to anyone about anything."

Cooper laughs.

"Yeah, don't worry about it."

"Hey listen, how're you fixed?"

"Me? Everything's okay."

"Work good?"

"Yeah, Graham keeps me busy."

"Right, right. Heard you're doing forensic audio restoration or something on unreleased demo tracks from dead people's archives."

"Yeah, something like that. You know, I've got a mountain of unopened letters here for you Jethro."

"Chuck 'em out."

"They could be important."

"After a year and a half? Doubt it. 'Sides, I contacted all the important ones. Had them redirected. Jethro hesitates. So how's everything else been going?"

Cooper gets it. She knows what he's asking. Her social life.

"Like I said, Graham keeps me locked in the studio or on location."

Silence stretches between them.

"What about you?" Cooper says.

"Yeah, the same. Not even got time to sleep. Punishing schedule, this is totally crazy stuff."

"Except you're on a Malibu beach with a Malibu Martini. What is a Malibu Martini anyway?"

He laughs again but this time it's half-hearted.

"I'll tell you one day."

"Oh, and thanks for the money you send."

"Yeah it's cool. I figured you'd still need it."

"The money's sitting in a bank account. I'm doing okay, Jethro."

"Yeah? Doing that well?"

Cooper waits, sensing another reason for his call.

"Listen Cooper… it's been a while."

She gets it. He's after a divorce. Cooper wondered when that would happen. She thought the papers would've been through the letter box within weeks of his leaving but when it didn't happen she forgot about it. She had other ideas but now they seem silly. A divorce would be best.

"You can have it," Cooper says.

"Have what?"

"Send me the papers."

"What papers?"

"You want a divorce, yeah?"

"Right, right," Jethro eventually says.

"That's why you're calling, yeah?"

"Course."

"All your clothes are still here. Your guitars, your equipment. We'll need to draw up something to do with the house."

"Yeah, I guess. I'd like to see my Les Paul and Gibson again. Clothes you can chuck out. I got more than enough T-shirts and jeans."

"And the house? We'll have to work out—"

"Yeah look, forget it."

"What do you mean?"

"Listen, I got to go."

"Oh. When do you want to talk about—"

"Catch you laters, yeah?"

Jethro hangs up.

Cooper's left with a silent line.

THE SUE BAXTER PODCAST
DR STEWART-WAY
I'm afraid there were no other options, Sue.
SUE BAXTER
So Jethro went through heartbreak the old-fashioned way?
DR STEWART-WAY
It appears so.
SUE BAXTER
Well he seems to have fared very well in the end. He's been seen with a string of girlfriends. But what of Cooper Hall? Are you still in contact with her, Dr Stewart-Way?
DR STEWART-WAY
We haven't heard from her in a long while.
SUE BAXTER
Is that normal?
DR STEWART-WAY
There's no reason to hear from her.
SUE BAXTER
So she continues to keep a low profile.
DR STEWART-WAY
Well, she's not in the spotlight the way Jethro T Hall is.
SUE BAXTER
So is their story over?
DR STEWART-WAY
I would say so.

1 2 1

JETHRO STARES AT his phone, feeling the punch in the gut.

It'd been so hard to call Cooper. It had been crazy mad to hear Cooper's voice after so long. The moment she'd answered a deep longing within him shot to the surface. Despite the glory, the fame, the tributes, the admiration, the awards, his life is empty. He'd had to steady his voice, make himself calm, speak casually, like everything was cool.

Fact is, every day his first thought is Cooper. Fact is, every night his last thought is Cooper. How she looks now, what she's up to, how she's getting on, all that stuff. It doesn't matter where he is, how busy he is, whether he's messing with The Crew on the tour bus, onstage, at the endless celebrity parties...

Or even kicking back on a Malibu beach with a Malibu Martini.

In every quiet moment Cooper is there, inside him. Inside him.

The worst thing is wondering whether she's seeing anyone. Every time he thinks she might be now, it makes him sick. Oh man.

Well anyway, Cooper sounds great.

Seems like her work is doing great.

It's just, after all that, it never occurred to him she'd stretch for a divorce. Not once. Never. And Cooper talked about it with the cool efficiency of an accountant adding columns in some ledger. Jethro knows Cooper feels nothing for him. He knows that. But to hear it in her voice.

He needs to get over it. Her.

Or…

That would be so easy, right? Book an appointment at Gateway House. He goes in, doc flicks a few switches, gets the treatment, comes out, basted, roasted, done. So easy. He'd smile up at the sky. He'd be like, why'd I wait so long? Yeah he could get the treatment and paint love by numbers too.

Except no, he can't. He just can't. When he thinks about it, he can't. Like it's betrayal to himself and Cooper. He gets why Cooper did it. She really did feel betrayed. He gets it. But he doesn't have that luxury of escape. That reason to have the treatment. It doesn't sit right with him.

So Jethro never makes the call. The easy one. The one to Gateway House.

Instead he made the other call. The hard one. The hardest one in the world.

And now Cooper is stretching for a divorce. Came out of her mouth easy, like she was ordering what to have on top of a pizza.

Wow.

Mind-blowing. A divorce. Never saw that coming, man.

Jethro sits in his car outside their old home. Her home now. He stares up at the darkened curtains of the bedroom. Cooper is in bed, behind that window, just a few metres away. A sheet of glass separates them, that's all.

Yeah so? What beach in Malibu? What Malibu Martini? He'd been in Malibu a month ago but it was only with the producer Wilson Thompson, his wife Courtney, their young son Dominic, and an always smiling, live-in nanny in a starched grey uniform called Engracia. Jethro'd gone for lone walks on the beach watching the sunrise, the sunset, having empty time, thinking of no one but Cooper. Wilson Thompson knew he still loved Cooper. He'd encouraged Jethro to call her when he flew back. It was so painful, missing her. The pain, the emptiness, it never goes away. Not even barefoot on a fine-sand Malibu beach, the ocean clear, the tide frothy, white, sizzling between toes like kisses, the sun, a big burning eye staring him down.

It never goes. The pain. You carry it with you.

Jethro has parked outside the house.

Their old house.

Her home now.

Just a few metres away. His old door key around his neck. Never takes it off, not even for a shower. Only at the endless airports when the metal detectors go off.

All he has to do now is call again, say guess where I am? She'd say you already said, you're in Malibu on a beach. He'd say actually I'm a bit closer. He'd get out the car, walk up to the front door, use the door key. Cooper'd rush down the stairs in surprise, delight, love in her eyes.

Love in her eyes.

Oh…

Yeah. Right. Right.

That's the bit he always crashes on. Love in her eyes.

Oh man. Cooper doesn't love him, doesn't love him, doesn't love him, SHE DOES NOT LOVE HIM. She can never love him again. It's impossible. Love – it's deleted. What is done cannot be undone. There's nothing there. There are no second chances. Not with Cooper.

So of course Jethro never gets out the car.

Never walks up the path.

Never uses the key.

There's never surprise on Cooper's face. A smile… Her expression of love, soft as cushions.

And they never fall into each other's arms.

Swell of music. Kiss. Roll end credits.

Jethro clenches his jaw.

There is no happy-freakin'-ever-after, get over it yeah?

Jethro finishes his rollup, pushes the nub of it into his tobacco tin, starts the car, pulls out. He's parked four times outside the house wanting to call, wanting to surprise Cooper.

He made it this far. He called her.

But this time as he drives away he knows.

Tears.

Tears falling.

This time.

Chest.

Chest tightening.

This time.

Heart.

Heart breaking.

This time.

It's the last time.

1 2 2

COOPER'S STILL LYING in the dark awake when there's the gentle squeak of the bedroom door. The soft patter of feet. Kelloggs leaps on to the bed, goes to Jethro's side, curls up on his pillow. It's where he sleeps now after his nocturnal jaunts. Cooper takes comfort him being there.

She reaches over, strokes him. His fur is cool, his paws cold and he has the smell of the night. He offers a lazy mew, then settles.

Cooper can't settle.

That call bothers her. She knows something's wrong with the call. She doesn't know what.

Outside a lone car starts up. Drives away.

Cooper lies there. A thought occurs to her. She sits up, switches on the bedside lamp, plumps her pillows upright again. Kelloggs lifts his head, looks around, then his head drops back to his paws, his eyes close into glossy slits.

Cooper puts on her glasses, picks up her phone. Jethro'd called. It'll be withheld but you never know. She finds the last number called. It's there!

She calls.

She hears the purr of his phone ringing. Cooper'd expected it to take time connecting to whatever exchanges around the world it has to go through but it connects straight away.

It rings.

Rings.

Jethro doesn't answer.

Rings.

He did say he had to go.

It clicks through.

"Jethro?"

"Hey it's Jethro. Be cool. Leave a message."

Cooper waits for the bleep. She leaves a message. Says what she wants to say. Hangs up. She resettles, takes Kelloggs, pulls him under the duvet and cuddles him.

Kelloggs can't believe his luck. He's not allowed under the duvet. He stretches out in the warmth of body heat, the cosy darkness warming his chilly fur. His cold paws warming against Cooper's hot chest.

He sleeps.

Cooper sleeps.

1 2 3

THE NEXT MORNING Cooper wakes to her mobile buzzing.
She peeks at who's calling, snatches the phone.

"Jethro?"

"Yeah, sorry to call so early again."

"You got my message?"

"Yeah."

Cooper looks at the clock. No wonder she feels like crap. It's
6.42am. Kelloggs wakes from the pillow beside her, obviously
he got too hot during the night. He sits up, paws the duvet,
attention-purring, staring at Cooper. He's ready for food. 0-60 in
seconds.

"Not now," Cooper says.

"Oh, yeah, sorry. I'll call back laters, yeah?"

"No. I was talking to Kelloggs."

Jethro gives a half laugh.

"Oh right, yeah. How is the breakfast cereal cat?"

"Yeah, he's good."

"Listen. Got your message. Had a think about what you said.
Fact is I haven't caught a single shut-eye since. I'm bushed."

"Isn't it late evening for you?"

"Oh yeah, yeah. Right, right... So listen... So okay I'm not
exactly in Malibu."

"Where are you?"

"Bit closer."

"You're in England?"

Sigh.

"Yeah."

"Then why—"

"Dunno. I don't know what's going on in my head, man. Anyway, I thought about... well about what you said on your message about how Daniel was playing my records that day."

The message. Cooper had told him everything on the message.

"I didn't even know he liked Gillespie," Jethro says.

"Jethro. Yeah, he doesn't."

"Then why...? Oh... wait... yeah, yeah. He was trying to impress the girl right? Araminta likes Dizzy, I remember her saying that night at The Savoy." He chuckles. "Hey, girl's got taste. And then yeah you mentioned the aftershave. And using our bed. That's why you got the new bed and did the whole makeover thing. I get it now. The brat wears my aftershave, he's in our bed playing Gillespie, and far as you know he's supposed to be back at uni. He copied all my moves on her. So, course it could only be me you'd expect to see. Guess I would've made the same jump if we'd reversed roles. I didn't know any of that stuff."

"You never gave me time to explain, Jethro."

"Yeah, right, right. My bad."

Cooper decides to mimic Jethro to lighten the mood.

"Hey, don't sweat it."

He laughs.

"Look, I still think you should've spoken to me about it. You know? Before you had the treatment but yeah I get it. You were crazy out your mind. I'd vamoosed on a tour. It's easy to think crazy stuff when your head's not on right."

Kelloggs climbs into Cooper's lap and pushes his nose into Cooper's face, his purr loud.

"Jeez, either that's you purring or Kelloggs's bought a guitar amp."

"He's hungry."

"What's new? Cereal killer cat's always hungry."

Cooper senses Jethro has more to say. She waits.

"Anyways," Jethro says, "I just shot the breeze with Harriet."

"When?"

"Like, five minutes ago."

Cooper glances at the clock again. 6.49am.

"Bet she wasn't overjoyed about the hour."

"Nah, she was totally cool about it. Eddsy gets up at five, you know that?"

Cooper remembers the early morning he'd surprised her in the kitchen after the accident.

"Yeah, I know."

"Harriet worries about you. She like told me something about the day after your car accident."

"What about it?"

"She said Eddsy caught you looking for sleeping pills and doing some weird stuff with a knife."

"Oh." The suicide implication hangs in the air unsaid.

"Anyways," Jethro says, "appreciate your filling me in on Daniel. I didn't know any of that. Guess Daniel tried to tell me several times and I stopped him cold. I didn't want to hear any of that stuff. I should be peeved at him."

"Yeah, don't blame him."

"Yeah, it's okay. I don't."

"And... I wasn't after a divorce Jethro. Last night when you mentioned it."

"Right, right."

"I thought that's what you wanted."

Silence. Cooper tries again.

"Jethro, is it what you want?"

Sighs.

"Who knows?"

"Anyway, I was thinking we should meet up and you know... And talk."

Again, the silence.

"Jethro?"

"Wait. Lemme think."

Cooper waits. Jethro comes back.

"I have some stuff scheduled that's all."

Cooper's surprised.

"I didn't mean today."

"What's wrong with today?"

More surprise.

"But you haven't slept since my message."

"Don't sweat it. On tour you have to catch the shut-eye when you can."

"You'll meet me?"

"Yeah, why not?"

Cooper has an idea.

"How about we meet up at some public place for a coffee or something?"

Jethro chuckles.

"You mean, like a secret rendezvous?"

"Yeah, if you want."

"Like, I have to wear a carnation or something?"

"We both could."

"Where you got in mind?"

Cooper thinks. Somewhere public where there could be distractions in case things get awkward. It comes to her.

"I've never been to the Natural History Museum."

"You're kidding me."

"I thought you knew that."

"I mean the location."

"Well… we don't have to."

Jethro's grin comes through the line.

"Nah, that'd be pretty cool."

COOPER'S WAITING INSIDE the Natural History Museum entrance. She walks in beneath the huge suspended skeleton of a blue whale called Hope. She learns blue whales are the largest mammals to have ever existed. Who knew? The 25 metre long skeleton looms down in a dive position so it looks more like a swooping giant bird with stumpy wings than a whale with lengthened jaws. Cooper cranes her neck as she follows the head all the way down to the pointed mouth. She fidgets and paces around the skeleton, preoccupied with how this meeting with Jethro will go.

Cooper stops at the plaque and reads about the whale. She learns the bones aren't that old. That the whale was trapped in a Thames tide in 1891 and after she died they excavated her.

Behind her a male voice clears his throat. Cooper spins around. It's Jethro. He's smiling, his handsome face thin. He taps a carnation in the lapel of his thick black leather jacket.

He sees Cooper's wearing one too. They laugh.

"Hey there." His voice sounds crumpled, like a well-used blanket.

Jethro and Cooper look over each other. Under his leather jacket he's wearing a grey T-shirt, jeans, trainers, and of course a bolero hat over his long hair. He looks a little too angular, too thin, but it's still the same Jethro.

Jethro in turn takes in Cooper's pretty V-neck pink top over a denim jacket, dark cotton skirt with flat heels. Her hair's down to her chin now, but she still keeps that cool, swept back gelled look.

They ignore the few visitors this early in the morning clocking him, pretending they haven't seen him, whispering after they pass, you know who that is? No, it can't be.

Neither Jethro nor Cooper know what to do. Hug? Kiss? In the end Cooper says hey.

"What happened to your combats?" Jethro says.

"Yeah well, I decided it was about time I stopped hiding behind them. I've got a better sense of the kind of people I want around me now."

Jethro nods at that, doesn't say anything more about it. Instead, he glances up at the 25 metre skeleton.

"Whoa, that bird's huge."

"It's a whale."

"No kidding."

"She's poised in a feeding position."

Jethro side steps it.

Cooper laughs.

"Don't worry, she wouldn't give you the time of day. Her diet's krill. Says so on the plaque."

Jethro shakes his head.

"Well, they haven't been feeding her. She's all bone."

*

In the coffee shop Cooper orders a cappuccino, Jethro orders Earl Grey, no milk and they perch on lightweight aluminium chairs. Jethro takes off his leather jacket and bolero hat, and combs his fingers through his hair. It sweeps over his forehead. He washed it this morning she can tell. He's trying hard. He places his hat on the table.

They talk about what they've been doing in the last year and a half, but really they're scouting each other out. A dance. A play of words.

Jethro tells her about how crazy life is now. Tells her what it's like to be on the road. All the backstage gossip. All the stories. The endless travelling, flying, coaching, singing, recording, interviewing, TV shows, podcasting. He says it's a crazy mad treadmill. Yeah okay it's fun, but after a while it's a treadmill.

Cooper tells him work's flooded in since she worked on The Shitty Squits album. About the software she'd invented. He tells her yeah he's heard her name mentioned in studios in hushed reverent tones.

As they talk Cooper sees Jethro's still in love with her. It radiates from him like heat. They interweave gossip like finely woven cloth, creating a continuous tapestry of conversation until it's over and they both stare into their almost empty mugs. He gets up, orders seconds. Cooper waits for him to return, rehearses what to say.

Jethro settles back in his seat, he clears his throat, something on his mind too.

"So, what's it like? Since the treatment, what's it like what you feel about me?" Jethro says.

Cooper thinks over the question.

"Feeling… it's not the right word."

He closes his eyes a moment at the hit. He opens them again.

"Right, yeah, right."

Jethro looks into Cooper's eyes searching for something there. Something of her he recognises. Her eyes, still just as beautiful. Still twin eclipses. Still the aurora of flaming amber stretching into the green of her eyes. But now all he sees is flat observation in the set of her face. The something else that used to be in her eyes, the vortex that drew him in, it's gone.

Cooper studies him too. Grey eyes. Just grey eyes. His face so tense, the corners of his mouth tight.

"I follow everything you do, Jethro. Your music's doing great."

"Right, right."

Jethro's unimpressed with the answer. He changes subject.

"Hey, you remember our first date after the picnic?"

Cooper smiles.

"Yeah. I thought you were hot."

"You do remember?"

"Course. You were in jeans and a white T-shirt."

"And you were in this sapphire satin dress with a silver shawl. You terrified me."

"I did?"

"You looked like you came from the planet femme fatale."

"You were nervous?"

"Nervous? Jeez was I. It's like the local restaurant wasn't good enough for you, Coops. Everybody was staring at you like you were Jessica Rabbit. Like you were going to slink on to a piano and sing something intoxicating. You remember that date, right?"

"Jethro, yeah I remember."

"I felt so underdressed."

"Yeah well, I thought you were this cool kid. Turns out you still are."

Jethro shrugs.

"Know what? After that evening I thought you'd say let's be friends again like we were before. I was crazy nervous when I asked for that second date. If my knees were maracas they'd have sounded like a pair of rattlesnakes serenading each other."

Cooper laughs.

Jethro continues.

"I kept thinking you'd give me the brush, like make some excuse or something and drop me there and then."

"I remember it differently," Cooper says.

"How'd you remember it then?"

"I remember fancying you rotten. You were so laid back and fluid. You always were, anyway." Cooper appraises him now in his T-shirt and jeans. "You haven't changed much at all. I felt so overdressed that first proper date. It shocked me you asked for a second one. I thought maybe you wanted to be friends again too."

"I wrote you that song, Cooper."

"I know. I suppose I was still young and insecure."

"You thought I'd walk away? We were friends anyway."

"On the doorstep I thought you'd mumble adios and go scuttle off and come back as a friend again, pretend that night didn't happen. I expected to go inside and cry my eyes out. Instead, you asked to me for a second date."

"You remember our wedding day?"

"Jethro, course I remember. My memory is doing great."

"Right, right, sorry. Kind of keep forgetting. So, you remember how I messed up my vows?"

Cooper laughs.

"You were supposed to say to love honour and respect but instead you said to love honour and regret. Had the whole congregation rolling in the aisles."

Jethro covers his face, his ears reddening.

"Oh man. That still makes me cringe so bad."

"Even the master of ceremonies couldn't keep a straight face."

Jethro jabs a finger at Cooper, his eyes glistening with amusement.

"YOU kept creasing up after that."

"Yeah, could you blame me? What a start to a marriage!"

They share the moment laughing. Cooper surprised by how much she's enjoying reminiscing. Jethro realises he's having a great time. Soon they both grow quiet again, both sip their beverages, both mirror the other. Jethro places his teacup down.

"Know what? I don't regret it."

"Don't regret what?"

"Marrying you."

"Oh Jethro."

"Not one day." His voice catches. "Not one."

Cooper reaches out but he lifts his teacup to his mouth at the same moment. Cooper's not sure if he meant to do that.

"I'm sorry, Jethro. I'm sorry what I did."

He nods accepting the apology, but it's clear to Cooper it's not enough for him.

"So like," Jethro says, "don't you feel anything at all? For me?"

Cooper thinks how to tell him. Saying it out loud would be a face slap. A punch. Instead, Cooper shakes her head slowly.

Jethro lets out a breath.

"Wow. Just wow."

"It didn't occur to me Daniel would do something like that," Cooper says.

"Use our bed?"

"Have sex. I didn't even know about Araminta."

"Yeah well, he's a teenager. He's got raving teenage hormones partying around inside. What do you expect?"

"A handful of years ago he was still on my lap, all bright and excited by fireworks and Christmas and birthdays. Suddenly he's a man? I kept asking myself where'd he go? That kid with the angel face and baby fat? Who's this stranger with a deep voice with opinions about everything? Who's this young man who shaves and gets tetchy? And now yeah... a girlfriend."

Jethro's eyes widen.

"What is it?" Cooper says.

"Jeez."

"Tell me."

"Does that like mean you don't love him either?"

Cooper shakes her head.

"It doesn't work like that. The treatment targets you."

"Just me?"

"Yeah."

"You sure?"

Cooper nods.

Jethro leans back in the aluminium chair, a look of relief relaxing his face.

Cooper knows it's her time to be direct.

"So, why'd you agree to see me today?"

Jethro picks up his hat, runs his fingers along the rim, suddenly self-conscious. Not the confident singer on stage, in interviews, waving to fans.

"Truth is, I need closure."

Cooper hesitates then. She'd wanted to ask him something but now she isn't so sure.

"Why'd you ask?" Jethro says.

"Yeah, nothing."

"Coops, I know you. What is it?"

Finally she feels a wave of bravery.

"I've got a suggestion."

"Yeah?"

"Come home."

Jethro leans back, stares at her. He puts his hat down.

"Firstly, I need more privacy than our old house can offer."

"And secondly?"

"My gut's in knots. I can't just come back."

"Why not?"

"Look, I got to ask, like what's in it for you, Coops? You've changed so much. Your hair's longer and even your clothes are different. Yeah okay, you sound the same. Yeah, you even act the same but it's your eyes. When you look at me, I can tell there's nothing there for me."

Cooper waits for more. She knows there's more.

"So, how'd you think this'd play out? This charade. You gonna pretend to love me or what?"

"I don't have to pretend, Jethro. You know I don't."

Now hurt and anger flash in his eyes.

"Then like, what's the point?"

"Jethro, we were always friends."

"We had intimacy, man. When we went for walks, we walked hand in hand. In bed we'd cuddle. Friends don't do that."

"Give me your hand."

"Oh man."

"Jethro".

Jethro looks away.

"I can't."

"I need to show you something."

Jethro sighs, puts his hand on the table, keeps it close as though coveting a deck of cards.

Cooper reaches over, takes his hand, draws it across the table. He doesn't resist. She weaves her fingers through his own. His fingers feel cool, feels familiar to her.

Jethro's eyes fill at her touch. At the warmth. At the familiar shape.

"See?" Cooper says, "not too bad, right?"

Jethro looks at his hand as though it's a separate object. He tries to pull away.

"I can't do it."

But Cooper's grip tightens.

"We can learn."

He pulls again but Cooper doesn't release. He stops fighting. She literally has the upper hand.

"What about Daniel?" Jethro says.

"What about him?"

"What you gonna tell him?"

"The truth. That we're trying."

Jethro forces himself to look at Cooper then. He comes to a decision. He unpicks his fingers from hers.

"I don't buy it."

"You won't even try?"

"I just freakin' love you too much."

"That's why—"

"Know what? I kind of thought after all this time things would've cooled inside me right? But they don't. I've been everywhere. I've been all over Europe, USA, Canada, Australia, New Zealand, to freakin' Japan, man. It's like I've been away years and I think yeah, I'm cool. I'm over it. But guess what? My feelings for you were messing with me. They're rooted in there. I expected to come here and realise yeah I can take it. Yeah it's cool I can let go. But you know what? It doesn't matter where I go. The pain comes with me. It keeps freakin' hurting. Every. Freakin'. Heartbeat." His face screws up, his voice straining. "It doesn't stop. I can't take it, I just can't take it."

Cooper draws him close over the table, cups his face. Her action causes his dammed-up tears to spill. This time he can't force them back. He drops his head, his hair falling over his face hiding his shame, it tumbles over her hand. He absorbs the familiar warmth of her, lets it seep in.

Cooper sweeps his long hair away from his forehead with her other hand. The gesture is intimate.

"It's okay. Ssh. Ssh it's okay, it's okay, really it's okay."

They stay like that. He takes several shaky breaths until he can compose himself. His voice is a whisper.

"You think we could try?"

Scared hope, terrified hope.

Cooper smiles.

"Yeah, I really do."

Jethro nods, wipes his face on his sleeve, the boy he never stopped being. He stands up, drawing his chair back so abruptly it startles her.

"Look, I need to go." His voice is suddenly assertive. He's fighting his vulnerability. He can't help it.

"But—"

"Yeah, I'll think about it." He picks up his hat, puts it on.

"Laters, yeah?"

"Okay."

Jethro makes to leave. He walks a few paces, stops, turns back.

"Coops, what you just did... When you consoled me."

"What about it?"

"What did you feel?"

Cooper won't lie.

"I didn't want you to hurt."

"But you felt nothing for me, right?"

"I care what happens to you, Jethro."

"But you felt nothing? Not even a spark of what you felt before? Nothing?"

Cooper doesn't say anything. What can she say?

Jethro's jaw tightens. He backs away, holding his hands up as though surrendering. Walks off.

1 2 5

IT'S SATURDAY AND Eddsy has a surprise for Harriet. He's
full of anticipation. He can't wait till he gets home and tell
Harriet what he's done. No, not tell her. Show her.

He drives home, parks in the garage port. He walks to the
front door, impatient now. He's been waiting all afternoon.
Can't wait to see Harriet's face when she knows. He knows
she'll be happy. He opens the front door. He calls out his
homecoming ritual.

"Home!"

Harriet calls out.

"Yay!"

He thinks he hears her in the sitting room. He walks in.
Harriet's squatting on the floor in front of a side cabinet, legs
under her. She has the cabinet door open. On the floor where
she's kneeling she's leafing through a photo album. Simply
Red's playing from a classics 80s radio station.

"What're you doing?" Eddsy says.

Harriet looks up.

"Sorting old family photos. Here, take a look at this one of
you."

Eddsy doesn't move. He grins. Harriet sees him grinning.

"What is it?" Harriet says.

"Got a surprise."

"A surprise?"

He sees a miraculous change in Harriet's face. Her eyes
widen. Her cheeks blossom. She sits up straight. Like she
knows. Like she already knows. She has a look of elation.

Eddsy grins.

"Guess what it is?"

She does little excited claps with her hands, her eyes so wide, so bright, so expectant.

Eddsy's delighted by the reaction. He has never seen her look so happy. So joyous.

"Ah, you've guessed."

Eddsy's jacket is bulky at the front. He unzips it a little. A face pokes out. It's a dog. The dog's eyes are brown. The dog's eyes are curious. The dog's eyes are timid. The dog's fur is caramel brown with a black glossy muzzle. The dog sniffs the air. Yaps when he spots Harriet.

Eddsy is still grinning, looks up from the dog to Harriet.

For a second what he sees surprises him. But it's gone in an instant.

Harriet shoots up, a smile broadening on her face and she rushes over. She coos, takes the puppy and cradles him to her. Laughs.

Harriet hugs him.

Kisses him.

She swaddles the dog in her arms like a baby and Eddsy knows he did good.

"Oh, he's lovely," Harriet says. He's warm. He's wriggly. Harriet rocks him but the dog struggles in her arms, legs in the air, one oversized paw tapping the side of her jaw, his tail swatting against her.

Harriet sits him on the sofa. She tucks her legs under herself, wedges herself into the corner of the sofa like a cat. The dog climbs up, scrabbles into her arms, licks her face. She laughs. Eddsy watches her. The dog looks from Harriet to Eddsy then back to Harriet. Yaps again. Harriet laughs.

"Where'd you get him?"

"Rescue home."

"Where's the mother?"

"Didn't make it."

"Poor thing. Does he have a name?"

"Diesel."

"Hello Diesel." She shakes his giant paw. "What is he?"

"Labrador."

"I love him. He's gorgeous. Is he ours?"

"Yeah."

"How old is he?"

"Two months."

"Is that all?" She looks at Diesel. "Is that all you are? You're nothing but a baby." She ruffles the fur on Diesel's belly. He yaps.

"I love him already. He's really ours?"

Eddsy grins.

"He's ours."

Diesel struggles so Harriet plops him down on the sofa once more and introduces herself. The dog looks at her, waddles over to her, tumbling over on the too-spongy cushions.

She laughs. Eddsy loves to see Harriet laugh. Loves to see Harriet happy. Bringing home Diesel was the best thing he could do. The right thing. He sees they're an inseparable team already. Harriet and Diesel.

Only one thing bothers Eddsy.

Eddsy leaves, goes back to the car, takes out the doggie crunchies, tins of dog food, a litter tray, litter grit, a dog basket, a food and water bowl, a lead, a collar. He struggles to bring them all in, sees Harriet through the window talking to Diesel in baby tones. She's saying you're beautiful aren't you? Yes you ARE. Yes you ARE. Diesel responds by yapping as though answering her. Eddsy must be wrong because look at Harriet now. She's so happy, so engrossed in Diesel.

Eddsy finds a place for all the dog stuff in the kitchen.

Still, he can't shake that image.

For an instant Eddsy thought he'd spotted a micro expression suddenly flash on Harriet's face a moment after she'd spotted Diesel's nose peeking through his zipper. But it was so fleeting

461

he can't be sure. A moment later she'd leapt up and snatched Diesel away, making all sorts of appreciative noises.

Still.

For a second, a fraction of a second, a fraction of a fraction of a second Harriet had looked, well,

Disappointed.

1 2 6

IT'S THREE WEEKS before Jethro calls again. Cooper's on a call to an electronics company. The company rep is extolling the virtues of a revolutionary new digital audio converter they want her to endorse. As the man waxes lyrical on the incredible signal-to-noise ratio and faithful dynamics her phone beeps, another incoming call. Jethro's name flashes up and she cuts the call short. Jethro sounds exhausted.

"Hey, Coops."

"Hey."

"I've been thinking stuff through."

"Yeah, I guessed."

He gets straight to the point.

"I don't think it's such a great idea. Us getting back together."

"Jethro—"

"Come on, hear me out. What you're suggesting doesn't make sense to me. I don't get why you'd want us to live like that. I figured it's something to do with Daniel, right? Like you kind of want him to feel things are back to normal. Well, that ain't a good reason to keep us together Cooper. So yeah, the upshot is, thanks but no thanks."

"Don't you think—"

Jethro remains steadfast.

"I love you to death Coops, you know that. This is the hardest thing I've ever had to say. Speaking with you, meeting you at the museum, all that's been killing me. I'm in a bad place right now. I needed to see if I could learn to be over you. I was totally unprepared. I'm not over you. But I need an ending now. Things have to end or I'm going to go insane."

"Can I say something?" Cooper says.

Jethro continues as though not hearing her.

"I mean, at the museum I got nothing from you. There wasn't even smouldering ashes. The grate was empty like there'd never been a fire. So, you know what? I'm totally impressed with Gateway House. They did a fine job. They wiped your hard drive clean, man. I kind of thought they'd at least be something left."

"Jethro—"

"Cooper, you like fired your piece last time. All you need to say now is sayonara. See you around."

He goes to hang up.

"Jethro, please wait."

Cooper hears his heavy sigh. He's struggling to keep it together.

"You think Daniel's the reason I want you back yeah?"

"Course, what else?"

"Daniel's not six anymore. He's hitting twenty-one pretty soon."

"So?"

"He's not the reason."

"Then what is?"

"How can Cooper explain this to him in a way that'll make sense?"

"I want to spend the rest of my life with you, Jethro."

An intake of breath.

Then.

"Nah, I don't buy it. That doesn't even make sense."

"It's the right thing to do."

"What're you talking about? You don't feel anything for me."

"That's not what I mean."

"So, like, what am I missing Coops?"

Cooper knows what she's going to say next will hammer home his point rather than hers. She says it anyway.

"The Gateway Programme turned out to be a gift."

"A gift? It's a gift? A GIFT?"

"When I loved you, it wasn't real."

"Like, this is so interesting." Annoyance in Jethro's voice now. "Keep going. Really I'm laughing on the inside."

"It was a hypnotic spell. Feelings like that… they were illusions."

"Illusions?"

"My feelings tinted everything I knew about you Jethro. I've come to realise that tint isn't who you really are. The tint was something I did to myself. You're so much more."

Jethro sounds incredulous.

"You're saying when you loved me it was a tint?"

"I guess. Kind of."

"A TINT?"

"Hear me out."

"Sure. Fine. Keep firing."

"Love is the most amazing feeling in the world. But it's kind of costly."

"What does that mean?"

"It makes us fragile."

"What're you saying? We were strong, not fragile. We were a good team. We were happy for like more than twenty years, Cooper."

"Yeah, we were."

"So, what do you mean fragile? That doesn't even make sense."

"I guess I'm saying love isn't as strong as you think. It's like China. It's brittle. You drop it once it breaks. It doesn't just break. It shatters. It shatters into a billion pieces."

Cooper closes her eyes a moment imagining the day she thought she'd found Jethro in bed with another woman. She sees herself floating over the shoulder of the other version of herself by the bedroom door. The sickening pain she felt for him is as alien to her now as waking up in the sulphur of another planet.

"When I loved you," Cooper says, "it was kind of like standing at a cliff edge, enjoying a beautiful sunset, unaware the cliff could crumble any moment. Right now, I'm standing on a beach and I still get to enjoy the sunset."

"Quit with the metaphors."

"You see what I'm saying, right? There's nowhere to fall. Nothing to break. Jethro I'm free from heartbreak with you."

"So, like if everyone had this treatment that'd like make us all automatons. I mean really, you think what you're saying makes sense?"

"I don't know about everyone, Jethro, I only know about me. That day I thought you'd cheated on me something inside me broke. No matter what I did I couldn't escape it."

"Yeah, but when you found out it was Daniel you'd have been relieved."

"Truth is I don't know if I'd have been around to find out."

Cooper lets her words sink in. The significance. The meaning.

Jethro can't speak for a moment. He can't. He doesn't know how to respond to that. He knows she's right. But it's a totally messed up way of looking at things. A flare of anger.

"What can I say to that? Cool. You totally win the argument. Slam dunk. Case closed."

"Oh Jethro, I'm not trying to win anything. I'm trying to tell you The Gateway Programme saved me. Not just my life, it saved me in a different way too. It made me realise the problem isn't about you and it isn't about me. It's love that's the problem. When love's involved we're all ticking time bombs."

"Love is the problem? Wait. You're saying LOVE is the problem? Love is why we have Daniel, man."

"Yeah, I know."

"Love is why we were made for each other."

"Yeah."

"So, what does that even mean?"

"All I can say is The Gateway Programme gave me back self-control. I wasn't a slave to my feelings for you anymore. I could decide things for myself."

"I never once took away your control."

"Yeah, I know."

"So, where're you going with this?"

Cooper tries to piece her thoughts together. It feels like she's trying to explain colours to the blind. She continues.

"Funny thing Harriet said to me. She said I saw what I expected to see through the bedroom door. And she said that wasn't a reflection on you. It was a reflection on my own insecurities, my lack of trust in my own self-worth. I thought that little of myself. But know what? They're gone, the insecurities. They're really gone. Love distorts reality. It's a carnival mirror. The Gateway Programme fixed the mirror straight. I guess I'm trying to say I see you as you really are."

"Which is what?"

"I no longer exaggerate the importance of you in my life."

"You just said that for real? Cooper you're telling me what I already know and the blow doesn't hurt any less. You know how to shoot low."

"No, you don't get me. I'm saying you can't hold me back anymore."

"Hold you back from what, Cooper?" Jethro sounds exasperated. "I've never like held you back from anything. Not ever."

Cooper knows she's making a big hot heap explaining it.

"I think I've discovered something greater than love," Cooper says.

"Wow. Greater than love. Wow. You're coming out with them today."

"I'm not scared of losing you anymore but that doesn't mean I want to lose you. I want to be with you for a positive reason not a negative one, don't you see?"

"Yeah you're totally selling this to me. Well guess what? I'm not sure I buy that. You're sure that's not the treatment screwing with your head? Maybe even the car crash concussion somehow baking in with the whole messy stew? Time was you used to say I completed you."

Cooper remembers that. They'd often fold into each other's arms and she'd feel vulnerable and fearful he'd leave her one day. She'd say how Jethro was her missing piece.

"Yeah well, I was wrong," Cooper says. "You can't complete me Jethro because there's nothing to complete. I am complete already. And you're complete already too Jethro. We all are. Love kind of makes us feel we're not. But it doesn't mean we're not right for each other. There is no one like you, and I'm not interested in anyone not like you. Don't you see that's amazing? The fact I can say that even though I don't love you?"

Cooper hears a noise through the phone.

"What're you doing?"

He exhales.

"Just lit up. So let me get this straight. You don't love me, right? That's a given."

"Yeah."

"You say you've found something greater than love?"

"Yeah."

"Way I hear it, you could walk away and be fine right?"

"Yeah."

"You don't need anything from me?"

"No."

"So, walk away."

"I don't want to."

"But where's the me in the equation? Where do I fit in with your amazing discovery?"

"It's you I want, Jethro."

"That's your argument? You want to be with me even though you don't love me?"

"Yeah."

Another pull. He exhales in a rush, bursting to make his next point.

"Okay, here's a scenario. What if I get fed up? What if I want someone else?"

"Then you go."

"Just like that?"

"I'd be okay. I'd still care for you. I'd get on with my life, Jethro."

"You can still love other people, right?"

"Yeah."

"It's only me you can't love?"

"Yeah."

"So, what's to stop you falling for some other guy?"

"That's just it. I don't want to."

"You don't want to. You can decide just like it's a switch?"

"That's what I'm trying to tell you. I don't want anyone to love. I don't want romantic love at all. All I want is you, Jethro."

"Your world sounds horrific." He takes another pull. Holds it. He lets it out.

"Wow." His laugh's sharp, acidic. "Wow. This is something crazy. I can't believe what you're coming out with."

"Jethro look, meet me again."

"Yeah, you know? That's not happening. It won't wash with me this time. You have no idea how you're completely screwing with my head."

"I promise if after we meet you still want us to go our separate ways, that's fine. I'll never ask again."

Another pull on the rollup.

"Yeah?"

"Yeah."

"The last time you'll ask?"

"Yeah."

"What's the point?"

"Give me a chance to show you something."

"Show me what?"

"I have to show you."

Jethro crushes his rollup out. Out of frustration more than anything else, he agrees.

"Fine. Okay. Cool. Whatever. Where this time?"

COOPER AND JETHRO arrange to meet on Waterloo Bridge
that evening. Jethro is early, pays the cab driver, steps out,
waits. There's a chill in the air. He pulls down his bolero hat
low, lifts the flaps of his black leather jacket and tightens his
grey scarf. Underneath all he has on is a thin Harley Davidson
T-shirt and jeans and he wishes he wore something thicker.
Minutes later a minicab pulls in on the bridge and Cooper steps
out. She's in a scalloped top, blue dress with a 2/3rd waist
denim jacket that nips in. She wears thick black woollen tights
and flat heels a touch of lipstick. Jethro's breath catches at the
sight of her. Excitement turns into a stomach-twisting ache
when he remembers a part of Cooper is gone, the most
important part.

He meets her at the curb as the cab pulls away.

"You're in a dress," Jethro says.

Cooper dismisses it with a hand flick.

"Yeah, wardrobe's changed a bit."

"You look great."

"Thanks."

Cooper embraces him. He hugs her stiffly back. He looks
around.

"So, what're we doing here?"

Cooper turns, looks behind her.

Couple of years ago our lives changed in that building right
there.

Jethro follows her gaze. Then he sees it. The Savoy.

"Oh right. Yeah."

"So, I have a good feeling about this place. This area. About tonight."

"Come off it, Coops."

"Really. I think tonight our lives are going to change again, only this time, I think it's for the better."

Cooper walks over to the balustrade. She leans over, looks at the black water beneath them. Low clouds tinged the colour of tobacco from sodium street lights. The street lights look pretty, daisy-chaining the embankment. Several lights from boats harboured or moving in the distance wink and bob on the expanse of water. Jethro joins her, leans on the metal rungs beside her. They both take in the illuminated buildings fringing the river. Behind them vibrations from traffic pass through the girders up their legs. It's not lost on Jethro it's the bridge nearest The Savoy.

"I remember everything from the very first time Jethro," Cooper says. "Our history isn't gone."

The wind picks up and almost lifts off Jethro's bolero hat. He slaps a hand over his head, holds his hat in place. Cooper's dress flutters and Jethro can't help admire seeing it ruffle and ripple against the curve of her calves.

"Jethro, remember when you came back from that tour with Sabre Light you said there was something different about me? You said I seemed spicy."

Jethro extracts a green tobacco tin from his back pocket, opens it, pulls out a half used rollup, lights up, takes a pull.

"So what?"

"That was after the treatment."

"Yeah Coops, I know. I didn't get it was because you weren't in love with me anymore."

"Actually, there's more to it than that."

Jethro takes a long pull, keeps the smoke in, feels it seeping into his blood, relaxing him like balm.

"Yeah? Like what?"

"Before the treatment I'd forgotten how good-looking you are."

He turns to her.

"What'd you mean?"

"After twenty years, the novelty of seeing you goes."

"Coops, that's normal. None of us gets that thrill for long."

"Well, I did when you rolled into the kitchen after that European tour."

He chuckles.

"I must've looked like crap."

"Yeah, you looked completely beat. You were all unshaven, all sweaty and stuff. But there was this beautiful man leaning in the kitchen doorway looking cool. Know what I thought?

"Go on."

"I thought wow."

Jethro turns to Cooper.

"That's flannel. Gran used to call what you're saying flannel."

"I'm saying I was attracted to you. It's like my head reset."

Jethro frowns.

"I don't get it. We both know you can't feel anything for me anymore."

"Yeah, but I'm not talking about love. I'm talking about attraction. I fancied you rotten again. When you said you liked how I'd changed, it was my attraction you liked."

"Yeah?"

"Attraction is attractive."

Jethro stands there a moment, absorbing the statement. He doesn't know what to make of it. In the distance the long dark shadow of a boat motors toward them, a single searchlight mounted on the bow throwing a triangle of light on the water. He works something out in his head.

"You saying you think you can like, learn to love me again?" Jethro says.

Cooper drops her gaze. She shakes her head no.

There Cooper goes again. She does it every time. She lifts him up then cuts off his legs before he can stand. His emotions jump and dive like a button happy kid in a lift. First Cooper wants a divorce. Then nah turns out she doesn't want a divorce. She wants to see him. But nah she doesn't love him. But yeah she's attracted to him. But nah she can never love him again. Man, he was being well and truly filleted and battered. How much more could he take?

Cooper clicks her fingers, breaking his thoughts.

"Hey, mister."

Jethro looks up, not realising he'd drifted away.

"You ever think about us?"

Jethro gives her a sarcastic laugh.

Cooper raises a conciliatory hand.

"Yeah okay, dumb question. I just need to tell you it's here now."

Jethro's about to take another pull.

"What is?"

"The attraction."

"Yeah? You getting a kick from seeing me right this minute?"

Her cheeks blush. He hadn't seen that in what? Years.

"Yeah, well it's a rush."

"Well shucks. Guess that's all it takes for a solid relationship nowadays."

Cooper doesn't let up. She's not going to let him dismiss it like that.

"See, both times I've seen you it's been like the first time."

"Well, how about that? How about that? So let me get this straight. You're saying you fancy me again?"

She nods.

"What's so funny?"

"You realise what you're saying, right?" Jethro says.

"I'm not the robot you think I've become, Jethro."

"Nah. That's not it. You're saying you've turned into a fan that's all." He shakes his head. "You're unreal. You fancy me but you can't love me. I've heard it all now. Jeez."

A lorry thunders past and the vibrations roll under their feet.

"I want you back," Jethro says.

"But that's all what I want too. That's why—"

He shakes his head.

"You didn't hear me. I want YOU back. The real Cooper."

"I am the real Cooper."

He glances out at the black river again. The boat with the headlight is closer. Light radiates from the bow, picks out eddies in the water like white commas floating on the dark toffee-coloured surface.

"Know what? Even crazier. Even now I'd give you a kidney if I had to." He gives a cold hard laugh. "I'd feel like the biggest sucker on earth doing it, but I'd still do it."

"Why?"

"Don't you get it? That's what love is. It's sacrifice. You had me life and soul. You OWN my soul." He kicks the metal railing with his ankle boots. "I can't do crap about it."

"I know it hurts, Jethro."

"More like torture. Thing is you're supposed to reciprocate, Cooper. That's what love does. Makes us look out for each other. If all you can do is fancy me what's the point? I got tens of thousands of fans like that. You know my manager says I get offers of marriage every week? Some of them only teens too. And the selfies they send... Jeez."

Jethro stares out at the water again searching for the boat. It's gone. Passed under and out the other side unnoticed.

"I still have this urge to look out for you I guess," Jethro says. "Can't do a freakin' thing about it."

"I'd give you a kidney too."

Jethro looks at Cooper.

"You'd give me your kidney?"

"No I'd pick one up from the bakery. Yeah, course mine."

"Bakeries don't—"

"I know!"

He smirks. "I only get one?"

"Yeah well, I'd save the other one for Daniel in case he needed it one day."

"Nice. You just one-upped me. You know you can't donate both kidneys right?"

Cooper puts on a posh accent.

"By George, I never thought of that."

He makes an apologetic smile.

"Yeah, sorry."

Cooper pushes herself off the balustrade.

"Fancy a stroll?"

"Now?"

"No tomorrow. God Jethro, what's with you tonight?"

Jethro joins her and they head toward the South Bank liking her familiar sarcasm, enjoying the sweet sting of it.

"You're feisty this evening."

"Good," Cooper says, "'cause I've got something to tell you."

1 2 8

IT'S TAKEN WEEKS for Eddsy to realise what's been troubling him. In that time, Diesel has settled in. He has a stainless steel bowl of water and another one for meat and crunchies. He has a leather collar which says Diesel and a telephone number on a little brass medallion the size of a 2p piece. He has a chewable marrowbone and his own rubber ball. He chases the ball all over the kitchen and keeps forgetting walls and chairs and table legs and kitchen units are in the way, keeps crashing into them. Harriet loves him to bits and picks him up and hugs him all the time. He's too young to take out on walks yet, but he adores the patio and jumps and yips around it like his little bum's on fire. He yaps and scrambles and rushes around with zesty energy and abandon and they both laugh at his daft antics as the day passes.

Now Eddsy is in bed in the dark. Weeks it took for him to realise. Weeks since he brought Diesel home. Weeks. It was that look of disappointment on Harriet's face. No doubt about it, she loves Diesel but that look of disappointment, it haunted Eddsy for three weeks.

Now he knows why.

So that's where the booklet went. Thinking of Adopting? He'd looked for it in the glove compartment. He'd been sure that's where he'd put it. He looked for it, it wasn't there. He looked in his jacket pocket. He looked in his coveralls. Then he'd forget to look further. Then he'd remember. Then forget. Remember. Forget. Now he remembers. Only this time he knows why he can't find it.

Eddsy sits up, switches the bedside light on.

Harriet is curled up asleep. Diesel is in a dog basket snoring. His snoring interrupts at the light, he pops open an inquisitive eye.

Eddsy taps Harriet's shoulder.

"Wife?"

JETHRO TAKES ONE last pull on the stumpy rollup, crushes out the tip on the edge of his tin, pushes the wasted stub inside, snaps the lid shut, slides it into his back pocket. He's waiting for Cooper to say her piece and shoves his hands into his jacket pocket as they walk along the bridge towards the South Bank. Okay, Jethro says, what have you got to say?

Cooper suddenly rushes ahead of him, turns, faces him, walking backwards. She throws her arms out and hollers as though screaming into a canyon.

"I DON'T LOVE YOU JETHRO!"

Jethro stops, staring at her.

She laughs. The wind whips at her hair, longer than he's ever seen. At the museum she'd had it gelled back. Now it's almost to her shoulders. His heart, a physical pain in his chest, yearns for her to come back to him as she was.

"Did you hear me?"

Jethro uses a finger to shake out his ear.

"Nah, don't think so."

She giggles.

"I DON'T LOVE YOU JETHRO I DON'T LOVE YOOOOOU." She spins around on the YOOOOOU. "Do you hear me now?"

"Like seriously? What're you doing?"

"Oh Jethro, I wish you felt it. I wish you felt it too."

"Are you on something?"

"It's so freeing. It really is. I DON'T LOVE YOU JETHRO!"

A Mini Cooper toots as it passes. Laughter and cheers come from inside the car. The irony of the car's make and model isn't lost on them. Jethro starts walking, pulls at Cooper's arm.

"Okay, you can cut it out now."

Cooper yanks away, laughs.

"You're more embarrassed by what people think than of letting go."

"Coops, this isn't normal for you."

"Consider it my new normal."

Jethro can't help smile. He remembers.

"Well, it's kind of you I suppose."

"Kind of?"

"Like when we were first going out remember? You'd do impulsive things. Somewhere along the line I guess you stopped. So wait, we came into central London so you could holler from Waterloo Bridge you don't love me?"

"Yeah. Why not?"

"That's completely crazy."

She grins.

"Yeah, isn't it?"

Cooper throws her arms around him. He gasps when he sees her eyes close up. He can't help it.

Those eyes those eyes those eyes. Twin solar eclipses. Those eyes. A corona of amber flames lick out from the aurora, the deep dark coppery greens flaring from the black centre. Those eyes. But the vortex. Where's the vortex?

Cooper presses her lips to his ear, whispers.

"I don't love you, Jethro."

The anvil drops hard in his stomach. Reality check. He pulls back.

"This is so confusing," Jethro says. "This isn't you and yet somehow it feels like when I first knew you."

He gazes into her eyes, her arms hooked around his neck. He feels himself weakening.

"I'm not, you know," Cooper says.

"In love with me?"

"Not in the slightest. Not even a teeny bit."

Cooper's acting like the most love-struck teenager Jethro's ever seen. He can't help it. He's drawn in and fascinated by her. But another part of him is breaking. He grabs her wrists from behind his neck and pulls them away.

"What are you doing?" Cooper says.

"You're telling me you don't love me and showing me you do."

"I'm not showing you I love you. I'm showing you I want you, Jethro." She tries to slip her hands back around his neck. Jethro backs away.

"This is too much."

"I WANT YOU, Jethro."

"Like what does that even mean?"

"It means what it means."

"You want the security of a relationship? You want things the way they were? What is it you want?"

"Right now, I want to share this moment with you. Here. That's all."

Jethro shakes his head. He looks at her. Those eyes. The way she's looking at him. Those eyes. Twin eclipses. Makes his heart race. Those eyes. No vortex. Makes his heart ache.

Cooper sees the confusion. The pain. The turmoil. She knows he's fighting it.

"Thank you."

"For?"

"Agreeing to meet me again," Cooper says. "I know it's hard for you. But I wanted you to see I'm more me than I've been in a long time. I want to tell you things I don't think I felt the need to before."

Confusion, confusion, she's confusing him.

"I love you Cooper but—"

"I don't love you, Jethro."

"Yeah," sighs, "exactly."

"Doesn't this feel exciting to you? Doesn't it feel fresh and new and different?"

"For the wrong reasons."

"What rule book says it's wrong?"

"You say you want to be with me?"

"Yeah."

"I don't get why."

"Can't want be its own thing? I want to because I want to."

"What happens if you stop wanting me?"

"Won't happen."

"It could."

"Yeah, but it won't."

He perseveres.

"What happens if you stop wanting me, Cooper?"

He'd used her name. He wants an answer.

"What happens if you stop loving me, Jethro?"

"Won't happen."

"Ah."

Jethro opens his mouth to speak. He has no argument. He's beat.

"Jethro, let's just be and see where it takes us okay?"

"Yeah, very Zen."

"I can't love you—"

"Newsflash."

"But I don't need to. I care what happens to you anyway."

"Nah kid, you don't. When Cooper doesn't respond Jethro adds, "Yeah well it's not enough. Tonight's all about you trying to persuade me to come home, right? So, what if I don't come back? What then? You walk away without a backward glance, right?"

"Guess so."

Jethro shakes his head.

They continue along Waterloo Bridge, nearly at the south bank.

"It's like you're living on rails. Like it's all a formula."

They come to the end of the bridge, make their way down some steps, stride along a wide expanse, past the National Theatre and find a stretch of grass. Cooper drops on to the grass and sits cross legged.

"There're benches over there by the river," Jethro says.

"Yeah, I'm happy on the grass."

Jethro joins her, sits opposite, also cross legged. Passers-by see two figures steeped in shadow with passing interest only. Sitting like this reminds Jethro of something… Yeah. The picnic. That day he declared his love. That day he'd nervously sung her the first song he'd ever written. They'd sat opposite each other that day cross legged too. Only it was day, a warm day, filled with the hum of summer, the heady haze of love, it was in the countryside, it was the beginning of something. Now it's night, it's cold, it's in the city, the end of something. Is this the parenthesis of their relationship?

Cooper shivers. Jethro takes off his jacket, drapes it over her shoulders. He's left in only his Harley Davidson T-shirt rippling in the breeze.

"You didn't need to do that, but thanks."

Jethro shrugs, looks out at the river. He knows Cooper can't love him. What is it he wants from her? What is he hoping for tonight?

Cooper interrupts his thoughts, looking serious now.

"Jethro?"

He looks at her, dejection in his eyes.

"I am still your wife."

"I know."

"I am still your wife."

"Like I said, I know."

"So, we need to call a truce."

Jethro's about to protest again. He doesn't. For their last few meetings all he'd done is fight her. Pull her in while shoving her away. Invite her. Oppose her. Accept her. Refute her.

"I'm a complete mess," Jethro says.

"I'm sorry."

Strands of Cooper's hair cling to the corner of her mouth. He reaches out to flick it away before he thinks to stop. Such a natural, intimate action. The north south divide bridged, at least temporarily.

Across the Thames, the Savoy's windows illuminate figures moving inside. Almost two years ago they were there, neither knowing how different things would be after that. Cooper braces herself before speaking.

"Look, some stuff I've been saying and some stuff I'm gonna say tonight is going to hurt. I don't mean it to. You just have to hear me out, okay?"

"Okay."

"You ready?"

Fire away.

1 3 1

IN BED, WHEN Eddsy taps Harriet's shoulder, he finally knows what he has to say. Harriet makes a noise in her sleep.

Eddsy clears his throat, voice firmer.

"Harriet?"

Harriet turns over. She blinks. She sees his bedside light is on. She looks confused. He called her Harriet. Not Wife. His serious voice.

"What's going on?" Harriet says. "Why're you sitting up?"

Diesel lifts his head from the dog basket. His mistress is awake. His master is awake.

"You," Eddsy says, "took the booklet didn't you?"

Harriet blinks before speaking, clearing her head. She instantly knows what he's talking about.

"I found it in the van when you were getting petrol."

"Me and you got some talking to do."

Harriet sits up, sleep gone, watching Eddsy.

Diesel detects a change in the air, a fizz, a crackle between his mistress and master.

"I've got a question I need to ask," Eddsy says.

"Okay?"

Eddsy knows there's going to be concerns. Lots of concerns. Worries. Lots of worries. Obstacles. Lots of obstacles. Hurdles to leap and jump. Maybe even rejections. He knows that.

Harriet asks again.

"What question?"

But Eddsy also finally understands that look of disappointment in Harriet's eyes when she met Diesel. It wasn't

Diesel's fault. She'd loved him the moment she realised she had a dog. No, the disappointment was for the moment between what she thought Eddsy was going to tell her, and revealing Diesel tucked in his jacket. That fleeting expression, a moment before the disappointment had been something else. Something important.

Hope.

It'd taken him weeks to work out what was so obvious now. Here he is, a middle-aged man who owns and runs six successful garages yet he'd been so slow. Eddsy steadies his gaze on Harriet.

"Would you like to adopt a child with me?"

He watches her then. For a moment Harriet doesn't react. Then a smile forms on her lips. Her face brightens. Her shoulders lift.

And that look in her eyes… Oh that look. Elation. Eddsy was right. He was so right.

Quietly. Ever so quietly, her tears fall.

"Husband. I've two words to say back."

"What's that?"

Harriet gives a series of little excited claps.

"Yay!"

Diesel yaps, leaps on to the bed, headbutts Harriet. They laugh at Diesel's clumsiness as though he'll never become accustomed to those clown-sized paws.

Eddsy's laughing, but stops when a thought comes to him.

"Hold it. That's only one word."

Harriet doesn't hesitate. She stands up on the bed, does a war-dance with hands in the air, repeating what she'd already said, only louder.

"YAY! YAAAAAAAAY!"

COOPER IS CROSS-LEGGED on the mound of grass in front of Jethro with Waterloo Bridge at his back, knowing she's about to say something important, hoping she can convince him.

"I've been thinking about how we used to be," Cooper says. "How amazing it was, yeah? It was as close to perfect as I can remember. But know what? I came to realise something about the way we were. How selfish I was."

Jethro looks at her.

"Selfish?"

"We want to be loved right? That's how the world works. Love validates us. Makes us feel worth something."

"I guess that's true."

"But what happens when someone leaves us, or dies?"

"We hurt."

"Why?"

"Because we loved them."

"Maybe it's because we lose that validation too, Jethro. The way I am now I don't need your validation anymore. What the treatment did was clear the path to make me realise I can endorse my own self-worth. I don't have that selfish need for you to do it for me anymore."

Jethro shivers, draws his legs up and wraps his arms around them partly from the breeze, partly because it's a self-comforting gesture.

"See," Cooper says, "I've come to realise love makes you believe you're worth less than the person you love. Loving Daniel is different. He's our child, right? Harriet and Eddsy?

They're family. But loving you the way I did… That kind of love explodes into existence. It's one without choice. It only works if it can be circular. If the other person can reciprocate. But what happens if the other person dies? If they leave? If they do something that breaks you? What's left is a void. You suddenly feel valueless. That's when it hurts. And know what? I know how bad it can hurt."

Jethro gets what Cooper's talking about. The day she thought he'd betrayed her.

"I know you love me, Jethro. I see that greed you have for me. And I see that pain inside you 'cause I can't return your love the way you want me to."

"Yeah well, it was good. You made me feel good."

Cooper nods to herself, as though confirming something.

"You know what you're saying, Jethro? Replace love with the word drugs and you're saying drugs made you feel good. Heroine, cocaine, ecstasy, love, it's all the same thing. What you're saying is you need your fix of me or you suffer."

"So, what do you need of me then?"

"Nothing. I don't need you, Jethro."

"Oh man."

"I'm sorry. But all that hurt you're going through isn't coming from me. You're doing it to yourself."

The logic makes sense to Jethro. He's creating his own pain. But logic and love is oil and blood. They don't mix.

"You know I said I'd give my life for you? I meant it."

Jethro's mouth presses into a tight line before speaking. The cynicism is still there.

"That right?"

"See, love isn't there to make that a pre-condition of our relationship. There's no contract. I'm not compelled or manipulated by feelings to do it. I simply choose to do it. I can as simply choose not to. But I choose to, Jethro. Don't you see how amazing that difference is?"

"I guess I need to understand why you'd make that choice then."

"So okay look, here's a riddle: What's a prison cell with the door permanently open?"

"I don't know, what is it?"

"It's a room. It's just a room, Jethro."

"What we had was good."

"Yeah, it was."

"I was happy to be with you Cooper. I didn't care about anything else."

"Jethro. Honestly. This is better."

He sighs. "Yeah. For you right? For you." Jethro ponders her point. "So, you're saying my love for you is selfish too?"

"Maybe all love is selfish. When the treatment took my feelings for you away it cleared the fog like sunlight after a misty dawn."

Jethro gazes out at the Thames.

"You've never asked me to take the treatment too. Why?"

"That's not something I can decide. That's something you have to do for you."

"I won't ever take it you know. Not ever. No way."

"Then that's okay. That's your choice."

"You think it's a bad choice though, right?"

"No Jethro. It's just a choice. It's neither bad nor good. It's a decision you make that's all. It's only a decision. It's what we do as a result of a decision that's important, not the decision itself."

"I don't get you. Why do you want me when you can't love me?"

"That's my point, Jethro. I just do."

"So, it's penance – you wanting to be with me?"

Cooper shakes her head.

"It's not a sacrifice, Jethro." Cooper takes a moment to reflect. "I want your company. Our companionship. Our understanding of each other. I want you around so I can continue to grow with understanding and share the world with you beside me."

"And that's it? You want to understand me? Am I such an enigma?"

"No Jethro, it's not that kind of understanding. The world keeps unfolding. We keep unfolding. You'll do things that'll surprise me. I'll do things that'll surprise you. I want us to unfold in this unfolding, surprising world together."

Jethro tries to get it. Really, he does. But his frown deepens, desperate to grasp her meaning.

Cooper sees that sadness and she's desperate to break into it. But somehow she's not cutting it with Jethro. If she could just get through to him. She needs to think, think, how can she get him to understand?

A text pings Cooper's phone, then Jethro's. They both glance at their screens. When they see the message from Harriet they smile.

So. Harriet and Eddsy are going to apply to adopt. Harriet's text explains how they'd both secretly wanted it, but didn't know the other did too, and what daft idiots they both were.

Cooper and Jethro return congratulatory texts. They put their phones down. The brief breathing space they both needed.

Cooper shakes her head. Isn't it odd how people devoted to each other can still harbour thoughts so deep, the other can't fathom them? Then she frowns.

"What is it?" Jethro says.

Wait. I just need a moment.

Cooper closes her eyes. She too had her own deep place, a place she'd learned to find. A place of serenity. A truth. A centre. A core. A singularity. A place that is the whole of her. A place she'd found once before in a hot bathtub at Harriet's.

There.

She is there. She floating in the centre of something so profound because it is so simple. Cooper whispers from that place. Any louder and she'd break the delicate thread she's found.

"I've discovered an alternative to love," Cooper says. "What I have I can't destroy because there is no creation. All I can do is choose to accept or not. Our relationship had a tangle of conditions and codicils. It was an either/or thing. What I'm offering now is not either/or, Jethro. I'm offering you And. If I choose you, it's because it's what I want not because I'm compelled by love to. I can choose to walk away. I choose not to."

"But why ME? What do you want from ME?"

Cooper smiles. The answer's so clear to her.

"I choose you because I choose you. I want you to simply have me. All of me for all my life. It's what I choose. I'm giving you all of myself without condition. It's a gift, Jethro. A gift to a man I know is good. All you have to do is say yes. It's that simple. It's not a sacrifice, not a conditional offer, not penance for what I did. I just give you me. I give you me."

Jethro is stilled. "That's beautiful," he says finally, his voice soft.

Cooper opens her eyes.

Her eyes.

Those eyes, those eyes.

The way she's looking at him. Those eyes. The way she rests her gaze on him makes everything fall away. Those eyes. He's Lifted. Suspended. The cold is gone, the breeze is gone, London is gone. It's only Jethro and Cooper facing each other.

And there's suddenly a presence in Cooper he can't define. Maybe it's what she said. Maybe it's how she said it. Maybe it's the serenity in her eyes. But the moment calms him. Is he imagining it? Is it real? What Jethro's seeing… the way Cooper's looking at him… what she'd said… it's like love. But love somehow beyond love. Love reimagined maybe. A kind of ancient wisdom perhaps. How can that be? How can it?

Jethro shakes his head to correct his vision. This isn't right. It can't be. He looks at Cooper again. The calm stillness in her is still present. In her eyes. Something so deep, so truthful he'd sink to his knees if he wasn't already on the grass. Jethro chokes up, knowing Cooper is telling him a truth so fathomlessly deep and eternal it seems to come from beyond her.

Cooper too senses the change in Jethro.

She stands up. Offers her hand.

Jethro stands up, looks at her hand.

"Let's go home Jethro. Please. I give you me. Give me you."

He nods, hardly able to breathe. Takes her hand.

Then they do.

They go home.

1 3 3

FOR A WHILE, things go great.

Cooper and Jethro buy a new house in the affluent Highgate area of north London, one with a high walled front, an electric security gate. A separate letter box on an external wall. The postman pushes stuff into the letter box. They collect their mail from the other side of the wall.

They visit a local restaurant, find themselves chatting about everyday things like they always did. Her tastes haven't changed. Her thoughts and feelings and opinions are no different.

At the restaurant they order a bottle of wine.

A second bottle.

By the end of the evening Jethro's holding Cooper's hand across the table, she's letting her hand be held, he's smiling at her, she's smiling back, he's gazing into her eyes, she's gazing back, he's squeezing her hand, she's squeezing back. He starts to believe she loves him. That's what it feels like. She loves him.

But.

Yeah, but.

Something is wrong.

They go home. They make love. He makes love. She has sex. It's perfect.

Jethro drifts off, a tiny voice, small, reminds him she doesn't love him. Doesn't matter. He holds her, she holds him, they fall asleep holding each other. He is happy now. So so happy. Really. Yeah.

But.

Yeah, but.

Something is wrong.

They go to a movie together.

When the movie's over they walk home arm in arm like always and discuss the movie like the always did before. Cooper expresses her opinion, Jethro expresses his. They argue about the movie in that analytical non-aggressive way.

It's all normal.

It's like before. Better perhaps.

Jethro finds it harder to tell if there's any difference between Cooper now and Cooper then. Is there? He can't find any.

But.

Yeah, but.

They head off to a funfair, something they haven't done since their youth.

They have fun together. Laugh together. On the roller coaster Cooper shrieks, buries her head into Jethro's shoulder, grips his arm when the roller coaster dives, laughs when it swoops up, as he waves his hands in the air, as she grips his waist. He teases her about it.

Cooper gets her own back when they go in bumper cars, chases him all across the rink to teach him a lesson, bottom lip folded in with gritty determination. She's gonna get him no matter what. Jethro can't get the hang of the wonky steering. Cooper bashes him time and again. He tries to get behind her but, he only spins impotently in place. She expertly sweeps around him, crashes into him and he's begging her to stop, laughing. They're both laughing.

But.

Yeah, but.

Daniel's with Araminta in Jethro and Cooper's home. It's a day later before Daniel says something.

Like what's with you two anyway?

Jethro stops tickling Cooper on the sofa, looks at them.

What do you mean?

It's like I've come home to a couple of naughty schoolkids. That should be me and Araminta, not my aging parents.

Jethro looks at Cooper.

Cooper looks at Jethro, they burst out laughing.

Daniel's perplexed. Araminta's in awe. She leans over, whispers to Daniel, I hope we're like this in twenty years.

But.

Cooper and Jethro invite friends around for dinner.

Their friends notice how in love they are. Girlfriends corner Cooper in their large new kitchen, they envy her so much. They're envious about the house, envious she has a rock star husband, but what they're really envious of is Jethro's so in love with her even after all this time, despite all the newspaper stuff about The Gateway Programme. What else could it be? What's her secret?

Meanwhile male friends tell Jethro, Cooper's amazing. It's unbelievable you two have been together so long and look at you two. Wow.

Time passes.

More weeks.

Even more weeks.

Months.

Even more months.

A year.

Then a year and a half.

Then two years.

Their careers are doing well. Cooper's up for a major nerdy tech audio award in forensic signal processing. Jethro's written his second album and working on the tracks.

So things are going well. So well. Sooooo well.

There's still a but.

One night after they've made love.

After Jethro's made love and Cooper's released her sexual tensions, they lie in each other's arms in the dark. Cooper is drifting off in the lazy afterglow when Jethro murmurs something.

Cooper's eyes snap open.

"Huh?"

"Nah, it's cool," Jethro says.

"No, what?"

"It's cool. I know the answer."

"Yeah, but I don't know the question."

"I thought you were asleep."

"What's the question?"

Jethro hesitates.

"I said if you don't love me, I can't tell." But he says it in such a way with such a tone that he's really asking do you love me?

Cooper is careful with her response.

"Jethro, you know the answer."

It's cool. Yeah, it's cool.

"I choose you."

"Yeah Coops, I get it. Shouldn't have asked."

They are both silent.

Cooper snuggles into him like a cat hungry for heat. She has her ear pressed to his bare chest, his heart thumping into it. She has one knee over his stomach. She draws herself tighter around him like she's protecting him. Like she's showing him she chooses him.

Maybe he can't unsee the illusion. Maybe it fools the eye but.

Something is wrong.

He can't fool the brain.

Cooper's eyelids flutter down. She slips away.

Jethro's eyes stay open, staring, staring, just staring.

Something is wrong.

1 3 4

SOMETIME DURING THE night Cooper wakes.

She's not sure the time it is, checks her phone. It's 3.17am. She stretches over to Jethro's side, finds the bed empty. She expects he's gone to the loo in the dark.

A little time passes.

Cooper micro dozes, becomes aware he still hasn't returned. When she checks again, Kelloggs has curled asleep on his pillow.

Jethro's been gone a long time. She checks her phone. 4.14am now. Almost an hour since she last woke.

Cooper gets up. The en suite is dark. She steps into the hall. Where is he?

Everything is dark.

Everything is silent.

Cooper wanders down in the dark, palm pressed against the wall, a curved plane of their Regency house for guidance. She spots a pencil of light under the door of his music room. New songs often come to Jethro at night. She doesn't want to disturb the muse. She doesn't want to disturb him so she presses her ear to the door, smiling. She expects to hear a stray chord, a line for a lyric, a hummed melody, a rhythm track laid down, something like that. Instead no, that's not what she hears.

Cooper frowns.

Presses her ear even harder against the door to be sure.

Her frown deepens.

A minute later, two minutes, three, Cooper creeps back upstairs, goes back to bed.

Things were working out, they really were. Everything felt right, felt easy, felt natural, it really did. Jethro wants to be with her. Cooper wants to be with him. She has memories, such memories. She knows the shape and curve of him, the corners, the edges, the angles of his lips, the length of his fingers, the sharp chevron of his elbows, the lines and dips of him. She knows the aroma of him, how intimate, how soft, how sweet. She knows him, his mellow, happy, considerate, lovely, generous self. She knows the love of him, intense, powerful, homey.

All this time she doesn't know the heart of him.

These past two years they've been closer than ever. Doing things together more than ever.

Jethro does it for love.

Cooper does it because she chooses him.

And to everyone it looks like love too. Jethro can't unsee the illusion he knows it is, no matter how hard he denies it.

Cooper doesn't sleep.

No, Cooper doesn't sleep.

TWO MONTHS LATER

JETHRO WALKS INTO the house and senses something's wrong. He closes the front door.

The house feels.

Vacant.

He calls out anyway. Nothing happens.

He calls out again. Cooper still doesn't answer.

If the house is empty, Cooper's likely in her studio space or he knows she's on a location job, but not today. This time the house feels different. Feels.

Vacant.

He goes around the sitting room, the dining room, the kitchen, the utility room, the games room, peeks out to the lawn, she's in none of those places.

Jethro goes into the basement, a modest wine cellar to see if there's a light on. There isn't. She isn't there.

He calls upstairs again. No answer.

Goes in the bathroom. Not there.

Goes in the bedroom. Not there.

The other bedrooms.

Not in those places either.

Jethro goes to Cooper's wardrobe, shallow breathing, like a vice around his chest squeezing the air out. He opens it. Wooden and plastic hangers swing emptily. Jethro starts shaking. Legs feel weak. Sweat on his forehead. Sweeps his hair back.

He scrambles to open all four wardrobe doors. All her clothes are gone. All of them. All her shoes. Gone. Her bags.

Gone. Her hats. Every one of them gone. Every single internal shelf is empty. Jethro is shaking violently.

The back of the bedroom door, the lovely silk kimono dressing gown that should be there. Gone.

He goes to the chest of drawers knowing what to expect already. They're empty. No socks. No knickers. No tights. No bras. No jumpers. No T-shirts. Empty. Empty. He feels sick.

In the en suite bathroom.

The toothbrush, hair clips, scrunchies all gone. All her face creams, shampoos, conditioners, hairbrushes, combs, gone.

He makes his way downstairs. Everything shakes. His lips shake. His arms shake. His hands shake. His fingers shake. His legs shake.

Her coat's not there. Her jacket's not there. Her rain mac's not there. None of her scarves. None of her gloves. None of her walking boots.

He goes out to her purpose-built studio over the manicured lawn. Flings the door open. Jethro steps inside. Maybe there's one thing she hasn't had a chance to do yet. Maybe there's still a chance.

The studio is empty.

Everything is gone. The computer, the mixer, the rack of outboard gear, the speakers, microphones, all the cables, everything. It's all gone.

With shaking fingers Jethro calls Cooper's mobile.

The phone you are calling is no longer in service.

Pain in his chest now. He feels like he's falling from a long way.

He calls Harriet.

Harriet answers. She's tearful. "Yes," Harriet knows. Says Cooper called yesterday. "I'm so sorry Jethro, I'm so sorry. I don't know what's gotten into her. She forced me not to say anything. I begged her not to do this. I don't understand why she's doing this."

Jethro listens. He doesn't say anything. Everything shakes.

Next, he calls her friends. All of them. He gets nothing. Calls Graham Chambers after finding his number.

Graham says Cooper called yesterday. "Deplorable, old chap. Must be a blow. Must be. When I next speak to Cooper I'll tell her you called. Listen old chum. Tell you what? Why don't you get yourself a stiff drink and wallow for a while, eh? Grab yourself a bottle. What do you say?"

Jethro calls Daniel.

Daniel answers on the first ring.

"Dad."

"Mum's gone."

"Yeah dad I – uh – I know."

Even Daniel knows before he did.

"You know where she is?"

"No dad, I completely don't know."

"Her number's out of service."

"Yeah."

"What's going on?"

"Mum said she'd leave you a letter, yeah?"

"Where?"

"I don't know."

"What did she tell you?"

"That she's going. Dad I'm like, so sorry. It's all my—"

"It's nothing to do with you."

"Yeah, yeah I know. Mum said the same thing. But like I can't help it."

"It's not your fault."

"It kind of is."

"It is NOT your friggin' fault, you hearing me my man?"

A pause.

"Yeah, yeah, okay dad."

"What else did mum say?"

"Dad. I think you need to like find the letter."

"Did she call today?"

"No. She said she'd be totally too busy… you know… sorting stuff."

"You could have warned me."

"She made me promise. I'm sor—"

"Okay son, it's cool. My bad, my bad. I'll sort it out."

"I'm really—"

Jethro hangs up.

He goes from room to room. He can't find any letter.

Kitchen table.

No.

Bedroom.

Peels back the duvet, checks the pillow.

No.

Sideboard in the hall.

No.

Not in her studio either.

There is no letter.

Where is this freakin' letter?

Jethro realises there's one room he hasn't been in. His own music room. He goes in now. He walks in slowly. He goes to his desk. He finds his Gibson guitar laying across it. It's usually hung up on the wall with the Fender, the Aria, the Martin, the Les Paul. There's an envelope woven between the strings. The envelope has his name written on it. It's Cooper's handwriting. He spots a bunch of keys on his desk too. House keys.

Shaking. Shaking.

Jethro rips open the envelope, pulls out several sheets, recognises Cooper's handwriting.

Jethro, it starts.

That's as far as he gets.

Jethro collapses to the floor unable to breathe. It takes a while before he can bear to read any further.

JETHRO.

My lovely, wonderful, amazing Jethro. I've said I'm sorry in so many different ways I don't know how to say it anymore. When you read this you'll know I've gone.

Practical things first, right?

Okay, so the house. I know it'll be a financial burden as there were two incomes but I guess your royalties are going to be okay to cover them. I won't be coming back. I've also checked re-mortgaging deals and you'll be receiving stuff from banks about it. We'll sort out splitting things another time okay? I'm sure we can do this fairly for both of us.

The house keys as you can see are on your desk. I've not taken the big car. I bought myself a little Smart car that'll do for now.

I've already secured rent for an apartment and sorted studio space until I can sort myself out and get my own place.

There's a few other bits and pieces I've tried to sort out you'll find in this envelope. Also details on all the utility companies, TV licence subscriptions, that sort of thing. They're all in your name now. You may want to cancel some stuff.

Enclosed are divorce papers. I've already filled in my bits. You can fill in yours when you're ready. Please don't destroy them. I understand if you want to put them in a drawer and forget about them for a while. You'll know the right time.

Jethro, please don't try to find me.

It won't be long before I'm registered and yes you can find me if you want to. But if you do I'll have to move again and next time I'll change my name and everything. I've made it easy this time as we've still a lot to sort out and I trust you not to look for me okay?

By now I'm sure you've realised I've cancelled my phone.

No one yet has my new number. I won't be giving it out because I'm sure you can guilt any one of them to give it to you and I don't want them to feel pressured into doing that. I'll do all the calling for a while.

Any further dealings for things I might've forgotten I've asked Daniel to arbitrate between us for now. He said he would. I hope that's okay? It might seem like I've been thorough but I've had plenty of time to think about stuff.

Anyway, please respect my wishes Jethro. Trust me. I am doing this for you.

Now the important bit:

Jethro, I've had an amazing life with you.

I have never wanted anything else. These past two years together were amazing, weren't they? I didn't expect to have so much fun! I enjoyed every moment I spent in your company. I can't thank you enough for the way you tried to adapt. The way you made us feel as a couple filled me with a contentment I never had before. It felt whole and totally right. I take with me so many new memories. Our meals out, that trip to the Spanish islands, the walks, the mini breaks in hotels, the laughter. God the laughter! We've laughed a lot these past two years haven't we? Remember how I got you back on the dodge 'ems for teasing me about the roller coaster ride? That was priceless! But just as priceless I also take all those memories from the other me. You know, the ones where I loved you. They are all memories I will cherish the rest of my life.

I know you want to know why I left. I bet you've already guessed.

I know you were suffering Jethro. What we were doing second time around was torturing you. It took me a while to work it out but after I started seeing clues it became so obvious

– you fooled me for a while you clever thing ;) I tried so hard to be the old me but please don't think I faked any of it. I didn't. Just because I can't love you doesn't mean every word, every laugh, every moment wasn't real. But I realised I had to leave.

I HAD to.

Remember it was me who persuaded you to come back. I chose you. I did it willingly. But I know you wanted it to be like old times. So did I in a way. But yours came with the weight of something I no longer have for you. Still, you are worth more to me than you can ever know.

I hope it brings you some comfort to know I'm happy. I leave with a light heart. I'm full of expectation of a new life. Full of hope for a new beginning. You know I can't mourn our loss but it is still a loss and it still feels like a loss. If I were to try to explain what it's like for me I'd say it's like having lost someone special to me a long, long time ago. I'm long over the pain but I still miss that person very much.

I will miss you Jethro.

I will miss your company every day for the rest of my life. You will always be with me.

Learn to be happy my wonderful Jethro.

It's okay to take your time. Do what you need to do to come through whatever it takes. Harriet and Eddsy know everything. So does Daniel. Don't blame them for not warning you. I gave them an ultimatum. Bad I know, but it's on me, not them. Let them help you. They are our family.

About Daniel.

Daniel's upset by this. Try to remain strong for him okay? You need to be. We both love him so much and he will need all the support we can give him. He feels so responsible. We have to keep reminding him none of this is his fault. It was completely my own stupid, silly fault. Daniel and I already shared tears over this. I'm sure we'll share many more until we hammer it into his skull.

Anyway I'll speak to him once I've settled in. I'm glad he and Araminta have decided to get a flat together. She's there for him but we'll need to be there for him too. Please keep reminding him he's not to blame. I know you will.

Jethro, take comfort in knowing the me I am now is because I found you all those years ago. Despite what The Gateway Programme did, it is impossible to unwind you from the person I am. I am imbued with the imprint of your life entwined in twenty-three years of my own. Every twist and kink since then had you there shaping me as we grew around each other. We're like woven vines, aren't we? Now it's time for those vines to separate and grow new leaves. But don't forget our history is still there. The roots can't change. That's all a bit poetic for me eh? But Jethro I'm saying you shaped me into who I became. Schoolyard sweethearts right? No medical treatment can ever take away that history. Simply by being myself, you are with me always. It is that I carry with me.

I will always be in awe of you my amazing and wonderful, talented Jethro. Believe me when I say I admire and adore you more than I could have ever appreciated before.

Be brave for me Jethro. I know you can do it.

C.

PS: One last thing I need to tell you. It's a really horrible thing but you have a right to know. After I thought you'd betrayed me but before my treatment I had revenge sex. I'm sorry. It was horrible. Afterwards I felt soiled and disgusted with myself. I'm truly sorry. I know it will hurt you to know that. In a way I want it to make you angry because maybe it'll help you heal. I hope one day you find it in your heart to understand.

THEY HAVEN'T SEEN each other in twelve years when Cooper spots him.

Jethro.

It's in The Open Page Bookshop in Jiffy Street in a rural village close to Westport in County Mayo in Ireland. The village is full of historic grey stone cottages, a church spire, cobbled streets, even has a touch of the Mediterranean with its own Riviera culture.

Jethro is leaving the shop. He's thinking about how the tinkling bell reminds him of old-fashioned sweetshops. Glass jars full of boiled sweets glinting like colourful jewels in the sun, a bronze weighing scale, a white haired man behind the counter, a child's playful spark in his eyes.

Jethro's bought a book and is holding a carrier bag with The Open Page Bookshop printed on the side. Someone calls his name.

Please not a fan. Not today.

Jethro turns around, sees a woman with long hair and glasses on a spiral staircase peering at him. No not peering, she's smiling. An old fan who recognises him? He looks at her. Then his mouth widens into a smile. It's Cooper. She's a little older but it's definitely her.

Cooper clomps all the way down the steps in open-toe sandals. She's wearing a pair of practical stonewashed ankle high jeans, a mint green top, it looks just right. She always hated mint green before. It looks good on her. She's carrying a bundle of books. She looks amazing.

Jethro lets the door swing back behind him. The shop bell tinkles. He stands there, not believing what he's seeing.

Cooper approaches, smiling herself, not believing what she's seeing either. Jethro looks good. He's fuller in the face than she remembers but it's a familiar fond terrain. The same contours. The sweep of eyebrows. The carve of jawline. A few more lines around the eyes, the skin has more sun in it. He still has long dark hair with a lot more grey woven through it, the tips sun-bleached. Still his trademark bolero hat but now he has a goatee with flecks of grey. He's wearing a plain shirt and chinos.

Cooper rests her pile of books on a nearby shelf and he puts his plastic bag on the floor. She tucks a stray hair over her ear. They pause long enough to know things are okay. Then they laugh and embrace. They rock a little. They step apart and look over each other.

"Hey," Jethro says.

"Hey, mister."

"It really is you," Jethro says.

"So they tell me. So how're you?"

Jethro notices the subtle Irish lilt to her voice. Only a touch, but it's definitely there. He gives a questioning arch of an eyebrow.

"Wait a minute."

Cooper laughs, knowing he's picked up on it. She'd needed to reinvent herself. Needed a defining line between her old self and the new. Coming to Ireland and embracing its culture had been that line.

"Cooper. Your accent!"

"I know. I live here now."

"You live where?"

"Here. Callum Bay. Eleven years."

"Get out!"

"Honestly. I work here."

"In Callum Bay?"

"Here. This bookshop."

"Get the heck out of here."

"Truly. I own it."

"Oh my god, you OWN IT?"

A cashier, a woman of about twenty-five, looks up.

"This is just crazy. I walk into this random bookshop and you own it?"

"Ah well, I fell in love."

"Someone I know?"

"Not someone."

"What do you mean?"

"Fell in love with the country." Cooper looks around, taking her bookshop in. "Somehow it feels like home, you know?"

Jethro stares at her.

"I can't believe it's you."

"In flesh and bone."

"This is totally crazy."

She does another once over on him.

"Well, you're looking fine yourself. How's the music?"

"Music's good. But last I heard you were an audio engineer."

"Ah well I sold up. A piece of software to an audio company."

"Not Sonic Scalpel?"

"You remember. Graham Chambers got me on to a good royalty deal."

"That plugin's legendary, man. They're like Yamaha NS10s. Standard kit in every studio now."

"So they tell me, so they tell me. Anyway I got out the audio business. Too many home studios you know? Bought this bookshop, tucked some away for a pension and well here I am. Daniel or Harriet must've told you? Surely?"

"Well, they did say something. But why here?"

Cooper regards him.

"Ah, come on now. Open your eyes will you? It's a beautiful country. Rolling hills. Tons of landscape. The sea. The people here are nice."

Jethro takes her in.

"I can't believe this. The way you talk, the way you look. This is crazy."

"How's your watch looking?"

"Say what?"

"You think you might have a bit of time on your hands?"

Jethro laughs.

"Course."

Cooper goes to the cashier, hands her the bundle of slender books, says something to her, the cashier nods, glances at Jethro, nods again.

Jethro follows Cooper up the spiral metal staircase and Jethro's surprised to find a coffee shop.

Cooper orders two coffees from Darragh and introduces Jethro as her good friend. They nod to each other. Darragh wears a forest green apron with the name The Open Page Coffee Shop printed on it. He offers Jethro something to eat. Jethro glances at the stall. It has cakes, scones and pastries under glass lids. It has an old cash register made of shiny brass. The whole setup has a church fete olde-worlde charm to it. He declines. They find a table and sit.

"Well now, it's fine to see you Jethro."

"I still can't get over how you sound."

"You can't help it once you've settled your feet under the country. There's a spirit over here, you know? A real sense of home like I say."

Their coffees arrive. Jethro sips before speaking, enjoying the oaky hit.

"Hey, you like remember the Natural History Museum?"

"Uh-huh. You had Earl Grey."

"You really do remember stuff."

"Like I always said. The treatment you know? It doesn't—"

"Erase memories. Yeah, I remember. I'm teasing Coops."

They engross themselves in conversation. So many questions, so much talking. They find time slipping away as each catches up on the other's lives. The young cashier from downstairs appears, leans over Cooper, whispers something in her ear. Cooper introduces Neasa to Jethro who nods back. Cooper gets up, tells Jethro she'll be right back, don't go away now.

Cooper turns to Darragh and throws a thumb over her shoulder.

"That man moves, you wrestle him back to that chair you hear?"

Darragh laughs.

Cooper descends the steps, pauses, turns, looks at Jethro, appreciation in her eyes, her smile never leaving. Then she disappears.

Jethro glances around. Old dark floorboards that creak. Bookshelves everywhere give the place a higgledy-piggledy feel. A few book-rapt customers sit at nearby tables in front of mullion windows nursing hot mugs. Not a computer in sight.

Soon Cooper returns, settles into her seat pushing a stray hair over an ear.

"You know we have the Internet age now?" Jethro says.

"Ah, come on now. People come here to get away from technology, that's why we survive. But we'll order books online for you if we don't stock them. I have a Kindle, a Nook, an Android tablet, and an iPad. Beat that."

Jethro holds his hands up.

I surrender.

He drains his coffee.

"This coffee's so good it's off the scales."

Cooper orders another. When it arrives, Jethro takes out his wallet.

"I swear I will shove you out the window you open that. God's truth."

Jethro laughs, puts his money away.

They settle down to talking again. Finally, after several stories of their lives and a third cup of coffee and a moist wedge of an Irish cake called Barm Brack, Cooper enquires into his private life.

"So," Cooper says, "anyone special waiting for you back home?"

Jethro shakes his head no.

"You?"

"One or two along the way."

"One or two?"

Cooper nods matter-of-factly, pleased how open she can be with him. Twice Cooper had tried dating. It always came with a bag full of feelings to cloud her judgement. Cooper liked having a clear focused head and feelings always seemed to isolate her instead. She felt lost. As uncomfortable in a relationship as sitting on stones. It's now a well-known side effect for clients having been on The Gateway Programme.

Cooper pokes Jethro on the shoulder, grinning.

"So, why aren't YOU seeing someone, handsome fella you are?"

"I tried online dating. I tried hook-ups. I tried blind dates, though of course once they know who I am they're always more in love with the fame than with me. I tried parties, dinners. You know, the kind of things so-called friends inflict on you. I guess being such a well-known face I disappoint people who get the real boring old me. I dated a few models too."

"So, I saw in the papers."

"They weren't really dates, though. It was all for the papers around about the time of album releases. But I did date Katie Connor about four years ago. She's a model too. Well, ex-model. Now she's like a modelling consultant to the industry."

"Okay."

"Wait, I'll show you."

Jethro pulls out his phone. He flicks to his Facebook account. He pulls up a picture of them both smiling in a selfie at some do.

Cooper whistles.

"She's a nice looking girl. She looks familiar."

"She did billboard modelling years ago. Covers on the likes of Vogue and Marie Claire."

"So, what's the story?"

"I like went on five or six dates with her. We got on well."

"There's a but."

"Yeah."

"They say actors and models are very insecure."

"Totally."

"She worried about her fading beauty?"

"Nah, like the opposite. She told me a story. When she turned twelve she started to notice the attention of men. Says all her life her looks controlled her. She realised it was becoming an issue. Kinda reminded me of you, actually. Even went to a psychiatrist about it."

"What happened?"

"She married the psychiatrist."

"Oh shush now."

"No, really. They were like together nine years. She tried an online site, got over 2,000 requests the first day and crashed the servers. Some of them came from women. The site owners said she was by far their most successful client. They wanted to use her in their advertising."

"What did she do?"

"Closed the account."

Cooper nods at that.

"So, how'd you two meet?"

"Katie came to a gig. She went backstage with her celebrity pass and she asked if we could meet for a drink. I said sure and we met at a bar across town. She was already there when I got there, two lads chatting with her. I had to rescue her and we ended up at a restaurant. The poor lads totally had their tongues hanging out, but my autographs and selfies had them backing off."

"Was that what put you off?"

"I liked her. Astute businesswoman. And that she was shy. Truth was we never had anything to start with. No connection. After the fifth date or something I came clean. Told her I was sorry I wish I felt something but that I didn't. I was happy to be friends with her."

"She took it okay?"

"It confused her. No one ever rejected her before. Never had a relationship broken off like that. I told her it hadn't developed into a proper romantic relationship so like technically it couldn't be rejection. Anyway, she backed off, took it pretty well."

"So?"

"Well yeah that was the last time I dated. About four years ago now."

"And so you're here."

Jethro looks around.

"Yeah, I'm here. I'm like supposed to be visiting someone."

"In Ireland?"

Jethro nods.

"Anyone I know?"

Probably.

"Who?"

"You."

"Ah, come off it, you're putting one over."

"No, really."

Cooper settles her coffee cup down on the saucer, studies him. He's being serious.

"I thought it was about time I did. I knew you were living in Ireland now but Daniel told me where you were."

"So, you knew I was in this bookshop the whole time?"

"Daniel didn't explain anything just said go to this village. I asked him not to mess me about but he said relax, enjoy the place, I'm sure to bump into mum at some point. I've like been here eight days. It's a cool little village. I totally get it."

"Ah, Daniel could have told you where I was. I wouldn't hide anything from you, Jethro."

"Nah, it's okay. This village chilled me. I spent days walking and browsing. Tea rooms. An old junk shop. A jumble at the school. That lovely church with the stained glass windows. Second-hand shops. There's a music shop up the road I like to visit. A camera shop. The village hall. I even heard someone call out bingo in there. Can you believe it?" He laughs. "I liked knowing I'd bump into you. People didn't bother me much even if they thought I was someone they might recognise. The odd tourist but that was it."

Neasa appears again, leans over Cooper, tells her something. Cooper stands.

"Give me five, will you?"

Jethro stands.

"Nah, not this time, Coops. I've taken up too much of your time already."

"You can't be leaving already?"

"I'm at The Callum Bay's Heart Hotel."

"The O'Donnell's place?"

"You know it?"

"Course. Everyone does. Jannon and Viola O'Donnell. They've owned the place all the time I've been here."

"Cool."

"You'll come back later though?"

"No need."

Cooper looks at him.

"Oh?"

Jethro grins.

"'Cause I'm like inviting you for dinner there. How's 7.30pm sound?"

IT'S EVENING WHEN Jethro leaves his room and goes down to reception at The Callum Bay's Heart Hotel. He spots Cooper chatting to Viola over the welcome desk. He stops to take Cooper in when he sees how incredible she looks in her dress. She's as breathtaking as ever.

Cooper hears a noise, turns, sees Jethro's open mouth. Viola turns, smiles with approval at Jethro's reaction.

Cooper is wearing an emerald-green evening gown. The ensemble is astonishing. The dress is silk, a sheer elegant sheen that follows the contours of her body, flows like a waterfall cascading off her curves. She wears a simple silver pendant around her neck, silver drop earrings, a dot of ruby swings at the ends like spots of blood. It brings out the flame in her hair. Beautiful. He walks up to her, kisses her cheek.

"Wow. Wow. Just wow, Cooper."

Viola laughs, winks at Cooper.

"I think you have a fan."

"Cooper. You look totally out of this world."

Cooper lifts her dress a little to reveal walking boots rather than heels.

"Ta da!"

Jethro grins.

"Yeah, that's more the Coops I know."

She turns it into a curtsy.

"Well a fair thank you, kind sir."

Cooper checks him over. Jethro's in an open-necked crisp white shirt, dark corduroys, simple Italian cut blue jacket, a touch of cologne. Homme. For once he isn't wearing his bolero hat. She nods, smiling her approval.

Cooper tells Viola Jethro's her good friend from England. Though Viola greeted him well enough when he booked in The Callum Bay's Heart, tonight she's even more friendly.

"I didn't know you had such famous friends, Cooper."

A red-faced man rushes through a door behind the reception desk, a wide grin. Viola introduces him as her husband Jannon. He's a small round man with a face so flushed it's as though he's been standing at the mouth of an open furnace. He takes off his chef's hat, wipes his glistening forehead.

"Holy Mary, I'm up to ninety in there."

His white hair stands on end like flames from an albino fire. Jannon pauses, gives Cooper the once-over and his pale grey eyes moisten. He takes her hand.

"Sure, you're looking like a maiden of the seas, plenty handsome for an old man's eyes tonight."

Viola looks at him with a stern look.

"What're you saying old man?"

Jannon looks at her.

"What do you mean?"

"You eejit, you just about insulted the poor girl."

"What you talking about woman I insulted her? I'm telling her she's looking fair."

"So, every other time she's an old bicycle, that what you saying?"

Jannon's eyes widen.

"But I didn't—"

"You old goat."

"But—"

"Jannon, she's messing with you," Cooper says, laughing. "Sure, but it's only a bit of fun." Viola looks as though bursting to laugh, amusement glistening in her eyes.

Jannon looks at Viola, his eyes narrowing.

"Woman, I almost wet me knickers. I insulted her!"

"Oh get away with you. Go. Scat. Take your sourpuss back to the stove."

He grumbles and pushes through the door to the kitchen.

"Ah, don't be bothering me, you old wagon."

When he's gone Cooper leans into Viola.

"Oh Viola, you're a mean one."

"Ah now, shush will you. It's only a bit of gassing."

Viola escorts Cooper and Jethro into the Tudor-style dining room. The hotel is oak beams, creaking floorboards, soft pools of light and gentle guttering candles at every table.

When they're seated Jannon reappears with an open bottle of ruby red wine.

"Compliments of the house."

He holds the bottle by the base and pours them each a sample. They taste it. It's rich and flavoursome and both smack their lips with noises of approval. Jannon looks pleased and fills their glasses.

"It's a St Joseph red from the Rhône Valley. Tonight's theme is red, in honour of your red earrings. Go on the both of you, give it a lash why don't you?"

They both sample the wine and approve.

"I could get used to service like this," Jethro says.

"Ah, Cooper's bang on round here you know. As a good friend from England that makes you pretty dead on too Mr Hall. Even if you are somewhat famous."

"Make it Jethro."

Jannon continues.

"Cooper's done a grand job for this village, a grand job. Sure, but when the old library went you know what Cooper went and did? You know she only went and bought out the old library books and started her own lending library for free."

"Ah, it's not free, Jannon. How many times do I have to tell you?"

Jannon dismisses Cooper with a flick of the hand.

"Now what's a few coins to cover the cost of hiring the hall. I bet it doesn't cover everything. Them stinking counsellors stealing from the poor and shutting down the library, Jesus O'Mary. Every third Saturday this lovely youngwan here uses the old school, sets out pallets of books so Joe and his dog can waltz in, pick up a book or two and pay with a lick and a promise for as long as they want. In this here village everyone knows Cooper's pure class."

Jethro listens, raising his glass to Cooper, but she only shakes her head, rolls her eyes.

Viola appears with burgundy leather-bound menus, hands them out.

"Now you stop with your gassing Jannon O'Donnell and leave them two young'uns in peace?"

"What're you talking about old woman? I'm just—"

"Shush with you. Put the bottle down and vamoose."

Jannon ignores her and turns back to Jethro

"Come here and I'll tell you something, Jethro. Cooper's been running this newsletter for—"

Viola puts on a schoolmarmish voice.

"MISTER O'DONNELL!"

Jannon turns to her.

"I said put the bottle down. Go. Scat! Clear the scales."

Jannon stares at Viola as he thumps the bottle down hard on the table to make a point. He retreats but not before slapping Viola's behind and letting out a HA!

Soon they're gone and Jethro leans over, covers his mouth, whispers.

"Is everyone you know here this batty?"

Viola calls out over her shoulder.

"Careful young fella. I heard that."

They all laugh.

*

For starters Cooper has lobster bisque and Jethro, French onion soup. Soft hot bread rolls appear on the table and they enjoy it with a pat of thick, yellow butter. The main course arrives in stages, braised lamb in a red wine sauce for Jethro, roast duck in a thick red port gravy for Cooper. Then comes creamed spinach, sauteed mushrooms, steamed asparagus, soft buttery, baked Irish potatoes.

"This evening's theme is red," Viola says.

"In my honour apparently," Cooper says.

"Is that what the old goat said?"

"It's not true?"

"Ah, believe what you must. All I can say is Jannon's an old scoundrel."

For dessert Cooper has an Irish coffee, a thick band of cream floating over dark coffee laced with whisky in a wine glass. Jethro has raspberry jam roly-poly with thick sherry-laced creme Anglaise.

Afterwards, after the meal, after soft banter, after laughs and reminiscences, after jokes, shared stories from their lives together, stories from after they separated, after everything they lean back, stomachs full.

"If I have to eat another thing you're going to have to roly-poly me back to my room," Jethro says.

Jannon appears, crooks a finger and asks them to come with him. Intrigued they stand, follow him to two leather wing-backed chairs by a crackling cedar fire, a small mahogany table with fresh prepared coffee and two waiting brandy glasses.

"Jannon man, we're overwhelmed. This is beyond service."

"Nonsense, nonsense. Sit, sit the both of you. Tonight you're guests of the O'Donnell's. The evening's on us."

Cooper looks past Jannon and Viola smiles and nods.

They both protest about not paying but Jannon closes his eyes and raises a red palm.

"Now stop with your wailing. Nod and say thank you Viola and Jannon."

"But—"

"Cooper we fair love you like our own but so help me you need to know when to keep that trap shut and accept a modest gift. 'Sides, a few of the other villagers chipped in when they knew you were coming with an old fla— a friend."

Cooper feels herself fluster, embarrassed but grateful.

"Thank you Jannon, and everyone." She raises a glass to Viola and mouths thank you. Viola winks back.

"I'm like totally speechless," Jethro says. "Thanks, man."

"Keep the weight off your legs both of you and enjoy the rest of your evening," Jannon says.

They sink into their chairs, the leather hot from the fire and watch as Jannon pours them each a brandy.

"Let me tell you a little about Cognac."

Viola rolls her eyes and disappears, shaking her head.

"Cognac's a brandy right?" Cooper says.

"So it is. As is Armagnac and Calvados."

"Don't tell me they're all brandies from the different parts of France."

"Gold star for you missy. Cognac is wine distilled twice to create a rich smooth flavour don't you know. There are three distinct designations of Cognac. VS, VSOP and XO. You know what they stand for?"

Cooper and Jethro speak in unison knowing Jannon's enjoying his mini performance.

"No, Jannon."

"VS means very special Cognac aged at least two years. VSOP is—"

"Very special old port or something?" Cooper says.

"HA! Very SUPERIOR old pale aged at least four years. And XO is, can you summon a guess?"

Jethro looks thoughtful.

"Extra old?"

Jannon raises an eyebrow, impressed.

"Let's give your man a gold star too. It means the brandy has aged at least six years."

Jannon inhales the aroma from the mouth of the bottle for a moment, enjoying the heady fruitiness.

"Ah, this one is particularly fine. Aged over twenty years in oak barrels made from the wood of trees in the Limousin region of France. I think you should enjoy this one neat. Go on, swirl it in your glass, see how thick the liquid is?"

They both swirl the Cognac, study their glasses, enjoying the lesson, passing amused glances at each other like schoolchildren with the headmaster.

"That's twice distillation working at the liqueur. Sure, Michelangelo couldn't have made a better Cognac if he were a winemaker. Now close your eyes and savour the bouquet. It should be rich and heady, bursting with the grapes of the Elysian fields."

They do as he says, closing their eyes, inhaling the wine.

"Slip some on your tongue. You taste it? That's the rich sunshine ripening those dusty grapes. Be careful though. Cognac can whip your feet from under you quick as a scalping. Feel it light the way down your gullet? That's pure medicine to ease the digestion. Me? I like to savour brandy and coffee alternately. Brings out the best of both don't you know. Ah, the weight of coffee eased by the sweet depths of Cognac. Bliss. Bliss."

There's a moment of silence as they each sip their cognacs and make approving noises.

"Now I'll go and leave the bottle with you before the old wagon pesters me again."

Jannon places the bottle on the small table beside them as gently as placing a sleeping baby in a cradle, makes a formal little bow.

They applaud. Jannon raises his red palms.

"Enjoy. Enjoy the fire. Enjoy the rest of the evening. Enjoy each other's company. Enjoy!"

He backs away, they watch him leave smiling with the impression he's done this performance before for honoured guests. They enjoy the coffee, enjoy the brandy, enjoy the crackling cedar fire, enjoy each other's company.

After a while, gazing into the fire filled with the soft heady glow of a satisfied evening, Jethro sits forward in his chair, a second brandy swirling thickly in his glass. He looks thoughtful.

Cooper has been hypnotised by the cloak of the intimate evening. She pulls her gaze from the fire and looks at Jethro with a lazy smile. She runs her gaze over his lovely face. A tinge of sadness salts her heart. Jethro is staring into the brandy, his eyes preoccupied. Cooper realises there's something on his mind. She could always tell.

"What is it, Jethro?"

Jethro swirls the brandy, his gaze not lifting from the glass.

"Jethro?"

"Seeing you again today… it's so unfair."

Cooper leans forward. The haze blows away like mist in a breeze.

"Jethro, what is it?"

"How is it time has done nothing to you?"

"Oh shush, will you."

"It's not only that. Now you've this soft lyrical accent going on. All these years and all you've done is become an ever-more incredible woman."

Jethro lifts his gaze from the glass and looks at Cooper, the fire reflecting in his grey eyes like mirrors.

"You know, there hasn't been a single day I haven't thought of you, Coops. Not one. I tried to forget you, you know. Nothing worked. Not therapy, not holidays, not my work, not hobbies, not dating. And yeah, seeing you in Daniel's face haunts me every time I see him."

Cooper touches Jethro's hand.

"You've had therapy? I didn't know."

"Yeah, for a while."

"A doctor?"

"Bereavement counsellor."

"I'm sorry."

"Yeah, like three-and-a-half years I went to her. Didn't change a thing."

"Oh Jethro." She wishes more than ever she could love him again. Despite all she's said. She sees it. His torment.

"You were like totally in my dreams, in my thoughts, in everything I did. Know something crazy? I still talk to you, Coops. I tell you things, seek your advice about stuff. What would you think about this? Would you prefer this or that? What did you think about what happened in the news? How you'd like this film."

"I had no idea."

"I hated myself and I hated you. I couldn't do anything about it. Yeah well except get the treatment but I never want to do that, you know that. I know it wasn't your fault but I blamed you anyway Coops. I blamed you."

"Jethro."

"I blamed you."

"It's okay." Her voice is tender.

Jethro takes a moment before continuing.

"Anyway, I gave the counsellor up. A month later I tried another. Then another. And another. Took me ten years to realise none of them could help me. None of them could make me move on. I needed to get on without you. Just get past you. If you'd died it would have been better. Fact is you're still walking the earth, still somewhere, still smiling and laughing, still being Cooper. You know that song, I Wonder Who's Kissing Her Now? That's me. It was all that which made it so hard. That and knowing no matter how hard I romanced you I could never woo you back."

"I chose you anyway, Jethro. I left because you needed me to."

Jethro cups the brandy glass in both hands like he's cupping a hot drink. He swirls the brandy and watches the dark liquid skim around the belly of the glass. He takes a hard shot from it.

"Well… anyway it was purgatory whatever I did. It really is can't live with you, can't live without you."

"I'm sorry."

Jethro's stares into his glass looking wistful and introspective. In the background the soft murmur of other diners around them, the gentle notes of a classical quartet coming from discreet speakers.

Cooper acknowledges one or two familiar people as they pass with a smile and a nod.

"And know what? You've crafted this amazing life for yourself, Coops. You live in this make-believe village where magic seeps out the earth like morning dew. You seen the stars? They're so many it's like someone spilt sugar onto black velvet."

"That's because the streetlights go out at night. No light pollution."

"You know what? It's so you, Cooper. This place. Your amazing bookshop. The land's cradled you, the village has embraced you. How could it not? You're magical too."

Cooper wants to feel something. Something more than the thrill of his beautiful face, his eyes grey but not like coastal mist. She gives him a gentle smile.

"Now that's a lovely thing to say."

"This place needs to be in a Hallmark movie, man. Maeve Binchy could write the script."

Cooper smiles.

"You feel it too?"

Jethro nods.

"I know you've found home."

"It's the right place. As they say over here, it's grand."

"They love you, Coops. They're not just business or work colleagues, not even just friends. They treat you like family. Even the soil loves you. The truth is you belong here. And somehow you knew instinctively where you needed to go. How did you know? I'd almost believe something drew you here. It's like the village lassoed you and yanked you across the Irish sea."

She laughs.

Jethro looks up again, his eyes gentle, no longer anger, frustration, sadness, just a resigned acceptance.

"And I can tell you love it here, Coops." Jethro's lips become thin as he presses down on them. "The only thing you can't love is me."

Cooper realises then he's here for a reason. Something's happened.

Viola escorts another post dining couple into the sitting room. She attends another group at the other end, reclined on chesterfields chatting, port glasses by a chessboard game they're engrossed in. After she's finished with them she turns to approach Cooper and Jethro with a smile but a flicker of uncertainty crosses her eyes. They're in deep conversation. She tactfully changes direction before they spot her, attend to another party with a welcoming smile. She tells Jannon to leave them be.

"Why haven't you found anyone, Coops? Why didn't you at least try?"

Cooper considers lying to Jethro about relationships but she knows he's not here for lies. It would be the wrong thing to do.

"I miss you too much." She says it plainly in answer to his question.

Her answer surprises him.

"You... you do?"

"For twelve years I've missed you Jethro. I miss our life together. I've missed everything about us. Daniel tells me nothing about you. I asked him never to. Until today I had no clue what you were doing, if you were with someone, even if you'd had more children."

"That can't be true."

"It is true. You keep your private life out of the news. I had no idea what you were—"

"No, I mean about… about missing me."

"Oh Jethro, you're the one person I could never lie to."

"But why? You can still love anyone else in the whole world. You can't be saying no one's ever attracted your attention."

"That's not what I said. I could admire. I never wanted more than that."

"I don't understand."

"It's what I choose, Jethro. Like I always said."

"Is it atonement for what you think you did? Is it guilt?"

Cooper considers her answer.

"That was part of it once, perhaps. Not now."

"What then?"

"I've realised it could never be fulfilling enough. That wouldn't be fair on anyone I was with."

"So you have it too? This purgatory."

"Yes. I expect in my own way I have it."

They both gaze into the fire and let their respective revelations sink in. Even in silence they read each other well. It's a mutual intuition that doesn't fade with time.

"I will always love you, Cooper."

She smiles, reaches over and squeezes his hand.

"I know, Jethro."

"I wish I didn't."

"Fair play. I wish you didn't either."

Jethro struggles with the next words.

"Cooper?"

She looks at him.

"Would you… like ever consider taking me back?"

1 3 9

COOPER CAN'T BELIEVE what Jethro's just asked. They're nestled close in front of the cedar fire, each gazing at the other. She stares at him.

"I'd want to take you back."

"Yeah, but would you?"

Cooper shakes her head.

"I'm sorry Jethro."

Jethro gives a solid nod to confirm his own thoughts.

"You understand why don't you?"

"Yeah," Jethro says. "You'd like choose me in a heartbeat. But last time you realised it wasn't working out for me."

Cooper nods.

"You understand."

"I'd know you can't ever say I love you back and mean it."

"Yes."

"Even though you'd want to."

"Yes."

"Even though it wouldn't affect you one bit."

"Yes."

"So even though you choose me, you think it will destroy me to come back."

Barely a whisper.

"Yes."

Jethro swirls the brandy glass in his cupped hands, swirls it, swirls it. He stops. He puts his glass down.

"What is it, Jethro?"

He lifts his gaze, meets hers. The fire blazes in them.

"You know I can tap dance now?"

"Really?"

"Been doing it for like six years. They say I'm pretty okay."

"You'll have to show me."

Jethro makes a non-committal shrug.

"What is it Jethro? Why are you here? You're not on your deathbed are you?"

"Nah. It wouldn't upset you even if I was.

Cooper looks away for a second but says nothing.

"Sorry. Sorry Coops, that was low. I didn't mean it. I'm sorry."

"Shush. It's forgiven."

Jethro stands.

"Look, it's late. I need to walk you home."

"Ah, there's no need. This is a small village. I'm two minutes away."

"Yeah, let me."

They return to reception. Viola gets Cooper's coat. Jannon reappears from the kitchen. Cooper embraces them both, thanks them both for the amazing evening. Jethro shakes both their hands, tells them how magnificent the evening was. They step out into the night air so crisp it almost crackles. After a minute they get to Carlisle Street.

"We're at your bookshop again."

"It's where I live."

Jethro looks up at the cottagy flint building. It's like something out of Dickens.

"You live here?"

"House next door down the little side street."

They step down the cobbled alley. The streetlights don't reach the passageway but a porch light the colour of candle flame is on. They stop at the front door, both draped in the soft glow of the light. Cooper turns to Jethro, faces him.

"Thank you for a lovely evening, Jethro."

"It was cool to see you too, Coops. Really. I'm just sorry—"

Cooper places a finger on his lips.

"Ah now, shush will you. There's no need. When do you leave?"

"How do you know I do?"

"You've your own reasons why you're here now. I don't know what they are but I know seeing me was part of it. I know you well enough to know asking me back wasn't why you came."

Jethro shoves his hands in his pockets, kicks an imaginary stone.

"Tomorrow."

"So soon?"

"As you said, I needed to see you first."

"What have you been trying to tell me all evening?"

Jethro takes a moment to phrase his response. He looks down the alley. It fades to darkness. Like his pained heart it leads to the unknown, the unexplored.

"I need to get away. Completely away. Like totally change direction. Start somewhere else. A different place, a different country."

"I see."

"It's what I need, Coops. I realise that now. You still feel so close. Too close. I need a different sky, a different world. I need to be somewhere else."

"You're going to emigrate?"

"Yeah, something like that."

"Where?"

Jethro considers his answer.

"The Arctic Circle. Bermuda. Darkest Peru. Who knows?"

"Does Daniel know?"

"He knows."

"But you will tell him where? Don't cut him off Jethro. That wouldn't be fair."

"Nah. Course I'll tell him when I know myself."

"I'm sorry you're still suffering, Jethro."

He gives a wistful smile.

"Yeah well, you know. Accepted. I know you are too. Even if it is a different kind of suffering."

"It is."

To anyone passing by they'd look like two lovers in a shadowy alcove, not quite saying goodnight. They stand so close. So intimate. None would see the impossible plate of glass between them. All they can do is gaze at each other through it.

"I expect this is goodbye," Cooper says. She studies his eyes. The light from the porch catches them. Grey. The coastal mist, now gone, belonged to her once. Lines around his eyes deeper yet still so attractive. Only now a sad wisdom in the turn of his mouth, the shadows of his brow, the hang of his shoulders.

He touches her lips with his. A light touch gentle as a snowflake. It melts just as quickly. Then he wraps his arms around her. Protective arms. Wings. She nuzzles in there cocooned for a moment. She'd choose him in a heartbeat. She would. But it's not love. No. Not love. She'd destroy him. He needs love.

After a minute they peel apart.

"You're shivering, you'd better get in the warm."

"Yes. I'd better."

Cooper opens her front door, steps in but Jethro doesn't move.

"You won't come in?"

"Nah, Coops. This is it."

"Jethro I'm so sor—"

Jethro presses a finger to her lips.

"Shush now, there's no need." He smiles mimicking what she'd just said to him. No one has ever known her the way he does. No one ever will.

"Go in, close the door. Enjoy your life, Coops."

"Yes."

Jethro smiles, boyishly.

"It's a cool life. I'm envious."

Cooper nods. She feels something delicate inside her. Not love.

He steps backwards, fades into the shadow of the alley, his eyes on her. A voice comes from the darkness.

"I'm happy for you, Cooper. Really. Thank you for once being my beautiful wife. Thank you for our amazing son. I'll love you always."

Cooper feels an urge to cry out to shout to scream back. PLEASE!!!!! STAY!!!!! PLEASE JETHRO!!!! But it's not there. It's not love. There are no miracles.

Not even tears.

Cooper closes her eyes leans against the door.

Feeling a strange, empty sort of nothing.

THE SUE BAXTER PODCAST
SUE BAXTER
Have you ever treated any other notable celebrities?
DR STEWART-WAY
Well I can discuss one interesting case.
SUE BAXTER
Please do.
DR STEWART-WAY
We once had a case where the celebrity's management agency
contacted us. They wanted us to treat an obsessive fan. We told
the agency the fan would have to volunteer to a psychological
assessment first. Obsessive fans often have underlying mental
conditions. Surprisingly, the management agency followed
through. They'd contacted the fan and offered him a fee to
undergo assessment and treatment. From what I gather the fan
agreed but only in return for a private dinner with the celebrity
rather than a fee. We didn't think it was a good idea but the
agency struck a deal anyway. They organised a dinner with the
celebrity and fan under close supervision. During the meal the
fan even went down on one knee to propose.
SUE BAXTER
The celebrity is a woman?
DR STEWART-WAY
Yes.
SUE BAXTER
I take it she turned the proposal down?
DR STEWART-WAY
I'm sure it was graciously done.

SUE BAXTER

Why would a fan agree to the arrangement then? Surely if the fan is in love with a celebrity whose work brings joy they wouldn't want to destroy that joy by agreeing to undergo treatment.

DR STEWART-WAY

Quite simply the fan didn't believe the treatment would work.

SUE BAXTER

Did you meet the star?

DR STEWART-WAY

We dealt with the management agency. We didn't meet the celebrity.

SUE BAXTER

So what happened?

DR STEWART-WAY

A few weeks after the treatment the fan called to thank us. He used to post on YouTube and TikTok and various other online video sites of the times he'd disrupt the artist's live performance such as jumping on stage and dancing with the singer, or hugging the celebrity if she was out and about. He called them video trophies. After completing The Gateway Programme, viewing these videos embarrassed him. He took down all videos within 24 hours of the treatment.

SUE BAXTER

So it changed him?

DR STEWART-WAY

What he'd considered romantic gestures he now realised was inappropriate behaviour. He said his former conduct horrified him when he became aware what he was doing was harassment. He described all the letters, emails, tweets and other social media comments as deranged behaviour. The treatment had been tantamount to sobering up and discovering on Monday morning he'd behaved appallingly at the office party on Friday night.

SUE BAXTER

So, a good result.

DR STEWART-WAY

Oh there's more to the story. The fan then went on to say his obsession had lost him his job and had caused depression and overeating. He described our treatment as a miracle cure. He began eating healthily, started an exercise program, and focused his attention on studies rather than the celebrity. It was an astonishing turnaround.

SUE BAXTER

That's quite an endorsement.

DR STEWART-WAY

The results surprised even us. The treatment had a worthwhile effect not only for the celebrity but also for the fan. He is now in a healthy romantic relationship and studying for a degree in fashion, something he always wanted to do but never pursued. There's also an epilogue.

SUE BAXTER

Which is?

DR STEWART-WAY

After the transformation the fan asked to meet the celebrity again. She granted a meeting though both were reportedly very wary of the other and it was once more under close supervision. The record label weren't keen. However, the fan wanted an opportunity to apologise for the way he'd hounded her for years. They met and things went so well they've since become good friends. Apparently they Zoom each other at least once a week and talk about something they're both obsessed with – costume design. I believe he's designed a few stage costumes for her since and he and his girlfriend even stays as a guest on her ranch.

SUE BAXTER

Good heavens. Quite a turnaround. Now talking about celebrities, it's a decade or more since Jethro T Hall and his wife Cooper separated, re-coupled, and separated again. In fact

I've recently heard unconfirmed rumours about their meeting again. Is this something you're aware of Dr Stewart-Way?
DR STEWART-WAY
Actually Sue, it's interesting you should ask that question…

1 4 1

IT'S MIDNIGHT.

Cooper's in bed. She's heard nothing from Jethro since he left four weeks ago. She considered calling him once or twice. She never does. It would not be the right thing to do. Cooper has no idea when he plans on emigrating. She wonders if he's asleep right now.

Where he is.

If he meant it when he asked her for another chance.

She's been wondering that one for four weeks now. Four weeks.

Still.

Cooper has resigned herself to her life. She will end her days here running a shop, enjoying this chocolate box village, her friends. Life is good. It is. How could she be happier?

She begins to drift off when the phone beside her bed buzzes and lights up. Cooper snatches it up, undoes the charging cable. Jethro's name's on the screen. She answers.

"Jethro?"

"Hey, Coops. Sorry to call so late. And don't worry. Just 'cause I'm calling late doesn't mean anything's wrong. Everything's cool."

He knows her so well. So well.

"You're calling to say you're going?"

"Actually, I've already gone. I sold the house a while ago. Was renting for a bit. But like would you mind opening your front door? I'm totally freezing my goolies out here."

Cooper sits up.

"What did you say?"

She hears the scrape of heels on the cobbles outside her window. She crawls out of bed, looks out. She sees the black velvet figure of a man in the alleyway.

"Man, I didn't realise you get power cuts here."

"Streetlights are out by midnight," Cooper says. "I thought you knew that. In winter they go out at eleven." Cooper slips on her dressing gown, finds her slippers, musses her hair in the mirror to take the pillow kinks out.

Jethro chuckles.

"That's so cool. No one goes about at night here."

"Well, no one innocent."

"Who said anything about innocent?"

Cooper feels the familiar churning in her stomach. Expectation perhaps? But of what? She dismisses it. Cooper goes down, opens the front door. Jethro's on the doorstep, lit now by the soft ambient light of his phone.

Jethro cancels the call.

Cooper cancels the call.

"Hey, Coops."

Before she can respond he steps over the threshold.

Her stomach tightens. It's not love. Definitely not love. But something.

"What's going on? Why're you here?"

Jethro closes the door behind him, leans on it. Even in the dim upstairs hall light Cooper sees the change in him. It's in his face. His expression, the sense of loss in him, the sadness, the pain is all gone, all of it gone. It's as though he's come to terms with something. His relaxed features surprises her.

Jethro's voice is quiet in the library-silence of night.

"When I was last here, I realised it."

"Realised what?"

"When you care about someone and you're willing to care for them like you love them, enjoy their company like you love them, want them like you love them, then walk away because you can't love them, what is that?"

"I don't understand."

"Any ideas?"

"Are you talking about when I left all those years ago?"

"I hated that you took the treatment."

"Oh Jethro. How many times—"

He rests his index finger on her warm lips. His finger feels like a cold steel rod. She feels a charge at the contact.

"I'm trying to tell you something I learned about you, Coops."

"About me?"

"Specifically about you."

"Jethro, you know I can't ever love—"

"Sssh, will you let me finish? When everything went down, we tried over right? We took a second chance."

"Yes."

"See, that's what totally confused me, Cooper. You were so happy, so normal the second time around. So contented. You seemed… satisfied."

"Yes."

"Even though you said you couldn't love me, and even though I knew you didn't, you still acted the same and felt the same to me. But what was going on in my own head tormented me. Truth is if I didn't know you didn't love me, I'd never have guessed."

"So?"

"Then you upped and totally went. You left that note on my guitar and vanished."

"I had to, Jethro."

"That's what I didn't get."

"But Jethro, you know the truth."

Jethro lets out a quiet chuckle.

"Will you like stop interrupting? I'm trying to tell you something. See that note you left was crazy. You wrote the word

HAD in capitals. You even underlined it. You HAD to leave. I didn't get it. I went out of my mind."

"I'm sorry. I wasn't trying to be enigmatic."

"But I needed to know why you HAD to. What had I done?"

"Jethro you hadn't done—"

"Then one day when I was like deleting all the security footage from our house cameras. Remember those? The motion sensing cameras? After the break-in?"

"So?"

"There was one in the hall. A camera."

"So?"

"I saw you on it."

"Saw me what? Leaving?"

"You know I often mess around in the studio if I can't sleep right?"

"Course.

"I was in my studio… working late one night."

Something switches on in Cooper's head. A memory. The one of her waking to find Jethro gone from the bed during the night and going downstairs to listen at his studio door.

"Oh. Now he knew."

"The security camera caught you in the hall, Coops."

"The hall lights were off."

"Infrared cameras. They see in the dark."

"I didn't know that."

"So, I saw you come to my music room door. You like never opened it. You put your hand on the door handle even. Then you pressed your ear to the door."

"I remember."

"You were there a long time. Then you were careful to take your hand off the handle so I wouldn't hear it jostle. You turned around, went to bed. Man, that completely confused me why you did that. I didn't get what you'd heard."

"I heard—"

Jethro raises a palm.

"Yeah Coops, it's okay, I get it now. You heard my song to you."

Cooper's voice is soft.

"Yes."

Jethro's eyes dim for a second, the sadness momentarily back.

"Tell me Coops, what's my song about?"

"Ah, come on now."

Jethro searches her eyes.

"Please."

"You sang about a lonely love."

"You understand what I was singing then?"

"Jethro, of course. You were singing about how lonely you were even though I was back in your life. How your love was lonely without mine in return. And that, no matter what, such a one-sided love was breaking you apart."

Jethro presses his lips together, contrition evident in his face.

"You weren't ever meant to hear it, Cooper. It was just me, spilling my stuff."

"I know. It's okay."

"I guess that means you know I rerecorded that song with new lyrics?"

Cooper nods.

"Why did you?"

"Oh Coops, it was too private with the original lyrics. I didn't want the world to know the real song. I turned it into a commercial version, that's all. I still have the original."

"It's a beautiful song Jethro, even with the changed lyrics. The song is still about me. That's why you sing it so forlornly. You disguised it well. Only now it's called Oh What a Fool, but I know the real title is My Lonely Love. I even remember the first verse."

Jethro's surprised.

"You do?"

Cooper clears her throat, starts reciting the first verse.

When she's done Jethro smiles, but the smile is sad.

"You do remember."

"It's not like your other songs."

"I'd probably been listening to too much Frank Sinatra and Dean Martin. Coops, you were never meant to hear it."

"Jethro, that song is why I wrote the letter. I could never have voluntarily hurt you. It wasn't until I heard that song through the door, I realised how much you were suffering. Well after that I saw clues all over the shop. You'd stare at me looking downhearted. Then when you caught me watching, you'd beam as though you were happy happy happy just to cover it up. Oh and the over enthusiastic reactions to anything I surprised you with. Sometimes I know you'd be awake studying me when you thought I was sleeping. Sometimes when you got up from bed I'd press my hand into your pillow and it'd be damp. Jethro you weren't happy no matter how hard you tried to hide it. You remember when we had to put Kelloggs down?"

Jethro shakes his head.

"They were bad times."

"I saw your heartbreak, Jethro. We left the vet without him and your face was so grey you looked like you were going to pass out. We got home and you slumped in a chair and I put the kettle on for a bit of tea and while I waited I swept up his cans of food, took away the water bowl, gave it all to our neighbour, collected all his toys up and tossed them in the pedal bin. You watched me do it. I was only doing a bit of business but you watched me wipe away his existence."

Jethro nods.

"I knew you were being practical. I'd have done the same eventually."

"That's just it Jethro. It's always been how I deal with things and you know I loved Kelloggs. But I didn't think. I didn't give YOU time to grieve. I was blind to your feelings now. I started to wonder how many things I'd done without thinking of you. That I was this mechanical wife going through the motions without noticing the nuance of your feelings. It was like Groundhog Day."

"Groundhog Day?"

"Sure, you know, the film with Bill Murray and Andie MacDowell."

"I know the film, Coops. What do you mean?"

"Bill Murray's trapped in a time loop in a snowy town when the same day keeps repeating, right?"

"Yeah, I remember."

"Well now, there's this bit of a scene where he's snow fighting with Andie MacDowell, having fun. Then these kids join in and Bill Murray and Andie MacDowell end up tumbling into each other in the snow laughing and kissing, both feeling something electric for each other."

"Okay, so?"

"Well, the same thing happens the next night, but this time Bill Murray's agenda is different, he just wants to bed good old Andie. So, he says all the same things and does all the same things he did the last time like he's reading a script. Only Andie MacDowell doesn't feel anything for him this time around. She's confused by his behaviour so when he tries to kiss her, she pushes him away."

"I didn't push you away, Cooper."

"I never pretended to love you. We were recreating all the things we did together before my treatment. But I realised we'd created our own Groundhog Day. I wasn't feeling it like you."

Jethro shuffles, looking down at his feet.

"Right, right."

"I only picked up on things after that night. That's when I started looking for them. And even then you probably picked up on ten times more things every day I wasn't aware I was doing. It was bleeding you out. We both wanted things to be the same but you started to see the cracks. Sure enough, I might as well have been a Stepford wife."

Jethro smiles.

"Ah."

"What do you mean ah?"

"AH!"

"Stop ahhing and tell me."

"You've just proven something to me."

"What do you mean?"

"Coops, this is like going to come as a surprise."

"What is?"

"I've had it confirmed."

"Had what confirmed?"

"Well, thing is, you love me, Coops."

Cooper cocks her head.

"Haven't you heard what I've been saying? You know I don't. Jethro you can't delude yourself that I—"

"Sssh."

Cooper ignores him.

"Look, we both know the treatment cut all feelings I had with you Jethro. I can't love you but I also can't hate you."

"You know the front garden to our old house?"

"We paved over it."

"You remember why?"

Cooper thinks back.

"We got fed up with all those weeds. They kept returning."

"What if I told you the weeds still came back?"

"It's paved."

"Between the paving stones, Coops. They're tenacious little devils."

"So? What're you saying Jethro?"

"You still care about me, right? That's what you used to say after the treatment."

"Course I care for you, but that's just a baseline empathy. That's what they said I'd be left with."

"Yeah? Really? That's all?"

Jethro pauses, waits for Cooper to think through what he's saying.

"Honestly, it's not love Jethro. It's not. I also cared for Bill Murray and Andie MacDowell in Groundhog Day but I don't love them. Sure, I'd be sad if they died but I wouldn't mourn them. I wouldn't for you either, just like you said at the Callum Bay's Heart Hotel."

"You're sure about that, Coops?"

"It's true."

Jethro's eyes are full of amusement. Why's he looking so playful?

"See, I went to visit Gateway House to ask the docs something. I asked them what happens if you continue to stay with someone after taking the treatment."

"So what?"

"They said something really kinda interesting."

"Why? What did they say?"

"They said now they know for sure new events continue to create new memories."

"Sure, but that's obvious. I could've told you that, Jethro. It's not memory that's affected, it's feelings."

"Ah."

"You keep saying that like you know something."

"AH!"

"Stop ahhing and tell me!"

"Coops, your old memories of us together have no feelings connected with them, right?"

"Course. That's the way of it."

"But what if you remain with someone after the treatment?"

"What about it?"

"Those eighteen months we created new memories together."

"So what?"

"It's called neurogenesis, man. See the thing is, the brain's plastic. It's malleable. New memories create new links."

Cooper stares at him.

"So?"

"New links also means new emotional links." Jethro chuckles. "Interesting right?"

"What're you saying?"

"It's like the weeds in the drive. They come back because little bits of earth start to build between the paving bricks in the driveway again. Seeds blow in and lodge there. Then they grow. The weeds start to appear even though you paved over the old garden. Weeds under the paving start to break it up. Leave it long enough and it breaks up all the paving and turns it into earth. What's left is a wild garden."

"You're saying my old memories of us is like the paved-over garden? The new memories are like weeds?"

Jethro's smile widens.

"That's it, totally."

The churning in Cooper's stomach she always feels around Jethro. Could it be a flutter? The way she snatches her phone up whenever Jethro calls. Could it be more than passing curiosity? The racing of her heart in his company. Could it be— Cooper slaps Jethro on the arm.

"Ow!"

Cooper hits him again.

"OW. Stop that."

"You!"

"What about me?"

"You're telling me my love is like a weed."

He laughs.

"Well yeah, kind of."

Slaps him again.

"Ow! Cooper will you, like, stop that?" He thinks back to when he tried to tell her, her eyes were like suns and moons, how she stung him with slaps then too. That day. All those years ago.

"They're sure about that? Dr Applegate and Dr Stewart-Way?"

Jethro rubs his tender arm.

"That's what troubled me about you leaving. See, if you didn't feel anything for me, it wouldn't have bothered you I was falling apart, basic empathy or not. You'd have stayed with me. Don't you see? You left so I could move on. You did it for me, Coops. You were already contented we were together again. What you did was sacrifice your own happiness for me."

"That's what you think?"

"Cooper, you're not listening. You left not because you didn't love me. You left because you did love me. You didn't even know it. That's why you HAD to leave. And, well that's why I contacted Gateway House after all these years when I reread the letter, when I saw the security footage, when I finally understood."

Cooper considers it. Is it possible for twelve years she's been denying herself what her heart already knew?

Cooper frowns, not daring to believe it.

"So… it's true? I love you?"

He grins. "Yeah well, only you can know that for sure."

Cooper looks at him. Stares. Misty grey not like… like… She studies his eyes. Misty grey not like… like… No. Wait. Wait. WAIT. She feels herself falling into his grey eyes. Falling and tumbling. Tumbling and somersaulting. They were. THEY WERE! THEY REALLY WERE! Misty grey like coastal fog. Her heart. Her heart. Oh god her heart. How it's racing, pounding, thrashing. Suddenly she's a teenager again.

"Oh my god. I love you? Oh my GOD. I LOVE YOU JETHRO!"

He sweeps her up then. Arms like wings fold over her. She feels it. It's love it's love it's really love. She feels it searing through her. No longer restrained and bound up. Now it unleashes and expands and floods her like alcohol, overwhelming her.

They embrace a long, long time.

When they separate, Jethro clears his throat.

"Something else."

"You mean there's more?"

"Coops, you were right. You were so right."

"About?"

"It's all stripped away. Everything. It's insane. I never knew."

"What're you talking about?"

Wait, let me quote something someone once said to me. He closes his eyes as if to recite a sonnet. "There is something far richer than love. You don't realise it until you strip love away and start over."

Cooper looks at him.

"Jethro, what have you done?"

"Guess."

"Anyway, I didn't say richer than love. I said greater than love. You learn to value yourself again, beyond love. So even if I choose to fall in love, I've learned how to get the balance right."

Jethro's smile is smug.

"That's right."

Cooper narrows her eyes.

"You've done something."

"They've refined the treatment a lot since you know, Coops. And you're right the memories don't go."

Cooper looks at him sideways.

"I thought you were never going to take the treatment."

"Well, that's because I'd have taken it for the wrong reasons. This time, I did it for the right reasons."

"What's the right reasons?"

"Cooper, I want us to create new memories together. New memories with fresh emotions."

"So... now you don't love me?"

"Cooper, the moment you opened this door tonight you took my breath away and my heart took a rocket ship to the moon. Suns and moons, remember?"

"You're supposed to be emigrating, surely?"

Jethro gives a knowing smile.

"Ah."

"What do you mean ah?"

"AH!"

"Stop ahhing and just tell me."

"If you can call it that."

"What does that mean? Where are you going?"

Jethro's smile lingers. It's a teasing smile.

"Wait a minute. Have you moved… here? To this village?"

Jethro's smile widens, a cheeky glint in his eye.

He clears his throat, embraces Cooper around the waist once more, pulls her close and whispers into her ear.

"Yes."

1 4 2

EDDSY AND HARRIET have fostered nine children over the years.

Some were teens. Others younger. They even had a sweet little three-year-old girl at one point, blind from birth. All had troubles in some way. Today they're welcoming a new boy who's thirteen. He'll be with them for something like six months, at least initially. His name is Anele. The name Anele means the last one. If he settles with them then perhaps it'll be his whole life. Then he really will be the last one. They knew all the other children were on loan. Anele though, they want to adopt if things go to plan. They've all written to each other before. All met before. He's even stayed before.

Anele's biological parents are South African but they gave him up after several troubling years because he had one leg longer than the other. At Anele's birth his father's face darkened and he stormed out of the hospital at the atrocity a child of his should have this.

When Anele was four and people said how he was starting to look like his father his father began beating him. To his father, it was an insult. But you could barely see Anele's bruises under his dark skin. It broke Karabo's heart to let him go. She had to. Anele wouldn't have survived.

It broke her heart.

Anele's been with four families over the years and spent time in a children's home. Because he's so quiet the other children bullied him and the staff often barely noticed. Such is the intelligent trickery of children. Three of the foster families were good or okay, one not so great.

Anele is thirteen now. He liked Harriet and Eddsy the first time he saw them. He hides behind thick glasses and avoids eye contact. He likes motor magazines, Marvel comics, computer games.

When Anele stayed with Harriet and Eddsy last time he got to visit Eddsy's garage and wow he was in heaven, fascinated by everything mechanical. He got to learn all about electric cars, even ripped his nice crisp shirt greasy and a rip in his trousers. He didn't care one bit. He grinned so much that day it was hurting his cheeks when he left.

Today Anele's excited about seeing them again.

He pushes the doorbell, grins at his chaperone Pamela as they stand side by side on the doorstep bouncing from foot to foot.

Harriet is upstairs giving Anele's room the once over. She's placed towels on the bed, a pair of pyjamas, new slippers, fresh toothbrush. She has a pile of action annuals. She's constantly adjusting things that don't need adjusting, restless with excitement. Meanwhile Eddsy is downstairs, pacing until he sees the social worker's car pull up through the window, the crackle of wheels on gravel. He calls out. He answers the door.

Anele and Pamela are on the doorstep.

Anele is grinning. His teeth so white and he looks so happy, so excited he's almost bouncing on his heels.

He's carrying a suitcase with all his worldly goods. In his other hand he's holding a bunch of daffodils. Pamela holds a folder pressed to her bosom.

Eddsy invites them in.

Harriet rushes downstairs saying oh gosh he's here, oh wow, opens her arms and Anele rushes into them and they wrap each other up. Already Anele's taller, more gangly, arms like long extensions from his body. Eddsy is sure he's topped another two inches since they last saw him. Anele presents Harriet with the flowers. She takes them, tears in her eyes. Eddsy looks at her, fighting not to choke up. Harriet is so happy. So happy.

Then Anele steps towards Eddsy.

Eddsy holds his hand out.

Anele takes his hand, shakes it. Then he rushes into Eddsy's barrel chest and throws his gangly arms around him too. Eddsy accepts it, embraces him, patting him on the back.

"You've grown," Eddsy says.

"Nah dad, you shrunk."

Dad.

Eddsy laughs, pride flooding into him, hearing that word.

Harriet lets out a little aw! Exchanges encouraging looks with Pamela whose eyes are soft and filling at the sight.

Pamela knows how good this is. She lives for moments like this. Positively thrives on it. When she drove Anele here, he couldn't stop bouncing his knees in his seat, a permanent smile on his lips. Now she knows for sure what she's seeing.

No doubt about it. Pamela smiles to herself. What she's witnessing, it's the birth of a family.

FIVE YEARS LATER
JETHRO AND COOPER step into a chugging London black
taxi cab. In the five years together, they've seen their son grow
up with his first love, Araminta, who now have a child together
called Lavender. They've seen Harriet and Eddsy's garage
business cease expansion as they became more and more
involved in the lives of so many children passing through their
home. They've even seen that lovely boy Anele, a shy, leek-
skinny teenager Harriet and Eddsy adopted, grow into a
confident, broad-shouldered young man who has a smile that
lights up the sky, studying mechanical engineering, specialising
in hybrid and electrically powered vehicles.

And they've felt each other grow closer than ever before.

As Cooper and Jethro settle in the cab, Cooper smoothes out
the pale golden satin evening gown she's wearing and adjusts
the blue shawl around her shoulders. Jethro's in a dinner jacket,
open white shirt, a bolero hat, his long hair swept over his
shoulders. He asks Cooper to shut her eyes.

"Where're we going?"

"You'll see."

"Not the Savoy?"

Jethro laughs.

"You know every year I take you to a different place."

"Where then?"

"Just somewhere nice."

Jethro passes a note to the cab driver, puts his finger to his lips. The cab driver gets the message. Drive. Don't say where. Keep schtum.

Cooper grins, loving the intrigue. Every year she likes the surprises.

As the cab driver negotiates evening traffic, he glances at them in the rear view mirror. He knows new love when he sees it. He enjoys seeing in-love couples in his backseat. Never tires of it. So, he's an old romantic? So what? Young, old, anywhere between. He's seen an eighty-year-old granny deaf in one ear in love with a man seven years her junior. He's seen eight-year-olds in adoration holding hands and gazing at each other and giggling. He's seen girl-girl love. He's seen boy-boy love. He's seen everything between. He looks at these two, notices they're both wearing wedding bands. He calls out over the throbbing chug of the black cab.

"Newly-weds?"

"We've been together for like five years," Jethro says.

"Yeah?"

"We were married twenty-two years before. Then we separated."

"No kidding."

"We even have a son in his 30s."

"This an anniversary or something?"

"No."

"Birthday?"

"Nothing like that."

"What then?"

"I decided to like treat my wife to a posh meal at a restaurant."

Cooper's eyes are still closed.

"Ah ha, we're going to a restaurant."

"We always go to restaurants."

"Not never seen that," the cab driver says.

"What do you mean?"

"Couple acting like you two after all those years. Not taken something have you?"

"Like what?"

"Dunno. Pills like the kids do. Or snorted something?"

Jethro smiles.

"Nah. We don't need that stuff."

The cab driver steadies his gaze over Jethro in the mirror.

"Hey, don't you look like someone?"

"Who?"

"Dunno. You look familiar. You kind of both do."

After a couple of minutes watching the couple as they whisper sweet nothings into each other's ears and alternately laugh, the taxi driver clears his throat.

"So, what's the secret between you two?"

"You want the truth?" Jethro says.

"Sure."

Jethro turns to Cooper.

"Should I tell him?"

She shrugs.

"Simple. Make every day like the first day."

The cab driver frowns. He still doesn't get it.

"You two look like my daughter with her new boyfriend sucking face under the porch light."

Jethro turns to Cooper. Looks at her beautiful face. The hair pulled up at the sides over her ears. Tendrils hang down either side, the fashion is like she's going to a Regency ball.

"Man, I can honestly say I wake up to beautiful twin eclipses every single day."

"And I wake up to coastal fog every day," Cooper says.

The taxi driver shakes his head. Eclipses? Coastal fog? These two must be on something. Or they're playing a game with him. That, he doesn't mind. It's nice to have silly, romantic company on his backseat, long as they don't get up to anything on his watch. Truth is he likes the couple. Makes his heart feel light. Makes the job worth doing, rides like this. He'd have something to tell the boys back at the rank. How this wacky in-love couple who claimed to be together for years were like the most sticky-sweet lovebirds he ever did see.

When they stop at the destination Jethro turns to Cooper.

"Your eyes still closed?"

She puts up a hand.

"Guides honour."

He helps Cooper out the cab, pays the cab driver and adds a folded tip, winks.

"Thanks for not letting on."

"No probs mate. Listen, how long you two lovebirds been married, really?"

"Twenty–seven years in total like I said."

The cab driver laughs

"Okay, have it your way."

Jethro turns to Cooper. You can open your eyes now.

Cooper looks around in delight.

"You dirty trickster, it IS the Savoy."

"Yeah, but I would've given the game away if I'd used their Roller this time."

"Then, I've a surprise for you too."

Jethro looks at Cooper.

"What do you mean?"

"Ah."

"What do you mean ah?"

"AHH."

"Stop ahhing and tell me what you mean."

"Well now, every year I call the Savoy and find out if you've booked a meal here. Turns out you did this year so guess what?"

"Go on."

Cooper gives a smug smile.

"I told the Savoy if ever you book a meal here then automatically book a suite too, but don't tell you, or me."

Jethro's mouth drops open.

"And guess what? It'll be the same suite we stayed in last time."

The doorkeeper opens the doors and they step into plush elegance.

The cab driver chuckles as he pulls away, forgotten by the couple. They're yanking his chain somehow, he just can't work out how. A story for the boys back at the rank, maybe. Maybe they can work it out.

Yeah. A story for the boys.

THE END

Thank you for reading

Amazon reviews are incredibly valuable to me. Please support my work by leaving a review there. Even if it's only a single line, I'll appreciate it. Every single review is genuinely important. I'm told Amazon's clever automated algorithms means it'll notice your review and count it specifically for that day onwards. It'll then automatically notch up the book's discoverability to other readers. All it takes is ONE additional review to get another person to see it who otherwise wouldn't have and if they order or review it, it starts to multiply discoverability, so you see how important your review is. Once reviewed, let me know and I'll be delighted to check it out. Also share your review on social media with the hashtag #LoveDeleted and encourage others to read my debut novel too.

If you can, your review on Goodreads.com helps too. Many readers find their next read there. Or, of course, your own favourite booksite.

Where did Dr Applegate Go?

Did you notice Dr Applegate disappears from Sue Baxter's podcast part way through Love Deleted? There's a reason why. The answer lies in a novelette called The Letter – The Dr Applegate Story. It's waiting for you free at:

PaulIndigo.com

You can read the first chapter on the next page...

1

Dr Applegate stares at the letter he's holding, hands trembling. He'd never known what it meant to be so shocked he needs to sit down before. He sinks into the leather armchair before his knees give.

Outside his Baker Street penthouse the morning sun is rising. The presenter on Radio 3 murmurs about the life and works of CPE Bach, introduces one of his harpsichord pieces. The piece starts, the harpsichord, clear and bright as shattering glass.

Dr Applegate reads the letter again, deliberating over each sentence. The letter's on 80gsm white paper. Times Roman font. Twelve point. Headline in bold capital. Parts in italics. Most in regular Times. His name on the letter.

Dear Dr Applegate.

He reads every sentence. Deliberates on every line. Every word. Right to the end.

No ambiguity about it. It tells him every terrible thing.

Ten minutes later, Dr Applegate stands up unaware of the time that's passed. He realises he's still wearing his gym T-shirt and shorts. Still has his trainers on. Still has the damp towel draped around his neck. He folds the letter neatly, returns it into the envelope.

He places the envelope under the 18th century French Ormolu clock set on a marble mantelpiece. Yes, that's what he'll do, wind the clock. Yes, he takes the key, opens the glass, winds the springs, one for the clock, the other for the chimes. His mind is numb. Anaesthetised. He closes the glass automatically, hangs the key on the back of the clock automatically. The envelope is firmly under it's feet.

In a daze he walks out the sitting room, all elegant mute grey, all gilt-edge furniture in striking relief – the mirror above the fireplace, the Louis 16th bureau, the tan leather sofa, the floor-to-ceiling bookcases, the ebony black baby grand piano. The lid, even raised expectantly, begging for someone to sit down, perform a Mozart or a Haydn or a Rachmaninov on it. But Dr Applegate doesn't play. Can't. Always wanted to learn. Never has. So, he is a successful man. Now he is numb.

What should he do? Where should he go?

Shower.

Yes.

Shower.

Dr Applegate steps into to shower. The water's freezing. He scrubs, barely noticing the hard horsehair bristles, the icy water, until he finds himself shivering yet burning from over-scrubbing, his skin raw. Numb. Numb inside. Numb outside. The letter. That letter. He grabs a towel, dries, slips into a robe, goes into the kitchen.

Do everything normally. Yes. After all, it's only a letter, that's all. Just words on a page.

What does he do after a shower?

He walks, paces, absently visits each room in his apartment. God.

Pacing. Hands through his greying hair.

Pacing.

He'll shave.

Yes.

Get dressed.

Yes. That's it. Do that.

It's just an ordinary day. An ordinary Tuesday, an ordinary, ordinary day.

Dr Applegate will have his protein drink, have his cereal muesli with chopped banana, read the newspaper over his black coffee. He'll dress in his dark suit, his crisp shirt, his polished Italian brogues.

He'll leave as normal in the lift cage, the exposed metal clanging as he shuts the polished-to-a-sheen brass gate. He'll say good morning to Carter who'll be having his doughnut and coffee at his desk in reception.

Then he'll get into his car.

He'll drive to work.

Yes.

He'll start another day.

Yes good that's good. Nothing more to do.

And of course wait.

Wait for the letter to come true.

Go to PaulIndigo.com to download the free novelette.

Acknowledgements

I'd like to thank several amazing people in alphabetical order, who read early versions of my manuscript or helped with editing: Ellen Cheshire, Joy Cheshire, Kathleen Kus, Karen McCreedy, Gill Mills, Beki Tonks, Tracy Wells. All made intuitive, perceptive comments and had thought-provoking ideas which resulted in what I consider a better version of the novel than I could otherwise have written.

I'd also like to thank members of the Thomas family:
Dr Peter Thomas for his fabulous contributions in ensuring the science of optogenetics reads authentically.

Dr Sara Thomas and Dr Richard Thomas for their valuable insights around the psychology presented in the novel (including a correction of a basic anatomical error!)

Finally, a BIG thank you to Brazilian artist Helio Teles (HelioTeles.co.uk) for his amazing artwork which inspired me to develop Cooper Hall's character. Without it, Cooper would never have been as striking a character.

If you'd like to know what Cooper Hall looks like, go to Paulindigo.com/#cooperhall

I'm grateful to all of you. You guys rock!

Made in the USA
Las Vegas, NV
06 October 2023

78650481R10333